Miss Nobody

Caroline Ross is the pseudonym for a young British writer, and Miss Nobody is her first novel. She is currently working on her second romantic novel.

First published 1981 by Judy Piatkus (Publishers) Ltd

© Caroline Ross 1981

Made and printed in Great Britain

Many of the characters in this book are fictitious, some of course are not, and I should like to stress that the events recounted are entirely of my own imagination. I have written *Miss Nobody* to provide pure entertainment and hope that nothing I have written will cause any offence to anyone.

FOR DANIEL

CAROLINE ROSS

Miss Nobody

PIATKUS

CHAPTER ONE

To an outsider it looked like any other day in the life of the world's busiest airport. Traffic moved in a steady flow under the concrete flyover which proclaimed 'Welcome to Heathrow'. The acres of tarmac were lined with planes glinting in the Spring sunshine – wide-bodied jets, 707s, big clumsy-looking freighters, towering above the clusters of tiny service vehicles.

Only an acute observer would have noted a momentary lull in the airport's activities. None of the huge silver giants had been lined up for take-off, and there had been no arrivals on any of the strips nearest the international terminal for some time. Inside the terminal, the vast chequered expanse of the arrivals area, usually crammed to bursting point twenty-four hours a day, was virtually empty. So was the visitor's lounge and the brightly-lit cafeteria. Even the clerks behind the message desks had disappeared into the back offices which overlooked the airfield.

So no one noticed the short, grey-suited man leaning unobtrusively on the gallery rail overlooking the concourse. Even if there had been the usual milling crowds, very few people would have noticed him. He blended into the background. It was his talent, his career. All that moved was his eyes, probing, scanning, with a constant impersonal watchfulness. And he wasn't alone. Poised at other vantage points there were other quiet, grey-suited men gazing down over the deserted concourse. Strangely, their eyes never met.

Any minute now. The airport security officer ran a hand over the familiar, hard, oblong shape of the two-way radio in his top pocket. He couldn't help feeling a surge of unprofessional excitement. For a moment he wished he was with the crowds of ordinary people packed into the visitors' gallery and the roof garden, their eyes fixed on the distant strip of cordoned-off runway. It wasn't the first time he'd been on duty for an occasion like this, but the old excitement never failed.

He leaned his elbows on the gallery rail. Without moving his head he let his eyes check the area beneath one more time. If he'd been asked what he was looking for, he wouldn't have known how to explain. His whole being was attuned to patterns – an unexpected movement, an unusual stillness, even something so apparently trivial as the way a man coughed or picked his nose. He thought of himself as a fisherman, poised above the stream, waiting for the big one.

Aha. He felt a tug on his imaginary line and tensed. Yes, he was right. Nicely tucked away behind one of the pillars supporting the gallery, in a convenient patch of shadow. Face well hidden under a grey hat. And motionless, too motionless. His sixth sense prickled. There was something wrong about that motionless figure. Why had she stayed behind in the concourse? Hadn't she heard? Why wasn't she with the other sightseers, nose pressed against the nearest plate-glass window? Wrong, definitely wrong. His breath hissed softly through his teeth. Nonchalantly he detached himself from the rail. This was it. The hunt was on.

Using the limits of his peripheral vision he monitored the grey hat as he went slowly down the gallery stair. Growing certainty hummed through his veins. There was something up, there had to be. The hat itself was a dead giveaway. It shaded her face too well and the colour was too drab. No woman in her right mind would wear a hat like that on a fine Spring day.

Who was she? Why was she here? Slowly, his feet noiseless on the closely woven carpet, he edged closer.

Now he was close enough for details. At the back of his mind he registered a subdued hum of expectation from the crowds packed into the viewing gallery. The flight must have arrived. With an effort he concentrated on his quarry. Face invisible, one hand resting at her neck, touching something he couldn't make out. No rings. Passenger or visitor? Behind her, just visible in the shadow, a small case. No labels, nothing obvious. But he prided himself on his ability to sum up the character, history and – most important – probable intentions of a passenger by one brief look at the case.

His senses prickled. Her case was old and battered, it looked as if it had been in someone's attic for years. Cheap cardboard, and the locks were partly rusted. If he could see her lift it, he'd know more ...

Casually he wandered closer. The subdued hum in the background had become an excited, wordless roar. But she still didn't look up. Just that unnatural stillness. What was she wearing? Dark, whatever it was; he couldn't see more. Damn that shadow.

Idly he walked over to the stamp machine set into the wall and fished noisily for change. Out of the corner of his eye he saw the woman register his presence with a start. He held his breath. Was she going to move away? He wanted her where he could keep an eye on her. She took a tentative step forward, hesitated, then retreated.

The time was ripe. At any minute the concourse might be flooded with excited people, it would be too late. He turned as if undecided, jingling a handful of coins.

'Excuse me ... you haven't by any chance got 10p?'

The woman jumped. This close to her he began to get a better idea of what was strange about her. Everything she was wearing, from the battered hat to the long rusty black coat with the scrap of black fur at the collar, looked as if it belonged to someone else. Nothing fitted, she looked as if she'd been left out in the rain. He was right, he knew it.

The pause seemed endless, as if she wasn't even going to answer him. Then her chin came up and she shook her head, a small, abrupt movement, and murmured something he couldn't catch. He bent forward, saw as he glanced down faded cotton stockings like his mother used to wear, ending in small brown sandals that looked as if it was only polish that held them together.

He put the coins back into his pocket, letting a couple slide through his fingers. They clinked on to the tiles and rolled off obediently in opposite directions. It worked. The woman bent down automatically to help him pick them up, giving him a glimpse of one side of her face.

His jaw dropped in shock. It wasn't what he'd expected at all. She was young, a girl, hardly even a woman. Pale skin, wide-set eyes, a drift of freckles over the straight short nose. One dark plait at the base of her neck. No make-up, the curve of an unplucked eyebrow, on one thin cheek what looked like ...

She caught his eye, flushed and looked down again. The hat brim blocked his view once more. Without looking up she handed him back the coins. The tips of her small fingers were red and rough.

He blinked in confusion, trying to re-order his thoughts. This was no terrorist or undercover agent. She was too young, for one thing, too obviously at a loss. The grey hat, her shyness, her presence down here rather than up there with the rest of the excited crowd – well, with what he'd seen in that one glimpse of her cheek that was understandable. He remembered his own daughter at that sensitive age. His vision of a case packed with explosive began to fade. But she was still a bit of a mystery. He'd give a good deal to know exactly what it did contain. After all, his instincts couldn't have been entirely wrong.

Quickly, he made up his mind. At all costs he had to know more. Professional pride was at stake.

'Excuse me, are you lost? Can I show you the way to the viewing gallery?'

He could place an accent, give or take a few hundred miles, anywhere within the English-speaking world – even, on his good days, the Indian sub-continent. It was almost a party trick.

Again that aching pause. The girl's hand went up to touch

whatever it was she had round her neck, hidden under that unseasonable coat. It seemed to reassure her. Her chin lifted.

'No ... no, thank you. I'd rather stay here.'

Her voice was clear this time, but it almost defeated him. From the dress and the plait he'd made a guess at American Mid-West, but the voice was a puzzling mixture. At the end of the sentence was the faint teasing upswing of the South ... A crystal clear picture swam into his mind. Scarlett O'Hara eating a peach, perched lazily on a swing hung between two magnolia trees; in the distance a big white house with pillars and porticoes ... That was it, the South. Only there was something else, much harder to define, an accent that seemed much closer to home ... a sort of soft brogue. It was a mystery. He shook his head and gave up. But he'd have one last try to find out what was in the case at least.

'Here. Let me help with your case.'

He bent swiftly down and took hold of the handle.

'Oh no!'

To his astonishment the girl snatched the handle away from him. He let go immediately and she clutched it to her chest. Her cheeks were flushed. He caught a glimpse of two brown-lashed eyes staring defiantly back at him under the disfiguring hat, then she looked away again.

He felt as guilty as if he'd tried to steal the Crown Jewels. He cursed his curiosity now. Even though, in the few seconds he'd actually held the case, he'd found the answer to at least one question. He didn't know what he'd expected when he'd picked it up. Anything but that pitifully obvious lightness, and the sad little rattle of some small possession – probably a cake of free airline soap – falling to the bottom. He looked away tactfully as the girl checked the rusty catches. He cursed himself again. After all, everyone had their pride.

Well, at least the mystery was over now. In his pre-occupation he'd missed the big arrival. Already people were filing back into the concourse, chattering excitedly. Soon everything would be back to normal. By this time His Royal Highness would be well on his way to Windsor, probably heartily relieved at the successful completion of another Commonwealth tour.

He couldn't help turning back to watch the small, shabby little figure with its straight back and bent head walk slowly away across the concourse, wearing her fancy-dress hat and carrying her make-believe case. She paused under the yellow perspex signs, hesitated, then made her way towards the Underground. He stared after her. He'd never see her again, and yet he had the strange feeling she still had hidden away somewhere – in a secret compartment, perhaps, or inside the lining of that shabby coat – the answer to a question he hadn't even thought to ask.

'Here he comes!'

A buzz of excitement went round the crowd gathered underneath the Henry VIII gate as the powerful maroon Rolls with the royal crest blazoned on the side swept up the incline towards the Lower Ward. Above the massive twin towers of the gate rose the golden stone battlements of Windsor Castle itself, the most ancient royal palace of them all. For nine long centuries, ever since 1070 and William the Conqueror, the medieval fortress had stood and resisted the assaults of every usurper. It had been held for Richard Coeur de Lion against his treacherous brother John; even Cromwell's men, who stabled their horses in the chapel nave and used the castle as a gaol for Royalists, could not destroy this last royal stronghold.

Now, set like a great golden jewel in the 5000 acres of rolling green parkland known simply as the Great Park, the Castle rested solid and secure behind its mile-long battlements. Inset in the massively thick stone walls, quarried from glacial deposits ten miles to the south, were narrow slits through which defenders once loosed a hail of arrows; three holes above the Henry VIII gate enabled them to pour molten metal and boiling oil on anyone attempting to force an entrance. Beyond these formidable defences was a totally enclosed, self-sufficient community, with its own chapels, libraries, galleries, gardens and orangeries, dominated by the magnificent Round Tower, standing proud on its Norman foundations and topped by the royal standard, and the huge State Apartments, ranged round the formal inner Quadrangle in the Upper Ward, overlooked by the proud bronze statue of King Charles II. South the Castle faced the small township of Windsor, with its winding alleyways and cobbled streets; North it overlooked the dizzying drop across the Thames to Eton College and the breathtaking background of the Chiltern hills.

But the crowds of onlookers outside the Henry VIII gate and lining the broad drive leading to the Lower Ward had no attention to spare for the grandeur surrounding them. All eyes were fixed on the approaching Rolls as it swept past and up towards the Upper Ward, past the timbered Horseshoe Cloisters, heading for the private royal apartments.

'Did you see him?'

A young girl with her hair in bunches clutched her friend's arm eagerly.

'Of course I did!' Her friend tossed her mop of blonde hair. 'Didn't you notice? He smiled at me!'

The other girl drew in her breath sharply.

'Oh Julie, he never did! You're making it up!'

The blonde shook her head triumphantly.

'No I'm not. When he waved, he looked right at me, and smiled. I saw him.'

Her friend bit her lip, then couldn't resist the temptation. 'What was it like?'

Julie smiled conspiratorially.

'Oh, you know ...' She groped in her mind for a clearer memory of that dim figure in the back of the car, a face tanned beneath crisp dark hair, a pair of penetrating blue eyes ... And that smile, had she imagined it after all? No, she couldn't have. 'It went right through me, here.' She laid her hand on her heart, which was in fact beating much faster than normal. 'It made me feel ... I don't know ... special somehow.'

She sighed. Her friend watched her face in silence, waiting for more. It came.

'You know what?' There was something in Julie's voice that made her friend eye her suspiciously. 'I'm going to do it after all!'

'You're not! You'd never dare!'

'You just watch me.' Julie's eyes were sparkling. 'I'll never get another chance.'

'You're crazy. You'll never get away with it.'

'I don't care. It's worth it.' Her friend struggled for a moment between disapproval and envy. Envy won.

'Honestly Julie, you have all the luck. I wish he'd smiled at me.'

Together they settled down to wait.

Inside the castle apartments preparations for the annual Order of the Garter ceremony had been under way for days. Under the experienced eye of the Master of the Household, aided by extra staff drafted into service from Buckingham Palace for the occasion, the complex arrangements ran with well-oiled efficiency. The corridors and galleries were crowded with footmen, their spectacular gold-braided scarlet livery, knee breeches and flesh-coloured stockings set off by the drabber colours of the senior staff, sober in black and gold, spotless white wool breeches and black buckled pumps. Ladies in waiting, women of the bedchamber, equerries, private secretaries and messengers were sent scurrying at the bidding of the Master of the Household. Members of the Castle's permanent community – the lay clerks, housed in the Horseshoe Cloister, the Master of Choristers, the Military Knights of Windsor, even the Governor of the Castle himself, could only stand by and hope to keep out of the way of the annual invasion.

The Upper Ward, on the sunny Southern side where the family had their private apartments, was a hive of female

activity, as maids plumped each cushion on the priceless
Louis XIV brocade chairs, swept and polished and dusted till
every surface shone. The high Gothic windows added by
King George III had been washed down with chamois
leather then finished with silk rag till they glowed like
diamonds. In each private sitting room books, games and
refreshments had been laid out for any members of the
Queen's party who might prolong their stay. Vases overflowed with fresh flowers from the formal garden, alongside
bowls of selected fruit, including the first small sweet oranges
from the orangery.

But the Master of the Household's chief concern lay
elsewhere. Thirty of his best men had been delegated to just
one room in the State Apartments, the huge, lavish Waterloo
Chamber. There they'd had been hard at work since before
dawn in preparation for the banquet preceding the procession, overlooked by the ranks of gold-framed portraits
that flanked the wood-panelled walls – from Archduke
Charles to the Duke of Wellington himself, sword in hand,
staring sternly down at the chamber that commemorated his
famous victory over Napoleon. Under the battery of demanding eyes the footmen hurried to lay out the gold plate
and wine flagons on the sideboards. The Grand Service, as
befitted a banquet for the most exclusive company in the
world, already glittered in all its glory on the 170 foot long
solid mahogany table, alongside the settings of sparkling
Louis XV Sèvres.

Light fell a full sixty feet from the intricate ceiling with its
Grinling Gibbons carvings picked out in gold, and glinted
off the lustrous cut glass as it received its final polishing. The
gold and scarlet chairs were lined up with military precision
behind the sculptured white linen napkins. Finally, between
the pyramids of fresh-picked flowers, so heavy that it took
three men to lift each one, the five-foot tall solid gold
candelabra were set in place.

The Master of the Household surveyed the Waterloo
Chamber and nodded once. Almost without pausing he

hurried through to the Garter Throne Room, where Her Majesty would preside over the investiture of new knights before the banquet. Here blue, the blue of the Order of the Garter itself, was everywhere, set off by the lustrous panelling and the full-length portraits of sovereigns in their Garter robes. Compared with the lavish Waterloo chamber it had a muted grandeur, as befitted the oldest order of Christian chivalry in the world. Ever since 1349 the twenty-five knights of the Most Noble and Amiable Company of St George, named the Garter, had had one motto – 'Honi Soit Qui Mal Y Pense' – 'Shame on he who thinks the worst' and one duty, to uphold the rigorous laws of chivalry.

The Master of the Household paused for a moment, caught up by his sense of times past. History was alive in this room. Six centuries ago King Edward III, dancing with the Countess of Salisbury, gallantly picked up her fallen garter, and declared, 'Let no one think ill of it.' So began the ancient order of chivalry. Was she, had she been his mistress? No one knew, no one would ever know. That was the essence of chivalry. To defend the honour of your lady with your life, if necessary.

Chivalry . . . it had been a reality then. He had a sudden, confused image of the court as it must have been all those centuries ago, glowing, bawdy perhaps, but magical . . . and the King's defiant, gallant gesture, the essence of courtly love. Would any modern man do the same? Maybe chivalry was well and truly dead, though a romantic like himself preferred to think that its spirit at least lived on in this tall wood-panelled room, where the elderly knights gathered once a year to pay homage to their sovereign lady.

A familiar sound roused him. The King's Change, rung out by the eight bells from the Curfew Tower, as they'd done every three hours since 1477. Quickly he banished his moment's nostalgia. There was so much that still had to be done if everything was to run smoothly. The Prince of Wales, just back from his Commonwealth tour, was expected at any moment. It made for a tight schedule for him, but he'd said he'd be back in time for the annual ceremony, as one of the Knights, and he was a man of his word.

With one last glance behind him the Master of the Household left the Garter Throne Room and headed briskly for the kitchens below stairs, noting with approval the two footmen walking slowly through the corridor swinging their censers of smouldering lavender. Time was pressing, but details mattered ... He frowned and hurried towards the stairs. He must check that the rounds of tender milk-fed veal for the flétan au vin blanc were of prime quality and the spring duckling well-plucked, and then there was the last-minute decision to be made, with the aid of the sommelier, between the Mazis Chambertin and the Hattenheimer Mehrholzen '64.

Outside the State Apartments the maroon Rolls whispered to a halt in the inner quadrangle of the Upper Ward. Calmly, oblivious to the anxious group gathered in the arched doorway awaiting his arrival, the Prince of Wales strode smoothly up the steps to the private royal apartments, followed by his detective. His tall, slim figure showed not a hint of tiredness; he moved like the athlete he was. Despite the rigours of the long flight his simple, excellently cut grey suit was immaculate. He paused to exchange a few words with his equerry, bringing a smile to the man's face. Despite his schedule, the Prince always had time for the small courtesies.

Then, still moving with that smooth, deceptively slow stride, he disappeared through the archway.

Back in the Lower Ward the crowd was growing. The route which the royal party would take from the Upper Ward to St George's Chapel before the investiture service was lined with the proud helmeted figures of the Household Cavalry, swords in hand, golden plumes fluttering in the Spring breeze, thigh-length black boots a gleaming contrast to their scarlet tunics. The initiated could tell which regiment the individual men belonged to by the grouping of the gold buttons on their tunics. Behind the Guards, cordoned off, the crowds milled eagerly, jostling for a better viewpoint. The experienced onlookers had brought shooting sticks to sit on and packed lunches for the long wait.

Wedged between a cordon pole and a white-gloved bobby, Julie heaved an impatient sigh.

'God, I'm hungry.'

'You can't be. I thought you were in love.'

Julie blushed scarlet.

'Ssh, you fool ...' She shot a nervous glance at the tall policeman. 'Someone'll hear.'

Her friend giggled. The tension of the moment was infectious. She still thought Julie was just bluffing, but there was a determined, all-or-nothing look on her face that she'd seen before. She shivered in anticipation.

Slowly, the hours passed. The crowd stirred restlessly, but the guardsmen stood proudly immobile. At last a ripple of noise from the Upper Ward announced that the procession was under way.

'They're coming!' Julie's face went suddenly pale. The two girls craned their necks round the cordon. Their eyes went wide. Slowly, ankle-length blue velvet cloaks sweeping the ground, the Knights of the Garter advanced towards them. The crowd fell silent. It was a moment straight out of medieval history. The graceful white plumes fluttered from their velvet caps, the insignia of the Garter gleamed on their left shoulders, above the heart.

A quiver of disappointment went through Julie's friend.

'But they're *old*.'

'Of course they are, silly.' Julie's eyes weren't even on the solemn procession of Knights, she was looking beyond them. A sigh of intaken breath went round the crowd. The royal party were in view. First the Queen and Prince Philip, behind them the Queen Mother and ...

Julie gripped her friend's arm.

'There.' Her voice was hardly above a whisper. '*He's* not old.'

18

Silently they watched the Prince of Wales draw nearer. The long velvet cloak and dashing plumed hat suited his tall figure. He looked like a medieval prince out of a Holbein painting, dare-devil blue eyes dancing in a tanned face. He was smiling down at his diminutive grandmother; with one hand he brushed back a straying lock of black hair.

Julie shrank back behind the policeman.

'I can't do it.' Now it came to it, he was so much more real than that quick glimpse she'd seen in the car. There was something about him, the way he carried himself, that made it quite clear who he was. Feeling suddenly small she half turned away.

'Chicken!' Her friend hissed in her ear. 'I knew you'd never have the nerve!'

Julie hesitated. The Prince was almost abreast of them now, his gaze straying over the crowd, smiling.

'There, he's looking for you! Just like you said.'

Julie gazed open-mouthed. She was so close she could see the heavy gold tassels on his cloak. She was mesmerized. In the dream she felt his brilliant blue eyes pass over her without a trace of recognition.

'Go on!' She felt her friend's hand hard in the small of her back. Suddenly she was through the cordon, dimly aware of a gasp from the crowd. Everyone seemed frozen to the ground. Still in a dream, her heart pounding deafeningly in her ears, she ducked past a guardsman. There he was. His face was the only thing she could see. It wore a faint frown. Her heart sank. She felt someone grab her arm and shook herself free. She'd said she'd do it, now she had to. With one last despairing lunge she rushed forward. The next thing she knew she was lying face down on the hard macadam. Around her she heard a gasp of shock, then a faint titter from the crowd. I tripped, she thought, stunned. Waves of embarrassment ran up and down her body. She closed her eyes tight, hoping she could disappear. Someone grasped her roughly by the shoulder.

'No. Wait.'

The voice was quiet but authoritative. The rough hand retreated.

'Have you hurt yourself?'

She looked up. It was him. The blue eyes looked straight into hers. She shook her head dumbly, feeling her cheeks go scarlet.

'Here. Let me help you up.'

Everyone else was smiling, laughing at her, but he wasn't. His mouth twitched, but his eyes were sympathetic. The blue cloak swirled around her, strong arms lifted her and she was on her feet. Dimly she heard the click of cameras. Then, to her scalding embarrassment, the crowd began to titter. She looked down, thoroughly mortified. Everyone was staring at her now, laughing behind their hands.

Suddenly the Prince stepped forward. The laughter died away. With one hand he doffed his white-plumed hat, with the other he raised her grazed, dirty hand to his lips. His eyes, the last twinkle of suppressed laughter gone from them, raked the waiting faces.

'Honi soit qui mal y pense ...'

There was a stunned silence, then a spontaneous roar of applause went up.

Dazed, Julie watched as with one last smile for her the Prince rejoined the procession. She hardly felt it as a security official whisked her out of the way and off to have her grazes seen to. The last face she caught sight of was Stephanie's, awed and envious behind the cordon. Proudly she walked past the curious crowd, conscious of the eyes on her. She knew she'd never be this close to him again ... but this was something she'd have to tell her granchildren. That one day, she'd felt like a Queen.

Hours later, the investiture service over, the royal family gathered in their private apartments. The incident during the procession, which could so easily have soured the occasion, was uppermost in their minds. The press would have been only too willing to make the most of such a heavensent opportunity.

Charles, his face showing for the first time the accumulated strain of the past weeks, stretched his long legs out towards the empty grate. The Queen eyed her eldest son sympathetically.

'I'm glad to be back.' Their eyes met in mutual understanding. They both knew how welcome it was to be for a few moments off-stage, away from the public spotlight.

'I thought you handled that very well.'

'Thank you.' He smiled. 'It's not the first time, after all.'

'I know.' As the eldest son and heir to a kingdom, Europe's most eligible bachelor, nearing thirty, at an eminently marriageable age, he was bound to bring a flutter to the hearts of impressionable young girls wherever he went Some were after publicity, some were more innocent.

'Poor little girl.' He shook his head wryly.

'Poor little girl?' The Queen Mother chimed in from her seat by the window overlooking the Quadrangle. 'I doubt if she'd like to hear you call her that.'

The Prince smiled.

'I know.'

He stirred restlessly in his chair. If only they knew, these aggressive, aspiring femmes fatales who threw themselves at him on beaches, in crowds, on isolated ski-slopes, how unattractive he found them. Some sensitive chord in him winced whenever it happened. That vain, probably silly little girl today, for instance. How surprised she'd have been to realize that he'd found her infinitely more sympathetic with her grazed hands and embarrassed face than rushing towards him with the glassy-eyed determination to kiss him in public written all over her face.

With the ease of long practice he dismissed it from his mind. He was home now, with a clear week to recuperate before the next round of royal duties, beginning with the Trooping of the Colour. He stretched again and rubbed his hand across his face.

The Queen Mother rose to her feet.

'Well, Charles, I must get back to the Lodge.' The Royal Lodge, set in the Great Park, was her pride and joy, as well as her home at Windsor.

She reached up to kiss her tall grandson.

'Hot toddy and bed for you, my dear, that's what I would advise.'

With a last smile she left the room. But the Queen remained. Charles waited. He knew there was something she meant to say to him, perhaps something arising from the incident this afternoon.

She was looking meditatively into the empty grate.

'You know, Charles ... there's one sure way to avoid that kind of ... ... unpleasantness.' She glanced up.

He waited for her to say more, but there must have been something in his face that deterred her. Her frown cleared and her face softened. She hesitated.

'Tell me, is Henrietta coming down for the weekend?'

He hid a smile. Perhaps it was always this way between mother and son, he didn't know. But he felt he could read her mind as clearly as if she'd spoken her thought aloud.

'I don't know yet.' His mouth twitched, then he took pity on her. 'But I'd intended to ask her tomorrow evening, after the Opera.'

'Good.' The Queen nodded briskly. The brilliant blue eyes, so like his own, only a shade lighter in hue, returned to their contemplation of the grate. 'She's a nice girl.'

'And a suitable wife.'

'Of course.' The Queen looked up, met his eyes and burst out laughing. 'Charles, you wretch, you knew all along!' She shook her head and rose to her feet. 'I'll leave you now, you must be tired after the journey. Sleep if you can before dinner. Anne and Mark will be here.' She paused at the doorway.

Charles stifled a sigh. Gently he bent and kissed his mother on both cheeks, Continental-fashion. How often he'd thought of a family of his own, children ... Only some stubborn, romantic streak had kept him single up till now. What was he waiting for? He found it difficult to explain even to himself.

Silently the Queen admitted defeat. After she'd gone Charles went into his adjoining bedroom and stretched out full-length on the covers, letting his exhaustion wash over him at last. Somewhere, perhaps, there was the right woman for him. What would she be like? For a moment he tried to picture her. He felt so sure he'd recognize her if he met her, and yet he couldn't summon up her face. All he could see was a composite of all the girls he'd ever known and loved for a time – but never enough.

At last he gave up the struggle and let sleep take him. His last thought was of Henrietta. Lovely, laughing Henrietta, her blonde hair sewn with diamonds, glittering like a jewel herself in the darkness of the royal box at Covent Garden. And if, in the shadows behind her, he thought he saw another girl's face, the face of a mysterious stranger, who was to know or care.

'Well, there it is, dear. Do you want to take it or not? Better make up your mind sharpish, I've got some stew on downstairs.'

The landlady watched curiously as the girl in the grey hat walked slowly across the room and stood by the window. She didn't seem interested in the fittings, just the view. Well, perhaps that was all to the good. This room was always the last to go; it was the stairs that did it. And though it was central, really quite close to the bustling shops of Kensington, no one could deny it was the wrong end of the High Street, tucked away in the decaying back streets between the Olympia exhibition hall and the railway line.

'Well?'

The girl didn't turn round. She hadn't had a good look at her face yet, it was hidden under the hat brim. Funny how she didn't take it off.

'I'll take it.'

The landlady heaved a sigh of relief, and turned to business.

'That'll be seven pounds a week.' She scanned the girl's clothes, taking in their shabbiness. 'In advance.'

The girl dug into her coat pocket and took out a creased brown envelope. The landlady's doubts returned as she saw how little money it contained. Carefully the girl counted out the notes and handed them over. The landlady hesitated. Obviously it was no use asking for a deposit. But there wasn't much worth breaking up here anyway.

'All right, dear. I won't be troubling you again till next week.' She handed over the keys. 'No baths after 11 p.m. and quiet on the stairs, mind.'

The girl nodded and put down her case.

'Thank you.'

The landlady hesitated at the door. There was something about her new tenant that piqued her curiosity.

'Here. Let me hang up your hat and coat.'

'No!' The girl took a step backwards, then recovered her poise. 'It's all right, thank you. I'd like . . . I'd like to settle in first.'

'Please yourself.' The landlady gave a sniff and closed the door behind her.

The girl listened tautly to the sound of the woman's footsteps as she went down the stairs, then breathed a sigh of relief. Like a statue coming suddenly to life she hurried over to the window. A smile of pure delight spread over her face. The glass could do with a clean, but to her the view was magic. It was hers, for a whole week, hers alone. Way below was a sea of green leaves, blotting out the back yard. Beyond that was a blackened brick wall, and beyond that the mysterious glinting tracks of a railway line, what looked like hundreds of them, weaving in and out of each other in their own intricate pattern.

She leaned on the sill, her exhaustion forgotten. It seemed as if the whole world was spread out in front of her, the London air so clear that she could see the little blades of grass and even tiny white flowers growing between the tracks.

She stared up along the track. The sun was just dipping down, topping every edge with gold. One small blue cloud floated motionless beside it, with a few specks of birds circling lazily through it. Suddenly she felt a surge of hope. She'd come this far, surely, somehow, she'd get there in the end. Looking down on the sunset like this she felt that anything must be possible, even the task she'd set herself. Because she had to succeed. If she failed ...

She turned away from the window abruptly, blotting out the thought. The room was small and crowded with an odd assortment of furniture. An iron-framed bed with a faded candlewick spread. Two armchairs that had seen better days. A large cabinet made of some strange yellow wood that looked as if it had once been intended for mixing cocktails. The walls had been recently painted, but the new paint ended in a wavery line before it reached the ceiling. And the carpet had been patched so many times, it looked like a map of the world.

She smiled again. The golden light made everything in it look beautiful to her. But it would have been beautiful anyway, because it was hers. The first room of her own she'd ever had. All her life, as far back as she could remember, she'd had to share. First in the orphanage ... she suppressed a shudder, and lifted one hand to touch her cheek. Five years ago, when the Principal had summoned her to his study and told her about the Foundation, it had seemed like a miracle. Apparently there were people in America who cared about girls like her, even though they'd never met her. People who remembered their own Scottish ancestors, who'd fled from the English persecution centuries ago and taken refuge in the Southern Seaboard states, where the pines and Atlantic winds reminded them of home ... Escape ... and all because of this. She touched her cheek with a wry smile. It must have been awkward for the Principal to have her around, living proof that the system didn't work, that slip-ups happened.

But she'd been too young to think like that then. All she'd thought of was escape. From the dark, airless corridors with their smell of cold linoleum and over-cooked porridge. From the loneliness in the dormitory late at night, when all the other girls were asleep. From feeling ugly and worthless and alone. A nothing, or worse than nothing. A nobody.

She'd resolved then never to come back. All she'd wanted to do was forget, make a new life. But she hadn't realized you couldn't leave the past behind. And her past was here. The Robertsons had been kind, busy people; they'd given her a taste of what a real family was like. Which only made it worse, somehow, not to have one of her own. Mrs Robertson had even cried a little when she'd said she was coming back. And given her the black coat, too warm for the Carolina winters.

Slowly she slipped the coat off her shoulders and hung it on the back of the door. The golden light was fading now, and so was her exultation. She caught sight of her face reflected in the dressing table glass and halted. Conflicting thoughts filled her mind. She'd grown so used to avoiding her own reflection, it was second nature. Just as she'd got used to wearing a hat whenever she went out where strangers might see her.

But maybe now was the moment to change all that. Resolutely she knelt down on the stool, glad the room was almost dark. In the old glass with its silvering of dust her face looked very pale. Her eyes, which the girls at the orphanage had called mud-coloured, had dark blue stains under them. She stared for a moment at this stranger's face, then deliberately tilted her head so that her cheek came into full view. Her mouth tightened. There it was. Neither worse nor better than she'd expected. High on the cheekbone, the pale raised line that would mark her out forever.

She traced it carefully with her fingers. She'd done that so many times over the years she should be used to it by now. In the beginning she'd had the crazy idea that one day, by magic, it would just disappear. Each morning she'd rush to

26

the mirror to see if the miracle had happened. Then she'd grown wiser. Instead of looking in the mirror she'd searched other people's faces. She'd had a fantasy ... one day she'd meet someone who'd wave a magic wand over her and make the scar invisible. Look straight into her eyes and prove it didn't matter. But little by little she'd given up hope of that too. It was too much to expect, just a silly childish fantasy. But it had got her through the years.

And now ... Carefully she unclasped the locket from round her neck and laid it on the dresser. Her eyes went from the locket to the scar and back again. Had it been worth it after all? Her lips tightened resolutely. It had to be. Inside, she knew she had something to offer. She just had to find someone who wanted it.

She turned away from the mirror and unpinned her hat. With awkward fingers she unravelled her braid and spread her hair out on her shoulders. It was no use thinking about the past. She had to make do with what she'd got.

Quickly she unpacked and undressed. She had so many things to do tomorrow. First, and most urgent, she had to earn some more money. The flight had eaten deeper into her savings than she'd thought; she had barely enough left to live on for a week. She'd been lucky to find a room so cheap.

The bed was cold and hard, the sheets and coverings worn thin. The soft blue square of the window now held nothing but darkness. For a moment she felt desperately alone. There was no one, anywhere, who cared whether she lived or died. No one even knew where she was.

Then, on one of the buildings on the other side of the railway line a lighted sign sprang out of the darkness, bright as the fourth of July. It said, in glowing red letters, 'Take Courage'. She smiled to herself. It seemed like a message. She closed her eyes, slid one hand round the silky coolness of the locket, and fell asleep.

'Piers! Watch out!'

Without turning, Piers knew from his team-mate's

anguished bellow what he would see – the Prince of Wales, polo-stick swinging at a lethal angle, his pony's ears laid flat to its head, charging towards him at a rate of knots.

Evasive action was out of the question. He ducked his chin harder into the leather strap of his cap and braced himself for the collision. Half a breath later it came, jarring every bone in his body. He caught a glimpse of the Prince's face, alight with the joy of battle, but there wasn't time for more. By the time he'd righted himself, his pony's muscles bunching with the effort, the Prince was racing down the field towards the goal, pursued hell-for-leather by the rest of Piers' team.

They didn't catch him. There was a whoop of approval from the onlookers as the goal went home. Begrimed and grinning, his faultless white breeches and gloves mud-spattered, the Prince rode back, his lean form swaying easily in the saddle.

'What happened there, Piers?'

Piers smiled back ruefully.

'A slight case of absentmindedness, I think Sir.'

Together they dismounted. The rest of the teams were disbanding too, it was the last chukka. The Prince ran an expert hand over his pony's shoulder.

'Not lame is she, Sir?'

'Julietta? No, she's as frisky as a two-year-old.'

They walked back companionably to the clubhouse. Despite his own performance, Piers was pleased with the day's practice. It was a perfect Spring day, ideal for polo at Smith's Lawn, the ground neither hard nor soft. And he needn't feel too ashamed of that last goal. The Prince was well nigh unstoppable when he was in this mood.

A lad took the two ponies and they went in to change, their long boots clumping on the wooden floor. As always Piers was aware of the omnipresent detective waiting discreetly outside the door, but he'd grown used to that. He and the Prince had been childhood companions, schoolfriends and now team-mates. He probably knew more about the heir to the throne than anyone in England.

'Hey, Piers.' The Prince's tousled wet head appeared over the shower stall. 'What do you think about marriage?'

Piers blinked. He might know the Prince well, but he still had the ability to surprise him.

'I try not to, Sir. Even the thought of it brings me out in a rash!' Hiding a grimace of stiffness he bent to retrieve his bar of soap.

'No, seriously ...' The Prince was towelling his hair vigorously. His blue eyes snapped with energy. Piers marvelled, wishing he could manage to keep himself in such good condition.

'Well, Sir ...' He hesitated. 'Did you see the papers this morning?'

'No, haven't had time. Had they anything special to say?'

'Not really, Sir. Just some more stuff about "Charlie's Angels."'

The Prince laughed. 'Is that all? I'm used to that. But you've dodged my question again. I may have to throw you in the Tower.'

Piers sighed and gave up on the soap. His back was aching too much.

'Well Sir, it's not a fair question really. Marriage is different for different people.' He wished he could think of something more profound.

'Is it?' The Prince's eyes held a look of interest. Encouraged, Piers made his way to the nearest slatted bench.

'If I'm going to be serious, Sir, I have to sit down.' He breathed in deeply. 'If I may say so, Sir, you've always seemed to have a pretty good idea of what you feel about marriage. From what I read in the newspapers, that is.'

'You mean about marrying a friend rather than someone you're madly in love with?' Piers nodded. 'Hmmm ... I know. And it all sounds very sensible when I say it.'

'Has something happened to change your mind, Sir?'

The Prince frowned. 'No, not exactly ... I just don't know how I feel about it any more. After all, one could go on being sensible for the next hundred years, and where would it get one?' Piers kept quiet. 'That's why I'm asking you.'

Piers sighed. 'I'm not much help, Sir. I don't think I've met the right woman yet. You know, the one you don't even have to ask because you know the answer and you know it's right. I suppose for me the whole idea of marriage is in a way ... incidental. Nothing to do with the real thing. Does that make sense?'

Charles nodded. He was listening with his usual intent, courteous interest. Piers hurried on:

'But for all I know it's just a question of timing. You know, one reaches a certain age, one does certain things ... one leaves the nursery, shedding salt tears, one goes to school, one leaves home, one reaches voting age, one marries ...'

The Prince looked at him with a glint of amusement.

'That explains a great deal. I'm not eligible to vote and I haven't left home. No wonder I find it hard to make up my mind.'

Piers smiled.

'Anyway, I'm the last person you should consult, Sir. I've never even plucked up enough courage to ask anyone to marry me.'

Charles looked at him again. His face wore a pensive look.

'Neither have I, old chap. Neither have I.' He paused. 'And the thing is, I'm only allowed to do it once.'

He gave Piers a quizzical smile. 'So.' He clapped him on the shoulder. 'I think that's enough fresh air and interrogation for one day, don't you?' He swept up his cap and whip and headed for the door. 'That is, unless you'd like a quick run round the Park?'

Piers groaned, then said with as much dignity as he could muster, 'I'd rather not, Sir.' At this rate he'd be spending the night in a sitz bath.

The Prince paused at the door. His smile faded, to be replaced by an expression Piers hadn't seen before. Puzzled, undecided ... almost at a loss. He tapped his whip restlessly against his thigh.

'Is anything the matter, Sir?'

'No ... yes ... I don't know.' The Prince suddenly ran his hand through his hair, making it stick out on end. 'I've been overworking, I think. I need a change.' A thought struck him. 'Wait a minute ... maybe you can help me there.' He spread his hands wide in a gesture of mock appeal. 'Tell me, Piers ... what can I do that's different? Without stepping out of line of course?'

'Well, Sir ...' Piers racked his brains. Then a thought struck him.

'There's the Beggar's Banquet, Sir.'

A gleam of interest entered the Prince's eyes.

'What's that?'

'It's our annual charity ball, Sir ... Same as usual, only this time we're asking everyone to come dressed in rags. I know you don't usually come, Sir, but perhaps this time ...'

The Prince paused, tapping his whip meditatively. Then he smiled.

'It's a thought, Piers. It's certainly worth considering.' His smile broadened. 'A Beggar's Banquet ...' Suddenly there was a mischievous glint in his eye. 'Maybe I will come at that. It sounds like fun.'

CHAPTER TWO

The next day she knew what she had to do. She dressed hurriedly and scraped her hair back into a tight braid at the back of her head. She had to look neat. She threw on her coat and rammed the grey hat well down on her head, locked the door with her brand new keys, mentally resolving to grease the squeaky hinge with the cake of airline soap when she got back, then marched down the stairs before she lost her nerve.

Once out in the street, she almost turned back. She didn't really know how to go about it, but she knew what she was looking for. First of all, she needed money. She'd never get any further without it. Only there wasn't much she could do, apart from cook and clean and make herself useful. And it would be better if she looked for something where she wouldn't be on show too much. She wasn't ready to face up to strangers yet.

The first employment agency she tried wasn't helpful. They were looking for secretaries and receptionists, though they did ask, hopefully, whether she'd had any training as a nanny. The second offered her an interview for a job as a wages clerk, but she realized that the journey to and fro from her room would swallow up most of her earnings, and she'd never be able to save the amount she needed. In any case, there was no certainty she'd get the job. As the girl in the agency pointed out, if anyone with 'administrative experience' turned up, the firm would be a fool not to take them instead.

It was proving even more difficult than she'd thought. She bought a loaf of bread in a corner shop and spent her lunch hour in the park. She ate as much as she could and fed the rest to the birds. Then she went back to the search.

It was the same story. Eager, smartly painted girls lost most of their enthusiasm when she admitted she'd not had a job before. They seemed to think that meant she'd never worked. Looking back, she realized she'd worked all her life – first at the orphanage, where she'd learned to wash up almost as soon as she could walk, then at the Robertsons' farm, where there was always work to be done. More work anyway than sitting behind a desk.

By the end of the day she still hadn't found a job. But she refused to give up. And at the last agency she tried, a small one hidden away down a back alley above a tobacconist's shop, her luck turned.

It was different from the others. Instead of crisp, louvred blinds at the windows there were faded brocade curtains. Round the walls, instead of enticing job cards, were framed photographs of country houses, neatly labelled. Northwick Manor. The Wealds. Park House.

The elderly woman who interviewed her riffled through her file of situations vacant, and drew out a card.

'Not very much money I'm afraid.' The woman scanned the card. 'But it's an excellent situation. A very good family, of course. And with your ... er ... limited experience ...' She slid her glasses down her nose and eyed Rose. Her eyebrows rose as she saw the scar. She picked up the card and seemed about to replace it in the file.

'I don't mind about the money.' She did, but any job was better than none.

The woman hesitated. 'You'll have to live in, of course.' She obviously hoped that would put her off. She couldn't know that was just what Rose needed. With her living expenses paid she'd be able to save. She didn't care how long it took – six months, a year. At least it was a start.

Reluctantly the woman consulted the card and picked up the telephone.

'Hello, Lady Osborne?' Her voice changed, suddenly smooth and unctuous. 'This is Miss Prine, of the Clarendon Domestic Agency. I have an applicant for the post of live-in maid in my office; perhaps you would care to arrange a time for an interview?'

There was a long pause, during which Rose could just hear a high-pitched rapid voice. It sounded, even across the wire, shrill and demanding.

'I see. I see. In that case as soon as possible.'

Within a few minutes everything was arranged. And within half an hour Rose was standing outside a tall Knightsbridge house consulting for the hundredth time the scrap of paper in her hand.

8, Carlton Place. This must be the place. It had to be. She leaned against the stone balustrade and looked up. The house was so tall and imposing it made her dizzy just to look at it. It rose straight and solid, a five-floor block of blood-red brick, each window picked out in brilliant white, the balcony railings beetle black. More railings loomed ominously out of the balustrade, each one topped by a lethal-looking gold spearhead.

She looked round, mustering up her courage. It was very different from any other house she'd been in. The Robertsons' plain, low, white-painted farmhouse had been nothing like the size of this. The orphanage had been almost as large, but grimed with Edinburgh dirt. This one looked big enough to house a hundred orphans, but belonged to just one family. More windows than you could easily count, and in front of each a white box packed with tightly regimented spring flowers. Broad stone steps, flanked by two half-crouching lions, led up to a vast black door. The brass figure eight gleamed unmistakably on the front.

Taking a deep breath, she opened the wrought iron gate and went up. She could hardly reach the bell-push, set in its elaborate enamel scrollwork. Deep inside the house she heard a man's voice raised in irritation and a woman's voice replying. Then the rapid clack of heels across a hard floor. Abruptly the door flew open. A sour-faced brown-skinned woman in a smart black and white uniform that was one size too big for her, appeared in the doorway. It was obvious from her face that she was expecting someone else.

She looked Rose impersonally up and down and then said
something Rose didn't catch. Seeing Rose's blank expression she threw up her hands and eyes and began to point
back in the direction she'd just come.

'Tradesmen, tradesmen!'

Rose tried to explain she wasn't a tradesman, but the
woman just shouted louder. Taking Rose's arm in a sharp
grip she gestured towards a much smaller door at the side of
the house, with no number and a plain white bell-push. Then
she slammed the door.

Taken aback, Rose stood on the steps, her lips set in a grim
line. She looked at the small black door and small white bell.
She was beginning to understand. One door for one kind of
people, another door for the other kind.

But she had no choice. She drew up her head and went
back down the steps towards the small door. As she edged
her way down she noticed how much darker and dirtier it
was down here, below street level. A row of dustbins
welcomed her, one of them almost overflowing.

Just as she was about to press the bell she heard a car draw
up outside. Instinctively she leaned back against the wall
amongst the garbage. Overhead she heard the slam of car
doors, then steps going slowly up to the front door. It swung
open almost immediately.

A man's voice, deep and cultured, with a slow drawl to it,
spoke overhead. Cramped in her hiding place under the
stairway, Rose was glad she couldn't make out the words.
The door closed again and she breathed a sigh of relief.
Quickly she brushed down the collar of her coat where it had
collected dust and spider's webs, and reached up again for
the white bell. To her dismay she heard the door above open
again. There was no time to hide this time. It was the same
man, she recognized his voice, but this time he was accompanied by the most beautiful girl she'd ever seen. Sleek
golden curls, a bright red mouth, long slender legs in pencil-

thin heels. The man, his face indistinct, took her arm as tenderly as if she was made of glass.

Her heart racing, Rose forced herself to freeze on the spot. She'd be all right, if only they didn't notice her. The girl's heels clacked down the steps, a wave of delicate perfume wafted down after her. Rose held her breath. They were almost gone. She closed her eyes, willing them not to discover her, and leaned back under the protective darkness of the stairwell.

Crash! To her horror the slight movement dislodged one of the dustbin lids. With a sound that seemed deafening to her ears it fell resoundingly onto the stone flags.

'Henrietta!' It was the man's voice again, only this time clear and authoritative. She heard him stride swiftly back up the path and swing back the wrought iron gate.

'What is it, Sir?' The girl's voice this time, with a note of alarm in it. Her heels clacked more tentatively as she followed him up the path.

'I don't know.'

They were back on the steps now. Rose tried to speak, to say something, anything, but nothing came out.

'Hello? Is there anyone down there?'

The man sounded angry. He was leaning over the balustrade now, she could see the outline of his head and shoulders.

'Show yourself!'

The note of authority in his voice was unmistakable. Rose felt the blood rush into her cheeks. This was worse than anything she could have imagined. What would they think of her? It looked as if she'd been eavesdropping, or worse. Mustering all her courage she stepped out from under the stairwell.

'Who is it, Sir?' The girl's voice.

'I don't know.' Rose was glad it was getting dark and he couldn't see her face. He was just a vague dark outline against the sky.

'Let me look.' The girl's head appeared at his shoulder. Her hair glowed fair against the man's dark head; she looked as if she was surrounded by light. Her gaze swept over Rose, then she gave a little laugh of relief.

'It's all right, Sir, it's nobody. Just one of the servants. Mother was expecting a new one.' She turned on her heel, throwing her loose silvery wrap round her bare shoulders. The man hesitated a moment longer, staring intently down at Rose's face. She lowered her head, hiding her face under the hat brim from that penetrating gaze. Then he too made his way slowly down the steps and into the waiting car.

Still frozen to the spot, Rose heard the powerful engine draw away. Moving very slowly, she turned back to the small black door. She should have known. There were two kinds of people, and that was the way things were. Wherever you went. There was no escaping it.

Her hand hovered over the bell, then her lips tightened. With one hand she tugged her hat straight, with the other she tucked in a stray wisp of hair. Her face was very pale. Her head up and her back very erect, she went up the steps. Now there were two bright red spots of colour in her cheeks. She reached the iron gate and turned back to look challengingly up at the big house. It stared back at her blankly. The stone lions looked haughtily down their long noses. On an impulse she stuck her tongue out at them, then closed the gate behind her with a defiant clang. She didn't know what she was going to do. All she knew was that she couldn't go back to being a servant. She belonged to herself. Her self respect was all she had. If she lost that, she'd die inside.

When she reached the end of the street she turned and began to run.

Laughing and chattering, the crowd spilled out of the red plush, brightly-lit interior of the Royal Opera House and into the cool Spring night. Some piled into waiting taxis, some began to make their way in small groups down Floral Street towards the new Covent Garden piazza for more discussion of the evening's performance of Don Giovanni over a late-night supper. Others, resplendent in long evening dresses, diamonds and furs, were whisked away to the exclusive clubs of Mayfair in their chauffeur-driven cars.

With the ease of long practice an usher escorted the Prince of Wales and his companion from the royal box to a discreet side exit. The unlicenced maroon Rover was waiting close by, the engine already purring smoothly. Without a word the detective slipped into the front seat beside the chauffeur, his eyes flicking briefly over the street ahead. Inside a minute the car had slipped unnoticed into Bow Street and away.

Henrietta leaned back luxuriously in the deeply cushioned leather seat and glanced at her companion. The Prince seemed preoccupied this evening, but that wasn't unusual. His black brows were drawn down over his eyes in an introspective frown. She knew better than to distract him. Though they'd known each other for years, ever since childhood, she'd always sensed this reserve about him. He could be extraordinarily charming, extrovert even, but there was still an invisible screen around him which set him apart. Vaguely, she felt he needed that screen, that aura of faint untouchability. No matter what, he was still the Prince of Wales. But she'd only once seen him exercise the full power of his authority, on an over-familiar and over-excited journalist. Then, the effect had been chilling. From the man's eyes, she'd seen he'd never forget it. What was his name? Earnshaw, that was it.

The Prince, suddenly aware of her eyes, turned his head and smiled.

'A good performance, I thought.'

'Yes Sir. The tenor was in fine form.' She hesitated. They hadn't had the chance to talk much before the curtain went up; that strange little incident outside the house had almost made them late. It had brought home to her once again how careful the Prince had to be, how alert. The paparazzi would stop at nothing for a story. But luckily it had been nobody. She'd had to admire his self-control.

Perhaps that was the reason behind his preoccupation. Or it could be his work; she'd lost track of the number of organizations of which he was President or Chairman, but she knew their demands filled most of his time. Far from being a mere figurehead, he threw all his efforts into what he did. That was one of the things she'd never been able to understand about him, his total dedication. If only there weren't quite so many demands on his time. The glamour of being seen with the Prince of Wales was irresistible, but there were disadvantages ...

Unconsciously she stifled a sigh. The Prince threw her a quizzical look.

'Tired?'

'No, Sir.' Guiltily she remembered he'd just returned from a taxing tour. 'But you must be.'

'I am, a little.' Now she could see in the light from the streetlamps that his face, normally lean, was a little more fine-drawn than usual. A spasm of disappointment went through her. That meant, most likely, that he'd be taking her straight home.

The Prince shifted a little in his seat. A sudden, rueful grin transformed him for a moment into the mischievous boy she'd known when she was only a small girl in pigtails.

'Stiff, too. I had a hard session at the sticks this afternoon.' Again she marvelled. He drove himself so hard, filling every minute of his time.

'And how is your second string, Sir?' It was an old joke between them. The second string was his beloved and extremely expensive team of six Argentinian-bred polo ponies. The first string, of which she herself was an honoured member, were the team of equally well-bred and young women whom the press kept bringing forward as eligible wives and future Queens.

The Prince smiled.

'Fighting fit. Julietta put me quite to shame.' But now that preoccupied shadow came over his face again. Was it something she'd said? She puzzled over it as the car slipped smoothly through the late-night crowds in Knightsbridge and Sloane Street. She'd been right; he wasn't taking her on to Annabel's or, which would have been even nicer, post-theatre supper in his suite of rooms at the Palace.

Her last hope died as the car murmured to a full stop in Carlton Place. Anxiously she racked her brains. Had she said or done anything wrong? She couldn't have. She was always so careful. It was probably just as he said, he was tired.

He handed her punctiliously from the car.

'I'll see you to your door.'

Together they walked slowly up the steps, his arm lightly supporting hers. Regretfully she acknowledged that his manners were perfect, so perfect she'd never be able to tell what he was really thinking. She glanced up at him. In this light his dark face looked distant, mysterious, that aura of untouchability even stronger.

'Won't you come in for a moment?'

He paused, looking down at her, unsmiling.

'Thank you, no.' Some of her disappointment must have showed on her face, because he took her hand and smiled. His touch sent a thrill of excitement through her. 'But I hope that you'll be able to come down for the weekend.' Another thrill went through her. Invitations to Windsor, given so apparently casually, were few and far between.

Looking down at her face, Charles hesitated. He cursed the strange feeling of restlessness he'd suffered from all evening, ever since the incident earlier. It wasn't so much the confrontation that had unnerved him, a lifetime's practice had trained him to deal with the unexpected, but the feelings it had aroused in him. For an eerie moment he'd felt trapped inside his role . . . and it had something to do with Henrietta.

He shook his head in exasperation at himself. Why was he so reluctant to commit himself? It wasn't fair to Henrietta. His gaze lingered on her face. She was very lovely. In her heels she was almost as tall as he was, but as softly curved as a thoroughbred filly, with that wonderful ash-blonde fairness you only found in England. How long had they known each other? Too many years to remember. And they spoke the same language, knew the same people ... She was so eminently suitable. Even the press agreed. There'd been another picture of her in the *Mail* only yesterday. She'd looked even prettier in the photograph than she did in real life. It had caught her best look – her brilliant smile – perfectly.

The pause lengthened. Quickly he made up his mind. It was time he made some sort of public statement.

'Had you thought of going to Warwick House for the Beggar's Banquet next week?'

Her eyes lit up.

'Yes, Sir, Piers did mention it. But I haven't got a rag to wear!'

He smiled, his strange mood lifting slightly. It was one of the things he liked best about her, her quick humour.

'Perhaps you would care to accompany me.'

'Oh Sir, I'd love to!'

There, it was done. It would mean a late night before the Trooping, but that couldn't be helped.

'The press will be there of course. I hope you don't mind.'

Her eyes were liquid as she looked up at him.

'Well, if we're all dressed as beggars, we'll all look equally silly, won't we Sir?' Her voice was light, but was that a speculative look he sensed in her eyes?

Quickly he bent to kiss her cheek.

'I've never seen you look silly in your life, and I doubt if you intend to start now.' The speculative look vanished – perhaps it was his imagination. Now there was nothing in her face but excited anticipation.

'I wonder who else will be there. I know Caroline's going. I wonder what she'll be wearing. *Anything* in her wardrobe would do, I expect ...' Abruptly she recovered herself. 'Are you sure you won't come in, Sir?'

Again that restlessness seized him. He had a quick picture of the house's interior: the spacious sitting room with its concealed lighting and perfect taste – Audubon prints, Dresden figurines, Persian carpets, Chippendale chairs: the French windows overlooking the garden, which Lady Osborne kept in excellent, almost military order, the beds as neatly coiffeured as Henrietta's glossy cap of hair. An ornamental yew hedge pruned into the shape of a chess piece – a knight – was the main feature of the garden. How many years did it take to prune and train a shrub into that shape? A lifetime, probably. He privately christened it the Prince of Wales – allowed to move two steps forward as long as he took one step sideways afterwards.

'Yes, I'm sure.' It came out stronger than he'd intended. For some reason, tonight, he didn't want to be indoors. This restlessness was filling him with a craving for something wilder, freer, he didn't know what. Suddenly he was sorry that he was spending the night at the Palace instead of returning to Windsor. Maybe it was the country air he craved.

Henrietta's perfect ivory eyelids, fringed with dark blue mascara, dropped. He lifted her chin and kissed her lightly on the lips. Her perfume – Chanel number 19, he'd given it to her himself – surrounded him.

'Good night. Sleep well.'

The door closed behind her and he lingered on the step for a moment, breathing deeply in the night air. It was after midnight, he was tired, but somehow he knew he wouldn't be sleeping well tonight.

Something in the air – Spring fever perhaps. Whatever it was, it filled him with a sudden irrepressible surge of elation. As if he'd escaped from something or someone. He waited an instant, trying to fight it down. He was after all the Prince of Wales, Duke of Cornwall, Duke of Rothesay, Earl of Garrick, Baron of Renfrew, Lord of the Isles and Great Steward of Scotland. There was no room in his life for impulse. Or was there?

He lifted his head. A few drops of rain fell on his face, cool and fresh as sea spray. Lord of the Isles . . . The nameless elation was back. He looked quickly to the right and left. The street was deserted. Without a moment's hesitation he raced down the steps and vaulted over the wrought iron gate.

CHAPTER THREE

'Got anything good, Palmer?'

The young photographer from the *Daily Mirror* had to shout above the boom of drums and clash of cymbals. His neck was festooned with equipment, Nikon clanking against Canon, adding their own random element of percussion as he craned to get a better view of the massed bands marching past.

James shook his head noncommittally. I wouldn't tell you anyway, he thought to himself. He was sweating in the unseasonable heat, made several degrees warmer by the crush of people, tourists mostly, who crowded the pavement. He wiped his forehead with his handkerchief, wishing he hadn't got so drunk last night. He couldn't take it like he used to. Not with Fabulous Forty staring him in the face. Still, he was glad he'd brought just the two Nikon camera bodies. Age and experience always won out in the end.

He could feel the pavement vibrating as the bands marched past. It was London's massed band season. He never failed to enjoy the sight. He'd got some good pics of the RAF motorbikers doing something complicated round a bollard – they were good value every year, obviously enjoyed every minute of it – but now pickings were thin. His sixth sense told him that it was probably time to drift up towards the Palace; Prince Charles was scheduled to arrive back from Windsor any minute, and it was always interesting to see who he might or might not have with him in the car. He'd just check out one more band, then trickle along with the other pressmen who were already beginning to detach themselves from the group and slope off back to the Palace gates to get a good vantage point before the rush. He chuckled. A lot of unsuspecting tourists would be getting the benefit of hard professional elbows just about now.

The spasm of amusement soon passed. That job for the Xiles was really giving him trouble. They were a new young band with big ideas and talent to match. They had their own sound – deceptively melodic, but with a bitter core to it. So the face they wanted for their first LP cover had to be special. Just a girl ... but special. He winced. A thousand pounds for the right girl. Easy money, he'd thought. But the deadline was nearly up, and if he had to look at another model's composite, all teeth and lipgloss, he'd jack it in on the spot.

The sound of the next band made his eyes brighten. All tanned bare legs, dancing golden plumes and sexy white boots, girl after girl, none of them, as far as he could see, old enough to vote. Ponytails too ... his toes curled with nostalgia. He focused in on a line of smooth brown thighs topped by earnest faces. The camera itself vibrated in his hands as they came nearer. They must have twenty kettle drums if they've got one, he thought, the rhythm pounding in his veins. You can beat my drum anytime you like, sister ...

He switched into overdrive, his whole being concentrated on the tiny rectangle of moving colour in his viewfinder. Then, with a last whisk of tasselled bottoms, a twinkle of polished brass and a nod of plumes, they were gone, far too soon for him. He lowered the camera, as always left empty by the effort of concentrating. He let a troop of massed bagpipes go by without comment. All he wanted to do now was rush back to the studio and spend a couple of hours in the darkroom. If they were half as good as he thought they were ...

He froze. Instinctively looked away, checked the image on his retina, looked back. Just a face in the crowd. But what a face ... To his photographer's eye it stood out like one broken pane of glass on a five-storey building. Instantly he brought up his camera with the black and white film and the long lens. If only she didn't notice him. As her face swam into focus, jerked into intimacy by the lens, he held his breath with excitement. At the back of his mind, with the certainty he'd learned to recognize, he knew that he'd just made his thousand. If only she kept still for long enough. As if she could hear him she stood absolutely motionless, her face turned towards the departing band. The white line of her cheek against the dark hair sent shivers down his spine.

Special . . . that was the only word for it. Exactly the face he'd been looking for. It would suit the Xiles bittersweet sound down to the ground. Beauty with a discord. A diamond all the more fascinating for being flawed. Beauty as old as the hills . . . but with the scar, modern as tomorrow. He couldn't have planned it better himself.

Already the other tourists were beginning to disband, milling around aimlessly, then splitting off to return to their cars and hotels. But the girl went on standing there, lost in a dream. James cursed as his cover began to disappear. Then suddenly her pose broke. She looked around her, seemingly aware of his eyes on her. Quickly he detached himself from the line of bobbies standing at the kerb and began walking towards her.

Don't panic, he muttered to himself. Don't panic, not yet anyway. But it was no use. Her eyes widened as she saw him and her face closed up. Hurriedly she lifted her hand. In it was a shapeless, battered grey felt hat, which she crammed down over her head, blocking out the whole upper part of her face.

To James the effect was as if someone had driven into his parking place before his very eyes. He almost shouted with outrage, then suppressed it into a whimper. Now she was turning, almost scurrying in her haste. All his hunter's instincts were aroused. He couldn't let this one get away – at least not without getting her to sign a model release form. That face was his, he'd seen it first.

As he set off in pursuit he heard from Buck House gate the buzz of excitement that heralded the arrival of the royal party. He ignored it without a pang of regret. He'd seen Prince Charles before, but the face was unique. He shoved one camera body into his pocket and fixed his best smile, gritting his teeth with the effort. As he swung into a deceptively slow stride he was already planning out the lighting – Rembrandt, high relief, low key, lots of texture. His last thought, as he rounded the corner into Queen Anne's Gate, was Christ, I hope she doesn't charge £200 a day.

It's a dream, it must be. Rose perched unsteadily on the stool and stared into the mirror. One minute she was listening to the parade – something she hadn't meant to do, only the Scots pipers brought back so many memories – and the next she was sitting here, in a photographer's studio at World's End, just off the King's Road.

World's End ... she hadn't believed him when he'd said where he wanted her to go. But she'd felt suddenly reckless, the sound of the pipes still in her blood. And she didn't have anywhere else to go. World's End was as good as anywhere.

'I want her just as she is, mind.' James frowned enormously at the girl behind her and made a slitting motion against his throat. The girl sniffed, obviously used to his threats.

'When Carole has finished messing about, come right on in.' Rose nodded, but his eyes had already glazed over again, as if he was thinking of something else. She didn't mind. She liked the way he looked at her face, closely but somehow impersonally. 'I need your face.' That's what he'd said, as if it didn't belong to her. So she'd made him a present of it. How could she refuse. He was the only one who'd ever asked.

'You'll have to take your hat off, love.' In a flash Carole whisked the grey felt away. Rose didn't even have time to cover her cheek, but the other girl wasn't looking. Her hands were busy unplaiting her hair.

'I'm a model too, you know.' She sniffed again.

'Really?' Rose stared at her, her cheek forgotten. It was

48

true, Carole managed to make being thin as a rake look like the only possible way to be. And round her mournful chocolate brown eyes was a wonderful gold line.

'Oh yes, I've done the rounds. Fashion mostly.' She struck a pose, making the pink nylon coverall look like a designer original. She glanced down at herself. 'Just editorial. No glamour, of course, I haven't got the tits.' Her eyes drifted over Rose's face. 'Never done character, either. What's it like?'

Luckily she didn't wait for an answer, but flipped open what looked like a fishing tackle box. While she scrabbled in it Rose sneaked a look round the cubicle. There was hardly room in it for two people and what seemed like a hundred assorted dresses, crammed onto a rack down the left-hand side. One was made up of nothing but shocking pink feathers. Behind her she could hear music playing. It was all a dream ... The naked light bulbs round the mirror began to dazzle her and she closed her eyes.

Carole's hands began to move over her face. She wanted to ask her what make-up she was using, but every time she opened her mouth she got a mouthful of face powder. It was probably something special. Maybe, in the photograph, the scar would hardly show at all.

'That's it.' Rose opened her eyes. With one sweep of her hand Carole tipped all the bottles back into her box. Rose kept her eyes fixed on the chipped white edge of the table top.

'Is it all right?'

Carole looked puzzled.

'Yeah, it's just what he wants, didn't he tell you? But don't you want to look?' Rose shook her head. The girl snapped her box shut and gazed at her with admiration.

'Cor ... you're a real professional.' Then, without changing her expression, she gave a sudden shout. 'She's ready, you old Bluebeard!' Seeing Rose's startled look she gave her a wink. 'Don't worry. He's harmless really.'

Afraid to smile in case her face cracked, Rose stepped through the battered wooden door that led from the tiny

49

cubicle. A carpet, hanging like a curtain over the doorway, came next, and then she was through into a room so big she thought for a moment she'd stepped outside into the street by mistake. High above her daylight filtered down through clouds of hanging dust from big skylights let into the arched roof. Ahead of her stretched acres of wooden floor. It was a huge space, almost as big as the airport lounge, but it had a familiar feel to it. Across the end was a balcony, ornately carved, and a circular stained glass window.

'It's a church!'

James' voice drifted down from the balcony. 'Used to be. Now it's just a monument to genius.' Now she could see him entangled with something round and metallic on a stalk, his hands full of trailing wires.

'Let's have a look at you.' His head popped up almost nervously. She steeled herself and looked up. The pause seemed endless. Maybe the make-up wasn't right. Maybe he'd change his mind.

'I don't mind having it done again . . .' Suddenly she knew how important this was for her. She wanted desperately, just once, to look like other people, even if it was only in a photograph.

He said nothing, but came down the wooden stairs with that worried, vague look in his eyes again. He was muttering to himself, sneaking little looks at her.

'This is for you.' He edged forward a stool, then stood, nibbling his fingers. She sat down and tucked her hands into her lap, suddenly conscious of the faded print of her dress.

'Is this dress all right?' Maybe he'd rather she put on the pink feathers.

'The dress . . .' he seemed stuck for words. 'The dress is . . . marvellous, fantastic, OUT OF THIS WORLD!' Suddenly he sprang into action, raced up the stairs and set off from somewhere a blaze of light.

'Look at me,' he sang out, way up in the balcony. 'Beautiful, beautiful,' he breathed, hidden behind his machinery. Beautiful . . . he didn't know what he was saying.

She hid a smile. For a photographer his eyesight didn't seem too good.

But after a while she almost forgot about him. The afternoon wore on; from time to time she heard Carole clattering in the tiny kitchen area, once she brought them each a cup of very strong tea, sniffing and saying 'Don't let it get cold.' But James never touched his. As the hours went by he seemed to move faster and faster, like a overwound clockwork mouse. Then, just when she thought he'd given up, he went over to the record player and put on some music.

The first notes sent a shiver down her spine. It was the music from the parade, the pipes high and sad as a bird's cry, or a baby's. Bringing back memories she'd thought she'd left behind. Herself, hardly big enough to see out of the window, high up in the orphanage nursery. There'd been a parade, only a small one, passing by in the street below. She'd heard the music and clung on to the window bars. The music pulled at her, she knew that if she could only follow it it would take her to the land of heart's desire. But hands tore her away from the window so she couldn't see any more, only listen to the music fading into the distance, never to return.

And then she'd been sent away. The music couldn't reach her any more. But once, she'd been standing beside the river, where the Cape Fear wound its way greasily through the marshlands, in autumn, watching the wild ducks fly Eastward overhead to their winter home by the estuary, where the river spread out and lost itself in the ocean. They flew so straight, no higher than they needed to be, knowing exactly where they were going and where they belonged, leaving the bitter inland cold for the warm, damp air off the sounds. They were going home. She'd heard the music in their cold little voices and thought, take me with you, and they had called back, one day, one day. But that day had never come.

'OK, that's it.' She blinked, still far away.

'Was it all right?'

He shrugged.

51

'Who knows?' But he looked pleased.

She was stiff as he helped her off the stool.

'Carole should have warned you. I'm a devil when I'm roused.' He disappeared, carrying his rolls of film, into an office at the other end of the nave. While she waited for him to come out Rose caught sight of some photographs hanging by their corners from what was clearly a common or garden clothes rack.

'Aagh!' One brown-stained thumb went over the face of the man in the photograph as James appeared at her shoulder. 'You don't want to look at those people. Take it from me, if you see someone dressed like that –' she looked carefully at the black jacket and white tie – 'do not give them even the time of day! Take it from me, they are BAD NEWS!'

'Then why do you take their picture?'

'Force of habit.' He waved a piece of paper in front of her. 'Sign here. Where shall I send the money?'

'What money?'

'Your modelling fee, of course.' She stared at him.

'Don't worry, I can afford it. I get paid, you get paid. It's all fancy ad budget money anyway. How about, er, fifty pounds?'

Fifty pounds . . . almost a hundred dollars. Enough, more than enough to take her the next step of the way. In a daze she signed her name and gave him her address.

'You don't know what this means to me.' She tried to thank him, but he waved her thanks away.

'There may be more later if they use it for the promotion.' He spun round, throwing his arms wide. 'And now, since we're both millionaires or soon going to be, it's time for – fish and chips!' He sank abruptly down on to the wooden floor and Carole appeared magically in the doorway carrying three steaming parcels wrapped in newspaper. They all sat down together on the scuffed boards and got their fingers greasy. Carole ate a lot for such a thin person. She finished first.

'Are you coming to the concert tonight?'

James clutched his head. 'Oh God. Can't do it, love. I

thought you were going to back me up at this other thing. You must, I'll suffocate all by myself amongst all the nobs.'

'And miss Split Rivett at the Odeon? You must be joking.'

Instantly James turned to Rose.

'But you'll be my blonde of the evening, won't you?' he wheedled, throwing a challenging look at Carole. 'It would be such a help to me in my work.' Rose caught Carole's eye. She was beginning to realize that helping James in his work could be a full-time job.

'Well, I . . .' A little stir of her old panic went through her. It was all right sitting here with just the two of them, but she wasn't used to appearing in public. Even with the make-up. Desperately she tried to think of an excuse.

'I couldn't go like this.' She indicated her dress.

James and Carole exchanged a glance. Carole smothered a giggle.

'Yes you could. No one's going to be dressed up. It's not that kind of thing.'

She hesitated.

'But I haven't been invited.'

James shrugged airily.

'That's OK. I'll get you in, and after that it won't matter. You'll see.' He smiled winningly. 'Come on. Don't you think you owe it to me?'

Put like that, it was impossible to refuse. James smiled in triumph.

'There's just one thing. You must promise not to wear that awful hat.'

'Oh, but . . .'

'It makes you look like . . . like a mushroom. I won't have one of my models looking like a mushroom.'

That did it. His face was so serious that the two girls burst out laughing. By the time Rose had wiped the tears from her eyes it had all been decided. She told herself firmly there was no need to be nervous. No one would notice her. She could leave early. Nothing bad could happen in just one evening. Even without her hat.

CHAPTER FOUR

A fusillade of flashes and a murmur of appreciation greeted Charles and Henrietta as the chauffeur ushered them out of the car. In the light streaming from the wide-open double doors of Warwick House Henrietta's dress was spot-lit, a bright flame of red with strategically placed tatters. Her hair was elegantly disordered, and on to her admirably straight nose she'd painted a line of fetching little freckles.

But the stir of appreciation and surprise from the pressmen hovering on the steps was more for the Prince of Wales' disguise. He was hardly recognizable. His usually immaculate blue-black hair was tousled, one lock falling rakishly over his forehead. The lower part of his face was transformed by a dark close-trimmed growth of beard, which gave him a sudden startling resemblance to his great-grandfather, King George V. In place of the familiar, sober-suited Prince was a tall, rakish, smiling strager, looking more as if he'd just stepped off a full-rigged sailing ship than travelled tamely by car from the Palace. His clothes carried out the theme. His dark blue fisherman's jersey was topped by a bright scarlet and white spotted neckerchief knotted casually at the neck. Faded canvas trousers and rope-soled shoes completed the disguise.

The pressmen's enthusiasm was catching. Henrietta posed prettily for them, her height conveniently matching Charles' with the aid of her needle-thin heeled sandals. Together they walked up the flight of broad stone steps, past the smilingly appreciative doormen, specially outfitted for the occasion in dusty top-hats and brightly patched topcoats and tails. One had stuck a huge daisy in his button-hole.

A sigh of disappointment followed their disappearance. Several of the pressmen began packing up their equipment, eyeing enviously the privileged few who had been issued passes which enabled them to cover the festivities inside. Only Earnshaw, a freelance known for his persistence as well as the ostentatiously shabby raincoat he wore to the most regal occasions, attempted to engage the royal chauffeur in conversation, but was swiftly moved on by the Prince's personal detective, who then settled himself expressionlessly in the back seat to await his charge's return.

Inside the tall, chandelier-lit hall of Warwick House, with its exquisite Adam plasterwork and famous balustraded staircase the Prince was welcomed eagerly by his host, warned of his arrival by the security men hired to cover the banquet. Flushed and proud, Piers knew the success of his function was now assured. A liveried footman helped Henrietta out of her shoulder-length black velvet wrap trimmed with trailing maribou, the doors to the reception room were thrown open, and the couple ushered in.

There was a moment's lull. Eyes turned, conversations stopped in mid-sentence, heads bent in whispered asides. Piers led the way. Without pausing the Prince, his hand under Henrietta's elbow, moved further into the room, seemingly oblivious to the battery of eyes turned in his direction. Little by little the party hum returned, this time with an added note of suppressed excitement.

'Come and have some beer, Sir!' Piers' whisper was conspiratorial.

'Beer?' There was a note of query in the Prince's voice.

'Of course, Sir.'

Piers, a special twinkle in his bright brown eyes, led the way towards the French windows flanking one side of the reception room. The crowd parted magically to let the royal party through, leaving a circle of charmed immunity. Through the guests Charles caught sight of a long walnut refectory table inappropriately covered with coarse gingham. A mountain of beer bottles, a mound of turkey drumsticks wrapped in paper, buckets full of half-opened oysters met his eyes.

He smiled. The beggars' banquet theme had been carried out with wit and imagination, if perhaps a little literally.

Reluctantly Henrietta took the bottle of beer which Piers uncapped and handed to her with a flourish.

Tentatively she drank. Mentally Charles commended her; though reluctant, she was game. He looked more closely at the bottle. The liquid had a remarkably fine head on it for beer, and a strangely pale colour. Henrietta sipped again, then her face cleared.

'Piers! How clever, it's champagne!'

Now it was the Prince's turn. Conscious of the party photographer at his elbow, he lifted a bottle to his lips and drank deeply.

'Good idea, eh, Sir?' Piers' eyes had a mad scientist's gleam. 'All specially decanted under pressure!'

'An excellent idea.' Charles nodded and smiled, lifted the bottle to his lips once more for the photographer, then turned to Henrietta. Her face was flushed and glowing as she revelled in the attention. His fatigue, from the long week spent working on the charter for homeless young people, lifted from him as he saw her excited face. It had been a good idea to come, the right idea.

With a firm nod and a quick smile he dismissed the photographer and moved away. It was better never to get stuck too long in any one place, any one conversation. Besides, this was Henrietta's evening; he wouldn't be able to stay as long as she might like, but he must give her the opportunity to mingle and enjoy it.

He glanced round the high-ceilinged ballroom, careful as always to look interested without staring at anyone in particular. His gaze, if prolonged, could halt conversations and paralyse perfectly self-assured people with the efficiency of a cobra's. It was one of the effects of his position – sometimes an advantage, more often a problem. But he'd learned to deal with it over the years.

Henrietta spotted a friend, and with one excited backward glance left him with Piers. Charles relaxed in the company of his old friend. He could feel the champagne bubbles buoying his tired body and mind. Piers pointed out eagerly some details of the decor that he hadn't noticed, the huge fake cracks in the french windows overlooking the flood-lit terrace, the rough matting laid in place of Persian carpet, with an area of bare parquet for dancing, the bizarre stuffed rats displayed in convincing if slightly moth-eaten attitudes underneath the banquet table. Listening with half an ear, he learned that a gypsy quartet was the next live band to appear. Someone had rigged up a brazier on the terrace outside and potatoes were being roasted to a chorus of squeals from smoke-begrimed girls. Huge daisies and what appeared to be nettles provided the floral decoration.

Aware of the covert glances from the female guests, some curious, others more openly flirtatious, Charles was glad of Piers' masculine chaperonage. Without appearing to do more than glance casually round the room, he assessed the girls in return. There were some real beauties here tonight. Long-legged, white-skinned, glossy-haired, like so many pretty circus ponies. Everywhere he looked were seductively lowered lids, heightened colour in the cheeks, increasingly animated gestures. Silk and satin and lace; old beaded dresses from the Twenties, grandmother's castoffs, everything artistically frayed and disarranged, tattered and patched for the beggar theme. But despite their clothes, none of these girls could ever be mistaken for a beggar. Their poise, the clouds of expensive scent that surrounded them gave the game away.

And none of them was more beautiful than Henrietta. His eyes sought her out. She was deep in conversation with a distinguished-looking older man dressed as a scarecrow. With some difficulty, he recognized the Chilean ambassador. Henrietta's face was animated, even though he knew the man's English left a great deal to be desired. What a splendid wife she would make.

And yet, he was conscious of a faint stir of disappointment. He would almost have felt better if there had been in the room a girl more beautiful than Henrietta. Perhaps that was only human, to feel that the grass should be always greener on the other side of the hill.

He shook his head in self-disparagement. The perfect wife. Did such an animal exist? Even if she did, he was hardly in the position to look for her. Tonight's disguise was only a temporary thing. Tomorrow, like the elegant old Georgian building he was in, he would be back in his normal state, all present and correct. The champagne back in its rightful bottle ...

With an inward smile he noticed the house detectives mingling discreetly with the revellers. They too were dressed in their shabbiest clothes, but gave their real identities away by their highly-polished shoes. Like him, they could never really hope to pass as anything but what they were. The job came first.

On the dance floor a couple was performing a bizarre dance which, from the amount of attention the official photographer was giving it, was sure to feature in tomorrow's paper as the Beggar's Bounce. It looked like fun. Perhaps in another half hour or so he would lure Henrietta on to the dance floor himself. Then it would be time to leave, see that she was taken home and head back to the Palace for an early night before the Trooping. What would happen at the party after he left he didn't know. For all he knew the guests might be merely pretending to have a good time for his benefit. It had been known to happen. Young and old, they all pretended. He himself was no exception to the rule ...

And then he saw her. Even from across the crowded ballroom, through the haze of smoke and jostling bodies, he could see that whatever she was doing she wasn't pretending. No one could pretend and look like that. Lost. Adrift. Her face was white, startling amongst the flushed faces round her. As if she was under water, drowning. Her eyes were huge and dark in her pale face. Instinctively he took a ster towards her. He would have done the same if she really was drowning, or an animal in pain. All his chivalrous instincts were aroused. There had to be something he could do.

At his side Piers looked up questioningly. Abruptly Charles pulled himself together. This needed caution, not only from his point of view, but because the girl looked as if she might turn and run at any moment. Disappear like a ghost. A ghost at the feast ... That face. From across the crowded room he could see the pale line of the scar that edged her cheekbone. A strange shock of recognition went through him. It wasn't a physical resemblance that struck him. It was her expression. Looking at her face was like looking into a mirror. She was like him, marked out forever, a perpetual outsider amongst the anonymous, laughing crowd. Everywhere she went people's first reaction would be to her face, never to her real self. He of all people knew how that could hurt. Her emotion was as clear to him as if he was feeling it himself.

And he had felt it. With dizzying suddenness he found himself looking down the years at a small boy, proud but panicking inside, on his first day at boarding school, surrounded by a crowd of other boys who wouldn't speak to him. Why? Becase he was different, set apart. He looked back at the girl. She was different too, with a difference that tugged at his heart and sympathies. And proud. Like that small boy, she wasn't going to turn and run, not yet. She'd die first.

He couldn't let that happen. But what could he do? He stared across the room. Common sense told him he'd better not get involved. But her taut white face and that odd sense of recognition told him that if he didn't help her he'd never forgive himself. The noise of the party forgotten, his half empty beer bottle in hand, he stood silent at Piers' side, his mind racing. Only long training kept his face expressionless.

No one, least of all Rose, noticed the direction of his gaze. The party was in full swing, a triumphant success. Rose pressed her back against the wall and half closed her eyes. It nad been all right to begin with. Despite the grandeur of the house she'd been reassured by the shabby clothes of the other guests. Some gaily flaunted gaping holes, torn stockings, patched and threadbare dresses, shoes with the soles flapping. She'd even felt relatively smart. Her blue print dress, though faded, was at least in one piece.

But then, as the evening wore on, a strange sense of unreality came over her. The guests weren't quite what they seemed. She began to notice details – the delicate gold bangles on one girl's wrist, the perfectly matched pearls round another's neck. The way they wore their defiantly shabby clothes, with such grace and confidence. The way they talked.

And then she'd seen her, the impossibly beautiful girl in red, the one who'd called her a nobody, and everything had fallen into place. It was all a masquerade, an elaborate joke. People with everything pretending they had nothing. Well, the joke was on her.

Her first impulse was to leave. But James had disappeared into the crowd and there were two sturdy detectives either side of the door leading out of the ballroom, checking guests' invitations as they went in and out. Without James she'd never make it.

Steering herself to walk slowly, ignoring the curious glances, she forced herself through the laughing, chattering crowd and found a quiet corner against the wall.

To hide her confusion and rebuild her confidence she turned to look in a big gilt-framed mirror hanging on the wall. Maybe she didn't look so out of place as she'd thought. But as soon as she saw her face all the blood seemed to drain out of her body. She tried to tear her eyes away but couldn't. Around her the din of the party was deafening; behind her she could see reflected in the mirror the other guests – dancing, laughing, chattering.

It was there. The scar. It wasn't hidden at all. Despite her loose hair and the touches of shadow Carole had put round her eyes it was still there. All her newfound confidence

crumbled away in that instant. No wonder people had stared
at her ... No wonder they were staring at her now.

She pressed her hand to her head. Faces, hostile curious
faces, were all around her, blurring and shifting. The hum of
voices swelled then died away. Other faces began to swim up
from her memory, faces from a nightmare she thought she'd
managed to forget. Alice and Nicola and Eileen ... She
shivered. Suddenly she was back, in another gaily lighted
room, another time, the years peeling back like the skin of a
winter orange. She could almost taste them, those dry winter
oranges they'd handed out at the orphanage every Christmas
Eve, a whole one each, such a treat ...

If only she could forget ... But now she was there again, a
girl of twelve, sick with excitement at her first grown-up
party, staring up at the great tree. Around her the big bare
basement dining room was transformed into an Aladdin's
cave of light and colour. Outside the uncurtained windows
thin snow was falling, already grey with Edinburgh grime,
but inside there was warmth and laughter, holly, mistletoe,
paper lanterns ... and in pride of place the huge tree, a tall
Norwegian spruce, a special gift from an anonymous bene-
factor. In honour of the occasion the Principal's wife had
brought out her best decorations, angels and snowflakes and
crystal balls in real spun glass, shimmering with all the
colours of the rainbow. They caught the candlelight, taking
her breath away. It was so beautiful ...

And she was beautiful too. She'd forgotten that feeling, it
seemed to belong to a stranger. For the first time she'd been
allowed to wear the locket. It rested warm and silver against
her neck, catching the candlelight from the tree. At the top
was a star. It shone out brightly, saying there's hope for
everyone. Dreams can come true.

She willed herself to hold on to that moment. But it was
fading. Now the nightmare was coming back in full force.
Alice and Nicola and Eileen. She'd heard scuffling and
giggling behind the tree and peeped through the lower
branches, where the needles were already browning. The

three bigger girls had got hold of a pack of cigarettes from somewhere and were lighting them off the candles. She tried to draw back before they spotted her, but it was too late.

'Well, if it isn't little Rose ...' Alice narrowed her eyes against the rising smoke. 'You wouldn't tell on us, would you, Rose?'

Rose shook her head. The three older girls eyed her.

'You look very nice today, Rose.' Alice's small eyes had an avid look. 'What's that you've got round your neck? I haven't seen you wearing that before.'

Automatically Rose's hand went to shield the locket. Suddenly the warmth of the party faded, she felt a chill of premonition. Alice moved closer. The acrid smell of the cigarette smoke filled Rose's nostrils.

'It's new, isn't it.' The note of envy in Alice's voice sent a shiver down Rose's spine. There was nothing the other orphanage girls coveted more than something new.

'No, it's not new at all.'

'Well now ...' Alice turned slowly to her two friends with a knowing smile. 'If it's not new, where'd you get it then?'

'It's mine. It belonged to my mother.' Why did she feel so breathless? Alice inched closer. 'That just proves what a little liar you are, Rose.' Her voice was soft. 'You never had a proper mother, everyone knows that. She just upped and left you when you were a horrible little baby.' She bent closer. 'Like a parcel.' She leaned back in satisfaction. 'So she couldn't have given you anything.'

Slowly she took her half-smoked cigarette out of her mouth, pinched out the tip and tucked it into her breast pocket.

'Liars shouldn't be allowed to have new things, should they Nicola? Should they Eileen?' The two girls shook their heads, smiling. Her heart racing, Rose backed away. The tree branches creaked above her head, blocking her escape. The three girls advanced. Suddenly Alice lunged forward. Her hand fastened round the locket and tugged. Rose heard the

63

fragile chain snap. Desperately she held on to the locket with both hands.

'Let go, you little beast!' Alice's voice was vicious in her ear. Rose felt the other girls grab her by the arms, felt her hands being prised open. She couldn't hold on much longer. With her last atom of strength she pushed Alice away. The effort made her reel, she clutched at the tree for support.

'Look out . . . it's going!' Through the roaring in her ears she barely heard Eileen's high-pitched whisper. It was enough to know that the locket was still clutched in her hand. Then she was falling, falling, dimly aware that all around her the delicate glass ornaments were falling too like huge tears, as the tree keeled slowly over with a crash of rending bark.

Then there was silence. Somehow, she got to her feet. The floor was covered in fragments of rainbow coloured glass and crushed candles. Dimly she heard the uproar from the girls beyond the tree. But it didn't matter. Her hand was cut, but she still held the locket, intact on its broken chain. Alice and her friends were nowhere to be seen.

Dazed, she looked round at the shocked, frozen faces. They were staring at her, all staring. A girl screamed.

'She's bleeding . . .' She took a step forward. Broken glass crunched under her feet. She raised her hand to her face. Something warm and wet was running down the side of her cheek. Only she hadn't cried . . .

The faces blurred, dissolved, shifted again. She was back in the present. She pressed her hand to her cheek. She'd known then, at her first and last Christmas party, that things could never again be the same. Something had been broken inside her and no one could mend it again.

But she wouldn't run. Not this time, not ever. She lifted her head proudly. She would outface them all. And hope that no one could hear her screaming inside.

But someone heard.

'Listen Piers.' The Prince spoke rapidly, turning his back

on the rest of the room. 'I have to go. I'll explain later. Hold the fort for me, will you?'

Piers looked surprised, but nodded, tipped an imaginary French legionnaire's cap. It was their old childhood code. It meant he'd do his best, come hell or high water.

Slowly, still keeping his face expressionless, Charles set out across the room, praying that nothing would panic her. How was it that no one else had noticed that small desperate face? They were all enjoying themselves too much. Perhaps Henrietta could help. He tried to catch her eye, but she was deep in conversation with Caroline, her bosom friend and sworn enemy of the moment. The two curly heads were pressed together, two pairs of hands waving in a glitter of unbeggarly rings.

At last he reached the girl. Her eyes were still lost in her own private nightmare. She looked as if she was trying to become part of the wall. Very gently, again with that troubling sense of recognition, he moved across until his body stood between her and the others. As his shadow fell across her face he could just see her eyes. They looked a hundred years old. She was so small that he had to bend towards her to see her face. With a small noise halfway between a gasp and a sigh she laid a hand on his sleeve. It rested there, tugging at the wool in a tight little grip, as light as a bird's. A whole lifetime of keeping his distance seemed to be destroyed in that moment. He bent down to hear her better, as if he could hear the beating of her heart.

'Are you all right?'

She shook her head.

'Is there anyone you'd like me to fetch?'

She sent an anguished look towards the dance floor, where the photographer had now joined in the mêlée. She shook her head again.

'Would you like to go outside?'

She nodded.

'Come with me, then,' he said gently. As he detached

her from her piece of wall like a limpet from its rocky home he signalled to Henrietta. She looked up and started to disengage herself from Caroline. But the small figure at his side stiffened.

'No, no!'

Suddenly she let go of his sleeve and ran blindly into the crowd towards the door, like a moth beating against a light. Quickly he shook his head at Henrietta. Puzzled, she shrugged and returned to her conversation.

As casually as he could, Charles sauntered out of the room. He felt as much as saw a hired detective drag himself away from the bar and follow him at a discreet distance. As he entered the hall he heard the doorman's upraised voice. He was standing in front of the girl, blocking the door, obviously suspicious of her sudden exit. Now he could hear her voice, breathless, with a curious lilting accent, trying to explain. In a few smooth strides he had caught up with her, only to be pained by the sudden panic in her eyes.

'It's all right, the lady belongs to me.'

The doorman looked flustered. His daisy buttonhole had wilted, much as the charm of the whole party had done for Charles.

'You'll feel better once you're outside.' He took her elbow, hoping the detective would have the sense to keep his distance. Clearly the girl was terrified of being observed. She had his wholehearted sympathy.

As they went down the steps he saw his own chauffeur and detective, parked patiently waiting in the Rolls. He glanced down at the girl. Clearly she hadn't yet recognized him. Her eyes still had that haunted look, as if she was past knowing anything. But this was no time for introductions. All that was important now was to get her safely away, if possible without involving his personal detective.

They both heard the click of the huge door behind them at the same moment, as the hired detective emerged and began to walk slowly down the steps. The girl took a step back. Charles made up his mind.

'Listen. You've got to trust me. We're both going to leave now. But you must do exactly what I do. Promise?'

She nodded. He heard her take a deep, quivering breath. He took her cold hand in a firm grasp. Slowly, hand in hand, they mounted the steps. As they passed the detective Charles' heart was beating wildly. The spirit of the adventure had got into him now, he was a boy again.

Slowly, she taking two steps to his one, they followed the stone path round the side of the house. Light spilled out from the party's uncurtained windows on to the terrace. Charles, straining his ears, could hear the scuff of the detective's shoes on the stone behind them.

Step by step they crossed the terrace, till they reached the brazier, now deserted but still glowing in the cool night air. Against the brilliantly lit scene inside the girl's face was a questioning shadow. The gypsy band inside began to play something wild and stirring; he was glad, it would cover the sound of their footsteps. He drew the girl closer. It seemed only a continuation of that first step he'd taken towards her. He bent his head, his mouth almost touching her hair.

'Listen. I'm going to put my arms round you. Trust me.' Carefully he raised his arm and slid it round her shoulders. He held her as lightly as he could, his hand just brushing her bare arm. Out of the corner of his eye he saw the detective turn away. He waited, hardly breathing. The scrape of a match, a flare of light, a surge of music from inside ... wordlessly he grabbed the girl's hand and ran, past the open door and round into the darkness at the back of the house. He'd been afraid she wouldn't come, but she ran with him, her feet noiseless on the dewy grass.

They froze and listened. He heard the slow step of the detective across the terrace, then silence as he hesitated by the door. They waited. The detective sighed, then stepped back into the party, closing the door behind him.

'Quick, before he finds out!'

He used to know the layout of this garden like the back of his hand, when Piers and he were boys. There was a secret

67

route they'd used, involving an old rain barrel, two crannies in the brick wall and some careful negotiation of steel spikes on top. He looked down at the girl standing obediently at his side. Would she be able to manage it?

He needn't have worried. She followed him like a shadow. On the other side he broke her fall and set her gently on her feet again.

Ahead of them stretched the deserted amber-lit street and beyond that the rustling darkness of St James' Park.

'We made it!'

To his surprise his voice was shaky with excitement, his heart beating faster than it had done for years. A surge of exhilaration filled him. He'd escaped ... maybe for only a few hours ... like a boy playing truant from school. He'd have to go back sooner or later, but meanwhile those stolen hours would be all the sweeter. For the first time in his life he could go anywhere, do anything, be anyone.

He straightened his neckerchief jauntily and looked down at the girl beside him. With a second stab of astonishment he realized that this was also the first time in his whole carefully guarded, rigorously scheduled life that he'd ever stood quite like this in a dimly-lit city street – alone, well and truly alone, with a girl.

Back at Warwick House the party was in full swing. No one had seen the Prince leave, but it was assumed, especially as Henrietta was no longer in view either, that the couple had left together. Those of the girls who'd hoped that later on the Prince might dance with them and give them a story to tell their grandchildren resigned themselves to the inevitable. Imperceptibly, with the Prince's absence, the atmosphere changed, grew more relaxed, rowdy even as the guests let off the accumulated tensions.

So it was that no one noticed Piers, an unusually serious expression on his face, leave the ballroom quietly and make his way down through the bowels of the fine old house towards the basement. He knocked on a small door leading to the basement pantry. A key grated in the lock on the other side, it opened a few inches and he was admitted.

Inside, perched uncomfortably on upended crates, a strange sight in the cramped confines in their beggars' motley, were Henrietta and the hired detective who'd been the last to see the Prince.

'Any news?' Henrietta's voice was sharp and anxious.

Piers shook his head and took a seat on a crate full of tins of stuffed vine leaves. He glanced at his watch. Three a.m. Only the three of them, plus the palace detective, knew about what had happened, and he hoped to keep it that way. At all costs the press had to be kept in the dark as long as humanly possible.

He glanced at his companions. Henrietta's face was pale and set, the hired detective's alternately resentful and disbelieving.

'I really don't think we should worry too much,' he said for the hundredth time. 'No one's to blame. If His Royal Highness wanted to get away I don't see why he shouldn't be allowed to. He made it quite clear that we weren't to worry. If he doesn't get in touch tomorrow, of course . . .' He left the sentence unfinished. In all their minds was the thought of what would happen if the Prince didn't turn up for the Queen's Birthday Parade the next morning. Headlines, speculation, storms of protest . . . the works.

'But what's happened to him, that's what I want to know.' Henrietta broke the silence angrily. 'I mean, he can't just have disappeared.' Her eyes were fairly snapping and two fierce red patches had come up under her powder.

'Mr Bridges was the last to see him, I believe,' Piers answered, stepping adroitly out of the line of fire.

'Well?' It was a demand.

The poor security officer began to bluster.

'It was on the terrace, Miss – er – Ma'am, with – um – a young lady. One minute they were – er – you know . . . and the next they'd disappeared. I assumed they'd gone inside to rejoin the – er – festivities, but . . .'

'You know? What do you mean. "they were – you know"?'
The detective flushed.

'Well, he – er, the Prince of Wales, His Royal Highness, I
mean, he had his arm round her ...'

Henrietta's lips tightened. There was an uncomfortable
pause.

'It seems only sensible,' she said at last, 'to find out who on
earth this ... girl is.'

Piers interrupted patiently.

'That's what we're trying to do.' He had every sympathy
for Henrietta. She was in a very difficult position which
could only get worse the more time went by.

'But why is it taking so long?'

'Well, you see, it's rather important not to draw too much
attention to the whole affair ...'

As he'd hoped, she took his point. The mileage the scandal
sheets could make out of such an incident needed no
explanation. The three of them fell into silence again. Piers
found himself reading over and over again the label on a jar
of preserved ginger rather than meet the eyes of his fellow
prisoners.

At last there was a knock on the door. It was the palace
detective, still calm and collected despite the late hour.

He addressed himself to Piers.

'I think I've found someone who may be able to tell us a bit
more about the young lady in question, sir.' He ushered in a
haggard-faced middle-aged man with a camera slung round
his neck.

'Well, who was she?' Henrietta demanded.

The man eyed her with open appreciation.

'I hate to disappoint a lady, but I don't actually know her
name. I'm afraid I've forgotten it.' He was obviously rather
drunk.

Henrietta's eyes widened.

'What do you know about her then?'

'Well ...' The man scratched his head. 'She's a good
model, if that's any help.'

70

'A model . . .' Henrietta thought rapidly. 'Then she must have an agency. Where did you get hold of her?'

The man hesitated, swaying slightly. 'Well, to tell you the truth, I picked her up in Queen Anne's Gate.'

There was a stunned silence. Henrietta shot Piers a look of pure horror. Conscious of the atmosphere, the man looked curious.

'I've got her address, though, if that's any help.' He peered owlishly round, patting his pockets. 'At least I thought I had it . . .' He scratched his head. 'Maybe I can remember it . . . somewhere in W14, I think . . . a rented room . . . I know I've got it somewhere.'

Aware of Henrietta's moue of distaste, Piers intervened tactfully.

'I don't think we need to worry about the address . . .' He saw that some of the bleary look had left the photographer's eyes. His curiosity was growing; it needed to be nipped in the bud. Hurriedly he thanked him, hoping that by morning he would have forgotten all about this bizarre late-night conversation.

'What's this all about? Is it some kind of joke?'

'Yes, that's it. Nothing to worry about. Sorry to have dragged you away from the party.' With a sigh of relief he saw the palace detective usher him smoothly out and re-lock the door. There was a moment's silence.

'Well, that seems clear enough.' He kept his tone deliberately non-committal.

'You're damn right it is,' said Henrietta. Her eyes were flashing. Anxiety fought with wounded pride in her face. 'No wonder he didn't want to be followed, with that kind of a girl . . .' She gathered her crimson skirts about her and rose to her feet.

'I for one,' she declared bravely, 'am going back to the party.' Her eyes glittered recklessly. 'Are you coming, Piers?'

Charles would want me to see she gets home all right, he thought. But it looks like a long night.

One by one they filed out, squeezing between the rows of

pickled tongue. They'd all gone by the time the hired detective managed to pin down what was wrong. He shook his head in confusion, remembering the small girl in the print dress, and the way the Prince had put his arm round her. Protectively.

'Funny ... she didn't seem like that kind of girl at all.' Sighing, he rose stiffly from his seat, his professional pride piqued that he'd been so neatly outwitted. But then he remembered the expression on the palace detective's face, and his own plight paled into insignificance. It would be his job to report back to the Palace with the unwelcome news.

'Christ ...' He let out his breath in a long whistle. 'I wouldn't be in his shoes for all the tea in China.'

Inside the great inner quadrangle of Buckingham Palace the pre-dawn flurry of activity was just beginning. Messengers, house servants, footmen and pages, tired after a night's duty, mingled with the usual stream of early deliveries in the stone-flagged courtyard. Above the Palace, still hardly visible in the murky light, the royal standard proclaimed in gold, scarlet and blue that Her Majesty was in residence.

Preparations for the morning's ceremony were even now well under way. But closeted in a room next door to the switchboard the Palace Press Officer, roused from bed, and the house detective on night duty eyed the panel of switches in growing dismay. Despite the earliness of the hour the lights were flashing almost continuously. Somehow, despite all the precautions, the news had got out. *The Times* and the *Daily Mail* night desks had already phoned through asking for corroboration, and it was only a matter of time before the rest of the press knew something was up. Heaven help the Prince of Wales if they once found out the truth ...

The Press Officer ran a hand through his hair.

'I don't know how much longer I can stall them.' He knew very well that as soon as the daytime staff came on duty the news of the Prince's disappearance would be all over the Palace as well. Wild rumours – kidnapping, a car crash, a sudden collapse – were already being whispered round the corridors.

'How long has he got?'

The palace detective consulted his watch.

'An hour, maybe two. But that's pushing it.' The two men's eyes met, both showing the same hint of sympathy for the Prince of Wales. But sympathy was a luxury neither of them could afford for long. The Press Officer voiced the unspoken thought in both their minds.

'I just don't understand it. Where the devil can he have got to?'

CHAPTER FIVE

Outside, soft Spring rain was falling on the city. It fell on the venerable old clubs in Pall Mall, the Athenaeum with its grand Parthenon frieze and statue of Minerva over the doorway, on the ancient Tudor quadrangle of St James' Palace where Mary Tudor died and Charles I spent his last days before walking to the scaffold, on the broad gas-lit highway of the Mall, stretching from Admiralty Arch to the east to the vast grey bulk of Buckingham Palace itself, where it nestled between the deserted streets of Belgravia and the rustling trees of St James' Park.

The Park itself was almost deserted at this late hour. The rain had driven the last of the late-night revellers home, and it was hours before the first early risers would be making their way to City offices. So the lake and its fountain were still, only the rain was making patterns and circles on the water surface. On their secluded island in the middle of the lake the ducks tucked their heads deeper under their wings. The willow trees hung motionless in the rain, their leaves pale and mysterious in the faint light. There was no one to notice the two shadowy figures that flitted silently over the arched bridge and down the pathway that disappeared between the trees.

It was dim here, away from the glow of the gas-lamps. Only an occasional light shone through the wet leaves above. Silence was everywhere, broken only by the gentle pattering of the rain. Charles hardly dared breathe in case he broke the spell. For him the familiar scene, which he'd overlooked so many times from the Palace windows during the day, was strangely transformed. Tonight, whether because of the rain or the silent figure of the girl at his side, it was an enchanted place.

He looked down at her. Rain beaded her face, covering her hair with little diamonds. She looked like a medieval princess. Or a mermaid. Something wild and fragile that might vanish if he broke the spell.

'This is a lovely place. Thank you for bringing me here.' She gave a small sigh. He nodded, knowing exactly what she meant. Suddenly the noise and excitement of the ball seemed a million miles, a thousand centuries away.

He took her arm.

'There used to be deer ... and then, later, Charles II made it into a pleasure garden for his lords and ladies of the Court.'

For a moment, with her arm resting lightly in the crook of his, he had the dizzying sensation that he was a cavalier walking with his lady through the pleasure garden. Coloured lanterns hung in the trees, around him was the rustle of silk and satin ... Then the image faded as suddenly as it had come, leaving him breathless. The past was alive tonight.

Slowly they made their way towards a bench sheltering under a massive old oak. They sat and looked out through the gauzy curtain of rain towards the lake. Without a word he slipped off his fisherman's jersey and hung it round her shoulders. She touched it wonderingly, as if it was a cloak made of the finest velvet. That same oddly protective feeling came over him. He fought back the impulse to put his arm around her.

'Good King Charles ...' Her voice was dreamy, with that soft lilting accent he hadn't managed to identify. 'He must have loved it here.' She turned towards him. 'He founded Carolina, you know.'

He smiled to himself. There was little he didn't know about his royal namesakes.

'I think that was Charles I.' The doomed Stuart king was one of his childhood heroes. So much grace and charm, and so little luck ... Then something else occurred to him.

'Carolina ... is that where you come from?' It could explain her accent, though there was some other more familiar element that haunted him.

He'd meant the question casually, but she didn't answer immediately. Instead she looked down. He sensed the tension in her as if it was his own.

'No ... not really.' She looked up again. He hesitated. He had no right to pry, but again he had that odd compulsion to help her. There was some mystery about her which called out to him. She pulled the sleeves of his jersey closer round her.

'Have you ... have you a big family?'

'Yes, I suppose I have.' He was taken aback at the sudden personal question, almost suspicious. But one look at her eyes, with their wistful, pleading look, made him feel ashamed.

'That's lucky.' She paused. 'I'd love to have a big family.'

'It has its disadvantages.'

'But it must be nice to know where you belong.' He watched her face. He had cousins in all the courts of Europe, but he'd never thought of it quite like that. A big family. Like so many other things, he'd taken it for granted, even permitted himself a certain degree of irritation.

'Have you no family of your own?'

She shook her head.

'None at all?' He tried to keep the disbelief and surprise out of his voice. Surely it wasn't possible for someone so young to be so alone. Then he remembered his first sight of her. Lost, adrift. His first impression had been right. She had no one.

'It doesn't matter, though. I can take care of myself.' He heard the proud independence in her voice and for some reason it brought a lump into his throat. He'd offended her.

'Tell me about Carolina, I've never been there.' She looked at him defiantly, testing him out. Something in his face must have reassured her. Little by little, with a few more questions, she told him what he wanted to know. There wasn't much to tell, but reading between the lines, listening to the cadences of her voice rather than what she had to say, he began to understand.

'It didn't sound so bad at first. No one had treated her

77

cruelly, there were laws against that kind of thing nowadays. No one had beaten her, or starved her, or dressed her in rags. For an orphan, she'd been well-treated. But that was all.

Somehow, that was the worst part. From her simple, matter-of-fact account, he realized that she hardly knew what was missing. How could she? No one had kissed her, or held her hand, or comforted her when she woke up with a nightmare. She'd been fed and clothed and sent like a small parcel from one 'home' to the next. And here she was, sitting like a prim little old lady on the park bench next to him. The loneliest person he'd ever met. So used to the feeling she wasn't even conscious of it any more.

When she'd finished he sat for a long moment in silence. He didn't know what to say. Her life had been so different from his. He'd been surrounded with attention, perhaps too much attention, from his earliest days, his every need catered for. And yet . . . perhaps they weren't so different after all. All her life she'd been looking for someone who would forget who she seemed to be and reach through to the real person underneath, the one who longed to belong somewhere but had never had the chance. Was he so different?

'What's your name?' Her voice was shy, tentative. Ready to be rebuffed at the slightest hint. He hesitated. Here was his opportunity to play safe. An easy lie. After all, they would hardly be likely to meet again.

But he didn't.

'My name is Charles.' It was out. He had a sudden dizzying sense of freedom. This was becoming a night of firsts. That was the first time in his adult life that he'd ever had to introduce himself.

'Like the king!' Her face was transformed with pleasure. For a long moment they looked at each other. He had the eerie sense that he was drowning in her eyes. Around them the rain fell softly, ceaselessly. He could feel it damp against his skin. Desperately he fought to keep his balance. Somehow she'd got under his guard, like the rain.

'What's your name?'

Suddenly shutters came down over her face. The brightness faded. She looked away, biting her lip.

'I'd rather not say.' He stared at her in astonishment. She was more guarded than he was.

'Why not?'

She shot him a pleading look.

'You'd only laugh. I don't want to spoil it.' She looked away again, her lip trembling. Suddenly she reminded him of one of his small cousins in need of comforting.

'You can tell me. I won't laugh, I promise.'

A long pause. She pulled at the frayed cuffs of his pullover sleeves, picking at the unravelled wool.

'Tell me. We're friends now.'

Another pause. Then, in a voice so small it was barely audible:

'Rose.'

'Rose. It suits you.' There was something fresh and unopened about her, the promise of summer to come. She was a wild hedgerow rose, so pale it had no colour, just fragrance.

'You didn't laugh.' Her voice was distrustful.

'No. Why should I?'

Her eyes searched his fiercely. Then she lifted one hand and touched her cheek.

'Because of this, of course.'

She turned her face away, unable to bear his gaze.

'Oh, that.' His heart turned over with sympathy for her, but he deliberately kept his voice casual. 'I hardly noticed it.' Suddenly it was very important to make her believe him.

She looked steadily into his eyes. He thought he glimpsed tears on her eyelashes, mingling with the rain. But she blinked them away.

'You're just being kind.'

He shook his head.

'No. Trust me.'

Again she looked into his eyes. Again he had the feeling that the earth was swaying under his feet.

'I don't understand ...' Her voice was a whisper. 'What makes you so different from everyone else?'

Her eyes seemed to be reading his soul. A shiver ran down his spine. She was right. He was different. He'd seen so many faces – the shattered faces of Battle of Britain air veterans, the sad little faces of handicapped children in hospital, the gaily painted and scarred faces of tribal Africans and aborigines. It had taught him to discount appearances and look for what mattered, the person behind the mask. By now it was second nature to him. The only way to survive.

'Who are you?' Her eyes searched his face. He had a sudden mad impulse to tell her everything – not just who he was, but what had made him who he was. How he'd cried on those long train journeys from Balmoral to his first boarding school, before he'd learned what was demanded of a future king. Somehow he knew she'd understand. But he fought back the impulse.

'No one special.' He smiled. 'Just someone who likes you.'

Her answering smile transformed her whole face. Suddenly she lifted both hands to her neck. They came away holding something that glinted silver in the moonlight.

'Here.'

Clumsily she stuffed what she was holding into his hand. He knew instinctively from the way she looked at him that it was something very important to her.

'I've never shown it to anyone before.' Her voice was gruff. He held the object gently in his hand.

'Are you sure ...'

She interrupted him before he could finish.

'Yes, I'm sure.' She looked down. 'We're friends now.'

Slowly, he opened his palm, aware of her anxious eyes fixed on him. Dimly he was conscious that they had passed the point of no return. Even more dimly he heard a voice inside him saying, what have I done?

'It belonged to my mother.' Her eyes were fixed on his face, waiting for his reaction. Again he heard that note of pride in her voice and his heart turned over.

Very carefully he picked up the silver locket and held it to the light. The rain was easing now, grey dawn was beginning to glow through the trees. It was a simple enough trinket, a classic silver oval faintly engraved with scrollwork that had been worn away by time and handling. The chain was broken, the two loose ends held together only by a knot. Compared with the priceless treasures he'd grown up with it was nothing. And yet he was aware that he held her reason for living in his hands.

'It's old, isn't it?' Her voice was anxious.

'Yes, I think so.' He turned the locket over, looked for and found the hallmark. He'd never been particularly interested in silver, but in a lifetime's close association with the nation's treasures, he'd picked up enough knowledge to tell her that.

'Look, here.' He held the locket out for her to see. The marks were worn, but still readable. 'Here's the lion rampant of England. And here's the crowned king.' The tiny bearded face was smiling under his crown. He remembered now. George II was the only king that smiled, on silver anyway.

'That means it's over two hundred years old. Early eighteenth century, anyway.'

Her eyes widened. He wished he could tell her more.

'Can I open it?'

She nodded. He felt for the catch and the tiny door swung open. With a pang of disappointment he saw there was no portrait or memento inside. The locket lay open and empty in his hand, like a shell with no pearl inside.

'My mother meant me to have it. It was round my neck when . . . when they took me in at the orphanage.' She looked at him hopefully. 'That means she meant me to have it, doesn't it?'

He nodded. 'I should think so.'

She needed some certainty in her life, it couldn't hurt to agree. She paused, staring off into the trees, then took a deep breath.

'So maybe she wanted me to look for her, later on?'

He hesitated. He hadn't expected that. He turned the

locket over and over in his fingers, conscious of her eyes on him, hardly knowing what to say. It was an old piece, the sort of thing that was usually a family heirloom, handed down from mother to daughter in an unbroken line. But that didn't necessarily mean what she thought it meant. He found it difficult to meet her confident gaze. She seemed to sense his doubt and looked away again.

'I'm going to look for her anyway. I have to find out about myself, who I am. I'm sure I can find her, if I look hard enough. Especially now I know a bit more about the locket.' She looked back at him. Her lips were set in a determined line, but her eyes were pleading. 'You don't think I'm crazy?'

'No.' He couldn't disillusion her, destroy the resolution in that hopeful face. 'I'm sure you'll find her.' If she can be found, he added silently.

'At the orphanage ... did they tell you anything about her?'

She bit her lip.

'Not exactly. It was another woman who brought me in. They couldn't trace my real mother, she didn't leave her name.' She looked away. 'But I don't think they tried very hard. I shall find her.'

His heart sank. It was a common enough story – a young girl trapped with an unwanted baby, poor probably, with no one to help her. It must have seemed like the best way out. And now ... it was hardly likely after all these years that she'd want to be found. He looked at the girl beside him, so small and determined. For a wild moment he wanted to protect her from almost certain disappointment. He was so rich in names and titles and relations, if only he could lend her one, give her a place to belong. But that was out of the question. He couldn't even mend her broken chain for her.

His unseeing gaze fell back on the locket. Something scratched roughly on the inside caught his eye. He held it again to the light.

'What is it?'

'I don't know ...' It was some sort of emblem, the outline

strangely familiar. It seemed like ... but it couldn't be. In a dream he laid the locket on the bench between them and slid off his own signet ring, the ring worn by the Prince of Wales since time immemorial. He held the two up together, frowning.

Stamped deep in the 24 carat gold of the signet ring was the Prince of Wales' emblem, so familiar to him that he hardly noticed it any more. The three curled plumes set in the royal coronet, with his motto, Ich Dien, blazoned underneath. And there, roughly scratched as if with the point of a knife inside the locket, were the same three plumes ...

Silently, he held the two out to the girl. Her eyes searched his face.

'I don't understand. What does it mean?'

'I don't know.' He took back the locket, half expecting the three plumes to have been a trick of the light. But they were still there. He shook his head, trying to clear it. He had the eerie feeling that he was caught up in events beyond his control. What link could there be far back in the past between him and this girl? A girl he'd never met before and would never see again.

He shivered. Reality was beginning to intrude into the dream. And it was getting lighter by the minute.

'I must go.' He rose abruptly to his feet. Her startled gaze met his. He didn't want to watch her face; suddenly he wanted to turn tail and flee. She rose too; in the grey light she looked very pale. For the first time in his life he had no idea what to say. The laws of etiquette simply didn't govern such a moment. But all he had to do was leave. In two hours time he would be on Horseguards parade, taking part in the ancient annual ritual of the Trooping of the Colour marchpast, surrounded by familiar ritual and ceremony – a million miles away from here.

She stood with her head bowed. For an awful moment he thought she might be crying. But when she lifted her head her face was clear. Somehow that moved him more than anything. He could see written into it all the goodbyes and rejections of her young life. No, she wouldn't cry. She'd learned not to.

Solemnly she unwound the trailing sleeves of his jersey, shook off the raindrops and handed it back to him.

'Thank you.' Her bare arms looked very pale in the dawn light. She gave a slight shiver and he had to fight back an impulse to put his arm round her.

'There's no need to thank me.' His own voice surprised him by its hoarseness. Suddenly he felt exhausted, as if he'd been ill with a long fever.

'Yes there is.' Her manner was oddly formal, it pained him. What had happened to that mysterious sense of ease between them? Deep inside he knew the answer. He'd destroyed it deliberately. He had to. It was safer for both of them that way.

But she wouldn't let him go just yet.

'You saved my life. Back there at the party. I shall always remember that.' Ruefully he realized her manners were better than his. She'd remembered to thank him.

'It was nothing.' From somewhere he forced a smile. It had been easy. He'd had nothing to lose. But then she didn't know that.

She didn't return his smile.

'Perhaps I can do the same for you some day.'

His heart constricted inside him. She was so small, so earnest, all her soul in her eyes. And how could she know that their worlds were light years apart, their meeting for these few hours a fluke, something out of a child's fairy story?

'Perhaps.' Still he lingered. She looked so small and defenceless, her eyes dim pools of light.

'Will you go home now?' His voice was softer than he'd meant it to be.

'No. I think . . . I think I'll stay here a while.' A tiny smile touched the corner of her lips. 'It's so lovely here.'

A sudden spasm of anger seized him. He looked around the Park. With the growing light the magic was fading. It was cold and grey and sodden, the paths littered, the grass worn away by too many uncaring feet. He could have shown her so many lovelier places ... but that was impossible.

'This is goodbye, then.' He took a step towards her, held out his hand.

'Goodbye.' Her voice was only a whisper, her hand cold in his. For a long moment he scanned her face, knowledge of it seeming to sink into his bones. Then she turned her head away so that only the good cheek showed.

'Rose. Don't do that.' Her wide, frightened eyes met his. She was very close. He could smell her fragrance, a faint flower scent, rain. Behind that, the hint of tears. Suddenly he knew he couldn't leave her like this. She'd given him, for one magical night, a gift beyond price, the freedom of the city. He would never forget it.

Very gently he bent his head and brushed his lips across her scarred cheek. Her skin was very soft, he felt a pulse beat under his lips.

Somewhere a clock chimed deeply. He leaned back, suddenly dizzy. The ground seemed to sway under his feet. It was like leaning back from a precipice. His breath came unevely. Wide-eyed, they stared at each other.

'There. It's invisible now. No one can see it.' His voice was hoarse, his mind spinning. One kiss – hardly a kiss – and what had happened to him?

'Really?'

'Yes, really.' The scarred and maimed and wasted, they'd queued in medieval times to be cured by the King's miraculous touch. Suddenly he felt full of power. Just looking at her face made him feel like a king.

'Rose.' He gripped her arms so tightly he could feel her trembling. He had the sudden impression he could lift her up and carry her away in his pocket. His wild rose ...

'Tomorrow ...' he remembered the clock chiming and laughed 'No, today ... I want to see you.' It was madness of course, but he couldn't let her go. Not like this.

'Will you come?' He knew she would before she nodded. She belonged to him.

He thought rapidly. Where could they meet? Somewhere where their two worlds touched. There, he had it. Swiftly he scrawled a place and time on a scrap of paper, remembering with one last impulse of caution not to sign it.

She looked down at the scrap of paper.

'Will you be there?'

She nodded wordlessly. Seeing her face, knowledge of what he'd done rushed in on him. Quickly he comforted himself with the thought that if the worst came to the worst, if daylight brought him to his senses, there was no real need for him to turn up. But it had been worth it just to bring that light into her eyes.

Carefully she folded the scrap of paper and tucked it into her pocket. The clock chimed again. It was getting dangerous for him to stay.

He released her and stepped back. She was smiling at him fully now, her cheeks flushed pink. He took a few paces, hesitated, turned, almost expecting her to have vanished like a dream. But she was still there, a tousled, bright-eyed little figure in a faded blue dress. She waved. Without the feel of her in his arms doubt crept in on him again. He felt a last impulse to warn her somehow that not all fairy stories had a happy ending.

'Rose ...' His voice carried faintly against the growing hum of traffic from the Mall. 'If I'm late ...' If I'm late, it means I'm not going to be there, he'd meant to say. But she didn't allow him to finish.

'I know. I'll wait.' Her voice was eager. He turned away again, fighting back a pang of guilt. He'd done his best. It was in the lap of the gods. One night, moonlight, rain ... it wouldn't take her long to recover. She was young. But as he strode quickly up through the willow trees towards the palace three words echoed in his mind, spoken with touching certainty. 'We're friends now.'

She watched him till he was out of sight. Then she sat

down again on the bench. In a dream she noticed she still held his ring. She half rose to call him back, but he'd gone. It didn't matter. She was seeing him again. He wanted to see her again ...

She raised one hand to her cheek. There was a glow deep inside her. It had to do with the dawn light, the dew on the grass, the touch of the wind on her bare arms. He'd kissed her, there. With one kiss he'd made her childhood fantasy come true.

The glow deepened, strengthened. It was sweet and cold at the same time, like vanilla icecream. It made her want to laugh and cry, shout and sit still. It frightened her, but she didn't want it to go away. Her life was just beginning ...

A stir of movement through the trees caught her eye. It was a man, too far away to see clearly, wearing a shabby beige waterproof, collar turned up against the rain, watching her curiously. She smiled straight back at him. No one's gaze would ever trouble her again. The miracle had happened Nothing could hurt her now.

CHAPTER SIX

Moving as one man the 1500 massed guardsmen, every gold buckle and braid gleaming in the brilliant sunlight, swept stride by metronome stride down the Mall towards Horseguards Parade. Their progress and speed between Chelsea barracks and the open-air parade ground had been calculated and checked by the Garrison Sergeant Major's pace stick weeks in advance, to allow for every possible set of weather conditions from sleet to fog. But this fine Spring morning heat shimmered off the deep rose pink macadam of the Mall, burning off the last of the night's rain. The most famous military pageant in the world, only cancelled twice in its long history, once for the Kaiser, once for Adolf Hitler, was once again under way.

The drum major sweated under the weight of his burden and the responsibility of keeping exactly 116 beats to the minute – not 115 or 117, but 116 exactly. His eyes flickered from side to side as he marched, noting the brass numbered markers discreetly set into the macadam at pre-ordained intervals, dividing off each section of the mile-long route. The guardsmen, in their turn, had been up at dawn for weeks drilling until each stride was precisely equal to the next, with its own inexorable geometry. Each face, pale and set in the heat, looked identical under the tall black bearskin, with the characteristic chinstrap hiding the lower half.

Palest of all was the royal standard bearer, guarded on either side by his colour sergeants. At all costs the standard must not be allowed to touch the ground; it was the regiment's most revered possession, and the highest possible honour for an ensign in the British Army. Weeks of special weight training in the barracks gym had stiffened his biceps, but once on the parade ground it would be sheer nerve he needed, with all eyes fixed on him as he swung the ten foot long standard in and out of the white leather hip holster.

The sea of scarlet and black rolled unstoppably on, the onlookers silent, awed by the show of discipline, the men made into machines, the split-second timing. But only the Queen, her retinue and invited guests – plus those lucky few who'd been able to obtain tickets on the black market – would be able to witness the parade itself from the stands in the huge, echoing well of Horseguards itself.

The massed regiments swept past St James' Park, crowded with onlookers, and into the arena. The tiers of guests round the square shifted in anticipation. The clock began to strike the magic hour of eleven. On the third stroke the Queen, a tiny erect figure on her tall black horse, entered the square. Her face under the specially adapted headdress, made using only female bearskin, was unsmiling, as befitted her role as Colonel-in-Chief of her troops. She too had sacrificed weeks of preparation, to enable her to cope with the strain of riding sidesaddle and controlling her mount through the long hours of ceremony.

Behind her rode the plumed, jostling ranks of the Household Cavalry, the ancient regiments of the Life Guards, Blues and Royals, founded by Charles I as his personal bodyguard. The glittering mass of cuirasses, gold helmets and nodding plumes, accented by the dazzling, blancoed white of cross-belts and gauntlets, was headed as always by the Prince of Wales, wearing the full dress uniform of Colonel of the Welsh Guards. In the high-collared crimson tunic, three foot tall bearskin, black breeches and white gauntlets, he was distinguishable from the men who followed only by his military sash and the indefinable poise of his lean figure.

Already the heat had built up in the stone and concrete square. The horses, tired and calm from their special early morning exercise, stood quiet, heads drooping. As the marchpast proceeded, the Queen and her retinue sat motionless, in their most testing annual ordeal. Like clockwork the guards wheeled and turned, scarlet and black interleaving endlessly to the screams of command, the Colour hardly fluttering in the still air.

The sun climbed the sky, beat down ferociously on stone and concrete. The guards swung into the giant Spin Wheel, a movement performed only by these favoured regiments. The spectators fanned themselves. A guardsman fainted, then another. Photographers craned to get a better view. A fainting guardsman was always worth a picture. Those heavy bearskins and double-breasted woollen tunics were better suited to Winter in the Crimea than a scorching June day. That, combined with the emotional strain of this once-a-year command performance, was often enough to tip the balance.

At last came the presentation of the Colour before Her Majesty. The standard-bearer's crisply white-gloved hands trembled as he re-seated it in its holder. An audible sigh, half relief, half disappointment, ran round the arena. All eyes were fixed on the Queens' upright figure.

Only a few of the most observant spectators sensed rather than saw the uniformed figure immediately behind her sway suddenly in his saddle as if overcome by the heat. His horse, alarmed as the reins dropped from his rider's hands, threw up its head and shifted. The guardsman nearest to the Prince of Wales tensed for action, not daring to move too soon in case he drew attention to his difficulties.

Only he could see how deathly white the Prince's face had become, as if all the blood had drained from his body. Out of the corner of his eye he saw the Prince grit his teeth and with a superhuman effort straighten his body in the saddle. His hands tightened round the reins again and with a murmur he soothed his nervous horse.

At last, the ceremony was over. The guardsman breathed a sigh of relief. On the long ride back down the Mall towards the Palace he kept his eye on the Prince's back, noting how stiffly he held himself, quite unlike his usual supple style.

Again, as they entered the inner quadrangle of the Palace, he was the only one to see the Prince slide off his horse and lean against its side, his head down. But there was nothing he could do to help. Torn between anxiety and protocol he dismounted. Relieved, he saw the Prince straighten up and catch his eye. With hands that shook visibly the Prince unstrapped his bearskin. His hair clung damply to his forehead. He took a deep breath and shook his head like a terrier. The guardsman saw for the first time how exhausted he looked, as if he'd been up all night. But then the Prince's charming smile flashed out.

'I must be getting old!'

He turned briskly on his heel and ran lightly up the steps. The guardsman watched him go and wondered. The Prince looked exhausted, but underneath his exhaustion there was something else – a sort of exhilaration. It reminded him of something ... He thought for a moment, his hand rhythmically stroking his horse's neck, then he had it. It was the way he'd held himself as he went into the Palace – tired, clearly, but head up, braced to face whatever came. Like a knight going into battle for his lady.

Inside the Palace Charles rubbed a hand over his freshly-shaven chin. There'd been barely enough time for him to shave and change into his uniform before the ceremony, but he'd made it by the skin of his teeth. The sleepless night and the heat had almost put paid to him out there, but somehow he'd summoned up the strength to survive.

And now ... there was another challenge to face. He squared his shoulders and tried to clear his mind. In his exhausted state the familiar great hall dazzled him. Ahead of him the Grand Staircase swept majestically up towards the State Apartments, veined Carrara marble offset with opulent Regency balustrading. For a moment its outlines blurred and he felt the ground sway under his feet. The contrast was too much. Only a few short hours before he'd been sitting bare-headed in the rain, anonymous and strangely light-headed, with a girl from nowhere ... And now this.

With an effort he brought himself back to the present. There were things to be done, explanations to be made.

A footman appeared at his elbow, splendid in his scarlet and gold livery. With a shock Charles realized that a primitive tribesman would have been hard put to it, asked to choose between them, to decide which was the heir to the throne. Again he fought back the wave of disorientation.

'Yes?'

'Her Majesty is waiting for you in the Audience Chamber, Sir.' The footman's voice was cultured and deferential – many of them were Old Etonians – but his eyes showed an unmistakable spark of curiosity. Obviously news of his unscheduled absence had got out.

'Thank you.' Charles hesitated. Perhaps he should change, give himself a chance to gather his wits together. Then his head lifted. There was no sense in putting off the moment any longer. He might as well face the music sooner rather than later.

He handed his bearskin to a waiting page and turned back to the footman.

'Lead on.'

The Queen's Audience Chamber was one of the rooms in the private apartments along the first floor of the North Front, overlooking Constitution Hill and Green Park. As the footman threw open the door and ushered him in, Charles was conscious of the anachronistic figure he must present, booted and spurred in this gracious, elegant room with its soft green walls, delicate gold slubbed silk armchairs and intricate plasterwork ceiling. He caught sight of his face reflected in the gilt-framed mirror above the fireplace. Drawn, pale, eyes bloodshot. The very picture of a soldier home from the wars.

'Good morning, Charles.'

The Queen was sitting by the half-open window. A welcome breath of fresh air drifted in from Green Park, refreshing the stillness in the room.

'Good morning.' He bent to kiss her, aware of her surprised look as she took in the fact that he hadn't yet changed out of his uniform, aware too of the unspoken relief in her eyes. Spread out on the mahogany table in front of her, instead of the usual state papers, was the morning's newspaper. With a pang of anxiety he wondered if the story had already broken, then he noticed with relief it was open at the crossword page.

'How have you managed today?'

He knew he was skirting the subject of his disappearance, putting off the moment of truth, but he had to find the right words first.

The Queen smiled.

'I haven't got as far as I should. I'm stuck on three down, and it's only four letters.'

Glad of the diversion, he picked up the paper.

'Let me see . . . "Girl on the way up, a common climber."'

In his exhausted state the answer hit him with an unpleasant jolt. With an effort he controlled his voice.

'Have you tried Rose? As in climbing rose?'

'Of course . . . yes, it fits.' The Queen laid the paper aside and turned to face him. Quickly he tried to shake off the apprehensive feeling the crossword clue had aroused in him. He needed to feel sure. But it left a bad taste in his mouth. A common or garden climber . . . could she be? His Rose?

Deliberately he banished the thought. The Queen, her eyes so like his, only bright blue where his were dark, was waiting for him to speak.

'Well?' She spoke softly. There was sympathy in her voice but her eyes probed his anxiously. 'What happened last night?'

So simple a question, and so difficult to answer. He himself still wasn't quite sure. What had possessed him to act so contrary to his character and training, to jettison the habits of a lifetime and go chasing a will-o'-the-wisp? Surely not moonlight alone. For lack of a better explanation he chose the simplest one.

'I met a girl.'

In a few short sentences he told her everything. Everything, that is, except what really mattered – and that he couldn't explain even to himself. When he'd finished she sat without speaking for what seemed a very long time. Then she looked up. Her expression was puzzled.

'Let me see if I've understood.' Her voice was clear and incisive. 'You attended a party, you met a girl, you spent the night talking to her. That I can understand.' Her lips curled into a quick smile. 'Though why you should have chosen anywhere so uncomfortable as a park bench is a mystery to me.' Then her frown returned. 'But what I find hard to understand is why you felt it necessary to keep your whereabouts a secret.'

He shook his head.

'It's not like you, Charles. I . . . we were all so worried. And the press . . .' She left the sentence unfinished.

'I know.' He knew, none better, what a risk he'd taken. It was the sort of story every newsman in the country would have given his eyeteeth for. 'I'm sorry. I just can't explain it. It was . . . an impulse.'

Hardly the word for that strange, irresistible current of attraction that had drawn him to her side and kept him there, but he couldn't think of a better one. In less enlightened days he supposed he could have said she'd put a spell on him.

'And you say this girl didn't know who you were?' The Queen's voice was disbelieving. He nodded.

'But in that case, why didn't you tell her at the earliest possible opportunity? Surely that would have been only fair?'

'Yes . . .' His knees were beginning to give way and he sank into the chair opposite. None of his behaviour made any sense in the clear light of day, he knew it. 'I'm afraid . . . well, the question didn't arise.'

The Queen faced him, her blue eyes piercing.

'Didn't arise?'

'No.' Recklessly he lifted his head. 'I didn't want to tell her. I wanted to be ... just myself.'

'Oh Charles ...' She reached over and laid her hand on his arm. Her sympathetic gaze met his rueful one.

For a long moment they sat in silence. The ormulu clock on the mantel chimed once. The sound seemed to wake the Queen from her reverie. Suddenly she rose to her feet, one hand resting on the back of her chair. There was something indefinable in her expression that made Charles uneasy.

'There's something I think you ought to know. This girl may not ... may not be quite as innocent or as ignorant of your identity as you supposed.' The Queen looked down, hesitated, then made up her mind. 'I expect she told you that she worked as a photographic model?'

'A ... a model?' Pure astonishment took his breath away for a moment. Anyone less like a model he'd never met. At last he recovered his voice. 'No. That's impossible.' It was laughable. 'You must have the wrong girl.'

'No, Charles.' The Queen's voice was sad. 'It's been confirmed. I'm afraid it may be you that has the wrong girl.'

He looked down at his hands. The room was spinning round him, everything falling apart. Could he have been so wrong? Could he have been, quite simply, taken in? But her face, those wide-open trusting eyes ...

'Charles!' The note of alarm in the Queen's voice made him look up. Her eyes were fixed on his hands. 'Where is your ring?'

He looked down automatically at his left hand. Against the tan of his skin, the betraying pale circle where it should have been showed up stark and clear.

'Oh no.' Their eyes met.

'You didn't ... you didn't give it to her?'

'No.' He put one hand to his forehead. His mind was spinning, he no longer knew what was real and what wasn't. All he remembered was showing her the ring and then – nothing. He stared once more at his hand, realization rushing in on him. That sad little story of hers, guaranteed to arouse his sympathy ... could it all have been a lie?

'No, I didn't give it to her. But it's possible she may have it.'

'I see.' The Queen looked suddenly drawn. The same thought was in both their minds. The afternoon editions. Headlines: Wild rumours. Denials from the Palace ... 'In that case there's nothing we can do but wait and see.'

CHAPTER SEVEN

'Don't do that!'

Rose jumped in alarm. A blue-uniformed man was staring down at her.

'Don't you know it's an offence to feed the pigeons inside the station?'

She shook her head. The man sighed and moved on. Surreptitiously Rose slipped one more crust under the bench, then dusted off her hands. She was too excited to eat anything herself. The station was swarming with people, all looking very purposeful. They all seemed to have places to go to and people to see. There were only a few people standing still like her. A woman with two children, one hanging on to each hand, staring distractedly at the travel indicator. A man in a battered hat and dirty beige waterproof, propped up against a pillar outside the bar, reading a newspaper, with a circle of cigarette butts round his feet. The news vendor inside his brightly-lit kiosk, meditatively peeling an orange.

It was nearly time . . . soon she'd see him again. In a sudden panic she left the bench and hurried into the ladies waiting room. In the mirror she stared anxiously at her face. There were smuts on her nose and her hair was tangled, but she hardly recognized herself. Her face was glowing, her cheeks flushed. And the scar . . . she told herself firmly that it hardly showed at all. He'd said it wouldn't. The memory of his lips on her cheek sent a shiver down her spine. For the first time in her life she'd felt safe, cherished, with his warm hands resting on her shoulders. As if she belonged.

'The 3.45 for Bristol Templemeads, calling at . . .' The announcer's voice boomed round the station, startling her.

Outside she could hear a train hissing, ready to leave. Her heart in her mouth she rushed out again into the smoky air. It was nearly four o'clock. Only ten more minutes to go.

Her bench was still vacant. She sat down, trying to still the frantic beating of her heart. To calm herself she felt in the pocket of her dress and took out the twist of brown paper. She unwrapped it carefully and tipped the ring out on to her palm. It rolled and winked like a piece of trapped sunlight. She wondered if he'd missed it yet. There was a worn bit under the loop where his finger had rubbed it, he probably wore it all the time. So it was like holding a little piece of him.

He'd be so glad to have it back, she knew. With fingers that shook a little she wrapped it up again in its protective brown paper, and looked up at the station clock. Only three minutes left now. She wished she was wearing something brighter. Would he be able to make her out among all these people? She was as close to the clock as she could get, just as he'd said.

There. Four o'clock. 16.00, take away 12. Any minute now she'd see his dark curly head making towards her through the crowd. Though of course he might be late. He'd said that. He'd wanted her to wait for him.

She bit her lip and caught the man in the battered hat staring at her. His expression made her nervous, there was something knowing and expectant in his eyes. She looked away quickly.

The clock again. Surely that much time couldn't have gone by? It had gone so slowly before, and now ... She stood up, straining to pick out just one face in the crowd. Perhaps something had happened to him. Perhaps the clock was wrong.

'Excuse me, does that clock have the right time?'

'No idea, love, I just work here.' The news vendor lobbed his orange peel with practised accuracy into a nearby litter bin. Her disappointment must have showed in her face because he relented and looked at his watch.

'I make it nearly half past four, is that good enough?'

Unable to reply, she nodded and turned away. All round her the station seemed to be getting bigger and bigger. Suddenly she thought of something.

'Excuse me ... Is this ... this is Paddington station?'

The man laughed.

'If it's not, I'm out of a job!'

'Oh. Is it ... is it the only Paddington station?'

'Only one I ever 'eard of.'

He turned back to his customers. Hardly knowing where she was going, Rose wandered back to the bench. The pigeon she'd fed earlier still strutted hopefully amongst the dust and crumpled sweet wrappers.

'No,' she whispered, dazed. 'I'm sorry. It's not allowed.'

The pigeon's round pink eye was expressionless. Soon it wandered away. Rose went on sitting on the bench, trying not to look at the clock. But the big black numbers went on changing, carving up the minutes like knives, whether she looked at it or not.

The plain black Austin slowed and made an unexpected right turn down a narrow incline. It eased carefully over the uneven pitted surface, glided through a deserted carpark and came to a halt just beyond a taxi rank.

'I brought you the back way, as you requested, Sir.'

'Thank you.'

Charles was glad the chauffeur didn't turn round. The back of the man's head was immaculate, as was his white shirt collar and neatly brushed jacket, his voice deferential. But since the morning Charles' nerve ends had been rubbed raw. He was well aware what he was doing now defied explanation. It was rash, dangerous, possibly fatal. He could be walking straight into a set-up. But he had to know.

The warm metal shape of the locket in his jacket seemed to be burning a hole right through to his skin. With an effort he resisted the temptation to take it out once more. It was his one hope. The business over the ring had shaken him more than he could say, but when he'd found the locket he'd realized that the whole thing could, just possibly, have been a mistake.

If I see her. If I can just see her, it will be all right. He clung to that like a talisman. But somehow it was getting more and more difficult to remember exactly how it had been. And it was only last night ... But if he could just talk to her, he knew she'd be able to explain ... somehow.

'Shall I be coming in with you, Sir?'

'No. Thank you.' Dammit, he couldn't remember the man's name. He was falling apart. If only he could get rid of that bitter, burning sensation, centred on his stomach. The suspicion that he'd been betrayed ...

With a quick glance up and down the side street, he left the car. The well-trained chauffeur averted his gaze and folded his arms behind the driving wheel. Charles strode away, feeling suddenly naked and vulnerable. He was mad to be doing this ... it was the action of a foolish love-struck boy.

In the shelter of a portico he paused, felt in his pocket and drew out the pair of heavy-rimmed spectacles. He looked at them with distaste and almost changed his mind about going on. Yet another disguise. Only this one no light-hearted romantic masquerade. His whole future depended on its success.

He slipped them on. Head well down he left the sunlit side street for the echoing grey dimness of the station interior. Once inside he paused to get his bearings and let his eyes get used to the light. So far so good. Not a flicker of recognition on the preoccupied passing faces. Bitterly he congratulated himself on the last, deeply ingrained instinct of caution that had prompted him to choose a public place for their rendezvous. There was always safety in numbers ... if he hadn't singled her out from the crowd in the first place he wouldn't be in this position now.

Unobtrusively he removed the glasses and shot a quick look round the concourse, pretending to polish the lenses as he did so. His Cambridge University acting experience was coming in useful at last. All round the entrance were stands selling magazines and chocolate and fruit. When he'd told her to meet him here he'd not thought the view would be so restricted. For a moment he despaired of ever spotting her in the vast dingy place. The station clock, he'd said, visualizing a big round face rather like a grandfather clock. But there was nothing like that here. And he couldn't go on polishing the glasses forever.

Then he saw her. The jolt of recognition stopped him in his tracks. Suddenly he knew how afraid he'd been that she wouldn't be there. But she was, sitting on a bench by the ticket office, knees pressed together as if she was in church, her face turned to something or someone he couldn't see.

Slowly the tension began to drain from his body, and something else welled up that wanted to run shouting and singing across the grey tarmac into her arms. She was real. She was there. How could he ever have doubted her? He took a step forward. In his mind he was already beside her on the bench, his eyes following hers to see what she saw, feel what she felt. He had that same eerie sense that they were two parts of the same person in separate bodies. Nothing could keep them apart, they belonged together.

But what was she looking at so intently? Was it that man in the crumpled fawn raincoat and disreputable hat, standing reading a newspaper outside the bar, with an expression of elaborate disinterest. Something about the man tugged at a familiar chord. He looked closer. It was the way he was standing . . . and the profile under the hat brim . . . surely he'd seen that face before . . .

A scalding tide of recognition washed over him. Everything stopped. In slow motion Charles felt himself step back automatically out of the line of view. He knew that clever face under the hat only too well. And he knew how clever and persistent the brain inside the hat could be. Earnshaw. Best and brightest of the columnists. He always got his man.

So why was Earnshaw here? His eyes moved slowly from the man's figure to the girl's. Was he mistaken, or did they exchange the briefest of glances ... He couldn't blot out the truth any longer. They were both quite clearly waiting for someone, and he knew only too well who that someone must be.

The relief he'd felt earlier turned to ashes in his mouth. All of a sudden the girl on the bench seemed like a stranger. Disjointed memories of the things they'd said to each other came back to him, only this time they were blown up in bold black capitals across the newsstands, like lines from a bad play. The locket ... the ring ... how neatly planned and executed it had been, to look like an exchange of lovers' tokens. How cleverly he'd been stalked and trapped.

Then she moved, and it was as if she'd touched his naked heart with her hand. For a moment it was like the first time, across a roomful of strangers.

But he drew back into the darkness. Across a crowded room. How could he have fallen for that ancient cliché? But he knew better now. His mouth tasted of salt, he'd bitten his tongue. Funny, he hadn't even noticed. Pity he couldn't have bitten it off completely, yesterday evening, a mere twelve hours ago.

The glasses hung uselessly in his hand. He stared at them, a small bitter smile touched his lips. Enough of this charade. The party was well and truly over. He turned, savagely, and crunched them under his heel.

He's come! I knew he would. He promised. Rose raced down the stairs, all her tiredness forgotten. She hadn't expected him to find out where she was staying so quickly, but she'd known all along that he'd come as soon as he could. Hadn't he warned her he might be late? Her hands were shaking so much with excitement that she could hardly get the bolt back on the door.

She'd been so sure it was him on the other side of the door that when she finally got it open it took her a long time to stop smiling. The man standing there smiled back. Despite the sunshine, he had a hat and coat over his arm. She looked behind him, she was so sure that Charles must be there somewhere. But there was nothing.

'Could I trouble you for a glass of water?'

She hesitated, still dazed. It wasn't surprising he was feeling the heat, if he'd been wearing that hat and coat. She turned round to go and get him some but when she reached her room she realized he'd followed her silently up the stairs.

'May I sit down?'

Perhaps he was feeling faint. He dropped his hat beside him and draped his coat with its chequered lining over the arm of the chair. There was something strangely familiar about that coat. She handed him his glass of water, but he shook his head.

'Please excuse my little subterfuge ...' His eyes flicked busily about the room. A chill of apprehension went through her. 'After all this time I feel like an old friend.'

'All what time?' Fragments of memory were coming back to her. The man in the park, his coat collar turned up. The man at the station, wearing a hat this time ... but the coat, surely it was the same one? She looked at it more closely. The lining was torn. That didn't seem to fit in with the way he sat in his chair, so precisely, like a cat at a mousehole ...

'Don't worry.' He took out of his coat a small pad with a pencil in the spine. 'You don't mind, do you? Helps jog the old memory.'

The chill reached deeper into her bones.

She'd never seen anyone look less forgetful.

'What do you want?' She sat down rather suddenly on the edge of the bed. Her knees felt weak. He stared down between her feet at the case under the bed, eyeing the labels.

'So you've just come from America? That's interesting...' His voice was thoughtful. 'Better and better ... Shades of Edward VII ...' He jotted something down in his pad.

'What do you want?' She was beginning to feel unreal. He seemed to take no notice of what she said at all.

'Well, that depends.' He eyed her considerably.

'On what?'

'On what you have to offer.'

She felt a desperate little laugh rising in her throat. Offer? Her?

'I don't know what you mean.'

'Oh well, if you want it spelled out ...' With an impatient sigh the man whipped out a folded paper from his coat, flicked it open at the front page and dropped it neatly at her feet. She stared at it uncomprehendingly. Most of it was taken up with news of some Middle Eastern riot. In the corner there was a large photograph under the heading 'Charlie slums it!' It showed a young man smiling and drinking out of a beer bottle.

She looked closer. A thrill of recognition went through her. Puzzled, she picked up the paper. It wasn't just any young man, it was Charles, her Charles. She read on. 'The Prince of Wales in fine form at Beggar's Banquet ...'

The room went black. Slowly she felt the newspaper slip out of her fingers. What did it mean? It couldn't be true ... He would have told her. Someone would have told her. Her mind began to whirl. Fragments of their conversation rushed back into her memory. One by one the pieces began to click into place ... his reserve, the difference she'd sensed about him ... it all made sense.

She felt a huge yawning emptiness open up inside her. She'd felt so close to him, and now ... The smiling face in the photograph mocked her.

'I take it you know who that is?'

She nodded wordlessly.

The man's bright eyes probed her face.

'For a moment there I thought ...' He paused interrogatively.

She shook her head, unable to answer. Her mind was racing desperately. She must think fast. If only she could stop thinking of Charles' face, his warm hands on her shoulders ...

'Why ... why are you so interested in him?'

The man made an exaggerated face.

'For the same reasons as you, my dear lady. For what I can get. After all, it's open season on royalty, isn't it? Don't forget I saw you in action. That was a nice little number you pulled outside Grosvenor House.' She flinched. So he'd been there all along, watching and listening in the shadows. And they'd never known.

'I just think we can help each other, that's all.' The man smiled winningly. 'I'm not the only one, you know. They'll all be after you soon. I just happened to get here first.'

'So what do you want from me?' At all costs she must keep talking, try and fight the rising waves of nausea.

He rolled his eyes to the ceiling.

'What do I want? Whatever's going, of course. The Story. The works. The front page. Syndication. World rights. You name it, I want it.'

'What story?' She swallowed hard. 'There isn't one. We just ... talked.'

'Now now, don't knock it.' The man's eyes grew eager. 'It's got plenty of potential, worked up a bit. The Beggar's Banquet – what could be nicer? The Prince and the beggar-maid ...' His eyes flicked expressively round the room. 'Romantic interlude in the park – moonlight, roses ... It'll go down like a dream, I promise you. Frilled out a bit, of course. Leave that to me.'

His face grew animated.

'Just think, this will make you a celebrity. You'll be able to do anything you want – interviews, articles ... people will come and ask you for your autograph. You'll also –' he paused weightily – 'you'll also be considerably better off. Depending on how ... cooperative you are, you might see anything from £3000 to £30,000 out of this. That is if you give me a free hand ... poetic licence and all that ... back me up all the way ...'

He leaned forward. 'I expect you could use the money.' His gaze lingered on her cheek. 'A little plastic surgery, perhaps? You could change your whole life ...'

His face was very close to hers. She could see the way his

eyebrows grew together over his nose, or would have done if he hadn't plucked them. For some reason that repelled her more than anything. As if he'd stop at nothing to have things the way he wanted them.

'No.' The nausea was threatening to overwhelm her now. He wanted her to put a price on Charles' head. Soon there would be nothing left of those few precious hours. Little by little he was destroying everything.

'No?' His surprise was almost comical. He sat back, frowning in puzzlement. Then his face cleared.

'I suppose you're worried about the publicity angle. No need to be. It'll all blow over soon enough and you'll have nothing left except happy memories and a nice little nest egg. There's no harm in it, really. Everyone's interested in the royals, especially when they ... er ... kick over the traces. And remember, you'll never get another chance like this. Might as well get your money's worth.' Suddenly his eyes narrowed. 'Unless of course you've already done so.' His mouth went white at the corners, then twitched into a smile.

'Clever devil ... he must be catching on.' He cocked his head on one side. 'OK, what's he given you to keep quiet? A measly couple of hundred? I'll top it.' He scanned the room, noting the patched carpet and uncurtained window. 'Or maybe something unnegotiable. Jewellery? No, he didn't have time ... Come on, you can tell me. It's nothing to be ashamed of. With any luck it'll be traceable and then we can work it into the story.'

Before she could stop herself her eyes went to her coat pocket where the ring was still in its brown envelope. The man's face twitched.

'Aah ... so he did give you something!'

'No.' With an effort she made her voice calm and convincing. The man eyed her.

'Mean sod. All you could expect from the richest young man in Europe, I suppose.'

Suddenly she couldn't bear it any longer. She picked up

the newspaper and handed it back to him. Then she stood up.

'I'm sorry. I'm afraid I can't tell you anything.' She pointed to the face in the picture. 'You see ... I don't know him. The one I know is a completely different person.'

Slowly the man rose to his feet and picked up his coat and hat. His eyes were unreadable.

'Well well ... so you're holding out for the big one after all.' He shook his head disparagingly. 'Girls ... they never learn. Always hoping for something more. Settle for what you can get, that's my motto.' He shrugged into his coat. 'You think you're going to see him again, don't you? Well, take it from me, even if the thought had crossed his mind, which I doubt –' he dusted the brim of his hat and sent a contemptuous look around the room – 'he couldn't afford it, not in his position. You come much too expensive. Think of what he stands to lose. Country estates all over England. £100,000 a year. Wall-to-wall blondes. I can't see it, can you?' One by one he did up his worn leather buttons. 'Unless of course you've got royal blood in your veins?' A small smile twitched his mouth as he watched her face. 'No, I didn't think so ...'

He paused at the door. A sudden savage glint came into his eyes then was as suddenly gone.

'I mean ...' he let his voice trail off. 'Paddington station! The oldest trick in the book. A brush-off is a brush-off all over the world.'

She took a step towards him. He lifted a hand.

'Don't worry, I'm leaving ... But I won't say goodbye, just au revoir. In case you change your mind.'

He paused one last time. 'Remember what I said, though. It's no use waiting for him to get in touch. Noblesse oblige and all that. He's got better things to do.'

CHAPTER EIGHT

High in his sound-proof box, the TV announcer spoke excitedly into his microphone. 'Well, for once it looks as if the tradition of First Day Ascot rain has been soundly beaten ...' His voice rose to a higher pitch. 'And here at last is the Royal Procession, led by Her Majesty the Queen ...'

Down below him the famous old course, the showplace of English racing, was a blaze of colour in the brilliant sunshine. The royal carriages swept down the last quarter of the Old Mile and the band of the Welsh Guards struck up the National Anthem. The crowd cheered. The famous Windsor Greys, Cardiff, Sydney, Rio and Santiago, tossed their heads with high spirits. Harness jangled, the solemn-faced top-hatted postilions tightened their grip on the reins, the Queen smiled and waved. Beside her was Prince Philip and two guests from the traditional Windsor houseparty always held for Ascot week, the Queen of Denmark and her escort. Behind them, in the second carriage, resplendent in full dress regalia of top hat, white waistcoat and tails, was the Prince of Wales, accompanied by the Queen Mother and the Grand Duchess of Luxembourg. The fashionable crowd in the white-railed paddock and royal enclosure craned for a better view. A flutter of excitement ran round the gathering; Royal Ascot was now open.

'Yes, it's a real strawberries and cream English Summer's day,' declared the TV announcer. Down in the royal enclosure the first champagne corks were popping. The Prince of Wales doffed his hat to greet a tall blonde girl in a brilliant green chiffon dress, topped with a wide-brimmed jade green coolie hat. Cameras zeroed in, admiring glances focused in on her from under the assembled toppers. Even in that rainbow of silks and jewel colours she stood out by virtue of the little finishing touches to her outfit; the single scarlet flower pinned to her hat, glossy scarlet sandals, immaculate enamelled nails. The Prince of Wales, smiling easily, escorted her to a good vantage point for viewing the first race, the Queen Anne Stakes.

Charles looked down at Henrietta, caught her eye and smiled. It wasn't difficult. She was pretty as a picture. Only someone who knew her as well as he did would have noticed the hint of suppressed anger that lent an added brilliance to her beauty. He had to admire her composure. She must be consumed with curiosity about his disappearance from the Beggar's Banquet, but she knew her royal protocol well enough never to expect an explanation unless one was volunteered. And this time, none would be forthcoming.

But even her vivid face couldn't lift his preoccupation. He found himself fingering the empty space where the ring should be on his left hand and restrained himself with an effort. How many days had it been now? Almost a week. Every day the same dread, every day the same doubt as it came to an end with no sign of the story breaking. Doubt growing gradually into certainty. The ring had not been returned. That could mean only one thing.

He forced himself to concentrate on the familiar scene ahead of him. Every day that went by was a milestone, a sign that he might, just possibly, have got away with his indiscretion. That he was safe. Free to return to his well-ordered routine. Ascot ... then Balmoral in August. Windsor for the weekends ... Sandringham for Christmas ... Winter sports in Gstaad ... the opening of the polo season in April ... then Ascot again.

'Which do you fancy, Sir?' For a moment he thought Henrietta had read his mind. None of it, he almost answered, surprising himself. He forced himself to inspect the thoroughbreds now milling in the paddock, their jockeys busy adjusting girths and leathers. He caught sight of the royal colours, and the green with red epaulettes of the Aga Khan, distinctive amongst the crossbelts and hoops.

'How about number four, Sir, the chestnut with the sheepskin noseband?' Henrietta consulted her programme earnestly. 'Last Fandango.'

He watched as the jockey swung into the saddle and began cantering his mount towards the course entrance.

'No. See there?' He pointed to the filly's gait. 'There's too much knee action. It means the going's too hard for her, she won't last the course.' The Old Mile was the hardest eight furlongs in England, especially with the going good to middling.

'Oh.' Henrietta frowned prettily. 'Well, Sir, in that case I think I'll save my wager till later.'

She smoothed the jade green openwork silk gloves hanging at her wrist and peeped up at him roguishly under her hat brim. He smiled. It was the Ascot tradition that ladies weren't allowed to bet, unless they wagered only their gloves – and of course a gentleman was not allowed to win such a wager.

His spirits lifted a little. Tradition ... it could bind a life together quite adequately.

'And which race have you selected? The Prince of Wales Stakes?'

'No ...' Henrietta ran her eye critically down her race card. 'There are too many entrants. I think I'll try the St James' Palace Stakes instead. Do you think that's a good idea, Sir?'

'Yes. Yes, of course.' With an effort he kept his voice level. Dimly he heard the roar of appreciation that indicated the first race had started, out of sight by the Golden Gates. St James' ... was he to be cursed with echoes for the rest of his life? Suddenly the sweet scent from the white carnation in his buttonhole seemed cloying. To hide his disturbance he signalled to a bowler-hatted steward, who hurried forward. Champagne on ice, strawberries laced with double cream, curls of smoked salmon on the silver tray. For a moment the sight sickened him, then he rallied.

Quickly he filled Henrietta's long-stemmed glass, then waved the steward away.

Henrietta, the delicate glass in one scarlet-tipped hand, looked at him in surprise.

'Aren't you having any, Sir?'

He glanced at the champagne fizzing in her glass, then looked away. He could almost taste it, a sour, cold, bitter taste. That too held too many memories. What a fool he'd been. Anger at himself made his voice harsher than he meant it to be.

'No. Not today.'

Her face was justifiably puzzled. He'd used his royal voice, and he hardly ever used it to her. He smiled again and took her arm, adjusting the topper so it shaded his eyes. Suddenly there were too many people in the enclosure.

'Come on. Let's go up to the box. If you hurry I'll get you a grandstand seat.'

Smile, he told himself. There's nothing to it. All I have to do is keep on smiling. And avoid the champagne.

Rose dipped the wet cloth into the water once again, wrung it out, wiped her forehead and went back to the window. She rubbed hard, making the glass squeak. The she stepped back. It was now the cleanest window she'd ever seen.

She turned and looked round the rest of the room. Everything shone and sparkled. She'd beaten the carpet to within an inch of its life, polished the mirror. Not a speck of dust or dirt anywhere. No trace of the waterproof man.

And now there was nothing else to do. The damp rag still in her hand, she sat down rather suddenly on the bed. Dimly she realized she hadn't eaten since yesterday. She couldn't even remember going out. She rubbed her eyes. What day was it? They all seemed the same ... endless, endless days.

The first three days she'd had a crazy idea. She'd thought he'd get in touch with her somehow. Send someone maybe.

Write her a letter. It wouldn't be too difficult for someone like him to find out where she lived. And he had her locket after all, he knew how much it meant to her. That was why she'd started cleaning and polishing. Just in case he came. It helped her, made her so tired at night that she could sleep. Stopped her thinking.

But it was a crazy idea, she knew that now. Deep down she must have known he'd never come, she was just filling in time. Trying to pretend nothing had changed.

He's forgotten all about me. The waterproof man was right. For the first time she let the truth sink in. He was just being kind ... and now he's forgotten. For a moment she tried to imagine what it must be like to be a prince, but it was too difficult. She just had this stupid image of someone eating off gold plates. He hadn't seemed like that at all.

Slowly, she got to her feet. Funny that being hungry should make you feel so heavy, when it ought by rights to make you feel light. She found the ring and unwrapped it. The gold was a little duller now, cold on her hand.

Of course she knew what she had to do. Even though he had her locket, she had no right to keep his ring. Her fingers felt numb as she wrapped in into a secure ball and stuffed it into an envelope. She went to the mantelpiece and opened the tin where she kept her savings. There wasn't much left. Enough to buy food for another few days. She tried not to think of what would happen when it ran out. She just didn't have the energy.

She stuffed the remaining notes into her pocket and went down the stairs. The light in the street dazzled her. A man and a dog walked by on the other side of the road and a sudden pain went through her body. While she'd been waiting in her room, willing time to stop, life had been going on without her. Nearly a week had gone by ... anything could have happened in that time. He could have cut his hair ... gone to the other side of the world ... fallen in love.

Two men sitting on the steps opposite caught her eye. They looked as if they'd been sitting there for hours. A sudden feeling of apprehension seized her. She hurried past them. There was a corner shop at the end of the road, and a stamp machine.

Then a thought struck her. She looked back to see the two men watching her intently. Her breath caught in her throat as she saw one of them wearing a crumpled raincoat.

Slowly the men began to walk down the street towards her. There was something very purposeful in the way they walked.

She looked round desperately, her heart thudding. He'd come back . . . and this time not alone. The betraying packet seemed to burn a hole in her hand. If they caught her with it . . . Quickly she crossed the road to the postbox. There was no time even to buy a stamp.

The ring hit the bottom of the postbox with a dull thud. She drew a deep breath. Perhaps, unstamped, it would never reach him. But she couldn't think of any other way out.

Taking her courage in both hands she began to walk back up the street towards them, as if she hadn't noticed anything. They saw her coming and halted. They turned to each other as if in conversation. The waterproof man lit the other one's cigarette.

Willing herself to move slowly, she walked up the street until nearly opposite her house. The two men still lingered, she heard the murmur of their voices. Then, suddenly, she turned and ran at full speed across the street.

'Hey, miss!'

With trembling fingers she forced her key into the lock. She heard hurrying footsteps behind her and looked anxiously over her shoulder. A blinding flash of light almost dazzled her. Blundering into the doorpost in her haste she threw herself inside, shut the door behind her and leaned against it, panting. Her head was swimming, but through the door she heard voices clearly.

'Damn.'

'Did you get her?'

'No, I don't think so. Too far away.'

Another muffled curse.

'There may not be another chance.'

'Want to bet? She's got to come out of there sometime.'

'Maybe you're right . . .' The voices faded. She peered out through the letterbox. They were back on the steps again, waiting.

She bit down to stop her teeth chattering. Suddenly the dark staircase ahead of her looked threatening, like the entrance to a trap. There was no way out.

But why was the waterproof man still after her? She'd said no, she'd thought he believed her. Then, with a sinking feeling, she realized why. He wasn't after her at all, or only incidentally. He was after Charles.

She pressed her hand to her cheek. She couldn't let it happen. She knew what newspapers were like. Even if she didn't say anything, they'd make it all up, twist everything. And nothing she could do would stop them. The facts were there. He was who he was and she was nobody.

And not just that. With a jolt of pain she realized that even if she refused to say anything she would still be a danger to him. Just by existing. At this very minute he must be regretting he ever laid eyes on her.

But what could she do? Her eyes fell on a brown envelope lying on the floor by her feet. It was addressed to her. For a wild moment as her fingers struggled to open it she thought it was from him. But inside was a one-line note. 'Don't spend it all at once.' Signed in a scrawl, james. And behind it, five new ten pound notes.

Dazed, she held the money in her hand. Then her jaw set. She marched up the stairs and threw open the door of her room. It looked unnaturally neat, almost as if she'd left it already. She crossed to the window, lifted the sash and looked down. There was the familiar railway line. Often in the middle of the night she'd heard the announcements from her bed. 'The train standing on platform one is the night service for Edinburgh, calling at Carlisle . . .' Edinburgh . . . the name had sent a shiver down her spine, she'd turned over and gone back to sleep.

But now the time had come. She leaned forward. Below was a balcony, then a tree. Ahead the railway line and all points North. The only place she'd ever find a clue to her past. A shiver of apprehension went through her. What would she find? Without the locket, maybe her quest would be useless ...

She banished the thought. What was she frightened of? There was nothing here to keep here any more. She had money in her pocket. And no one to say goodbye to.

She grabbed her case, bundled her coat under her arm. A motorail express, already loaded, was waiting at the platform, its engine humming. There was no time to lose. At least then, whatever happened, he'd be safe.

She looked round the room one more time. It had been home ... she remembered how happy she'd been when she first saw it. Her own key, her own door. Well, that was over now. Her grey hat caught her eye. She'd almost forgotten it. She picked it up, then hesitated. What he'd said came back to her. 'The scar ... it's invisible now. No one can see it.'

She took a deep breath. Of course it wasn't true ... but oh, how much she wanted it to be true. She weighed the hat in her hands. He'd tried to help her. Now it was her turn to help herself.

Quickly, before she could change her mind, she marched to the window. The hat must go. Putting all her strength behind it, she hurled it out of the window. It went spinning and sailing down, away out of sight.

There, it was done. There was no going back now. Without a backward glance she climbed out on to the sill.

CHAPTER NINE

The big flat-bottomed ferry juddered and wallowed its way towards the setting sun. Above the sky was pure violet, below the sea was pewter grey, oily with calm. A tireless escort of gulls sailed silently above the ferry's wind-tattered blue flag with its diagonal white cross.

Rose clung to the front rail and looked down the glassy white side of the boat to the glassy black water below. By now she didn't care where she was going or what happened to her. She'd been so full of hope when she arrived in Edinburgh. But that was before she'd learned the truth.

She closed her eyes, remembering. How strange the orphanage had looked to her. Smaller somehow, much smaller than it had appeared to her in her dreams. New faces everywhere. A new registrar, young, overworked but willing to help. She'd given her the address of the woman who'd brought her in as a baby. More hope, mixed with fear. Would she still be there? Would she be able to tell her anything?

Then the long trail through the hilly backstreets beneath the castle. Even though it was summer the cold Northern wind sliced through her bones. At last she'd found the small house with its Bed and Breakfast sign.

A sour-faced elderly woman opened the door. But when Rose explained who she was and why she'd come a look of avid curiosity replaced her suspicion.

'Well now!' The woman bustled her into a damp, over-furnished parlour. 'Who would have thought it after all these years . . . so you're the poor wee babe.' She looked her up and down, her nose twitching with interest. 'Aye, you have a look of her, right enough.' She shook her head disapprovingly.

119

'Poor little mite ... she never should have done it. Unnatural, I call it.'

'Please, tell me what happened.' Rose could hardly control her eagerness. This was the first person she'd met who'd actually known her mother.

The woman snorted. 'I remember it as if it was yesterday. It's not the sort of thing you'd forget in a hurry.' She settled her back against an over-stuffed cushion. 'It was late, very late one winter night. Dirty weather. I heard the ring at the door and I almost didn't answer it. If I'd known, I'd have stayed right here by the fire.' She sniffed. 'But there it is, I didn't know. So I went to the door and there she was – no coat, no hat and a tiny baby wrapped in the crook of her arm. Well, I ask you, what was I supposed to do? I don't normally take in children, but I couldn't send a little mite like that back out in the cold. But what kind of mother would traipse her child through the streets like that I don't know ...

'Still, she said she'd just got back from a long journey, so being a fool I made the both of you comfortable in the best bedroom, seeing she was so tired she could hardly put one word in front of the other, and told myself I'd get to the bottom of it in the morning.

'But would you believe it, come the morning nothing would do but she wanted to be off again, leaving you with me!' The woman's eyes were round with outrage.

' "I'll be back by evening," she says, bright and breezy. Of course that wouldn't do at all, I told her so.

' "How do I know you'll be coming back?" I said to her. That stopped her in her tracks.

' "There's the baby ... of course I'll be coming back," she says, all wide-eyed and innocent. I had my suspicions then. She's thinking of doing a flit, I thought. I'll test her out.

' "In that case, you won't mind settling up before you go." That gave her something to think about, I can tell you.

' "But I've only enough for my fare as it is," she says. "I was going to bring some more money from home." I've heard that one before, I thought, but I still wasn't sure. There

120

was something about her I should have known but she quite took me in.

'So I thought a bit. In the end I said, "Why don't you leave something as security before you go, just in case."

' "But I haven't got anything," she said. But she had, a locket round her neck, I'd noticed it straight off.

' "What about that?" I said. I could see it was solid silver.

' "Oh no, I couldn't . . ." Yes, lots of excuses she made. But she had to in the end.' The woman nodded her head in satisfaction. 'And a good job it was too. Taught her a bit of a lesson. Because as you know she never came back.'

She frowned. 'Funny though . . . when it came to it I couldn't bring myself to keep the locket after all. Even though it was worth quite a lot of money. Solid silver and all. But there you were, a poor little mite with nothing . . . I couldn't bring myself.' She turned eagerly towards Rose. 'Did they tell you at the orphanage? I told them to make sure to tell you about the locket. I could have kept it . . .'

Rose shook her head. 'No, they didn't tell me. I thought . . . I thought my mother meant me to have it.'

The woman's lips pursed in a tight line. Her voice rose. 'That worthless girl? Nothing was further from her mind. A fine sort of mother she was. Best thing you can do is forget about her entirely.'

Rose looked down. Other words seared into her memory. 'You haven't got a proper mother . . .' It looked as if Alice and Nicola and Eileen had been right after all. The disappointment took her breath away. She'd never imagined anything like this. All these years the locket had been her one hope . . . but now she could see it for what it was. Unwilling payment for a sordid little debt. Proof of how much her mother must have wanted to be free of her. She'd given up the one thing she had of any value, just to escape . . .

'Tell me . . .' The woman's voice came from a great distance. 'Do you still have the locket?' There was an eager, sentimental look on her face. It was as much as Rose could do to answer.

'No, I'm sorry. I lost it. No, I gave it away.'

The woman's face fell, then sharpened. Now she was displeased.

'Well well, that's a surprise. Perhaps I should have kept it after all. Two pounds she owed me for the room, and I never saw a penny of it. Not to mention the trouble I was put to taking care of the baby. A whole day it took to go to the orphanage, signing all those forms, putting up with all their questions . . . anyone would have thought it was me who was in the wrong just because I'd forgotten her name.'

'Please . . .' With an effort Rose stemmed the flood. Not even a name . . . her last hope was gone. She dug in her coat pocket and took out a ten pound note. 'Let me pay . . . for the room and everything. It's only right.'

'Oh, I don't know that I should . . . it wasn't your fault . . .' The woman's eyes lingered on the money. 'Well, if you insist.' The note disappeared in a flash. There was an awkward silence.

Is that all, thought Rose numbly. A debt paid, all the ends neatly tied? The end of the road . . . She lifted her head. No, she wouldn't let it end like this. She'd come so far, she wouldn't give up now.

'Tell me, that morning . . . did you ask her where she was going?'

The woman frowned, racking her brains.

'Yes I did, it was only common sense. But she wouldn't give me a straight answer. Tir nan Og, she said. And where might that be, I said, never having heard of it. The end of the world, she said, with a funny little smile. But that'll be no help to you, I'm afraid. The people at the orphanage tried to trace her but they couldn't. As I say, there's no such place.'

'Tir nan Og . . .' For some reason the words sounded familiar. 'What language is that?'

The woman sniffed dismissively. 'It's only the Gaelic, I've no idea what it means.' Then she paused. 'Come to think of it, maybe she was a Gaelic speaker. She had the softness in her speech, it's not often you hear it this far East. I think it was the softness took me in ...'

A last forlorn hope stirred in Rose.

'Then perhaps that's where she was going – back home?'

The woman tossed her head. 'I doubt it myself. That's not the kind of girl that has any liking for her home and family.'

But Rose ignored her. 'Even so ... if I wanted to find someone who spoke Gaelic, where would I go?'

The woman looked puzzled. 'The West coast, of course ... The highlanders and islanders still hold on to it. Godforsaken places, though. You're not thinking of going there? Whatever for?'

Rose stood up. She didn't know herself. But there was nowhere else to go.

Late that same afternoon, after a winding mountainous train ride across the backbone of Scotland, she arrived in the small West coast port of Oban. It seemed to be as far West as she could go. And it was very different from the East. The air was soft and moist, the colours of the little fishing boats in the harbour muted and mysterious. Orion, Harvest Moon, Constant Friend ... and towering above them the ferry. Driven by an impulse she didn't understand she'd asked a friendly sailor on the quay where it was bound for.

He paused for a long moment, taking in her windblown appearance. His voice when he spoke had an odd lilt to it, as if English wasn't his native language.

'To you, the Western Isles.' His nimble fingers wound the heavy rope round its mooring as if it was weightless. 'To the mainlanders, Innse Gall, the islands of the strangers.' He stood up, wiped his hands dry. 'To me ... and to those who love them ...' He looked out to sea, a faraway expression in his pale grey eyes, 'they are simply Tir nan Og.' He smiled. 'I hope that answers your question.'

Tir nan Og ... that wild hope stirred again.

'What does it mean?'

The sailor looked at her quizzically. 'Ah, that is a more difficult question to answer. If you were a Viking, it would mean Valhalla. If you were sad and needing comfort, it would be the land of heart's desire. If you were a traveller it would be the end of the world, where you need travel no more. But if you want merely to know what the words mean, then it is an easy matter. Tir nan Og. The land of youth. Where the sun never sets and there is no time.'

So here she was. Looking out over the railing she knew he was right. This was the end of the world. There was no wind, only the onrushing roar of the boat engines as it heaved over the swell. The sky was immense, flickering with colour like a vast cinema screen. First cloudless ivory above the iron-grey water, then ripening to apricot, dusky blue, violet. Even though it was almost midnight the sun hadn't gone down. It hung there in the empty sky, edging every wave with green.

Suddenly she realized how cold and tired she was. There was no saying if her mother had ever come this way, no certainty that there would be anything waiting for her when she reached the islands. The strange impulse that had driven her to try and retrace her mother's footsteps was fading now. Here on the ferry, with nothing around her but sky and sea, she could feel that the world was huge, so huge there was no point in trying to hold on to anyone ...

And now she'd left behind everything she knew. She stared unseeingly over the waves. She'd never felt so alone. The image of her mother, carefully built up over the years, played over so often she knew it by heart ... Simple details ... a smiling face ... an open door, the flicker of a fire behind ... just the feeling of being expected, waited for ... Now that image was broken into a thousand pieces. She'd been so sure the locket had been meant for her. But now she knew that her mother was someone she'd invented. Her real mother was someone else, a stranger.

She shivered. It had been a day of goodbyes. Now there was nothing left, no point in feeling anything any more.

Then, down in the water, she saw what she thought at first
were reflections of the sunset, big sunset-coloured disc
shapes that flowed and eddied with the movement of the
waves. Each shape was surrounded by a cluster of tiny pale
purple shapes, transparent and dimpled like a photograph of
the galaxy. She hung over the rail and watched them drifting
serenely by just underneath the water like hidden planets,
comets trailing clouds of fire. Somehow they managed to let
the waves swell away under them while they stayed in the
same place, their long starry feathers twinkling away behind
them. Flowers in a garden that no one saw, patiently offering
up their colours to nothing and no one.

She closed her eyes. Maybe there was something left after
all. If she kept them shut she could see his face and the way
he'd looked at her. As if he really saw her. In his arms she'd
felt beautiful. And nothing could take that away.

She slid her hands inside her coat, hugging the memory to
her. She'd been like the underwater flowers. Waiting to be
seen, just once, in a lifetime of waiting. It would have to be
enough.

She could feel her heart beating, slowly and painfully.

Just for a second she'd felt his heart beat like that, strong
and comforting under his shirt.

The wind brought tears to her eyes. But out here there was
no one to see them. No one to hear her either. Perhaps the
wind would carry her message for her.

'I love you.' The words were strange and unfamiliar on her
tongue. She said them again, into the emptiness which
stretched in front of her and behind her

'I love you.'

There was no reply. She felt the wind blow her words back
to her with a seasoning of salt spray.

'Why?' said the wind.

She drew her coat collar tight around her cold body.

'Because. Just because.'

Almost five hundred miles away, the sun had already left the

London sky. But in the centre at least the streets were still ablaze with light as tourists and night-lovers roamed in search of distraction – through the tiny mysterious streets of Soho, with its hazy basement clubs and flickering neon signs promising sex that could be relied on, in the luxurious restaurants of Belgravia and Knightsbridge, where white linen tablecloths shone in discreet candlelight, and the streetlamps glowed amber on the faultless paintwork of Daimlers and Jaguars, in the marble-faced casinos of the West End where Arabs staked fortunes in order to be winked at by uniformed doormen, through to the seedier regions of Earl's Court, where the Australians prowled on their English outback and squabbled like dislodged starlings outside the closing pubs of the King's Road, to raucous shouts of 'Time, gentlemen, please!'

Deep in the City itself heat still smouldered as the central core of stone and concrete slowly released the stored energy of the day's relentless sunshine. But round Victoria station and Waterloo the streets, so crowded with secretaries and businessmen during the daytime, were almost deserted. Big Ben's illuminated face looked down impassively on the reaches of the Thames and Westminster Bridge. The Houses of Parliament were silent and dark. Trafalgar Square lay empty, even the pigeons and photographers at rest, the stone lions guarding the sights for tomorrow's influx of visitors.

The Mall with its gently glowing gaslamps was deserted apart from the occasional taxi taking the short cut through to the crowded West End. Outside the Palace the royal standard hung limply, hardly stirring. Every window on the upper floors of the Palace was open, but only a hint of a breeze filtered through the plane trees on the South side.

'It's after midnight, Sir. You asked me to let you know.'

'Yes. Thank you, John.'

The door closed silently behind the detective and Charles laid down his pen. It had been a long, hard day. He listened to the detective's footsteps receding down the corridor. He must be glad to be going home.

I'd like to be going home too. The thought rose unbidden in his mind. He rubbed his aching temples. What could he be thinking of? This, the great brooding bulk of the Palace, where he was born, was home, as much as anywhere. He had more homes available to him than anyone in the country, including two, Chevening, left to him in trust, and Georgian Highgrove, his latest purchase, that he'd never even lived in.

If only he could think straight. If only he wasn't constantly reminded ... Like this afternoon at Ascot. He'd survived that well, only to catch sight of a poster by the side of the road on the way back to Windsor. He'd glanced at it casually, his eye caught by the clever name. The Xiles ... some new group, probably. Then, as he recognized the face beneath the lettering every other thought had fled his mind. It was a clever photograph too. You couldn't decide whether the girl was plain or pretty. But however you looked at it you couldn't get away from the eyes, deep pools in a pale, flawed face. Her mouth was parted as if she was about to smile, but her eyes looked as if she was about to cry.

So there it was. Proof positive that she was what they'd said she was. Only for the rest of the day he'd been unable to banish that haunting from his mind, as if she was trying to tell him something. In the end he'd been driven to make his excuses and leave the houseparty. He'd driven the Aston at full throttle all the way back to London, Henrietta silent in the seat beside him.

And now at last he had what he wanted. He was alone. He got up restlessly and picked up one of his Eskimo soapstone carvings. A huge bull walrus, weighed down by its own tusks.

As one endangered species to another ... He gave a wry smile.

He'd envied the palace detective this evening, going home after a day's work well done. His wife would be waiting for him, eager to hear about the doings of the day and discuss plans for tomorrow.

Tomorrow ... He rubbed his eyes and stretched, letting the idea take hold. It was so tempting, an all-or-nothing decision ... like that time he'd taken the turn at Thruxton too fast in Graham Hill's Formula Two racer and nearly spun out of control ... the surge of adrenalin, the knowledge that nothing but luck stood between him and destruction ...

I'll do it, he thought suddenly. First thing tomorrow. No more looking back. No more wasted time. His mind made up, he fell into the bed and slept like the dead.

'Don't worry, just pretend you're the Queen of England!' The sailor called up encouragingly from the quay, his face a pale blur in the darkness. Step by step, her wet shoes just gripping the footholds, Rose edged down the companionway. By the time she'd reached the jetty the friendly ferryman had disappeared, leaving the quay deserted.

Behind her, suddenly, the ship's lights went off. She was the only passenger left. Most had left the ferry at other islands, only a few had stayed right to the end of the voyage and the last port of call. The last had disappeared with a wink of red tail-lights before she had time to realize this was as far as the ferry was going.

From below decks she heard a faint peal of laughter, then silence. Soon even the crew would be asleep. Now, without the ship's lights, it was even darker, like being inside a velvet-lined bag. Only one road led away from the small jetty, flanked by lamps so dim their light hardly reached the ground.

She lifted her head, trying to get her bearings. There was something different again about the air, not a smell, more a feeling. Something soft and fresh. No sound but the lap of water against the jetty. Not a bird, not a rustle, not a breath of wind in a tree. The sailor's words came back to her, unbidden. The end of the world ... but familiar somehow, as if she'd always known what it would be like ...

She shook herself. She was tired, she was imagining things. The long day with its disappointments had disorientated her. Now she needed more than anything somewhere warm and dry to sleep. But where?

Slowly, with only her own footsteps to keep her company, she began to make her way down through the dark shuttered shapes of one-storey houses. Perhaps there would be a hotel, a small inn, anything, even a lighted window showing that someone was still awake would do. But after only a few yards the street lights ran out completely and so did the houses. She felt rather than saw the land swim up around her in the blue-violet darkness.

What was that? A glint of light by the side of the road caught her eye. It looked like nothing more than a shining round hole through to the other side of the earth. A wave of dizziness went over her, for a moment she felt like an astronaut. Cautiously she moved over to investigate, and the hole turned itself inside out and became a pool of water. Scattered in amongst the grass were a chain of tiny lakes, each no bigger than a bathtub, glinting beadily wherever they reflected the sky.

Where am I? She tightened her grip on her case and pressed on. She had no idea where the road was taking her, but perhaps her mother, twenty years ago, had come this same way, going home. She stopped for a second and closed her eyes, willing it to be true. Help me find the way, she asked silently. I've come such a long way, don't desert me now ...

But the strange sense of being guided that had prompted her to take the ferry was gone. It was as if her mother had never existed. She opened her eyes. Darkness. Silence. It was late and getting later. Her feet in the wet shoes were cold and sore, and she still didn't know where she was going. Only that it was probably a wild goose chase.

'Ouch!' She tripped over a stone hummock and nearly fell headlong. From habit she clutched at the locket to check that the knot in the chain hadn't come undone. But of course the locket was gone ...

The tears in her eyes weren't just from the pain of her stubbed toe. Suddenly it seemed much darker. What am I doing here, she thought dully. I must be mad. There's nothing left, not even the locket.

She blinked hard. Her eyes widened. What was that, off to the left, low down on the horizon? A small, twinkling light ...

She hesitated only a moment, then turned and left the road. She had nothing to lose. Keeping her eyes fixed on the flickering light she edged her way forward. The ground was very uneven, full of large grass-covered lumps. Once she found herself ankle-deep in one of the icy little pools, but the shock was worse than the water. Her shoes were soaked through already.

Once, and once only, she looked back over her shoulder at the road. With a shock she realized she couldn't see it any more. And in the darkness that meant she'd never find it again. So there was no going back even if she'd wanted to.

She glued her eyes to the light. Now she could see where it was coming from. It was a single candle, set inside a tiny window very low to the ground. She could see an edge of drawn curtain behind the deep window sill, and a small vase of flowers.

Suddenly there was the creak of a door and a blaze of light. Something dark rushed towards her over the grass and flung its solid shaggy weight against her knees. A cold nose pressed against her hand, a hot tongue licked once, then it raced away again.

Against the light in the doorway stood a small figure.

'Welcome.' It was a woman's voice, warm and deep. She clicked her tongue chidingly at the dog. Rose hesitated. The woman was clearly expecting someone else. The candle in the window, the eager dog, the open door, the crackle of a fire inside ... Drawn irresistibly, she took a step forward. Now she could make out a halo of fine white hair drawn back, deep-shadowed eyes. There was something strange about those eyes, perhaps the woman's sight was failing. She opened her mouth to speak but the woman forestalled her.

'Well, come in then unless you want to spend Midsummer's Eve on the hill.' This time her voice had a chuckle in it. The dog's black and white face poked out

behind her skirts, grinning. Behind them both Rose caught a
glimpse of a scrubbed table laid with blue and white china,
firelight flickering off the rafters . . . warmth and light. Just as
she'd imagined it in her dreams . . . Another step forward.
She was so cold and tired, she could explain later. One more
step took her to the door. The candle guttered and went out.
The woman put a welcoming hand on her arm. They were
both nearly the same height. It was like coming home.

Henrietta curtseyed demurely.
   'Good morning, Sir.'
   Charles eyed her appreciably. In the mere twelve hours
since Ascot her appearance had undergone another sea
change. The flamboyant green and scarlet was gone, to be
replaced by something subtler, yet another foil for her multi-
faceted beauty.
   He succumbed to the familiar surge of attraction. She was
an extraordinary girl really. The heat was stifling, but her
gleaming gold hair was smoothed back into an elegant roll at
the back of her head, with one ingenious curl escaping down
her neck. Her dress was demure, cloud-grey and high-
necked, but so cleverly cut that it showed the movement of
her breasts beneath the fabric. The only real Henrietta touch
was the pale grey suede shoes with their narrow high heels
and open toes, from which peeped her insolently maroon-
tipped nails.
   Conscious of his appreciative gaze she reached up to
smooth her hair, unnecessarily, and he admired her grace
and the slender gold bracelet that slid along her perfectly
rounded wrist. It seemed a year since he'd last seen her rather
than a matter of hours. Enough time anyway to have
forgotten how she glowed, with a flawless lustre like the
pearls round her neck. Pearls, no less . . . He remembered the
days when Henrietta wouldn't have been seen dead in pearls.
'So ageing.' But that was before she'd learned you had to
make sacrifices to fit your station in life . . .
   Yes, she was eminently suitable. Even the press approved.

She knew how to dress, what to say whatever occasion, when to say nothing at all. She rode beautifully, and even if she drew the line at trudging the moors with a pack of muddy dogs she was an entertaining and witty companion round the fireside afterwards, with a glass of brandy glowing in her hand.

A rapid series of images flicked through his mind as he looked at her – Henrietta at the races, Henrietta at Sandringham in the autumn, sparkling in the blue, gold and white drawing-room created by Queen Alexandra, Henrietta dictating the colour of curtains and the lay-out of rooms at Highgrove, with her hair whisked back in a Hermès silk scarf, Henrietta at Windsor, lightly draped over a satin-covered Louis XIV sofa, Henrietta at Balmoral ...

A slight frown crossed his face. It was better not to think of Henrietta at Balmoral. Her image was oddly out of place in that timeless, turreted fairytale palace that Victoria loved so much.

'How lovely to see you again so soon.' He bent to kiss her cheek. 'I'm so glad you hadn't made other plans.'

They both knew his words were the merest courtesy; it was highly unlikely that she would ever turn down his invitation.

'It's such a fine day, I thought we might go for a drive. Then perhaps luncheon at the Pomme d'Amour – unless of course you'd rather eat first? Are you starving?'

'Oh no, Sir.' She looked at him from under her lashes. It was odd that they'd known each other so long and he still didn't really know what was going on in her head. But perhaps that was an advantage. 'I can wait.' She stroked back a wisp of hair and sighed. 'It's been so warm lately I've hardly been able to eat a thing.'

'Perhaps it's love,' he said lightly.

She looked directly at him suddenly, her green-blue eyes wide. Here was his opportunity. He should now fall on his knees and declare his intentions – then she would look away and blush, eyes downcast. 'Oh Sir, this is so sudden ...' And it would be over with. But not here, he thought. I want to be outside, somewhere I can breathe.

Once in the Aston he felt a little better. With the roof down and the rush of cooler air his mood lifted. The wind carried away the cloying sweetness of Henrietta's scent and the Aston was running smoothly. John, hunched up in the dickey seat, was his usual impassive self. Henrietta was used to his presence. With the ease of long practice she twisted a mauve silk scarf round her hair, leaned her head back and half-closed her eyes as Charles accelerated. He found himself smiling into the wind. His mind had been so full of other things in the past week that he'd almost forgotten his old pleasures. After all, they'd served him well for years, and he'd considered himself happy as a sandboy. He had a duty to be happy, in his privileged position.

He concentrated on his driving, allowing his fatigue to lift from him temporarily just as the wind lifted the heat of the city from his face. If only he could keep on driving, forget everything except the road ahead and the pretty girl beside him. What more could any man possibly want? A fine June day, the sun high overhead, a thoroughbred car, the statutory blonde ...

Now they were heading due West, slipping through the midday haze like a dream, everything going according to plan. He knew exactly where he was going to take her. Romantic setting, reasonable privacy, good visibility for John's security-minded conscience, a breath of fresh air in the muggy London heat. And something else that he craved so deeply he could almost taste it – a link with past innocence, a touch of something wild and free.

An odd sort of excitement took hold of him. Passersby glanced curiously at the windswept young man and the golden-haired girl, but he didn't care. Today he was a kamikaze pilot – death or glory time.

He felt John shift uneasily in the back seat as he did a particularly racy piece of gear-changing on the corner. It'll end in tears, he could almost hear him thinking.

But they were almost there now. One more sweeping bend,

and London was forgotten. Ahead, bathed in brilliant
sunlight, as unexpected as the sight of the ocean in a desert,
the wild rolling expanse of Richmond Park. Two thousand
acres of heath and woodland, big enough for wild deer to live
in, so there must be a few square yards of privacy for the
Prince of Wales. But today I am not incognito, he thought.
Today I am Doing the Right Thing.

With a flourish he swung the Aston through the tall
wrought-iron gates and into the park itself. It was almost
deserted. London was either lunching or away for the
weekend. In the distance, a herd of deer raised their heads
and stared, the big male motionless with his heavy antlers
still covered in velvet. The Aston was almost silent as it
purred along the still familiar road. Why hadn't he come
before? There on the right was the stretch of level ground
where he'd played football with the chauffeur as a small boy,
and lost his best belt buckle in the grass. It was all coming
back – it has been a real jungle for him then. Past the clump
of oak woodland, round that bank of ferns, and ...

He recognized it immediately, and turned the Aston off
the road into a suitable parking place. Henrietta looked up,
startled.

'I thought we were going for a drive, Sir?'

He suppressed a flare of irritation.

'I have a surprise for you.' As he'd expected, her eyes lit
up. Women were all the same under the skin. Smoothing her
skirt she slid gracefully out of the car, her high heels
crunching on the gravel. She shivered a little in the cool
breeze off the open ground, but refused to put on her jacket.
He took her arm.

This is it, he thought. He knew exactly the place he
wanted. All he had to do was get her there. But it wasn't
too far. All one had to do was leave the road and keep
walking due West and one couldn't miss it.

Up ahead he saw a couple striding along arm in arm, a big
leggy dog gambolling like a lamb around them. They were so
obviously together they didn't even have to look at each

134

other. For a moment a pain ran through him like an electric shock. He was interested to notice that after it had gone, he felt numb. It was an improvement.

'Ugh!' Henrietta shook her head violently. A bit of hair escaped from her hairdo and she pinned it back impatiently. She shook her head again, batting at the air. Puzzled, he looked at her, then noticed the cloud of tiny black insects floating above her head.

'It's all right. They don't bite, you know. They just tickle.' The look she shot at him showed that she wasn't too convinced. Tight-lipped, she went on, shaking her head from time to time, John following discreetly behind.

Charles felt his pulse beating faster. The trees almost hid it, but he knew it was there, just beyond. He'd never been allowed to go too close when he was a boy, but now he'd reached the age of discretion. There. That was it. He released Henrietta's arm, feeling the old surge of excitement. When he was a boy it had been the Sargasso Sea, that's what he'd called it, and he'd been overjoyed when he learnt from the chauffeur that they'd actually landed seaplanes there during the war. Imagine it – the big roaring machines coming right down in the middle of London, hidden behind the trees . . . It made anything seem possible. One day I'll fly one of those, he'd said. And he had.

Now of course the big stretch of open water had shrunk with the drought, leaving the band of mud and waterweed along the edge. But for him it was still the Sargasso Sea, with the same weeping willow hanging over, its fountains of leaves with their pale undersides reflected in what was left of the water.

He took Henrietta's arm again and was surprised to feel her resistance. Her pretty mouth was quivering in a pout.

'What's the matter?'

Her usual calm seemed to have deserted her.

'Where . . . where are we going, Sir?' Her voice was apprehensive. He pointed out a spot near the waterline, beside the willow. Her eyes widened.

'You mean ... right down there? In the *mud*?' Her eyes were round with horror. 'But I shall get soaked!' He glanced down, following her gaze, at her immaculate suede shoes. Now he understood her reluctance. His heart sank a little. It was not an auspicious beginning. But he mustn't let it sway him. He thrust his hand into his pocket with a surge of anticipation. But instead of the solid velvet-covered ring box he'd expected he encountered a cool, smooth, oval shape.

The locket. His valet, conscientious as always, must have found it in his pocket after that disastrous rendez-vous, assumed it was important, and discreetly transferred it to the suit he now wore. His fingers recoiled, but it was too late. The damage was done. Instead of Henrietta's face, still slightly flushed and pouting, he saw someone else's, glowing through hair wet with rain.

For a long frozen moment he stood there. Then, with aching slowness he withdrew his hand. It was no good, he couldn't go through with it.

'Of course.' He spoke gently, half to himself, half to Henrietta. 'I should have known.'

They walked back to the car together, in silence, his black head close to her golden one. The breeze had died away now and he felt the heat rush in again. Yes, he should have known. This wasn't the wild green fresh place he'd known all those years ago. Perhaps it never had been. He stared at the parched ground in front of him, the dry wiry grass. Everything was dry and worn and faded. People had worn it all away, making it into a desert. Even his Sargasso Sea. He hadn't known much geography then, he just thought the name sounded nice. But he knew better now. Even the Sargasso Sea, when you came right down to it, was just a tideless, salt-encrusted, weed-choked pond.

CHAPTER TEN

Rose straightened her aching back and leant on her spade.
Beside her the pile of fresh-cut peat, looking like chunks of
chocolate fudge, was growing steadily. It looked very
different from the hard dry squares which burnt to fine white
ash in the old range.

But it was getting late. Soon it would be time to go back to
the croft, where Catriona would be waiting. Rory, the old
black and white dog, who always liked watching other
people work, lifted his head expectantly, his eyes narrowed
against the sea wind.

She was getting to know and love the island. Though it
was so small it seemed different every day, the light changing
it from a bare wind-swept desert to a magical oasis inside a
minute. Even the tiny lakes that Catriona called lochans
disappeared at low tide and popped out again when the tide
came in. Only the peat scars remained. Rough grass and bog
flowers softened their outlines, but they were still there, signs
that people had lived here for centuries and would go on
living here, this year, next year ...

She shivered. Even though she was cutting peat for
Catriona's winter supply, there was no saying where she
herself would be by wintertime.

She bent and scrubbed at her spade with a handful of
marsh grass, thinking back to that morning after her arrival.
She'd woken up with a sense of dread, hardly knowing where
she was, but sure of one thing – she had no right to be there,
taking advantage of the old woman's hospitality. The bed
she's slept in was a little wooden box set into the wall, with its
own wooden doors. She'd pushed them open, letting in a
blinding surge of light, swung her feet to the ground and to

her astonishment touched bare sand. The first thing she saw was her clothes, hung to dry over the old range. The second was the old woman putting down a saucer for the dog.

'Excuse me ...' She hardly knew how to begin. 'I'd like to explain –' The old woman swung round abruptly. Her eyes probed Rose's face.

'Och, I've no time for explanations. Never have had.' She bustled away into a further room, came back with clothes hanging over her arm.

'But ... you were expecting someone ... the candle ...'

'Aye. It's the tradition, on Midsummer's Eve, to keep a candle in the window for a stranger.' The woman hesitated. Her eyes in daylight still had an odd filmy look to them, as if she could see things that other people couldn't. 'I knew someone would come. I have the sight, I can read the signs.' She shook her head in dissatisfaction. 'I thought it was you I was waiting for, and then again ... the token is missing.' She stared thoughtfully at Rose, then seemed to make up her mind. 'What is your name?'

'Rose.'

She nodded briskly. 'And mine is Catriona. And that is all folk have had to know about each other since the seals had ears.'

Unceremoniously she dumped the clothes on Rose's bed. 'There. Best put those on till your own are dry.' Her voice was gruff. Without a backward glance she clicked to the dog and went out, closing the door behind her with a bang.

Rose dressed slowly. There was a dark blue and beige striped woollen skirt, longer than she was used to, a soft, worn linen blouse and a short jacket in the same wool as the skirt. The faint smell of lavender drifted up from the material, as if the clothes had once belonged to someone else and had been kept in store for years. To her surprise they fitted perfectly, right down to the knitted stockings and sturdy black shoes. Maybe the old woman had had a daughter ... but then she wore no wedding ring and had the look of an old maid.

Dressed, she looked round the room. It was perfect, everything just the right size for a single person. Like a dwarf's house. The ceiling was low, the stone walls deeply inset with small windows, the wooden settle and three-legged stool all in proportion. And there wasn't one mirror.

The door swung open, letting in a rush of clean cold sea air. The dog skittered round her heels, almost toppling her over. The old woman seemed to have difficulty speaking. Her cheeks were pink, bits of white fluffy hair had come undone and were whipping round her head.

'Come. Come quickly.'

She grabbed Rose by the hand and almost dragged her through the door. Rose had a confused impression of sunlight and open air, then they were running, their skirts whipping in the wind, up a grassy slope.

At the top of the slope Catriona stopped. Rose looked down, breathless. Ahead the grass gave way to sheer, baby-smooth white sand. Beyond that, a single sheet of blue light, the colour so deep it almost hurt, was the sea. Above her a black-faced gull swooped and called with its small cricket-like voice.

'There.' Catriona pointed. 'It's not the token the sight showed me, but it is a sign for all that.' Like a young girl she scrambled down the sandy incline. Rose followed her. Now she saw what the old woman had been pointing at. Half in, half out of the water was a small boat, rocking gently on the tide. Its paint was rusty and flaking, the two simple wooden seats warped. Its bottom held a good six inches of water, on top of which a broken oar floated sadly.

Rose gave Catriona a puzzled look. The old woman was staring at the boat with an air of complete satisfaction. She leaned forward, scraped at the bows with a wrinkled finger.

'There ... do you read it?'

Rose bent forward. Faded and almost illegible in its design of entwined flowers was the boat's name. *Love and Honour*.

Suddenly her heart went out to the small vessel. Clearly no one had bothered to take care of it. One day it had simply escaped its moorings and drifted where the tide took it, ending up beached and useless, but still with a faintly hopeful air.

'Who does it belong to?' She had to fight the urge to reach forward and drag the boat safely on to the beach. It wouldn't take much to repair it – a lick of paint, some oil for the salt-rusted outboard motor, a new pair of oars . . .

The old woman turned to her, her hands on her hips. Her voice held complete certainty.

'It belongs to the sea. And now the sea has given it to you.'

'To me?' Rose felt herself sway as the wind caught her. She felt strange, wearing someone else's clothes, looking at someone else's boat as if she owned it . . . 'But how can it belong to me?'

Catriona's wrinkled face wore a smile. Her eyes were faraway.

'It was always yours. It will always be yours, as long as the sea beats on stone and a black cow gives white milk. It is the sign.' Abruptly, with one of the sudden changes of mood which Rose was learning to recognize, she turned on her heel and marched back towards the cottage. Her voice floated back over her shoulder.

'Best hurry if you want your tea with the heart still in it . . .'

And that had been that. Rose finished cleaning her spade and straightened her back. She was now the proud owner of a small, unseaworthy boat. One day, she might sail it round the coast, explore the island . . . go fishing, bring supplies back from Lochmaddy . . . there were so many things she wanted to do.

And yet . . . no amount of plans would cover up the fact that she didn't really belong here, no matter how much she'd come to like Catriona. She'd just been washed up on the shore like the boat, and one day the tide would carry her out again, empty except for her memories.

Briskly she picked up her spade and whistled to Rory to follow. It was no use brooding over the past. She'd had one

140

night of perfect happiness and that should be enough to remember. If sometimes, late at night, she couldn't help thinking of him, that was her secret.

The door of the cottage swung open as she neared it. Catriona must have been watching from the window. But when she saw who was standing in the doorway she felt her mouth drop open in surprise. It was Catriona, but not Catriona. She looked taller, beautiful, not a hair out of place. The dark skirt with its coarse hairy stripes was gone. In its place was an ankle-length full-skirted dress of amber wool, so soft and fine it fell without a crease or a fold. Over the dress was a delicate raw linen apron trimmed with spidery lace, and round her shoulders a crocheted woollen shawl the colour of fresh cream.

Suddenly Rose felt shabby and windblown.

'Catriona ... you look beautiful.'

'Aye.' The old woman's voice was pleased but impatient, an air of suppressed excitement in her gesture. 'But come away in.'

Rose stepped into the tiny hall and stared in amazement. The earth floor had been newly swept and sanded. A bunch of kingcups glowed in a pewter jar on the dresser. Fresh peat crackled in the grate beside the range, sending a plume of scented white smoke up to the low bogwood rafters. The bucket-sized iron kettle simmered on the range and the small table had been pulled out into the middle of the room. A shining white linen cloth covered it, stiff with starch, and on top, so crowded together that there was hardly room for the plates, was a real feast. A cold boiled chicken, pale and plump, sprigged with wild herbs. A dish of eggs, surrounded by tiny beets from the kitchen garden. Wicker baskets full of scones and bannocks, griddle cakes and oatcakes, pink-tinged scallop shells piled high with fresh and salt butter. New cheese. A bowl full of cairgein, just set and creamy, another bowl full of blueberries. And in pride of place, dark and rich as a hunk of coal, a huge round cake, its top paved with whole perfect almonds.

'All the way frae Edinburgh.' The old woman's voice overflowed with pride.

Dazed, Rose stepped into the room. It was dazzling. Everything shone with polish, the dark bogwood chairs, the settle, even the stone walls. And on the shelf above the fire, instead of the smelly mutton-fat tapers Catriona usually used, were no less than three real wax candles. Somehow that more than anything else made her realize how special today must be.

'Catriona ... is it your birthday?'

The old woman gave a snort of laughter, looking for a moment more her usual self.

'Och no, when you're my age ye've no cause to draw attention to the fact.' She paused, again that glowing look of anticipation in her eyes. 'It's just ... a wee celebration.'

She pointed to the mantelpiece, her expression mischievous. Lined up between the candles was an odd assortment of glasses, and right in the middle, in pride of place, a large dusty bottle full of dark brown liquid. 'The water of life!' Catriona gave an enormous wink.

But Rose was too preoccupied to respond. She was trying to count the glasses, but they kept merging into each other. All she knew was that there was a lot of them. A chill went through her, despite the warmth of the fire. Glasses. Lots of them. That meant company. Her mouth went dry. That meant people. Strangers. Pitying looks. What was it he'd said? 'It's invisible now ...' Oh, how much she wanted to believe him. Only now the time had come she didn't want to put it to the test ...

But it was too late. Already there were voices at the door, people spilling into the room. Catriona, regal in her amber dress, was welcoming them.

'Is that yourself, Moire? And little Eighrig too – aye, 'tis the witch herself talking to you.' The shy giggle of a small child. 'And did you save that tooth for the little people, like I told you?'

Behind them a tall young man with a weatherbeaten face

and the blackest eyes she'd ever seen, looking like a giant in the tiny parlour. Behind him more and more people she'd never seen before, a river of people, all laughing and chattering softly to each other in Gaelic.

Suddenly Catriona held up her hand authoritatively.

'Eisd, a chairdean...' Silence fell. All eyes turned to Rose. Catriona must be making some sort of introduction. Rose wished she could sink through the earth floor. More Gaelic, this time rapid and excited. More smiles. And then, all at once, they had glasses in their hands and were raising them – to *her*.

'Slainte mhor!' The smiles were wider now.

'Thank you ...' She didn't know what to do, in the end gave a shaky sort of half bow, half curtsey. 'Slainte mhor!' She hoped she had the pronunication right. More smiles. A glass was pressed into her hand.

'Ceud mile failte agus slainte mhor!' It was the young man again. The others nodded in approval. Tentatively Rose dipped into her glass, swallowed, then caught her breath. It was whisky, pure spirit.

Moire stepped forward. 'Failte do'no dthaich, a Floraidh.' She smiled shyly.

The young man lifted his glass high. His voice was loud and strong now.

'A Floraidh!' The other followed him, beaming. Rose felt tears coming into her eyes. Maybe it was the whisky. She blinked them back.

'Is that my name is Gaelic?'

'Aye, it is.' Catriona's face was flushed, her eyes gleaming. 'Those fine Sassenach names are too grand by half for us simple hill folk. Ye'll have to bear with it.'

'No, I like it, I really do!' A name of her own ... impulsively she leaned forward and kissed Catriona on her soft wrinkled cheek.

Suddenly, as if that was the moment everybody had been waiting for, the atmosphere changed. A little old man with baby-soft white hair brought out an accordion, a younger man so like him he must be his son brought out a battered set of bagpipes. Suddenly all the furniture was pulled back to the walls and everyone was dancing, laughing and jostling against each other in the tiny room. She found herself being whirled round in a kind of jig by the tall young man. Somehow, without noticing when, she'd learned his name was Iain Dhu.

With a last triumphant skirl the music came to an end. Rose wasn't too dazed to notice how cleverly the dancers each managed to end up right by their own glass. There was a flood of excited Gaelic, then cries of 'Moire, port a beul, port a beul!' Moire stepped forward, took a deep breath and launched into an extraordinary song, the words so fast they sounded like water gurgling down a drainpipe. By the end everyone was laughing out loud, more at the fact she'd managed to keep going than anything else.

But that wasn't the end. There were more songs, and each time the singer had to have another glass of whisky, and the rest had to show their appreciation with a toast. They only stopped once, for the ceremonial cutting of the big black cake. Catriona measured it out as if it was pure gold, frowning with concentration so that everyone would get a fair portion. The small girl's piece was wrapped in a handkerchief for her to take home, since she'd long ago climbed into Rose's box bed in the wall and fallen asleep. Catriona served herself last, slightly cross-eyed after her fourth glass, and Iain Dhu called out, winking at Rose to make sure she noticed.

'Dinna forget to keep back a piece for your pillow tonight, a Catriona Ruadh, it's never too late for a wedding in the house!'

Catriona frowned severely.

'I'll be doing nothing of the sort, Iain Dhu. 'Tis a grand cake, but not a wedding cake for all that – and 'tis yourself should be going up the aisle, not a puir auld woman like me!' She shot Iain a piercing look and he went scarlet while the women giggled.

Rose felt as if she was in a dream. How many times had she imagined a gathering like this? She could almost persuade herself these people were really her friends, that she belonged.

The cake was eaten, the candles burning down. But no one seemed to want to leave. They all seemed to be waiting for something. One of the women whispered to Catriona. She nodded and stepped forward, her arms lifted to take them all in.

'Moran tang, a chairdean ...' The piper smiled and ducked his head as she paid him a compliment. Then everyone turned towards Rose, still smiling and nodding. Solemnly Catriona spoke.

'I have been telling our friends that they have sung like angels and piped like the Devil himself. And now, in honour of a very fine ceilidh – and to show that you are truly one of us –' again the glasses went up '– they would like you to sing them a song.'

All the heads swung round to face her again. The candle-light reflected off the friendly faces, and Rose realized that with these people, whose faces were all marked by sun and wind, she hadn't thought about her scar once, past those first terrible minutes. And all they wanted in return for their friendship was a song.

In that case, they should have one. She stood up, straightened her dress. She was pulled and tugged and patted into a position in front of the fire, facing the rest. The piper, his face attentive, folded his arms.

'I would like to sing for you ...' Her voice faltered at first but their nods encouraged her. 'I would like to sing for you a song from another country, on the other side of the ocean.' They nodded wisely. Catriona had told her that many of the islanders had relatives in the Carolinas. Many had fled there when their own land had been taken from them after the '45 rebellion, and the links were still strong.

'It is called The Brown-Haired Lad.' It was one of the only songs she knew, a simple folk melody she'd learned in North

Carolina. In the Edinburgh orphanage she'd learned no
songs at all.

Slowly she began to sing. The words were simple enough.

> 'Oh I am sad for my dark-haired lad,
> Who smiled at me so fine,
> But he now lies alone in his bed,
> And I in mine ...'

Familiar though the words were, she felt she'd never really
understood them before. She'd had to come halfway across
the world to learn what it meant to lose someone you loved.

Her voice faltered, then to her amazement she heard other
voices joining in with words of their own, like waves in an
ocean swell.

> ''S mise tha fo mhingean,
> Mu'n ghille dhonn ...'

It seemed they knew the song after all. Their voices lifted
strongly, supporting hers with harmonies solid as rock. The
notes of the old lament echoed round the tiny room. The
words might be different but the feeling was the same.
Everyone had loved and lost, especially those ragged
Highlanders. They'd lost everything, even their own
country.

She sang on, trying to convey in music something about
the new country that had taken them in all those years ago.
The moonlight on the pines. Rain burning off the red clay in
summertime. The wild ducks. The way the new roads still
followed the old Indian paths. The shine on tobacco leaves.
Silky blond hair covering the new corn. The mountains you
couldn't always see but knew were there.

Little by little as the music flowed round her she could
feel the two halves of her life joining up. People were the
same anywhere – continents and seas might separate them,
but the words of a song could bring them together again.

She caught Iain Dhu's eye. Something in the way he looked at her sent a small warm glow through her. Suddenly she felt safe and protected. She'd never forget her own brown-haired lad, but much more than seas and continents stood between them now. And it was no use dreaming. All the songs in the world wouldn't bring him back to her.

But here . . . here was something solid and real, she felt it in her bones. Simple people. People like her. She felt the warmth spread. It had happened at last. She belonged.

CHAPTER ELEVEN

With a flourish Catriona set in the middle of the table something covered with a white cloth.

'And what are the three most beautiful things in the world?'

Rose held a hand to her aching head, and suppressed a groan. Not another riddle ... It was the day after the ceilidh, and she couldn't understand how Catriona could be so cheerful and bright-eyed after all that whisky.

The old woman, hands on hips, surveyed her with satisfaction.

'I see that I shall have to answer for you. The three most beautiful things are ... the full moon ... a ship in full sail ... and a woman with child.' She shot Rose a penetrating look, saw her startled face and gave a crow of laughter. Then she leaned forward over the table and whisked off the white napkin. Underneath was a wicker basket overflowing with blueberries and a small stone pitcher of cream.

'And the fourth is early bleaberries with cream fresh from the cow!' She took another quick look at Rose. It said quite plainly, aren't I a clever old woman.

Then, satisfied, she turned away and began to riddle the range, sending the pungent earthy smell of the peat wafting up to the driftwood rafters.

Rose smiled, then smothered a yawn. It was getting late. She'd be glad to have supper and climb straight into her bed in the wall tonight. But Catriona seemed to be in no hurry. She bustled about the room, but not really doing anything beyond setting out the eggs for boiling and putting the grey-brown oatcakes, butter and cheese on to their separate plates. She fussed over the table, dusting off imaginary crumbs, rearranged the plates, even lit the other candle. Ceremonially she put the kettle on to boil, wiped the eggs one by one and lined them up on the dresser, arranged the two mugs side by side on the griddle to warm.

At last, when Rose had already reached starvation point, she stood back and surveyed the table, hands on her hips. Then, just as Rose was about to sit down, she clicked her tongue in irritation.

'Och, I'll be forgetting my own name next. Why did ye no remind me? I've no salt for the eggs.'

Rose opened her mouth to protest; the crock of salt had been two thirds full only yesterday. But something in Catriona's expression silenced her. She knew the old woman in these stubborn moods, there was no reasoning with her.

'You'll be wanting a bit of salt for your egg.' Catriona's voice was matter-of-fact. It wasn't a question, it was a statement.

Rose's heart sank.

'My good friend Iain Dhu up by Houghmhor would spare us a cup of salt if a bonnie lassie like yourself were to go visiting him.'

Iain Dhu. That was the tall young crofter from the ceilidh last night. Now Catriona had on a deceptively sweet expression. That meant it was no use protesting. Rose sighed. Well, Catriona had taken her in and that meant she could send her out again, whenever she liked. If only she didn't choose such odd moments.

'Is it far?' She stalled for time.

'Och, no, it's only a step,' said Catriona airily. 'Two, three mile to the West across the machair will bring you right to his door. I'll be waiting on you.'

She handed Rose a cracked bowl from the dresser.

Reluctantly Rose unhooked her coat from the back of the door and went out into the darkness. Looking back she saw Catriona outlined by the light of her candle. There was still that odd light in her eye, but she was smiling. Rose shook her head philosophically. She must really want salt with her egg.

In the twilight, the island seemed enormous. As she felt her way along the machair she couldn't help wondering what on earth she was doing there. It wasn't like Catriona to forget the salt in the first place, let alone keep supper waiting till she came back, burning expensive candles in the meantime. Still, there was no understanding her. Quirky, that was the only word for Catriona.

Alone, the two, three miles stretched like magic into three, four. Around her she heard the sighing of the light wind in the grass, but nothing else. That was strange too. All the birds and insects had gone quiet, even though the moon was nearly full. Even the pale shapes of the sheep, usually so easy to startle, were motionless, like cardboard cut-outs of themselves.

By the time she reached Iain Dhu's cottage, she didn't know whether she should go in. All the windows were dark, perhaps everyone was asleep. But Catriona had been so sure ... Perhaps it was the wrong house. She looked round for the mountain to check that she'd come to the right place, but to her astonishment it seemed to have disappeared. Instead, rolling down from where the mountain should be, was a shifting, pearly, impenetrable mass, edging its way down across the machair towards the ocean.

There was something about the way it moved that frightened her. It looked so soft and slow, but behind the first waves there was more, closing in without a sound. She almost ran to Iain Dhu's door. If she hurried perhaps she could get back home before it reached her. She was relieved to see Iain Dhu's square, impassive face. He was so big and solid, his bulk was reassuring. His eyes lit up with pleasure when he saw her.

'Come in, come in.' His voice was very soft for so big a man. She looked at the room behind him, sorely tempted. It was plainly furnished, almost spartan, but spotlessly clean and neat. A fire of just the right size already laid, the fragrance of tea brewing.

'No, I can't. I must get back, Catriona will be waiting.'

151

Quickly she explained about her errand.

Iain Dhu frowned.

"I don't know what's got into the auld woman lately. She's as contrary as a cat with two tails. She's no business sending you out on a night like this.' He glanced over her shoulder at the mist. 'Surely you could stay till it clears?'

Again she shook her head. He reached behind the door for his coat.

'Then I'll come with you ... see you back safe to your door.'

'No, no.' Hurriedly she dissuaded him. He was clearly just about to have his own supper.

'Well now, if you're sure ...'

She said goodbye quickly, before she could change her mind. Catriona had put her on her mettle now. If the old woman wasn't frightened of the mist, why should she be? She was aware of Iain Dhu standing in his doorway watching her as she felt her way down the path. By the time she reached the end of the path she saw that the mist had rolled down even further. It was drifting along a few feet above the ground, looking soft and fluffy as cottonwool, blotting up everything it touched. She'd hardly gone a hundred yards when Iain Dhu's whole cottage disappeared, painted out by the mist. It was then that she realized she wasn't going to reach home before it caught her.

Within minutes the mist had reached her. She tried hard not to close her eyes as the strange white stuff eddied round her face. It was like being buried in a pile of wet laundry, it made her feel she couldn't breathe. All she could see was a few feet of clear air round her feet. Head down, keeping her eyes on the circle of ground she could see, she moved doggedly forward.

The mist kept teasing her. It threw the sound of her own breathing back at her, only magnified. It made her hear strange dull sounds in the distance and not know where they came from

But she kept on going. It would be all right if only she

could breathe, without the choking, mothy taste of the mist in her mouth. And if she didn't have the feeling, just because she couldn't see, that the mist was full of eyes, all watching her. Cold, dead, indifferent eyes.

She had no idea where she was or how far she'd come. Only the air tasted a bit different now, as if she'd somehow stumbled on to higher ground and caught the smell of the ocean. But if anything the mist was thicker here. And it had stopped moving. It just hung, blank and silent, looking so solid that it was almost a disappointment not to be able to push it away.

Gradually she found herself concentrating all her efforts on forgetting how tired she was. The mist had done something strange to her mind. It didn't seem to belong to her any more, it was just stumbling around like her feet, with no idea of where it was going. Dimly she realized that the mist was waiting for her to panic, so that it could take her over completely. She made herself concentrate on the ground, the only real thing she could see. It was getting uneven now, she had to be careful not to trip over large rocks in the way. She missed one hidden under the grass and spilled the salt. Carefully she scooped up as much as she could off the damp ground and went on.

Now she could hardly feel her body at all. The mist seemed to have invaded it. Her mind, faced with all the blankness, began to fill with images and memories, things she didn't want to remember. You're lost, lost, lost, said the mist. Nobody will ever find you. Nobody knows where you are, nobody cares if you live or die. You're nobody.

She stopped, shaking. Her newfound confidence was draining away. If only she could see. Anything would do. Anything but terrible soft blankness. She stiffened. Was that the glow of a torch? From somewhere, from everywhere, came a sudden high-pitched whistle.

'Is anybody there?' She shouted with the last of her strength into the swirling softness, but her voice was muffled by the mist. The whistle didn't come again.

153

I can't go on. The thought came to her quite clearly, like a voice. Very slowly she sank down on her hands and knees. There was nothing left of her strength. She propped the salt bowl against a small stone and herself against a larger one. The dampness was everywhere, hanging on her eyelashes, cold and sticky in her hair. She pulled her coat collar up. Mist filled her throat, she could taste it. A damp, graveyard taste. It was like being buried alive.

She clenched her teeth to stop them chattering. What would happen to her if the mist stayed on the hill all night? She'd heard stories about what could happen in mist ... Climbers so disorientated they walked for hours in circles, then died of exhaustion and exposure. It could happen even in broad daylight ...

Suddenly, somewhere ahead of her, she heard the scrape of metal on stone. A ghostly light loomed and shimmered. The same piercing whistle echoed through the whiteness, closer this time. She sat bolt upright, strained her eyes into the blankness.

Abruptly the mist threw up a shadow on its swirling surface. It was man-shaped but huge, bigger than any man she'd ever seen, with a halo of phosphorescence round its grotesquely misshapen head. The unnerving whistle shrilled again, seeming to come from all sides at once. Then, silently, the shadow resolved itself into a figure, face half-hidden by a bulky scarf, a storm lantern held above its head.

'Iain Dhu!' Her voice was a croak. She'd never been so glad to see anyone in her life. Without a word he stepped forward and swept her up in his arms, as if she weighed nothing at all. Slowly, unerringly, he began to make his way down the hillside. How he found his way she didn't know. She could hear the scrape of his nailed boots against the stones but he never lost his footing. Gradually the warmth from his chest seeped through to her chilled bones. He was whistling tunelessly through his teeth, an oddly comforing sound, the same refrain over and over, with pauses as he adjusted her weight in his arms.

Before she knew it he'd placed her gently on her feet right outside Catriona's door. Down here the mist was thinner. As he looked down at her she could see the condensed moisture beading his cheeks and brows. He was breathing hard, but it wasn't the exertion; his black eyes were snapping with anger. He gestured towards the closed door.

'Tell that interfering old woman that if she plays any more tricks like that she'll have me to reckon with.' He was so angry he could hardly speak. He stared down at Rose fiercely, almost possessively. Then, before she could even thank him, he was away. Two strides and the mist swallowed him up again.

She clenched her teeth to stop them chattering. What would happen to her if the mist stayed on the hill all night?

Catriona opened the door so suddenly that it was obvious she'd been listening.

'Well?' Curiosity vied with triumph in her expression.

'What do you mean, "Well?"' Realization dawned as Rose recognized the look in the old woman's eyes. That was a matchmaking glint if ever she saw one. 'Catriona! How could you?' She pointed behind her at the mist. 'You knew ... and yet you still sent me out?'

'Och ... a little bit of mist never did anyone any harm ...' Catriona's tone was placatory.

Rose shook her head in disbelief.

'Now I know what Iain Dhu meant when he called you an interfering old woman! You should be ashamed of yourself.'

Catriona sniffed, obviously not ill-pleased by the insult. They stood on either side of the deal table, staring at each other like two offended cats. Then suddenly something occurred to Rose. Against her will she bagan to laugh.

Catriona flashed her a suspicious look.

'And what might you be laughing at, may I ask?'

'Yes you may ... but I'm not going to tell you.' Rose succumbed to another attack of giggles. 'You'll have to guess. Go on, you're always telling me you have second sight.'

Catriona's nose quivered in irritation.

'I wouldn't so demean myself,' she answered tartly. 'But you'll tell me all the same. You'll not be able to resist it.'

And she was right, as usual.

'I'll tell you.' Rose snatched a quick breath before the humour of the situation overcame her again. 'After all that ... I've forgotten the salt!'

There was a moment's silence, then Catriona's face broke into an unwilling smile. The smile became a chuckle, the chuckle an outright laugh. 'That's no matter!' She grinned hugely between wheezes. 'I was so busy listening at the door I let the eggs boil dry ...' Still laughing, she buttered two oatcakes, sprinkled them ostentatiously with salt from the crock and handed one to Rose.

'Supper, mo chridhe?' Her wink was sly but very endearing.

'And peace with it?'

With as much dignity as she could muster Rose accepted the oatcake. Together, still laughing when each caught the other's eye, they sat down at the table.

The two figures, the tall broad-shouldered one in cap, Hunting Stewart kilt and well-cut tweed jacket, and the small plump one in an old blue mackintosh and disreputable felt hat stood silently side by side.

Around them the scene was bathed in early morning light. Mist floated on the surface on the River Dee. The sun was hardly up and the air had a distinct chill, even for midsummer. In the distance rose the delicate grey turrets and battlements of Balmoral, the grey Invergelder stone looking dream-like and somehow insubstantial against the dark pine-clad hills. It looked what it was; a fairytale palace built for love, conceived by the Prince Consort as a highland fastness for his beloved Victoria, safe from prying eyes in the shelter of the Cairngorms.

But the two by the river were blind to their surroundings. Both were fixed on something which might as well have been invisible in the fast-flowing water in front of them.

Suddenly the taller figure gave an almost silent curse and the shorter one sighed in sympathy. Charles reeled in his line in preparation for another cast. It was getting late in the year for salmon, but even so his touch seemed to have deserted him.

The Queen Mother looked up at her eldest grandson affectionately. He was so like her late husband. For a moment her mind went back to his courtship. It had taken him two years to win her, but he hadn't given up. He'd set his heart on her, ever since she'd given him the cherries off her birthday cake at that children's party. For some men love was like that. And Charles? He was looking so thin, and despite the good Scottish air his cheeks were still pale. He hadn't been out enough lately. And the frown between his eyes hadn't been there a few months ago ...

Charles caught her looking at him and glanced down at his grandmother. In profile her face was almost invisible under that beloved old hat with the scarlet feather stuck jauntily into the band, but he could just see the tip of her pearl earring. Trust his grandmother to come fishing in waders and pearls. She seemed happy just to watch this time, even though his coming up to Balmoral early in the season was all her idea. He'd been glad of the excuse to leave London.

He made another cast, aiming for a patch of less fast-running water, hoping to tempt a salmon resting in the shallows on the other side of the river. But his aim was out and the fly got tangled in the overhanging branches. The Queen Mother didn't say a word, though he knew she must be itching to take over. After all, she was the expert. He gave an impatient tug and the fly fell out, bringing with it a few leaves which fell into the river. Both of them saw the swirl of water as the salmon flicked his tail and made off lazily upstream for a safer refuge.

'Let's take a break.' The Queen Mother's whisper was conspiratorial. 'Let's pretend we didn't see that.'

They found a dryish patch of ground away from the river

and sat down. Charles fiddled restlessly with his signet ring, but his grandmother sat quietly, hands folded neatly in her lap, glancing from time to time at his face. It was an old habit of his, playing with the ring, but now he seemed to be trying to tear it off, and the finger with it.

'Is that the new ring?'

He nodded, holding out his hand for her to see.

She examined it with interest.

'The design ... it's very different.'

'I know.' The bitterness in his tone took her by surprise. 'That's the way I wanted it.'

She hesitated, then took the plunge.

'I never heard exactly what happened to the other one.' He looked at her levelly, then seemed to make up his mind.

'You'll be shocked.'

She smiled inwardly.

'I ... lent it to a girl. And forgot to get it back.'

So that was it. Her eyes rested thoughtfully on his averted face, suddenly profoundly interested in a dragon fly hovering over the water.

'She must have been a fascinating girl.'

'Yes ... I suppose in a way she was.'

She waited hopefully. Perhaps he would go on. She said nothing. Gradually the story came out, with long pauses in which he seemed lost in thought. As he told her her heart sank. She had seen it in her husband so often, and now she could see it in her grandson's face and hear it in his voice. So chivalrous, so romantic – and so ultimately vulnerable. No woman would ever dare be so once-and-for-all.

The story came to an end. Together they looked out over the familiar landscape. She must say something.

'And where is she now?'

'I don't know. Somewhere in London.'

'And what do you think her feelings are for you now?'

'I don't know. I thought I knew. But you know what they say about women.' His face twisted savagely. 'Writ in water and all that.' There was a short pause. 'I'm sorry.' He looked at her apologetically. 'It's just that it makes me feel such a fool.'

Diplomatically she kept silent. How much was injured pride, how much was real feeling? She looked again at his face. Injured pride alone never made anyone look so ill. A small chilly breeze fanned the air, waving the lime-green fronds of the young bracken. By autumn the bracken would be on fire with gold and red colour. By autumn perhaps all this would be forgotten.

'That'll blow the germs away.' She lifted her face to the breeze. Andrew used to try to explain to her that it was scientifically impossible for the wind to do anything of the sort, but Charles had more sense. He never even tried.

'Do you still think about her a great deal?'

He nodded. 'I don't mean to.'

'Then perhaps, just this once, you should take a risk. Find her. Ask her for her side of the story. No one need know.'

He gave her an appraising look. She returned it, trying to show him that as always his secrets were safe with her.

'What about that man from the press – do you think he could help you?'

'Earnshaw?' His laugh was humourless. 'It would be like walking into the lion's den. He's probably got her hidden away somewhere waiting for me to do just that.'

The Queen Mother sat racking her brains. What could she say that would help him? What could she say that he would believe? He must be feeling betrayed on all sides.

'This girl . . .' Her voice was hesitant. When she saw him stiffen she changed it. 'Your friend . . . she must have had some feeling for you. I know that, as a woman.'

Charles looked at her steadily. Please believe me, she repeated to herself. And then, please let me be right.

'Do you really think so?' He was so grown-up now, but something in his voice reminded her of the small boy she'd known.

'From what you've told me, yes.'

They stared at each other. Then, slowly, his face broke

into a smile. He shook his head.

'Grandmama ... If only I could find a girl like you.'

Ceremonially he rose to his feet and reached down a hand. Then, since her head hardly reached his shoulder, he bent down, tweaked up the brim of her hat and planted a smacking kiss on her cheek. In perfect agreement they hurried back to the river. The sun was well and truly up now, pure gold on the water surface. It was going to be another hot day.

Charles cast again. This time his fly danced nimbly out across the water, just where he wanted it. In the same instant, with a swirl of water and bubbles, the fly was taken. The struggle was short and the Queen Mother handy with the net. Within minutes, wet but triumphant, he had the salmon on the bank. It was a young cock fish, all of five pounds if he was lucky, with the orange cheek stripes and golden tinge of the freshwater male. Every scale shone in the sunlight. Carefully he unhooked the fly from its jaw. Apart from the slight tear there wasn't a mark on it anywhere.

He looked upriver. Only the strongest and most dedicated salmon would struggle through against the current to mate in the secret place where they were born. Gently, with both hands deep in the water, he lifted the fish out of the net. For a moment as he held it he could feel it pulsing with life. Then he released it. In a flash it slipped away, the only sign of its going the crest of water that formed ahead of it as it battled upstream. I hope you make it, he thought. One of us has got to.

His grandmother looked at him questioningly. Her surprise was quite understandable. For an ardent fisherman he had been a bit careless with breakfast. But he knew he wouldn't have to explain.

He offered her his arm. 'Shall we go back?'

She nodded at him, twinkling under the brim of her felt hat. 'Yes, let's. We'll just be in time to catch the morning post.'

Back at the castle the big sideboard that flanked one side

of the dining room was as usual covered in silver serving dishes – devilled kidneys, bacon, sausages, chops, kedgeree for the unsuccessful fisherman. But even the early start and the morning air hadn't restored his appetite. Still, breakfast was a ritual, in a life of pleasant rituals.

After it was over and his grandmother had retired to her room he lingered alone a bit longer than he should have, breathing in the scent of lavender through the open window that looked out on to the rose garden. By the lion-headed fountain he and Anne had played ambassadors, a game that involved endless bowing and scraping and face-pulling, and toasts of brackish water drunk out of the best wine glasses. Beyond the rose garden were the blue hills, already hazy on this fine summer morning. This isn't getting any work done, he told himself, and turned with a sigh to the day's mail, stacked neatly beside his plate.

Most of it had been forwarded from the Palace in London, but there was nothing with the small initials E.R. in the corner of the envelope, showing delivery by Queen's Messenger. Therefore nothing urgent. He relaxed. One parcel looked interesting. It was almost a work of art, it had been packaged and re-packaged so many times. At one point the Post Office had written on it No Return Address, at another some wag had scrawled in bright red capitals, TRY ASCOT. That had been briskly crossed out by someone else, and neatly printed underneath it was Re-packed by the Post Office.

He tested the parcel's weight in his hand. He'd long ago lost any enthusiasm he'd ever had for presents, but this one was like a message in a bottle – it was surprising it had found its way through to him at all. The parcels with no return address on them were usually destined for the waste bins anyway, long before he ever saw them. But each time someone must have opened it, seen what was inside, then solemnly packed it up again and sent it on through the system.

Curiosity made him clear the other papers away. Had he

ordered something for Henrietta and forgotten? Inside the functional brown wrapping paper donated by the Post Office was a twist of paper, rather dirty. Reluctantly he unravelled it, hoping there hadn't been some awful administrative error.

Something small and heavy fell out of the clumsy twist on to the linen table cloth. Slowly he picked it up. The familiar gold warmed to his touch. He turned it to the light. Ich Dien. I serve.

She sent it back. The words floated into his brain, but he couldn't take them in. After all this time. She sent it back.

He looked out of the window towards the blue hills. The hills and the roses were the same, and yet, trembling on the edge of his mind, was an enormous change. He almost expected to see the hills suddenly heave and crumble with it, like an earthquake. He held back the change as long as he could. Had she known from the beginning? Had she meant to betray him but changed her mind? Was this part of another plan?

He gripped the ring so tightly that it hurt the palm of his hand, and made himself say it again. The facts of the case. She sent back the ring. He mustn't go any further than that, not yet. One step at a time. But even as he said that to himself he could feel the walls crumbling, the roar of falling masonry as hope set in. At least now there was something he could do.

His eyes fell on his pushed-aside plate. He rose to his feet, feeling as if his legs didn't belong to him. He strode to the sideboard, whipped off the cover of the silver chafing-dish and helped himself to some more kidneys and four crisp rashers of bacon. He sat down again at the table, took a deep breath, and grimly buttered two slices of cold wholemeal toast. He knew what he had to do now. For his own sake. But he was going to need all his strength. This time the current would be against him all the way.

'We're here.' Iain Dhu's voice was matter-of-fact. He squatted down and spread his woollen jacket out on the ground. One by one, with the economy that characterized all his actions, he took out of his pockets a clean linen handkerchief, four oatcakes in a paper square, already buttered, two oranges, that must have come all the way from the store in Lochboisdale, and two silver-wrapped chocolate biscuits.

Rose looked round her. So this was the house he'd wanted to show her. It was a ruin. No roof, hardly any walls, just a line of tumbled stone marking out where they used to be, and the doorway, with the door long gone. But he was right. Even ruined, it was still a house. The room they were in must have been the séombar, the parlour, with a window overlooking the winding track that led down to the ocean and petered out in the bright green marsh dotted with marigolds and wild flags.

She sat down on the stone that Iain Dhu indicated. How warm and safe it must have been in winter, with the wind beating on the shutters and a big fire inside. She looked up: blue sky and a haze of clouds where the rafters should be, and in the middle of the séombar, just where she'd have had her rocking chair, was a strange ramshackle pile of stones.

As she watched, Iain Dhu bent down and picked up one of the stones that had worked its way loose. Carefully he wedged it back into the mound.

'Sith do d'anam, 'us cloch air do charn.'

Peace to thy soul and a stone on thy cairn ... now she understood. Adding a stone to the pile must be a way of showing your respect for the long-dead owner.

Quickly she got to her feet and hurried outside. On the shore she found the right stone. It was large, almost too heavy to carry, but rooted in a sand-filled crack right inside was a small, spiky dwarf hawthorn, with a few tiny deep red blossoms still on it. Hawthorn was good for the heart, that's what Catriona said. Somehow that seemed right.

Iain Dhu helped her manoeuvre the stone to the top of the cairn, where the tiny tree would get light and air. When it was in place they smiled at each other. Suddenly she knew they weren't guests in the house any longer. She'd brought flowers for the woman of the house, and now they were welcomed in.

'I'm glad you brought me here, Iain Dhu.' Politely he handed her an oatcake, holding it delicately by the edges. The sea air had given her an appetite and she bit into it eagerly. From somewhere a rock pipit gave its high chirping call, then stopped.

'I like this house.' Iain Dhu nodded and smiled. She'd never met anyone who spoke even less than she did. But it didn't worry her, his silence. It was like the silence round this house, it had the sound of the sea in it, if you listened for it. Almost without noticing it she switched to Gaelic. She had to practise, and here it didn't matter that she could only go slowly. There seemed to be all the time in the world.

'Tell me, Iain Dhu, who was it who lived here? Was it a very long time ago?'

'Aye. Long ago but long remembered.' He'd finished his meal already and was leaning back against a stone, meditatively peeling an orange. 'She was a brave lass, the lady of the house. She had the same name as yourself, Floraidh. That's why I brought you here.'

'What happened to her?'

'The Sassenachs threw her in prison after the Forty-Five. A year later they let her go ... but she never came back. The cause was lost by then, do you see. So she had no heart to come back.'

'And the stones? Some of them look very old.'

'Aye. The clan started the cairn, because she was born here, you see. Every winter the wind knocks down a few stones, but come the summer there is always someone, like ourselves, to build it up again. The clan will always remember its own.'

A small cool wind off the sea drifted through the roofless house, ruffling Rose's hair. 'The clan will always remember its own'. It must feel so good to know that everywhere you went there were people who'd welcome you, even if they'd never seen you before, because they knew you were the great-niece of their married daughter who'd married a Mackinnon and lived over by Kilbride. A whole close, warm, living network, built up over the centuries, bit by bit like a cairn, strong enough to stand up to the worst that could happen. So you were never a stranger, left out in the cold.

'Which clan is that, then?' Iain Dhu looked up in surprise.

'Why, Clan Ranald, of course. The best of all. Our motto is Dh'aindeoin co'theireadh e, Gainsay Who Dare.'

'Is that your clan too, then?'

'Aye, it is.'

'But how can it be? Surely then your name should be Iain Ranald, not Iain Dhu?' There was a moment's astonished silence, then he began to laugh, his black eyes dancing.

'But isn't that your name? It's what everyone calls you.'

'Aye, it's my name ... and not my name. You see, it's like this. Even on this side of the island there must be – oh – four Iains at least. So to tell one from the other we add on something to make it easier. Like with Catriona. When she was a lass she had the finest red hair on the island, so she was called Catriona Ruadh, Red Catriona. And so I'm Iain Dhu, because of my bonny black hair.' He shook his wiry mop comically to prove it.

There was a long pause. She was thinking furiously. She tugged at a piece of tough dune grass to cover her excitement.

'Can anyone have a name like that, then?'

'Aye, I suppose. I never really thought about it.'

'Could I?' He lifted himself up on his elbows and looked at her appraisingly.

'Aye, you could.'

'Would I be Floraidh Dhu, then?'

'No ...' He tilted his head. 'You're not one of the black ones. No. For you, I would find another word. You don't hear it so often, but I think it fits you better. Floraidh Donn, that's what I would call you.'

'What does it mean? What colour is it?' Maybe in Gaelic something better could be made out of pale skin and mousy hair and mud-coloured eyes.

'Well, in English I suppose you would call it brown.' Her

eyes filled with disappointment. 'But it's no ordinary brown, not the brown of the peat, it's lighter than that, not the brown of the bracken, either, that has too much red in it.' He looked at her appraisingly, narrowing his eyes. 'No ... there is no one English word for it that I can think of. Donn is brown with all the colours of brown in it together, like seaweed just from the water. Or the kelpie herself, the brown seal that some call grey for want of the right word.' His face cleared. 'Och, I have it now. It is like the bird we call dreathan donn, the brown wren, the smallest bird of all. That is donn. The colour of a feather. The colour of a bird on the wing.'

She smiled. He made it sound so pretty.

'Will you call me that? Please?'

His face was serious.

'Aye, that I will, Floraidh Donn.'

Floraidh Donn. She said it over to herself. She couldn't be a genuine member of the clan, that was too much to hope for, but a name of her own was the next best thing. A new name, for the new person she was going to be, fit to be introduced to the lady of the house she was sitting in.

'The lady of the house ... she must have been a great lady to have so many stones on her cairn.'

'Och no!' Iain Dhu swung round suddenly, his voice impatient. Clearly, she'd said something wrong. 'She was no lady at all.' He shook his head, trying to make her understand. 'Lords and ladies ... all of that Sassenach nonsense ... there's none o' that on the island. We don't believe in it. The saying goes: a King's son is no better than his company. And it's the same with the clan. Inside the clan there's no room for master and servant. Why should there be? The wind and rain treat us all equally. And a great house, with a great lady inside it all to herself, is no better than a small one – only colder in winter. It's the Highland way.'

Then his face softened. 'Aye, well ... there's a story I know that maybe tells it better. The clan chief went once to dine with the chief of the Lindsays in Edinburgh town, and

Lindsay set a fine table with real silver candlesticks, for he
was a terrible vain man, and a Lowlander to boot. But the
clan chief said nothing at all to these silver candlesticks, for
all his host's boasting. But when Lindsay came to the island
to dine, the clan chief had five tall Highland men bearing
torches behind his chair, and he said to Lindsay, "I doubt
if with all your silver and gold you'll ever see finer candle
bearers than these."' He paused. 'Do you see now what I
mean?'

'I think so.' But one thing still confused her. 'But what
about the clan chief? Surely he's more important than the
rest?'

'Aye ... but he belongs to the clan. He's not above any of
us. Even to his face I would never call him Sir, or any of that
Sassenach nonsense, because he and I are brothers in the
clan. We call no man Sir, least of all some pencil-pushing
government minister away there in London. That's why the
mainlanders call these islands Innse Gall, the islands of the
strangers. Because we belong to ourselves only, and the
clan.'

Rose leaned back against the stone. The moss smelled
sweet where she'd pressed it. Why couldn't it be that way
everywhere? Perhaps here was the only place in the world
where she and Charles could meet as equals. Here names
didn't matter, only the colour of your hair. No one cared if
you were rich or poor. No one looked down on you because
of where you came from or what you didn't have. Even if you
weren't rich or clever or beautiful or well-connected, they
didn't care – as long as you loved the land. The rock pipit
sang again, the wind stirred the dune grass. Something deep
inside her told her he would have loved the land.

'I wish ... I wish I could stay here forever.'

Beside her Iain Dhu's voice came, so quiet and low he
sounded half asleep.

'You could do that.'

She sighed. Yes, today even that seemed just possible. But
there was no use dreaming. Just as she knew Charles

wouldn't suddenly walk in through the wide-open doorway, she knew the island wasn't really hers, not to keep. Only blood relatives were allowed to inherit a vacant croft.

'No ... no ... how could I?'

She felt rather than saw the shadow against the sky as Iain Dhu sat up and turned towards her. When he spoke his voice was still soft and quiet, with that musing tone she'd come to know well, but his words took her breath away.

'That's no hard to answer Floraidh Donn ... There's a wee possibility that deserves consideration. You could marry me.'

CHAPTER TWELVE

The entire length of Oxford Street and Park Lane was a solid, unmoving sea of vehicles. Sunlight bounced and glittered off the black roofs of taxis, the cabdrivers philosophically rolling up their shirtsleeves, prepared for a long wait. Some wished they'd read their morning papers more carefully, others, better prepared, leaned back to enjoy the annual insanity and listen to the patient ticking of the meters behind their left shoulders.

Inch by irritable inch the traffic edged round Hyde Park Corner, past the cordoned-off wide expanse of the Mall, looking as temptingly empty as a prime Barbadian beach. Policemen, only taking time off to lift their heavy blue helmets off their foreheads to catch a bit of air, marshalled the traffic busily, proud to be on duty on this particular afternoon, with the Queen holding the first of her annual July garden parties. Pedestrians who attempted to enter the Mall on foot were politely turned back with a few words of explanation, but not before they'd caught a glimpse of the long black cars drawing up one by one outside the tall gold and black gates of Buckingham Palace.

Inside the Palace brilliant afternoon sunlight streamed through the open French windows of the Bow Room. As the guests entered from the Marble Hall they were silenced for a moment by the sight of the emerald green expanse of garden, thirty-seven razor-smooth acres of it, that unrolled in front of them, a vast living oasis right in the centre of dusty concrete London, protected inside the solid stone shell of the Palace. Awed, they stepped through the French windows and on to the wide stone terrace which fronted the lawn, where thousands of guests had already gathered. All the men, apart from the odd uncomfortable-looking eccentric in an ordinary business suit, were splendid in morning coats, striped high-waisted trousers and smooth grey toppers, their women a riot of parrot colours – white lace vying with flowered silk, crisp, tailored linen contrasting with floating cotton lawn. And the hats – straw boaters trailing ribbon, demure cloches in sugar pink or blue, wide-brimmed starlet fantasies in sophisticated navy or outrageous scarlet, hats made of daisies and cherries and feathers and net, hats that were hardly there at all and hats that couldn't be ignored.

But all of them, even the ladies in their summer colours, powdered and painted and perfumed to within an inch of their lives, were put to shame by the row of elderly men who stood on guard at the edge of the lawn. Magnificent as heraldic dragons, splendid with royal privilege and popular esteem, they let the sunshine do their work for them, picking out the brilliant scarlet and living gold and dramatic black of their medieval tabards. Each of them, by virtue of their dress, presented a piece of living history, straight from the days of the proud Tudor monarchs, who knew in their blood and bones (whatever their private lives may have been) that for public appearances there was no substitute for star quality. And that's what they had, these elderly men, all time-expired non-commissioned officers, who after a life-time of service had reached a kind of immortality – the custodians of the terrible Tower, the Yeoman Warders, known better by the familiar name which brought the past to life – the Beefeaters.

For the guests, dazed and disorientated by the colours, the crowd and the unbelievable sensation of actually being inside the Palace itself, for this one special afternoon, it was a relief to turn to the gaily-striped marquees set up on the lawn. Music drifted above the hum of conversation, a Gilbert and Sullivan selection played by two Guards bands, adding to the unreal, timeless quality of the occasion, evoking the palmy Edwardian days when garden parties were a part of everyone's lives. Inside the marquee the effect was intensified; light, yeast-baked scones, plain and sweet, set out on decorative doilys, tiers of triangular sandwiches filled with wafer-thin slices of fresh-cut cucumber and tomato, silver teapots filled with the best Indian tea, golden Victoria sponges packed with fresh Jersey cream and topped with Kentish strawberries. And everywhere the ushers, each with a yellow carnation in his buttonhole, ensuring that all went well and that guests were steered almost without noticing it into the right marquee.

By half-past three guests who had had the privilege of attending before had finished their tea and taken up their positions in front of the royal marquee, to be ready for the arrival of the royal party. First-time guests couldn't resist exploring the garden, trying to remember every detail for the rest of the family left behind in Winchester or Surbiton or Ullapool, noting the immaculately kept Aiton's Lake, where rosy flamingoes wandered, the great black mulberry tree planted for James I, when the grounds were given over to the cultivation of silkworms, the swings set out for the children, the tennis courts, the apple-scented chamomile lawns, the dignity of the avenue of spreading Indian chestnuts that gave shade where needed and hid the Palace gardens from the outside world. From time to time they stopped, trying to remember where they were, trying to catch the roar of traffic from Buckingham Gate and beyond, but without success.

But even the beauty of the gardens couldn't keep them from the main event. By no later than four o'clock all eyes were riveted on the garden gate at the North entrance. Conversation came to a halt, or proceeded only in anxious whispers as hats were straightened and imaginary crumbs brushed off grey waistcoats and silk laps. Finally, at exactly ten minutes past four o'clock, the royal party appeared at the North entrance. The hush deepened. Slowly, smiling in the sunlight, they advanced towards the assembled guests. Thousands of eyes followed as they proceeded on to the terrace, where specially selected subjects of the Duchies of

Lancaster and Cornwall had been gathered. Those nearest the terrace were able to catch snatches of conversation. Attention was almost equally divided between the Queen, deep in conversation with her Duchy of Lancaster's tenants, and the Prince of Wales, moving with his own inimitable grace among the Duchy of Cornwall contingent, many of them seeing their squire and hereditary landlord for the first time in person. For a moment history showed its power. Since the days of the Black Prince the Duchy of Cornwall had been the hereditary portion of the heir to the throne, and each man and woman on the terrace knew something of the history of the relationship between prince and people. Some were from the Scilly Isles (rent, three hundred puffins, decreased to fifty during the reign of Henry VI), others, very different in character, from the London borough of Kennington, just south of the river Thames, across Westminster bridge (revenue, from forty-five acres of prime inner city property in a decade of spiralling land values, a great deal more than fifty puffins).

Yes, times had changed. But as the Prince moved amongst his subjects, tall, smiling, his lean height showing to immense advantage in morning dress, it became apparent to the guests marshalled on the lawn below that some things never changed. Pride and excitement showed in the faces of the honoured few from the Duchy of Cornwall; they were glad to have this young, debonair, blue-eyed prince as their own. The guests on the lawn envied them the privilege. As they watched, they saw a stir amongst the Cornwall contingent. The security officers in the Prince's retinue looked round anxiously, expecting trouble, but the Prince himself ignored it. The man on his right tried to suggest that he move on, but he ignored that too.

And then, filtering through the back of the crowd where the stir had begun, came a strange little procession. The others parted to let it go by, beginning to smile. This was a definite break with tradition. A whisper ran round the crowd, the ones in the know spreading the word. The Prince saw the procession coming and frowned slightly, trying to make it out. Seven children, faces set and flushed with importance, each carrying something in their arms. One by one, the tallest first, they bowed and curtseyed to the Prince and handed over their precious burdens. A ripple of laughter ran round the assembled guests as the prince, his face serious but a smile tugging at the corners of his mouth, received in turn: a wooden pepperpot filled with black pepper, a home-made bow and twelve arrows, three stalks of wheat (one slightly bent in transit), a pair of spurs (cardboard, painted silver), and ... the ripple of laughter turned into a roar ... a live greyhound.

By now the story was out and the official photographers had gathered. The Cornishmen and women who knew about their own history had tears in their eyes; the little procession of rent-bearers had brought history to life again. The Duke of Cornwall, in the far-off days of Henry VI, had had his rent paid in many different ways – in money, of course – but also in pepper, the famous peppercorn rent. In a grain of wheat for each tenant. With bows and arrows. A pair of silver spurs. Even, for the royal hunt, a greyhound.

The children, shy now their presentations had been made, drew back. Discreetly the Prince transferred his burdens to his attendants. Then the tallest child noticed something wrong. One of the rents hadn't been presented. The smallest child, clutching its rent behind its back, was cowering at the rear, hoping not be noticed. 'It's your turn, Mary!' In the silence the anxious hiss was clearly audible. Another ripple of indulgent laughter ran round the audience. The Prince, ready to leave the terrace and join the guests on the lawn, turned back, smiling. Prodded by a succession of eager fingers and encouraged by the adults on the terrace the smallest child was gradually filtered through to the front. All eyes were fixed on the small figure, trying to make out the rent she carried behind her back. When she reached the Prince she stood nonplussed for a long moment, looking up at the tall figure, seemingly fascinated by his hat. And very reluctant to present her rent.

The Prince put her at her ease at once. He bent down, letting her see the hat at close quarters.

'Put it on!' The small voice was eager, setting the crowd tutting under its breath. But the Prince took no notice.

'If I put it on, will you show me what you've got behind your back?' The little girl thought it over, then made up her mind and nodded. With a smile the Prince donned his topper, tilting the brim rakishly over one eye. The girl gave a squeak of pleasure, drew her hand from behind her back and thrust something into his hand. The people watching craned to see.

The Prince of Wales held the offering in his hand for a long moment, the brim of his top hat shading his face. Then a sharp-eyed photographer who'd worked his way to the front spotted what it was. The word spread quickly. 'Of course . . . a rose, a rose!' They all remembered the missing rent now. Grains of wheat, silver spurs, peppercorns and – in those days a real luxury – roses. Now the Duchy of Cornwall's rent was paid. In full.

The Prince doffed his hat, his face impassive. He held the rose in his hand, appearing uncertain what to do with it. He glanced round at the expectant faces, shining with proprietary pleasure, and understood. With steady fingers he removed the white carnation from his buttonhole and handed it to an attendant. His face did not change as, neatly avoiding the thorns, he inserted the rose in its place. A small cheer went up from the Cornish crowd. Then, still graceful, smiling once again, he went down the broad terrace steps and joined his guests.

Hours later, long after the guests had all gone home, the Prince of Wales stood looking out over the deserted garden from his study window. On the table in front of him was a glass of water. In it stood the rose, drooping now on its slender stem.

His thoughts were far away. How sure he'd been that once back in London he would find her. His mouth twisted as he remembered his surge of hope when three days painstaking investigation had turned up an address.

But it led to nothing but an empty room. She'd gone, leaving nothing behind her.

Except one thing. Carefully he reached into his pocket and drew out the silver locket, running the broken chain through his fingers. It was all he had left of her now. That, and the scent of roses.

'Quick now! Push!'

Together they heaved and struggled, their bare feet sinking into the wet sand.

Slowly, inch by inch, it began to move. The tide, creeping nearer, lifted the rear end.

'We're almost there!' Rose dug her feet deeper into the sand. A grating, hissing noise came from underneath as the sand sucked away from the keel. She nearly lost her balance as with a sudden swish the boat leaped away from under her hands. Now waves were licking at its sides. With one last enormous heave they sent it swinging free.

Ignoring the chilly water that lapped round their ankles they both stood back and gave *Love and Honour* a critical going-over. For days now, in every spare minute, they'd been sanding and varnishing, caulking the seams with new tar and painting the hull. Iain Dhu had spent hours, cursing under his breath, with grease up to his elbows, dismantling and reassembling the small outboard motor. Rose had re-painted the faded flower garlands along the bows. Now the boat shone with colour, red and blue and green standing out against the golden brown of the newly sanded wood.

They looked at each other silently. Iain Dhu's eyes were bright with anticipation.

'Go on then ... What are you waiting for?' His expression was quizzical. Quickly she scrambled in. He followed more carefully, balancing their weight.

'We should have champagne, for the launching.' She picked up one of the oars and trailed it experimentally over the side. The blade was still warped but Iain Dhu had grafted in new wood to replace what had rotted. A shadow crossed her face momentarily. If only Catriona could be here ... But the old woman had looked frail this morning and insisted they go to the beach without her. She wasn't as strong as she pretended to be and Rose was glad she was being sensible for once.

She looked up to find Iain Dhu smiling at her.

'I've no need of champagne.' There was something in his eyes that made her blush. To hide her embarrassment she dug deep in her skirt pocket and took out the book.

'Page five, please.' She spoke sternly. 'And you must be very strict with me. No hints.'

'Me? I wouldna' dream of it.' He opened up the notebook, setting his face in the flinty-eyed expression of a spinster schoolmarm. 'Now then ... What are the spirits of the ancient owners of the land?' His Gaelic was soft and musical. She answered carefully, trying to get the intonations right.

'The spirits of the ancient owners of the land live on as mute swans, on Loch Druidibeg.' The legend was that they guarded the little children of the island, herding them away from dangerous water.

'How does a witch raise a storm?'

'By tying knots in a length of wool. As each one is unloosed, the wind rises.'

'What should you do to protect your house from the storm?'

'Put the head of the tongs in the fire.'

'What colour dye is got from the boiled roots of the marsh flag?'

She had to think about that one. There was so many colours to be had from different plants – yellow from green heather tops, red from sorrel, black from waterlily roots.

'Blue-grey.' It wasn't what you'd expect from the brilliant yellow flowers.

'What does the owl say?'

'When the owl is mourning, rain is coming.'

176

'How can you tell a fairy bull?'

'By his slit ears.'

'When would you go fishing?'

'Late to the loch and early to the river.'

Iain Dhu signed, and Rose hid a smile. He liked her to get at least one wrong. Now he was scanning page six, trying to catch her out by slipping in one that she hadn't prepared. His voice was elaborately casual as he asked her next question.

'How would you cure a cold sore?'

She paused as if she was thinking.

'Well now . . . I'm not sure.' Looking out of the corner of her eye she could see that Iain Dhu's face was alight with triumph.

'Would I bathe it with seawater?'

He shook his head.

'Would I rub it with mutton fat?'

Again no.

'I know. I'd make up a poultice of crowberry, marsh marigold and . . . and mouldy potatoes.' She was really inventing now. Iain Dhu's face wore a look of scorn. He opened his mouth to tell her but she stopped him just in time.

'No, wait . . . I have an idea . . . I think I know the answer.' Idly she trailed her fingers in the water till she found what she wanted, a fragment of slippery seaweed. She turned back.

'Yes, I remember now. If you had a cold sore, Iain Dhu, I know what I would do.' She lifted the scrap of cold, slippery weed, hiding it in her hand. Suddenly she pounced. 'I would put a slug on it!'

Iain Dhu's face was a study as the slimy morsel touched his skin. 'Ugh!' He recoiled, the boat rocked, the book went flying as he tried to wipe it off. When he found out what it was his face split into a reluctant grin.

'You knew all the time, you little devil.' His voice was accusing.

'No, no.' Rose smiled. 'It was a lucky guess, no more.'

He shook his head in mock disapproval and retrieved the

177

notebook from the boat bottom. 'I think that's enough book-learning for one day.'

A sudden roar of engines from beyond the white sand of machair made them both look up in surprise. A muddy green jeep with a cargo of uniformed soldiers, rifles on their backs, was speeding noisily Northwards along the island's only good road.

Iain Dhu frowned. Suddenly the light-hearted atmosphere was gone.

Rose watched his face. She'd often wondered about the soldiers on the island. There'd been some on the ferry, friendly enough but somehow out of place in this peaceful, isolated place.

'The soldiers ... why are they here?'

'You may well ask.' His face black, Iain Dhu picked up the oars and began to pull savagely away from the beach, as if he couldn't get away from the sight quickly enough. 'They belong to the rocket testing site, up by Iochdar.' He shook his head. 'That's if they belong anywhere on the island. They should never have come here. They have no feeling for the land or its people.'

A rocket-testing range ... Looking out over this peaceful empty landscape it was difficult to believe.

'Couldn't you stop them?'

He gave a grim smile.

'We tried. When they were extending the site, we lay down in front of their lorries along the causeway. But there were too many of them.' He grimaced. 'And they had too much money, government money. They bought their land, and we will never see enough money in our lives to buy it back again. So the land is theirs.' He rested the oars for a minute, his dark eyes burning. 'But the spirit of the land is not. That cannot be bought, for blood is stronger than the rocks.'

Again she studied his face. This was a side to Iain Dhu she'd never seen before. Things Catriona had said in passing, rumours she'd heard from the other islanders, began to come back to her. He'd joked about being a trouble-maker, but he seemed so quiet and gentle a man she hadn't believed him.

'Is it true then ... you were arrested?'

'Aye ... they took me in, as a warning. But I was only seventeen, they couldn't keep me. They let me go, with a caution.'

'And what happened then? Did you give up?'

He looked back at her with the glimmer of a smile.

'What do you think?'

Of course. She knew him well enough to understand that he was a fighter. His smile faded.

'But it's difficult ... there are so few of us left.'

She racked her brains.

'Couldn't you find someone ... someone with influence to speak for you? Take your side?'

'No.' His voice was bleak. 'There is no one like that anymore. Not for two hundred years.'

His eyes were distant. She knew he was thinking of the Young Pretender, the exiled King over the water, for whom the islanders had fought and lost everything they had. He turned back to her. His eyes were hard as stone.

'But we will survive. That's what the soldiers will never understand. We have learned to wait. They can take everything away from us – land, lives, beasts – but we will survive.'

He trailed the oars. 'There. This is what I wanted to show you. It explains what I mean better than I can say it myself.'

She followed his eyes. They'd reached a part of the coast she'd never seen before. High on a rocky outcrop overlooking the sea was a tall slender stone, looking as if it had grown out of the land. Wind and sea spray had eroded it, but the shape was still clear. Spare, upright, defiant, it looked out Westward. Carved in the granite was the faint outline of a strange cross.

'That's the cross of Iona, the ancient Celtic symbol. It's shape is old, far older than Christianity. Some say the Druids set the stone, some say it has always been there. It was there that the Bonnie Prince said goodbye to his people and vowed to return as their rightful King.' Iain Dhu's face lightened.

179

'And see that hollow at the base? They say that if two lovers join hands through the stone their love will last as long as the land itself.'

Slowly, deliberately, he shipped the oars.

'What do you say, Floraidh Donn?' His voice was casual, but his eyes were determined. 'Shall we join hands through the stone and see if it is true?'

Their eyes met. She knew what he was asking. He'd first planted the suggestion in her mind in the ruined croft. Since then he'd made no mention of it. But in his own quiet way he would go on asking until he had her answer. He was a fighter.

And it was such a simple question he was asking. If only she could give him a simple answer. But it was too soon for her to know what she really felt. She knew she'd come to rely on him in all sorts of ways, trusting to the strength behind his quiet exterior. And there were depths to him that she'd only sensed as yet. It would take a lifetime to learn the island's changing moods.

And what a life they could make together . . . His eyes held hers.

She saw reflected in them all the things she'd dreamed of and never thought could be hers. A husband and a house of her own. Right by the sea, maybe, like the ruined croft he'd shown her. Perhaps they could rebuild it together. She could put a herb garden at the back, sheltered from the sea wind, and grow all the herbs Catriona had taught her about. Self-heal and pennywort, lady's bedstraw and rest-harrow . . . In the evenings she'd be able to look out and see Iain Dhu digging lugworms for bait at the ocean's edge. Maybe she'd even be able to keep him out of trouble, find a better way to help the islanders . . . Maybe they'd have their initials carved, entwined, above the door . . .

She hesitated, torn with conflicting loyalties. It would be so easy to say yes. But would it be fair to him? She had memories too, of her own King over the water . . .

'I cannot wait forever, Floraidh Donn.' Iain Dhu leaned forward. His hand was warm on hers. I don't know, I don't know, she thought. Can I wait forever? Can I make myself forget him? Or am I like the islanders, sacrificing everything for the sake of an old dream?

He was very close. She could almost feel his lips on hers. If he kissed her, then surely she would know ... banish that memory of another kiss in a dark moonlit garden ...

They both sensed it at the same time. A flash of black and white bounding across the windswept grass towards the shore. Rory. Instantly Rose drew back. A stab of pure fear went through her. The dog was running silently, low to the ground. Something was wrong, terribly wrong.

His face set, Iain Dhu made *Love and Honour* fast. Together, running and stumbling over the tussocks, they followed the dog back across the machair towards the cottage. The door was open. Whining now, Rory disappeared inside.

As soon as Rose crossed the threshold she knew her instincts had been right. The kettle on the range had boiled dry and the air was full of steam. Iain Dhu plunged ahead of her to the closaidh where Catriona slept and went in without knocking. There was no sound of protest. That confirmed Rose's feeling of dread. Catriona would never have allowed that normally, she was as careful of her privacy as a cat.

Dreading what she might find, Rose followed him. She'd never been inside Catriona's bedroom before. It was pretty, the walls lined in faded flowered paper, lace curtains at the tiny window.

'Here, Floraidh.' Catriona was lying on top of the bed. Instead of her workaday blue striped drocaid she was wearing the saffron-yellow crotal-dyed wool robe she'd worn at the ceilidh. Against the golden material her face was white. 'Here, do me up at the back.' Her voice was a whisper. She gestured weakly towards the side fastening.

Her hands trembling, Rose fastened up the three hooks. Her eyes met Iain Dhu's across the old woman's body. She read in them her own certainty. Catriona's face had changed, shrunk in on itself. Suddenly she looked old and fragile.

181

There was no colour at all left in her skin, but her eyes, usually pale blue, had gone quite dark. A young girl's eyes in a dead face ... A lump came into Rose's throat. Suddenly she knew. The doctor had said her heart was weak. And now the worst had happened. Catriona was dying.

'I meant to do it before you came.' The old woman's hands plucked irritably at the covers. 'I want to be pretty when I go.'

'Oh, Catriona ...' Rose reached for the restless hand. 'You look beautiful, you always do.' The old woman smiled in satisfaction.

'Aye, well, that's as may be.' Her eyes turned to meet hers, and suddenly her face was serious. 'I'm glad you came, Floraidh. There's something I must tell you before I go.' Her voice was just a rustle, but the intensity in her eyes held Rose motionless.

Rory whined from the bedside, but Catriona's eyes didn't flicker. 'Hush, dog.' The fingers in Rose's grip trembled. 'It was a long time ago ... there was a lad. I wanted him, and he wanted me. We were to be handfasted through the stone. But I was proud then as I am now and could not have enough of courting ... so I sent him away.' She drew in her breath in a long sigh. 'Oh, but I wanted him ... Blue eyes he had. But I knew I could have him any day I wanted him, so I turned him away, time after time. You know how girls are ... I knew I could hold him with my long red hair ...' She moved her head restlessly on the pillow.

'Then one fine morning when the beasts were on the hill I listened for his step at the door and did not hear it. I learned from the village that he'd gone away across the sea. But I knew he would come back ...'

There was a long silence. Catriona's face softened, a touch of colour appeared in her thin cheeks.

'Did he ... did he come back?'

'No ... he never came.'

The words hung in the tiny room. Rose felt tears prick at the back of her eyes. She shivered. Catriona's eyes, alive and indomitable in her faded face, met hers.

'Aye, you feel it. It is the old blood calling. Always I heard it too, but I was vain and stopped my ears.' Her eyes were fierce now. 'And that is what I wanted to tell you. When the blood calls, answer it, because the day will come when you will not hear it any more. Then you will be like me, an empty house with the blinds drawn and no one knocking at your door but the wind and the cold sea air ... and nothing but your pride to keep you warm.'

Suddenly her fingers curled round Rose's in a grip of iron. 'Two crossing the ford are better together. You will remember that, little Floraidh? When the time comes? Will you promise me?' Her grip tightened. 'Listen to what your heart tells you ... Will you promise me that?'

Rose swallowed painfully, her voice coming out in a whisper.

'Aye.' She pressed the old woman's hand. 'I give you my word.'

Catriona's grip relaxed. She seemed to shrink inside her dress, as if it was only her iron control holding her up.

'I cannot say more.' She looked thoughtfully towards Iain Dhu. 'Will you help her, when the time comes?' He nodded, unable to speak. 'Aye, you're a good lad ...'

A lark sang from the mountainside outside the window. Catriona smiled.

'I have one last gift for you.' Her eyes moved slowly back to Rose.

'No ... I don't want anything.' The words burst out before she could stop them. Please don't die, that's what the words meant. Catriona seemed to understand.

'Would you refuse my blessing? I have no other kin to give it to.' Rose shook her head dumbly.

'May you have the art of the Druids for the luck of the wind, and the faith of Iona for the stilling of the waves.' Her right hand touched Rose's hair, then fell back. Gently she loosed the hand that Rose was holding and slipped it under her pillow. She drew out something that Rose couldn't see.

She held it tightly, obviously it meant a great deal to her.

Catriona closed her eyes, holding her secret hidden in her hand, and settled her head into the pillow. She was smiling again and her lips were moving. Rose had to bend to catch what she was saying.

'Och, Callum, Callum ... you were always a foolish fellow. But I liked you pretty well for all that. You've left it a wee bit late to come back to me, my fine lad, but now you're here you might as well hear it. I love you, mo chridhe. There, I've said it. And now let's hear no more of the matter.'

Her hand uncurled. Out fell a small dark fragment of something that Rose didn't recognize for a second. Then she saw what it was. A tiny dried-up morsel of Dundee cake. It must have been under her pillow ever since the ceilidh, waiting for Callum to come back. Carefully, fighting back her tears, Rose put it back in Catriona's open palm. The old woman's eyes half-opened for a moment. She clicked her tongue. Rory pricked up his ears and edged his way to the bedside, as near as he could get. He pressed his shabby grey nose against Catriona's wrist. It was the closest Rose had ever seen them.

'Daft auld dog,' said Catriona affectionately. She squeezed Rose's hand again. 'Take care of him for me. Don't let him at the new cheese, mind, no matter how he begs. It's too much for his stomach.' She smiled, her eyes closed and then, as gently as *Love and Honour* slipping out to sea, she died.

'She's gone.' Rose said the words numbly. She couldn't believe it. Catriona was as tough and vital as an old bramble, surely she could never be uprooted. There was a great aching emptiness inside her. There were so many things she'd meant to say, and now it was too late.

Aye, she's gone. Come.' Unresisting, Rose felt Iain Dhu take her hand. Suddenly she was grateful for his solid, comforting presence. Gently he led her out of the closaidh, and into the sunlight.

She stood by the cottage door, dazzled. The winding path

down to the sea was the same, the grass still grew, the lark was still calling. But everything was changed.

Iain Dhu put his arms round her. His touch melted the hard numb core of disbelief inside her. She began to cry. He held her close, murmuring Gaelic words of comfort into her ear. The rough fabric of his jacket tickled her nose. Catriona's words drifted back into her mind. 'Two crossing the ford are better together.' She clutched Iain Dhu's lapel, felt his voice reverberating through his chest.

'Don't worry, Floraidh Donn. You still have me. I will take care of you now.'

CHAPTER THIRTEEN

'What's the weather like ahead?' Charles spoke crisply into the radio, leaning forward to make himself heard above the clatter and roar of the engine.

'Perfect, sir! It couldn't be better.'

The enthusiasm and relief in the small tinny voice that answered him brought a smile to his face.

He settled himself back in the pilot's seat. It was a pure, cold pleasure to fly the luxurious Westland Wessex twin-engined helicopter. And the weather was perfect, or as perfect as anyone had the right to expect on the notorious West Coast of Scotland. It was still cold in the exposed cockpit but the sunlight was sending rainbow reflections off the rounded glass of the windscreen and the landscape below was as bright as if the Isle of Skye had been specially floodlit for his departure.

He turned his mind to the visit he had just completed, seeing again the wavery line of serious little faces in rain-dewed brown berets. It had still been grey when he'd arrived in Broadford, over two hours late, but he hoped he'd made up for it. It had been worth the effort just to see the Brownies in full regalia. Why were their ties never long enough to tuck into their belts? And why did little girls always stick their stomachs out like parade-ground sergeants? Some of them had almost fallen backwards with the effort.

He smiled to himself. At least he'd been able to brighten up those small, anxious faces. Nothing like royalty for instant sunshine on the greyest day.

Fortunately the Press had been happy too. They had their story, strong, simple and romantic, the first visit of a Prince of Wales to the Isle of Skye since the Forty-Five rebellion and Bonnie Prince Charlie, and would now be phoning it through to London, provided of course they could see at all through the haze of Drambuie, the famous, sweet but far from innocent Skye liqueur kindly provided by the reception committee.

But he had to move on. His schedule was a crowded one. Though he was leaving Skye behind his royal duties weren't over yet. He cast his mind's eye over the afternoon's arrangements. He was due to arrive in South Uist, the largest island in the isolated Western Isles group, in less than half an hour. It would all run like clockwork, knowing the military. Presentation to the site commander, brief introductions to the technical personnel, a swift look over the installation, a pause for light refreshment and then out to the waiting helicopter again for the solo flight back to Balmoral. Clean, painless, humane – the ideal visit.

And there ahead was his first glimpse of the treacherous Minch itself, calm and sparkling today. Oddly reluctant to break into that beautiful silent vista he swung the helicopter in a wide circle to take one last look at Skye.

Down below, overlooking the sea to the West, was a ragged little graveyard dotted with simple white stones. Most were grouped in pairs. Husbands and wives side by side so that rain and sunlight could fall on them together, just as it did when they were alive. How tiny everyone's life was, when it came down to it. How little anything mattered.

And yet ... if he had the choice, he would like to be buried like that, his wife by his side, in a simple, unfenced graveyard looking Westward out to sea. But he didn't have that choice. It would be the cold, dark grandeur of Westminster Abbey for him.

A bright green and red Highland bus threaded its way past the graveyard and disappeared over the brow of the next hill. It was no bigger than a toy, but for a moment he felt as if he was the one who was trapped. It was a foolish thought. He was free as a bird up here in the helicopter. He could go anywhere he liked, in theory. But there was one thing he couldn't do, which all the people in that bus could do without a moment's hesitation. Stop and get off.

Far away in his memory he felt a twinge of pain. He'd got off once, and it had been all he could do to get back on again. He thought fleetingly of the locket. He'd had it sent to a museum in Edinburgh, in the vain hope that they might help him trace her again. But he'd heard nothing. Maybe that was for the best. Freedom was an illusion. It was better to have a schedule, a reason to be somewhere, a job to do, every waking minute active, productive and accounted for. It was the easier way.

He blanked his mind, attentive only to the heartbeat of the powerful twin engines. Without a backward glance, at one with his machine, he headed Westward out to sea.

Rose cut the outboard motor and let *Love and Honour* drift. She should have headed for home hours ago, but something had stopped her.

Home ... a pang of sadness went through her. Catriona's cottage had been left to a distant relation in Fort William, so she couldn't stay there any longer. Iain Dhu had snorted with disgust, pointing out that it was highly unlikely the relation would ever actually live in the cottage, since 'it hasna the electric,' and maybe that was right. The factor would come and take away all the movable possessions, and the cottage itself would be left for the wind to whistle through it. Little by little the stones would shift, the roof would wear thin, till all that was left was a ruin, with the big old iron range rusting in the sea air.

But she had a home of her own, now. Iain Dhu had helped install her in the tiny shepherd's hut high on the mountainside. It had been empty for years; the islanders used to sleep in it when guarding their cattle during the summer on the mountain pasture, but it was a sound little structure. Iain Dhu had repaired the door and helped her move in a makeshift bed, complaining all the while that it would be much simpler if she married him and moved into his cottage.

But it was too soon after Catriona's death for her to think of marriage. There were so many things she had to work out in her own mind. She smiled, thinking of how hard Iain Dhu had tried to persuade her to go with him to Skye for his usual Friday night's celebration. He'd caught the ferry early that morning, and she suspected he wouldn't be back before Saturday, when his splitting headache would drive him home.

Perhaps she should have gone. But for once she'd wanted to be alone, to think. She'd felt oddly reluctant to leave the island, even for the beauties of Skye, which she'd never seen. Instead, she'd taken *Love and Honour* and sailed slowly along the deserted coastline. It was almost as if, like Catriona, she was waiting for some kind of sign, to help her make up her mind.

But now it was time to go home. Still, she lingered. It was so peaceful and silent. Not even a gull in sight. She seemed to be the only living thing in the whole landscape. The air was still, so was the water.

She leaned forward and re-started the motor. The determined put-put sounded thunderously loud in the silence. She looked up. There was a thick yellow haze where the sun should be. It reflected off the dead level, oily-looking water. She frowned, trying to pierce the milky haze. There was Ben Mhor, the cruabh, the crab-shaped cloud that lay North to South along the hill and said which way the wind would be blowing for tomorrow, shouldn't be far off.

But the familiar weather guide wasn't there. There was nothing but haze, closing in over the water. But behind it was a hint of movement. That was odd, there was no wind at all. The haze began to shift and billow, as if there was something behind it. Something ...

She drew in her breath with a hiss. She'd never seen anything like this, not even on the Cape Fear. Stretched across the southwest from one side of the sky to the other was the cruabh, or what was left of it. Pulsing, monstrous, so dark it was almost purple, it had swollen out of all recognition. And it was moving. As she stared mesmerized at the huge bruised shape she saw it boil up in the middle, sending out a spurt of vapour.

She groped in the bottom for the oars. The cruabh said only one thing. Go home. As fast as you can.

A sudden jolt almost sent her flying. The sea had come alive without warning, its jaws snapping. In the same moment a gust of wind from the southwest rushed into her face and made her eyes water. The small boat rocked and trembled as the water caught it broadside. Hurriedly she revved the outboard motor. The little engine shuddered into life and she breathed a sigh of relief. Maybe there was still time.

But when she looked up again her heart sank. Even in those few moments the cloud had grown enormously. Now it was almost black, a big black heart pulsing with energy. The wind was building too, breaking up the water. There wasn't a hope of getting home before the cloud caught her. This was just the beginning. Whatever the cloud had hidden away in its centre could only be worse.

The boat surged forward. She'd have to try and find somewhere to take shelter on the coast, find a safe place to pull in. If only she knew the coastline better ... It had looked safe before, but now the light was leaden, the rocks looked bigger and blacker and much more dangerous. Already the water was against her. Spray hissed up against the bows, the wind flung salty water into her face, forcing her to lower her head. The boat was slowing now, the engine spluttered and whined as it tried to make headway. The waves slapped against the keel, pushing it back. It was getting darker, nothing had any colour any more. She pulled harder on the oars. Even the bright yellow flowers she and Iain Dhu had painted on the handles had gone grey and dead-looking. Above her she could sense the storm building. It had come so fast. She had to find somewhere soon or there was no knowing what would happen.

A dark gap in the rocky coastline yawned in front of her.

Inside she could just see the glint of smoother water. It was some sort of inlet. In any case it would be safer there out of the wind.

The opening was just wide enough for the boat to enter. Steadying herself against the rocky walls she backed the boat in under the overhang. It was almost a cave, the water had hollowed out a space just large enough for her to shelter in. The rocks gleamed with moisture in the dim light.

Outside the wind was getting stronger. She huddled inside her plaid jacket, bracing herself against the gunwhale. If it came to it she would have to abandon *Love and Honour* and take shelter on land.

If it wasn't too late already . . . Through the cave opening she could see that an eerie twilight had descended. The cloud must be right overhead, it had blotted out the sun completely. Even in the shelter of the inlet she felt the water heave underneath her angrily.

Then she heard it. A steady beating sound, only small and somehow desperate as it came in snatches through the wind.

She edged closer to the cave mouth and looked out. The wind knifed through, above the sky was black from one side to the other. She searched for the source of the sound in the howling darkness. Deep in the murk lightning flashed. In the brief flare of light she caught sight of the waves rolling in from the southwest and couldn't believe her eyes. A tall, black unbroken line, a towering wall of water. Surely no boat's engine could survive against that. Seconds later thunder rumbled. The storm hadn't even reached its peak yet. She strained her ears to catch the beating sound. The wind dropped for a second and she thought she heard something. It seemed to be closer now, but she still couldn't see anything.

Lightning flashed again. In the white glare she saw something, swaying dangerously only a few feet above the water. It was a helicopter, a common enough sight on the run between the rocket-testing site and the mainland. But this one was trapped by the storm. The wind had got hold of it and was shaking it like a rat. She could hear the motor screaming as the pilot fought to keep it level. Then, as suddenly as it had appeared, the image vanished. In the darkness after the lightning flash she kept her eyes glued to the spot where she'd seen it, straining to hear the beat of the engine. If only she could see ... Then a chilling thought struck her. If she couldn't see, then neither could the pilot. Maybe he didn't know he was so dangerously close to the water.

The thunder rolled out again, deafening her. After it died away she listened again, expecting to catch the sound of the engine. But there was nothing. She put her hand to her mouth. She couldn't believe it. It had sounded so strong. It couldn't just stop. Could it?

She stared out through the cave mouth. She couldn't go out there, it was much too dangerous for a small boat. Even if the pilot had crashed, they would surely send people out to look for him. No one could expect her to go. It wasn't as if he was even an islander. Probably one of the soldiers from the missile monitoring site that Iain Dhu hated so much. No one on the island would thank her for trying to rescue one of them. Risk her life for no good reason ...

She reached behind her and started the motor.

The engine roared, missed a beat, then roared again. He felt the wind catch the rotors, felt the warning sideslip begin. He struggled grimly with the controls, held the helicopter level with an enormous effort. Beneath him, dangerously close, dark water glinted. Ahead of him was nothing but blackness.

Again the wind gusted violently. Above him he heard the creak and whine of overstressed metal. Sea spray dashed against the perspex screen, blinding him. The helicopter shuddered. Desperately he fought to keep it on an even keel. If only he could see ...

Suddenly a huge fist lifted the helicopter bodily and hurled it sideways. The joystick was snatched out of his hands. He felt the machine lurch to one side at a sickening angle, felt the rotors snatch into thin air, heard the engine, no longer under load, begin to scream.

Then he was plunging, plummeting down, his ears filled with nothing but the triumphant howling of the wind.

'Any news?' rapped out the clean-shaven middle-aged officer.

'No, sir.'

'Weather forecast?'

'South-Westerly gales, force 9, maybe reaching force 10 in the next hour, sir.'

The officer glanced out of the observation port. No luck there. Fierce black clouds scudding across the sky at a rate of knots. Damn island. Not a tree on it to break the gale. He tapped his pencil on the younger man's desk. They both had the same thought in their minds.

'Visibility?'

'Right down, sir.'

'Down? Down to what, man?'

'Nil, sir.'

The commander cursed under his breath. The young man kept his eyes on his work. When Old Frosty had this kind of emergency on his hands it paid to keep a low profile.

'Radar?'

'No trace, sir.'

'Keep scanning.'

'Yes, sir.'

The commander strode off, hiding his anxiety under a poker face. The weathermen had been so sure it was clear for take-off, and the Prince was used to flying solo. But even the local fisherman got caught out by these Hebridean quick-change acts. Still, he was a bloody good pilot. Then he thought of those scudding black clouds and the doubts rushed back. He glanced at his watch. No word from the mainland yet, but with a head wind ... And even if the worst had happened, there was nothing he could do till visibility improved. The coastguard had been alerted. All he could do was wait. These freak storms could rage for days or play themselves out in a couple of hours. All he could usefully do was keep his fingers crossed and contemplate the first draft of his resignation speech ...

He gritted his teeth. If it wasn't so nearly tragic, he'd have appreciated the irony. It was a cruel joke to have at your fingertips all the most sophisticated missile equipment in the world, and yet be unable to do something well within the capabilities of any twelve-year-old amateur radio buff – keep track of the heir to the throne.

He was on a roundabout. The painted horses were bucking and wheeling, the music roaring so loud that he couldn't tell what tune it was. Up and down he went, the constant movement making his head loll backwards and forwards.

But it was so cold ... He'd have fallen off hours ago if something or someone hadn't been holding him on. He tried to explain that he'd had enough now, he wanted to get off, but his lips were numb with cold and wouldn't move. Up and down, up and down ... Perhaps he'd have to stay on the roundabout for the rest of his life, getting colder and colder, so cold he didn't even shiver. Perhaps he'd never feel solid earth under his feet again, never be able to lie down and rest ...

The music roared on, fierce and distorted. The only part of him that felt warm was his head, it seemed to throb with the music. The roundabout was going so fast it was making him dizzy. He tried to hold his head with his hand and a sudden pain lanced through his shoulder.

His mind cleared. With an enormous effort he lifted his eyelids. Black, nothing but blackness. Salt water dashed against his face. The cold wet fabric of his life jacket was hard against his cheek. That was all he could feel. The rest of his body, apart from the warmth in his head and the pain in his shoulder, seemed to have disappeared. He stared out through his swoollen eyelids, his mind moving sluggishly. One black wave after another lifted him like a rag doll then

195

dropped him sickeningly, up and down, up and down . . . He forced his mind to obey him. Survival procedures. He had to keep moving, keep awake. Somewhere on his jacket there was an emergency flare . . .

But he couldn't move. His hands didn't seem to work. He was as helpless as a baby. All he could move was his eyes. He closed them, opened them again. It took all his strength. A thought came to him, from a long way away. This is the end. He could hear himself breathing, slow, hoarse, painful sounds. He looked up into the blackness. There should be a stars somewhere. There wasn't.

I'm dying, he thought calmly. He felt oddly lucid. Memories swam up clear as day in his mind. Dawn bird-song. Rain shining off the leaves. Rain shining on her face. Rose. Rose. Rose.

He fixed his mind on her face. The throbbing in his head had changed now, it was harder, more rapid. He was near the end now. The throbbing grew louder.

He blinked. This must be the end. A half-smile curved his lips. A vision swam up out of the blackness, something out of a nursery picture book. A little boat, so incongruously pretty he knew he'd imagined it. He gazed at it possessively. It was the last thing he'd ever see, he wanted to fix its colours in his mind. It reminded him of one he used to sail in his bath. And the throbbing – he could almost imagine the sound of a tiny outboard motor to match.

The mirage came closer. It was heading straight for him, like a friendly Labrador puppy looking for a game. A desperate chuckle escaped him. It will have a mermaid in it, he told himself. Just as he thought, perched in the stern, long seal-black hair gleaming on her shoulders and her pale face was a mermaid. He could see her small chin jutting with determination and her knuckles white on the gun-whale.

The boat edged closer. He could hardly keep his eyes open now, the vison dazzled him. The mermaid's eyes seemed to look straight into his.

Recognition jolted through him. He tried to speak, but it was too late. Her face blurred, water filled his mouth and he went spinning into blackness.

'Only a few more yards.'

She tried to keep her voice steady but she had hardly any breath left. His right arm lay like a dead weight across her shoulders. He could hardly stand, it was all she could do to keep him upright.

Braced together, they stumbled across the machair. The wind howled round them, knifing through their wet clothes. She could taste salt, feel the shudders that ran through his whole body. He was so cold, he was shivering to death. Her eyes strained into the blackness. Shelter, she had to get him into shelter.

She put her head down and pushed against the wind. Catriona's cottage had to be nearby. She could hear his ragged breathing, sometimes a muffled groan as he stumbled and jarred his damaged shoulder. He couldn't use his left arm at all, it hung useless by his side. They were going slower and slower, with each step she could feel the strength ebbing out of his body.

A blur of white in the darkness. Relief surged through her body. The cottage. The warm glow from the peats in the grate. Thick stone walls to keep out the wind. Hot water boiling in the big old kettle, shutters drawn against the cold a pile of rough woollen blankets instead of cold wet clothes ...

The door. Exhausted, she slipped out from under his arm. He leaned heavily against the wall, almost sinking to the ground. She caught a glimpse of his face and her heart lurched inside her. He was stark white, his eyes swollen half closed, his lips almost blue.

Hurriedly she fumbled with the latch, but the door didn't budge. She put her shoulder against it and shoved. It rattled but didn't shift. It was as if something was holding it back. She reached down, felt cold metal. A thick heavy iron chain

197

was strung tight through the latch, fastened off with a huge aluminium padlock.

'No . . .' A whimper of despair escaped her. She looked up at the shutters, knowing what she would see. Each of them was firmly padlocked. She leaned against the door, closing her eyes. She couldn't believe it. The islanders never locked their doors, they didn't believe in locks. But even Catriona couldn't help her now.

So it was up to her. She forced herself upright, put her hand on his good shoulder. After a long moment his eyes opened. They looked strangely unfocused through their swollen lids.

'Time to go.' She tried to make her voice matter-of-fact.

He stared up at her. Then, very slowly he shook his head. His eyelids dropped again.

Panic welled up inside her. She fought it down.

'We must go.' She shook his shoulder.

His lips moved slowly, painfully. She bent down to catch what he was saying.

'No. Sleep.' His voice was slurred and indistinct.

The panic welled up again. If he went to sleep now he'd never wake up, she could feel it. She shook him awake.

'No, you can't sleep. Not yet.' He looked round him, bemused. He'd obviously lost track of where he was. She tugged at him.

'Get up. You must get up.'

He stirred, winced. Slowly, painfully, he struggled to his feet. She could feel her heart pounding with the effort of supporting him.

'Now, walk.'

He took one step forward, then his legs buckled under him. Shakily he leaned back against the wall. The ghost of a smile went over his battered face.

'Can't. Sorry.'

She paused for a second to get her breath.

'You've got to. Lean on me, I'll help.'

He shook his head. The shudders were running through his body almost continuous now, he could hardly get the words out through his chattering teeth.

'Won't work. Too heavy.' His head dropped, he swayed. 'Get help.'

She shook her head. If only she could. How was he to know that the nearest cottage was four miles away, and that belonged to Iain Dhu, now far away in Skye. She swallowed hard, trying to make him understand.

'There isn't any help. Only me.'

His head lifted. She could see him struggling up out of a black pit of pain and exhaustion. Her heart went out to him. It was so clear that all he wanted to do was lie down and sleep.

'Nobody else?' His voice was hardly there, a hoarse whisper.

'Nobody.'

For a moment his eyes cleared. A light came into them, for a wild second he suddenly looked happy. Through the pain and fatigue and cold. It almost dazzled her.

With an enormous effort he straightened his body. Stiffly he reached his good arm round her shoulders and turned his face into the wind. The ghost of a smile was on his face again. A different shudder ran through his body. Astonished, she realized it was a laugh. She looked up at him questioningly. To her amazement, she saw one swollen eye close in a conspiratorial wink. His voice came in a ragged whisper.

'Lead on, Miss Nobody.'

A little thread of pure warmth ran through her body, wiping out the past. The old link was back, just when they needed it. It wouldn't last, it couldn't last ... but maybe it would be enough to save his life. 'Two crossing the ford are better together.' Catriona had said that. Well, this was their ford. What would happen if they reached the other side safely she didn't know. But for now, they were together. She braced herself under his weight. It was uphill to the shieling, but it was their only hope.

Time passed, measured out in aching steps and heaving lungs. Gradually more and more of his weight came to rest on her shoulders. But at least the wind was behind them now, gusting so furiously it almost blew them over. Propped against each other they managed to keep upright. Even in his half-unconscious state he was trying to help her, waiting patiently while she skirted a boulder, trying to spare her as much of his weight as possible. Somehow that gave her the strength to go on.

At last, a rough coat against her legs, a warm nose shoved into her hand. Rory. Iain Dhu's make-shift door swung open. The shieling. Home. Gently she led him to the plank bed in the corner. Rory followed anxiously at his heels, sensing his exhaustion. He seemed very tall in the tiny one-roomed hut, his head almost brushed the ceiling. Frantically she piled everything she could think of on to the bed, trying to stop his shivering. Her coat, all the blankets, her towel. He lay there unmoving, his chest hardly lifting and falling except for the shudders running through his body.

She hurried across to the fireplace. Just a few stones for a makeshift hearth and a hole above for the smoke, nothing like Catriona's big range, but it would have to do. Her hands, cold and stiff, fumbled with the peats and the matches. When she struck the light the figure on the bed stirred restlessly. The match trembled in her hand, quickly she put it to the peat. Rory watched her, his eyes gleaming, from his nest by the hearth. At last the peats caught, sending flame light flickering over the shieling. Moving stiffly, her skirt hampering her, she lit two candles. Her hands still shook with the cold, but there was no time to warm them. Hurriedly she went over to the bed.

In the candlelight she could see his face clearly for the first time. His hair was caked and matted with salt water, his face twisted with pain. Blue shadows were dark in the hollows of his eyes and high on one side of his head was a swollen red bruise she hadn't noticed before. It looked angry, but it seemed to be his shoulder that was giving him the most pain

It looked wrong, twisted out of shape inside his heavy flying jacket.

Anxiously she tried to think what to do. He would be warmer soon, but not unless she could get him out of his soaking wet clothes. He stirred, wincing as the movement reached his shoulder. Setting her teeth, she went to the upended wooden crate that served as her larder, and took out the kitchen knife. As carefully as she could she slit the thick leather sleeve of the jacket right up to the shoulder and eased it off. Underneath the flesh was swollen, the bones of his shoulder hardly visible. She eased off the rest of the jacket and cut away the shirt underneath. She had to be quick, he was shivering again. She padded the shoulder as best she could and covered him with a thick layer of blankets. Quickly she unlaced the heavy boots.

The fire was sending up a plume of white smoke now and the peats were crackling with heat. She leaned back, suddenly exhausted and cold despite the fire. It was the tension leaving her body. She smoothed the blankets over his chest, checked the padding by his shoulder. He was breathing more deeply now, colour was coming back into his face. She sat back on her heels and looked at him. It might be the last time she'd ever be able to look at him like this.

It was strange. Even half-unconscious, one side of his forehead angry red, hair matted and salt-tangled, his mouth twisted with pain, there was still something special about him. Different. She'd felt it that first time, and even the sea couldn't wash it out of him. It went deep down, even when he was asleep he couldn't hide it. Even lying here hurt and half-unconscious on her bed, helpless and exhausted, he was somehow set apart. She should have seen it the first time.

And yet . . . she hugged her knees with her arms . . . she still felt close to him. Maybe because she was different too. Not because of the scar, she could see that now, but the other things, the scars inside. Not knowing who she was. Always that emptiness . . . as if part of herself had been cut off and wouldn't stop aching. It put a barrier between her and other people. She'd blamed the scar, but she'd been wrong. With one kiss he'd shown her that ...

His eyelids flickered, he tried to turn his body towards her but the hurt shoulder stopped him. With a moan of pain he lay back, biting his lips. She winced too, the same pain seemed to go right through her. She was part of him. Even though she'd thought she'd never see him again, the link between them wouldn't die.

She shivered. It frightened her. It was too strong. And it was all on her side. It couldn't be the same for him, he didn't need her. Right up to the moment he'd seen her again he'd probably forgotten all about her. And now ... he was here now, but he wouldn't be for long. Fate had brought them together again but tomorrow it would all over. And no one must ever know about this night spent alone together. No one must ever know about the link. They wouldn't understand. To them she'd always be just a nobody.

Shakily she got to her feet and went to the fire. But the warmth from the flames didn't seem to get through. She was cold to the bone. She shivered inside her wet skirt, steam rising slowly from the material as she crouched by the peats. It was cold and clammy against her skin. She wrapped her arms round her body but that didn't help. She had to get out of her wet clothes, she'd never be warm again unless she did. She glanced over her shoulder. He was lying very still, his breathing slow but shallow. Hurriedly she pulled the blouse over her head, stepped out of the skirt and stripped off her underclothes. She was wet right through to the skin. She huddled nearer to the fire, feeling the salt water drying on her face and arms.

A murmur from the bed made her turn, startled. In the firelight she could see his head tossing on the pillow. Quickly she reached for her nightdress where it hung by the fire but before she could slip it on she saw his eyes open. They widened in his flushed face. She felt herself tremble. The murmur came again, so soft she could hardly hear it.

'Beautiful.'

He must be dreaming. With shaking fingers she pulled on the thick cotton, glad of the familiar roughness on her skin. When she looked again his eyes were closed, his head moving restlessly again. Beautiful ... she felt herself blushing and was glad of the half-dark. Of course he hadn't really seen her, he'd been half asleep. He wouldn't remember anything in the morning. But I'll remember, she thought, hugging the nightdress round her. Even if it was only a dream.

Another murmur came from the bed. Anxious, she edged closer. His face was flushed, too flushed. He looked as if he was running a fever. In his condition that was dangerous, it would use up the little strength he had left. But this time there was something she could do. She hurried to the row of herbs hung from the rafter beside the fireplace, running over in her mind all the things Catriona had taught her. When she'd saved them she'd never dreamed she'd need them for anything more serious than a bruise or a sprain or one of Iain Dhu's hangovers. She put the kettle he'd given her over the fire to heat, taking care as always not to fill it too full – it had a hole in the side which meant you could only put enough water in it for one cupful. Any more and it boiled over, dousing the fire.

When the brew was ready she added more cold water so that it wouldn't scald him and hurried back to the bed. His breathing was more rapid now and beads of moisture were running down his face, mingling with the dried salt. His skin felt burning hot, but he was shivering now as hard as he'd done when he'd just come out of the water.

She lifted his head, taking care not to jar his shoulder, and raised the bowl to his lips. He drank a little, but not enough.

'You must drink more. It will help you sleep.'

Obediently he drank a bit more. But then his teeth started to chatter so badly that she couldn't hold the cup to his lips.

'Cold. So cold.'

His voice came in painful gasps between the convulsive shudders that racked his body. She tried to hold him still and protect his shoulder but the shudders wouldn't stop. She looked round the shieling in desperation. Every ounce of clothing she possessed was on the bed and still he wasn't warm. She rose to her feet, undecided. Perhaps there was something else she could find, anything ...

His eyes flew open. His hand reached out blindly and grasped hers. It was burning hot.

'No. Don't go.'

He was struggling with the bedclothes now, trying to throw them back. His voice was thick and indistinct.

'I can walk. Don't leave me.' A shudder racked him again. 'Cold.' His hand tightened round hers, a groan escaped him. When it came again his voice was a whisper.

'Is it much farther?'

Her eyes filled with tears. His eyes were open but they were glazed, he wasn't seeing her. He was back on the machair, trying to plant one foot in front of the other, willing his exhausted body to keep him upright. Helplessly she pulled the blankets back into place and tried to get him to lie back. The convulsive shudders were tearing him apart, doubling the pain from his damaged shoulder.

'Help me. I'm drowning. Help me.' His body twitched, his head thrashed on the pillow. He was further back now, reliving the nightmare struggle in the water. She could see him straining, trying to keep his head above water, using up the last of his strength.

'Ssh.' She tried to soothe him but he didn't seem to hear her. The only thing that seemed to help was his grip on her hand.

'No!' He was shaking his head from side to side now, oblivious to the pain. He seemed to be trying to fight something off. The effort exhausted him and his head fell back. He loosed his grip on her hand. For a terrible moment she thought he was dead. He was so quiet he was hardly breathing. Then his eyes opened again and stared straight ahead, unseeing. The expression in them frightened her. Pure, cold, despair.

'Where are you?'

Her eyes filled with tears again. She didn't know who he was asking for, but she could tell from his voice that he'd practically given up hope. Gently she slid her hand into his.

'Ssh. Don't worry. I'm here.' Such a small lie. He didn't seem to hear her.

'Lost.' Blurred, unfocused eyes turned towards her, looked right through her. 'Lost. Cold. Where are you?'

The shivers were starting up again, shaking him like a rat. She looked down at him, biting her lip. Whoever it was he wanted, she was the only one he had.

Carefully she eased herself down on the bed beside him and lay full length. That way she could brace and support his body, like she had on the machair, stop some of the shivering. She wrapped the blankets tight round them, willing the warmth from her body to flow into his. It seemed to comfort him. His eyes closed, a long sigh shuddered through his body. Maybe the herbal draught was taking effect.

She closed her eyes and tightened her arm across his body. She could feel his dry, matted hair tickling her cheek, feel his warm breath on her neck. He was quieter now, deep in himself. The warmth from her body had soothed him. She was glad of that. It was all she could offer him, but maybe it was enough. Simple warmth, something anyone could provide, even a nobody. She held him closer, feeling the shivering recede. He was far away now. A pang went through her. Perhaps, deep in his mind, he'd found the person he'd been looking for. She forced the pain away. It was enough for her to hold him like this, just for one night. It had to be enough. The fire-light flickering behind her closed lids. Rory snuffling in his nest by the fire. The crackle of the peats. The smell of smoke. The beat of his heart against hers . . .

Maybe, just this once, tomorrow would never come.

CHAPTER FOURTEEN

Iain Dhu winced as the late morning sun hit him full in the eyes. He paused for a minute to take in a lungful of cool braeside air. If it hadn't been for yesterday's storm, he reasoned with himself, he wouldn't have had to wait for the Saturday morning ferry to get back to the island, and if he hadn't had to stay the night in Skye he wouldn't have drunk so much ...

He shook his head to clear his headache. The milk pail clanked against his side. He was looking forward to seeing Floraidh again, even though he'd only been separated from her for a day. He'd missed her. And he'd got so much news to tell her. And a surprise. He tucked the wooden chest firmly under his arm. He was dying to see what was inside it.

He blushed, only partly because of the effort of climbing the hill. He'd been really tempted this morning, when he'd found the chest delivered by the factor the day before, to have a good look inside. It would have been easy enough. The key was inside the envelope taped to the side, with 'For Floraidh' on it in Catriona's spidery writing. But something, maybe his half fearful respect for the old woman, had stopped him. She was dead and buried now, her cottage locked up by the factor and her bequests all distributed, but her spirit seemed still to be alive.

Thinking of what he'd seen on the ferry journey that morning he lengthened his stride. He could hardly wait to tell her, there hadn't been so much excitement on the island for a good two hundred years. Helicopters quartering the choppy water of the Minch like so many half-trained sheepdog puppies. High-powered boats cruising to and fro. The port full of men with loudhailers and more soldiers than he'd ever seen at any one time. And more arriving at the dockside by the minute. Not to speak of the newspapermen with their endless questions and loud Sassenach voices – the ferry had been full of them. He smiled with glee. They hadn't had much change out of him. If the military had mislaid one of their precious machines he wasn't going to be the one to help them find it.

He crossed the burn in one stride. As a lad he'd spent summer nights in the shieling himself, his feet found the path out for themselves. From here on you could follow the peat-brown trickle of water, ice-cold from the hilltop, or take the short cut across the tussocky grass. As he approached the shieling he gave it a critical going over. The piece of corrugated iron he'd pinned to the roof and weighted with stones was bearing up well. The door ... well, it was serviceable enough. One of these days he'd plane a bit more off the bottom so it opened easier.

Strange, though, for it to be closed so late. She was usually out and about by now, knowing Rory would keep a careful eye open for visitors. Undecided, he paused by the door. There wasn't a sound from inside the small stone hut. He set down the pail and tapped. From inside he heard Rory's low whine as he recognized a familiar scent. But no answering voice. Suddenly anxious – perhaps she was ill and needed help – he pushed up the latch and opened the door. There was a trick to it, always had been.

The door swung wide. Light streamed in after him, but still nothing stirred except Rory, who came and sniffed his ankles. His eyes went first to the fire. It was almost out. Automatically he set down his burdens and bent to shake down the ashes and add fresh peat. It wasn't like Floraidh not to bank up the fire, she must have gone out without the dog. He bent to fondle Rory's rough head.

'Where's your mistress then, old fellow?' Rory nuzzled his hand briefly then went back to his nest by the fire and dropped his head on his paws, his eyes bright in the half dark. The flames were catching nicely now, sending light flickering across the tiny room. 'Well now ...' Iain Dhu mused to himself. 'Where would she be on this fine morning?'

The faintest of sounds answered him. Startled, he turned towards the bed, straining his eyes into the dimness. He couldn't see.

'Floraidh?' He found himself whispering. 'Is that you?'

He reached behind him and swung the door further open to let more light in the room. It edged across the floor ahead of him. Now he could see a few details. A burnt out candle in a pool of wax on the floor by the bedside. Her best boots neatly lined up next to it. Further back, a pile of clothes that he didn't recognize. He felt his senses prickle, the hair lifting on the back of his neck. Somehow the whole atmosphere in the room had changed. It even smelled different. Salty, wild, strange ... he tried to pin it down. Familiar ... like the taste of your own tears. That was it. It smelled of the sea.

Hesitantly he took a step forward, half afraid of what he would see. For a terrible instant his whisky head told him he'd see Catriona, lying in state in her golden robe, ready to haunt him to the grave. But what he saw was stranger even than that. He stared down at the bed, unable to believe his eyes, straining to make it out. The image dissolved in front of him, then came clear again. Two dark heads, hair mingling, close together on the pillow. A man and a girl, both strangers. The girl's head rested just above the man's, her arm curled awkwardly but protectively around his shoulder. And the smell of the sea all round them. As if they were two pieces of driftwood washed up on the shore.

Iain Dhu held his breath, half expecting them to disappear. Both of them were whiter than the pillow they lay on. He'd heard about such things before. A sea maiden and her earth-born lover ... changeling children ... the old stories were full of such things. Then, suddenly, the lad shivered like a frightened pony and muttered something. Instantly the girl, deep in sleep as she was, tightened her arm round him, murmuring against his ear.

The spell was broken. All at once the picture dissolved,

reformed into something very different. Iain Dhu took a step backwards. Outrage welled up hot and bitter inside him, spewed out in a hoarse cry of rage.

'So this is why you wouldna come with me!'

His voice rang out in the tiny room, setting the tin plates rattling inside their wooden crate. Rory rose to his feet with a low growl. The girl on the bed stirred and her eyes flew open. The fear in them angered him even more. It confirmed his worst suspicions.

'So. What have we here?' His face twisted as he looked down at the bed. They were still laced together, they looked so comfortable. The shock in Floraidh's eyes was the only jarring note. Stiffly, anger pulsing down his arm like electricity he took the man by the shoulder. How dare he lie there so peacefully in her arms. If it came to it he'd pry them apart with his bare hands.

'No! Wait!'

Hair flying, Floraidh threw back the blankets and slipped out of the bed. Face to face with her he had to fight a pang of sympathy. She was so small, hardly a fitting adversary. And she looked as if she hadn't slept all night, her hair sticking up on her head and her small white feet poking out at the bottom of the thick cotton nightdress.

'Why?' It came out as a sort of groan. He looked at her pleadingly, searching her face for any sign of shame or regret. There was none. He clenched his teeth, tried to control himself. There had to be some sort of explanation, surely he couldn't have been so wrong.

'Oh Floraidh Donn ...' His voice came out thick and painful, he hardly recognized it as his own. 'Why did you not tell me? Why did you make a fool out of me?'

'Wait ...' Her expression was dazed, her voice still blurred with sleep, she swayed a little where she stood. 'It's not like that ... you don't understand.'

'No?' That was too much for him to swallow. He had to suppress a cold flare of rage. 'I am not such a fool. I have eyes in my head.' He grabbed her arm and wheeled her round towards the bed. The man lying there stirred restlessly, throwing back the blankets. A scalding tide of fury and resentment boiled up inside Iain Dhu as he saw he was naked to the waist.

'Get up, damn you!' A red mist began to gather in front of his eyes, his head began to pound. The man's eyes opened, he stared vaguely round.

'Yes, you, whoever you are!' The man's gaze wandered across his face. One hand stirred, lifted, then fell back.

'I'm sorry ... you seem to have me somewhat at a disadvantage.' The voice was low, but the accent unmistakable. The eyes closed again, the man turned away. His words rang in Iain Dhu's ears. A Sassenach. The red mist began to boil and thicken. A cold-blooded, toffee-nosed, smooth-talking Sassenach. Centuries of hatred and oppression rose up inside him, focussing on the motionless figure in the bed. The Sassenachs had everything, money, land, power, but it wasn't enough. They had to steal land that belonged to others, plunder it, make it their own ... draw all the blood out of it then throw it away. It was the same old story. Thieves, every last one of them. And now one had tried to steal his woman. But this time he'd gone too far.

Black rage throbbed through his body. Infuriated, he grabbed the man by the shoulders and shook him, hardly knowing what he was doing. All he knew was that somehow this rage inside him had to find an outlet or he'd choke. A long way off he heard Floraidh's voice, but he ignored it. 'Fight, damn you!' The man was a coward, limp under his hands, but he'd make him fight if he had to half-kill him first. The girl threw herself against his back, he shook her off without difficulty. Nothing could stop him now. Nothing and no one.

Suddenly a sharp pain nipped through his ankle. Surprise more than anything made him loosen his grip on the man and look down. The old dog, eyes tight closed, had fastened his jaws round his ankle bone and was worrying it busily, making up for the weakness of his grip by growling ferociously through his toothless gums.

'Och, no, Rory ...' Somehow it brought him back to his senses. The final betrayal. Shuddering with the effort of self-control he released his grip on the man in the bed. Slowly the red tide ebbed away from his vision. He was dimly conscious of Floraidh sobbing with relief. Moving like an old man he bent down and gently pried the dog's jaws loose.

The next minute he nearly fell as the girl pushed him out of the way.

'You've hurt him!' Her face was a blaze of anger. Speechless with astonishment he watched as she bent over the man in the bed, then flew to the hearth and lit another candle.

'I've no hurt him, Floraidh Donn. Only shaken him up a wee bit.' His bewilderment began to curdle into resentment. She had him apologizing now, when the wrong was all on her side.

With shaking fingers she put the candle by the bed, directing its light over the man's face. Against his will Iain Dhu took his first good look at his rival. Just what he'd imagined. A lean, pale, aristocratic face. Stubble dark against the ashy pallor of the skin. Eyes closed in dark hollows. A handsome lad – the sort of worthless good looks that women always fell for. And something else, something vaguely familiar ...

The eyes opened, looked straight at him. Blue. Unmistakably blue. The world lurched round him.

'A Mhuire mhathair! Holy Mother of God!'

It wasn't possible. But there was no mistaking it.

Stunned, he watched as Floraidh turned back the blankets. His mind didn't even have room for jealousy as her hands touched the other man's skin. The man shifted painfully under her hands and he recoiled. What had he done?

'Look!'

212

Floraidh pointed to the man's shoulder. Unwillingly, his mind still reeling, Iain Dhu followed her eyes. What he saw made him wince. The shoulder socket was badly swollen and inflamed, the nub of the arm bone loose and visible under the skin, clearly dislocated. Somehow the sight of it cleared his mind. The man on the bed became just a living thing in pain, like one of his own sheep caught in a crevice on the hillside. Energy flooded back into his paralysed limbs.

'Here.' He handed Floraidh the candle and directed her wrist above the damaged shoulder. He ran his hands over the dislocation, checking for torn ligaments. Floraidh watched him anxiously.

'What are you going to do?' He saw the doubt in her eyes and couldn't blame her for it. Minutes ago she'd seen him trying to choke the life out of the man whom he was now attempting to help. His patient moaned under the manipulation, but Iain Dhu's mind was remote now, concentrating on the job in hand.

'You must help.' His voice was curt. 'The shoulder must go back in, there's no time to lose.'

She drew in her breath with a hiss.

'You won't hurt him?'

His face was grim. 'Aye, I'll hurt him.' His expression softened as he saw her alarm. 'But I won't harm him, any more than he's been harmed already.' He took her other hand, placed it on the man's other shoulder. 'When I say, put all your weight here. He'll struggle when he feels the pain, but he must be still till I'm done.'

He looked down at his bare hands and took a deep breath, flexing the big muscles in his arms and shoulders. It had to be done quickly, the first time, or not at all. He braced one hand against the collar bone, fastened the other round the arm. The man stirred in his grasp, began to struggle weakly.

'Now!'

All his strength rushed into his hands. With a sickening, audible grate of bone against cartilage the joint moved, swivelled, snapped into place. The man made not a sound, but he felt his whole body stiffen, then slump.

'Is he all right?' Floraidh's face was twisted in sympathy.

'Aye.' He looked down at the man's face, grey now, and streaming with sweat. He was clearly unconscious now. 'Aye, he will be. The shoulder will be stiff and sore for a while, but there's no lasting damage done.'

'Is there not?' Floraidh's eyes looked straight into his. They were full of tears.

Gently he took her arm and guided her over to the fire. His anger had left him completely now, all that was left was confusion. He no longer felt as if he understood, he didn't know who to blame.

Her eyes fell on the wooden casket.

'What's that, Iain Dhu?'

'Oh, nothing. Salt for the sheep.' He didn't know what made him lie. Somehow he felt that this was all Catriona's doing. She was behind it really, she was to blame. He pushed the box away with his foot. It was better to have someone to blame. He didn't feel like giving it to her now anyway.

They sat watching the peats, just the way he'd imagined they would after they were married. Her in her nightdress, soft-faced from sleep. Him looking forward to the new day.

'Do you love him?' The words were out, harsh, abrupt, before he could stop them. She looked up, startled. He read the truth in her eyes.

'Och, Floraidh Donn ... How could you be so foolish?' He shook his head, hardly knowing which he was more sorry for, her or himself.

'But it's not what you think.'

He gave a short, hard laugh.

'And how could it be? He is who he is and you are ...' He left the sentence unfinished. Dimly he began to realize what he was up against. He of all people knew how a lost cause lingered, sacred in the memory.

'Listen, Floraidh Donn ...' He spoke urgently. 'You must forget him. He's not for you, even for a day, you know that.

214

Soon his people will come and take him away and you'll never see him again.'

'His people?'

Quickly he told her about the soldiers, the helicopters over the Minch, the boats, the newspapermen.

'No!' Suddenly her face was panic-stricken. She shot a quick look back to the motionless figure on the bed. 'They mustn't find him here!'

She was on her feet now. He rose and caught her by the arm. His suspicions were back again in full force.

'Why not?' What had gone on between them after all?

'Oh, don't you see!' She shook off his arm impatiently, scrubbed at her eyes. 'Because of what you said. Because he is who he is and I'm who I am. Because we should never have met in the first place.'

Anger filled him again. It was all right for him to state the blunt truth, but the idea of other people seeing it as well made made him boil inside.

'But you saved his life! They should be grateful! He should be grateful!' She laughed shakily.

'I know.' A shadow went over her face. 'But I don't want him to be grateful. And I don't want him to end up hating just the sound of my name. Because that's what would happen, after the newspapers were through.'

A treacherous flame of hope ran through him.

'Are you sure that's what would happen? How do you know?'

She looked down. Her voice was small.

'Never mind how I know. I just do.' She looked up, her eyes shadowed. 'You'll have to help us.' Us. The word burnt into his consciousness. 'Somehow we must get word out before they find him.'

Rory stirred, rose to his feet, barked once. Instinctively they both looked out through the half open door. He couldn't help a surge of triumph as he saw the four small figures making their way up the hillside towards the shieling,

The first two clearly soldiers, rifles pointing up behind their shoulders. Behind them, at a safe distance, two more dishevelled figures, one with a camera slung round his neck and carrying an aluminium case that caught the sun.

'It's too late.' He tried to keep the triumph out of his voice and failed.

'They're here already.'

The two soliders, slightly out of breath, paused halfway up the hill to resettle their rifles and catch their second wind. The plumper of the two squatted down and wiped his forehead, shooting an irritated glance behind him. The two journalists, purely by coincidence, had stopped too and were elaborately admiring the scenery.

'Dunno why they bother. Wouldn't fool anybody.' His companion shook his head in sympathy.

'There's no getting rid of them. It's a free country, you know.' They both laughed. 'Where've you been living, mate?' The plump one's expression was cynical. 'Wouldn't need us if it were.'

He cast his eyes up ahead, up past the brackish-looking stream to the makeshift stone hut ahead. To him it looked hopelessly rundown. Just then a tall figure came round the side of it and halted, looking down, arms folded.

The two soliders looked at each other in relief. Together they went up the last few hundred yards. Close to, the shieling looked even more of a ruin. The tall figure watched, unsmiling. The two journalists edged closer.

'Excuse me, sir ...' The leading soldier pulled out a list of names and consulted it, 'but are you Iain Macdonald of Clan Ranald of Ballybreck, near Houghmhor?' Bloody long names these islanders have, the soldier was thinking to himself as he tried to make sense of the outlandish spelling.

'I am.' The man didn't move. The soldier assessed the length and breadth of him and was glad he had company.

'Well, sir, there was an accident just off the coast last night ... did you notice anything unusual?'

'What kind of accident would this be then?' The young soldier blinked and cleared his throat. He had the fleeting impression that the big man was playing for time.

'We can't be sure at the moment, sir ...' He felt uncomfortably conscious of the two journalists well within earshot behind him, and his neck reddened inside the collar of his uniform. His voice became officious.

'Did you see or hear anything unusual last night at any time?'

The silence lengthened. The two soldiers found themselves shifting from foot to foot. The big man stroked his chin. 'Aye well ... I wasna here myself, do you see. But I hear there was a gey awfu' storm.'

The soldiers exchanged glances. The leader straightened his shoulders.

'In that case, sir, you won't mind if we take a look in your ... er ... hut.'

'What for?' The big man's face was bland. The soldier began to suspect that what local gossip said about his status as a troublemaker was accurate. 'Lost one of those clever gadgets, have you?'

'The authorities haven't ruled out the possibility of sabotage.' Crisply the two men moved round to the door of the hut, closely followed by the two journalists.

As they came into view a black and white sheepdog that had been lying on the rough grass outside the open door rose stiffly to its feet and growled.

'Will you call off your dog, sir.' The soldier's voice was firm. The big man looked at him consideringly.

'Aye, if you insist.' There was something in his tone the soldier didn't quite like. 'Lie down, Rory.' The dog sank back, still growling.

Resolutely, increasingly conscious of his audience, the soldier moved to enter the hut.

Crouched beside the bed behind the door Rose held her breath. She heard Iain Dhu's voice and another's, heard the

217

scrape of heavy boots against the hillside rock. The sheep moved restlessly, torn between the two humans they sensed in the corner of the shieling and the dog they could see on guard, head lowered, a few feet outside the door. The ram stood protecting his ewes, his splendid head lifted and yellow eyes flaring against the dog.

She closed her eyes. She could hear Rory's exhausted panting. He was too old and tired to work sheep like this. If only he could hold them long enough. More than he would ever know depended on it. A king's ransom ...

Charles stirred and moaned in his sleep. In an agony of fear she froze, willing him to settle again. The sheep flicked their ears nervously. One of the ewes trod in the still warm ashes of the peat fire and bleated in surprise. Charles stirred again. She covered his mouth with her hand, squeezed her eyes still tighter.

Suddenly a shadow loomed against her closed eyelids. Terrified, she opened them. A soldier was standing in the open doorway, filling it. She couldn't see his face, only his silhouette, with the rifle sticking up threateningly behind his back. The sheep milled in the cramped hut, close to panicking. The ram made a little nervous dash forward, his eyes gleaming in the half dark.

Abruptly the soldier recoiled, catching the barrel of his rifle on the low doorway. Smothered laughter from the journalists greeted his reappearance outside, breathless and scarlet-faced. Even his companion couldn't suppress a snigger. Framed in the dark doorway the heavy horns and baleful yellow eyes of a young ram appeared. Behind it the long black faces of two ewes and their lambs peered out resentfully.

'Seen enough, have you?' inquired Iain Dhu. His voice was solicitous. Ruffled and breathing hard, the soldier tugged at his jacket.

'Yes.' He cleared his throat, saluted smartly.

'Thank you, sir, for your cooperation.' His companion followed his stiff, embarrassed back down the hill. The two journalists lingered tactfully a moment until they'd gone by, then sauntered down after them.

Inside the hut Rose strained to hear, holding her breath. The mutter of voices – and then, at last, the clump of boots going down the hillside, much faster this time.

Then, to her relief, Iain Dhu's bulky figure in the doorway. The sheep scattered. Without a word he drove them expertly out of the shieling and called in the dog. Rory came straight to her, his tongue out, his thin flanks heaving with exhaustion. She buried her head in his ruff, took his old grey head in both hands. He'd used all his strength to help them.

She poured him water in a tin plate, but he was too tired to drink it. He padded straight to his corner and lay down, only his wise old eyes moving from Iain Dhu to herself and back again. He seemed able to sense the tension that filled the room.

'Thank you.' Her voice sounded small, inadequate. Iain Dhu looked at her levelly.

'There's no need. I'd have done the same for any poor hunted beast on the moor.' He hesitated, his voice gruff. 'I'll be away now.'

He turned, awkwardly, his eyes avoiding the figure on the bed. His glance fell on the half-full milk pail, forgotten by the hearth.

'Best cover the milk before it spoils.' He spoke automatically. For a moment it was just like it used to be between them, as if nothing had happened. Simple, casual, everyday. Then his eyes met hers and the illusion vanished.

'What will you do?' His voice was a whisper.

'I don't know ... wait till they've gone.'

He shook his head slowly, doubtfully.

'How will you get word out? The lines are down.'

He hesitated, then spoke with difficulty. 'I could take a message to the mainland. If you wanted me to.'

'No.' Rose knew what he was offering. He'd already taken a risk in defying the soldiers. If they ever found out he'd deceived them ... with his reputation he'd have much more to fear than a mere warning. She could never let him make that sacrifice.

'It'll be all right, you'll see.' She spoke with more confidence than she felt. 'They'll give up in a couple of days, then it'll be safe.'

He bit his lip. She could see that he was aching to be gone.

'Aye, well . . . you'd best stay inside, the both of you, till I give you the sign.' He hesitated. His eyes avoided hers. 'I won't come up. Not till . . .' with a jerk of his head he indicated the figure on the bed. 'I'll pile some stones by the burn, where you cross. Then you'll know it's clear.'

'Thank you.' It was all she could say. She had no right to ask him to help her any more.

Awkwardly he scooped up the wooden casket and tucked it under his arm.

'You see . . .' there was something almost pleading in his voice. 'If it was to come out, that I lied to the military, there'd be the devil and a' to pay.'

'I understand.' He'd risked too much for her sake already. 'No one shall learn it from me.' She said it in the Gaelic, for emphasis.

He looked at her uncertainly. She felt her eyes filling with tears. Already the trust between them, built up so carefully, seemed to be vanishing. She felt as if she was losing her only real friend.

He looked down. He seemed to be struggling with himself. Once again he made to go out, then turned back. His mouth opened, then shut. When at last he spoke his voice was thick.

'There'll be food left at night for ye, by the burn. I'll see to it.' Before she could thank him he was out of the door. It swung to behind him and she heard him latch it shut, locking her in her prison. Then she heard him set off down the hillside, whistling tunelessly through his teeth. Somehow it was the saddest sound she'd ever heard. She waited, rooted to the spot in the darkness, until she couldn't hear him any more. And long after that. Outside the little burn chuckled and sang as usual over the stones, on a distant slope came the baa of a sheep. But inside her there was silence. For the first time she knew what it meant to lose a friend. In all her life she'd never felt so alone.

CHAPTER FIFTEEN

He was safe. A thousand miles beneath the sea, deep in a coral cave, where the cold wind wouldn't reach him. The coral glowed with a warm golden light behind his eyelids. He let his tired mind and body float on the current. If he listened hard enough he could hear the mermaids singing ...

Drowsily he opened his eyes. The cave was still there. Rocky walls reached up over his head, from somewhere came the sound of trickling water. He let one hand trail over the side of his bed, touched sand. He was dreaming, he knew it now. He sifted the sand slowly through his fingers.

A rustle of movement came to him. He turned his head on the pillow. The source of the glowing amber light was behind her but he could see her shape distinctly, the small head, the ripple of hair down her back. The mermaid. He held his breath. He didn't want the dream to end, he wanted to see her face.

She bent, lifted something. A kettle. He frowned absently. It was strange, a mermaid with a kettle. But the dream didn't vanish. She poured water into a bowl, stirred it, then set it down beside her. Now she was kneeling down, with something else in her hand. Up and down, forward and back, graceful and sure as the swell of the sea, she was combing her hair. The light glanced through the shining curtain as she combed. He longed to touch it.

He must have made some sound in his dream because she stopped suddenly and turned towards him. He couldn't be sure in the dim light but her cheeks seemed to glow a deeper rose. Hurriedly, for a mermaid, she set down her comb and picked up the bowl. He watched her as she came towards him across the sand, balancing her bowl so carefully.

She leaned over his bed, lifted the bowl to his lips. The liquid in it tasted warm and bitter but not unpleasant. Green, like the sea. As she bent forward he caught her mermaid scent, wild, sweet, haunting.

'Hush.' Her voice was no louder than the sigh of the wind in a door.

'Sleep now.'

He fixed his eyes on her shadowed face. Her eyes shone, but they were sad. He wanted to take the sadness out of her eyes, he wanted to make her smile, somehow he knew her smile would be so beautiful he'd never forget it, but he was too warm, too peaceful. Against his will his eyes closed. He slept.

A hundred years later he awoke. Even before he opened his eyes he began to remember. The crash. Black icy water closing over his head. The agonizing pain in his shoulder. The throbbing in his head ... then, numbness.

But he'd survived. Experimentally he stretched his body, checked himself over. The sharp pain in his shoulder was just a dull ache. His head was tender still but the swelling had gone down. His ribs felt as if he'd been run over by a steamroller, and he was weak as a cat, but apart from that everything seemed to be in working order.

With an effort that made his head swim he sat up and swung his legs round off the bed. The golden light from his dream was gone, the room hardly recognizable in the cold grey dimness filtering in from round the badly-fitting door. With a spurt of relief he realized that the room was empty.

He shivered with the cold as he struggled into what was left of his shirt and heavy jacket. But there wasn't a moment to lose. He must get back, let them know he was alive, let them know where he was ...

But where was he? He stared round. It seemed to be some sort of one-roomed shack, a shed, almost a hovel. Bare stone walls, the cracks packed in with earth. An earth floor scattered with sand. A makeshift hearth built up with stones.

A door that didn't fit and looked as if it had been made out of driftwood. Two candles, or what was left of them, sooty smears of wick marooned in fat white pools of grease.

He grimaced. So much for his magical coral cave.

Then he froze. Steps outside the door, the scrape of claws on stone, a dog's whine. Suddenly, before he was ready, she was there. Automatically he rose to his feet, almost bumping his head against the smoke-blackened rafters. The dog darted in between her feet and went straight to a bowl of water by the hearth.

They stared at each other, the silence broken only by the dog's noisy lapping. That strange sense of recognition welled up inside him, draining his strength.

A metallic clank broke the spell. He looked down. She was carrying two battered pails, one of milk, one of water. Mermaid into milkmaid. The transformation was complete. And in a string bag hanging from her wrist, what was clearly the scaly legs and dangling neck of a very dead rooster.

And that wasn't all that had changed. He caught his breath. The pale, mouse-like girl in the faded print dress that he'd rescued and then befriended was gone. In her place was a vital, beautiful girl. Even in this dim light her face glowed, the skin was the colour of fresh cream against the dark wool of her loose jacket. Her hair, lightened by sunshine and sea air, tumbled round her shoulders in unruly golden-brown waves. The scar now hardly showed, serving only to accent the delicate line of her cheek-bone, adding a piquant note to the wide hazel eyes. She even stood and moved differently, her head high. She was transformed.

He found it difficult to speak. She was new, beautiful, disturbing ... his pulses told him that ... and yet there was still the same sense of recognition. She's found herself, but the old Rose that had moved him so deeply was still there.

Then, startled as he was, he became aware that she was breathing hard, as if she'd been running. He took a step towards her. Again he felt that impulse to protect her, to put his body between her and any possible danger. He stopped himself just in time. This wasn't the time or the place. But he must do something, say something ...

'You saved my life. Thank you.'

She looked up at him. He forced himself to meet her eyes. Years of self-discipline helped him keep his expression neutral. After a few seconds she looked away again. Her shoulders drooped, suddenly she looked tired.

'It was my privilege.' The formal words sounded odd, a mockery of what he knew of her. Suddenly he felt cheated. 'After all, you saved mine.'

Against his will he remembered their first meeting. That strange half-promise she'd made him. She'd kept her word, and he ... without her he would have died.

He looked back at her, words trembling on his lips. She was sitting by the unlit hearth, staring thoughtfully at the ashes. But she made no move to light the fire. So much had happened since that first innocent meeting. Now he could no longer pretend the outside world didn't exist. Now she knew who he was. Never again would he feel in her presence that magical, exhilarating sense of freedom.

'This is a mess.' Raw, honest, his own words startled him. It had all happened so fast. He'd meant to go carefully, give himself time to decide what to do.

'It will be all right.' She looked up at him from the hearth, her face determined. 'Look.' She pointed to the pail of milk, the incongruous limp form of the rooster. 'Iain Dhu put them by the burn. He said he would.' Her voice was full of pride.

'Iain Dhu?' His voice was harsh. The name struck an unpleasant chord. He searched his memory. Voices he'd heard outside the hut, strangely loud through his fever. Later just the two voices, hers and another's, low and conspiratorial. The shadow of a big man.

With a chill of foreboding he realized the truth. It all made sense. Her breathlessness. The provisions. The unlit fire.

'They're out there already, aren't they? Looking for me?'

She nodded. 'I meant to go down to the burn earlier,

226

before it was light.' She blushed. 'But I overslept.' She drew a deep breath. 'They almost caught me.'

'Who?'

It was a rhetorical question, he knew the answer before she gave it.

'Two photographers. It's all right, they didn't see me.'

Of course. It had to be. Slowly he made his way back to his bed and sat down. Suddenly he felt like an old man. He stared blankly round the room. He was trapped here as surely as if he was in a prison. And yet ... he reached out a hand and laid it on the cold stone. These tumble-down walls were all that had stood between him and disaster. For disaster it would be, if he was found with her, in these compromising circumstances. What a story it would make for the press. His nerve ends tingled. He didn't want that to happen. Above all, not now when he'd only just found her again.

'Did I do right?'

It was her real voice, raw with anxiety. He nodded wordlessly. He wished he could stop looking at her profile. His lips set in a grim line. It was much more of a mess than he'd thought. If he had to spend any length of time with her he didn't know what would happen. It was the effect she had on him. His senses spun.

'I must go.' His voice was harsh. 'As soon as it's dark. My family, they will be sick with worry. I must let them know I'm alive.'

She swung round to face him. There was something oddly resolute in her expression.

'No. I'm sorry, I can't let you do that.'

He blinked in astonishment. In all his adult life no one had addressed him quite so categorically.

Her cheeks flushed.

'You don't understand. It's because of Iain Dhu. The press ... they were here, with the soldiers. Looking for you.' Her eyes dropped. 'I knew you wouldn't want to be found here, with me. Iain Dhu ... he helped me hide you. He lied ...

227

it was the only thing we could do.' Her eyes lifted, met his directly. 'That's why I can't let you go. Not till it's safe. He did it for me. I won't let him suffer for it.'

'I see.' Exasperation and admiration conflicted inside him. So he still had some lessons to learn about loyalty. 'How will I know when it's safe to leave?'

'Iain Dhu will leave a sign by the burn.'

'This Iain Dhu ... is he to be trusted?' Her head reared up, her eyes met his accusingly. For some reason he felt faintly ashamed.

'Yes.'

'How do you know?' Suspicion was mixed with something else now, hotter, harder. How well did she know this man? They stared at each other across the tiny space, tension crackling between them.

'You don't trust anyone.' Her voice was quiet but it stung all the same. Anger flared inside him, making his head throb. No, he didn't. In his position trust was one of the luxuries he couldn't afford.

'If he is to be trusted, then surely he could get a message out for me? At the least he could telephone ... there'd be no need for him to give his name.'

'No!' Her vehemence took him aback. He stared at her blankly, unused to opposition. 'The lines are down ... he'd have to go in person. And I won't ask him to take that risk.' She gestured fiercely at the milk, the provisions.

'Don't you see, he's done enough. He's been in trouble before. If they found out ... I won't let him do any more.'

Her words rang in the silence. He heard the protective warmth in her voice, felt again that uncomfortable spurt of jealousy. He suppressed it with an effort. At all costs he must maintain some sort of detachment. Especially now. Grimly he forced himself to consider the circumstances. Whichever way he looked at the situation, fate could not have played a more cruel trick. She couldn't take a message for him in case

the press found out about them. And there was no one else
... So he was well and truly trapped.

How long would it be? A day, two days ... thinking of the
anxiety at Balmoral and the Palace he could only pray that it
was no longer. And that wasn't the only reason.

'I won't disturb you, I promise. You won't even notice I'm
here.'

It was as if she'd read his mind. She knelt down and began
to unpack the provisions. Her narrow shoulders, turned
away from him so deliberately, made him feel ashamed. She
was so small ... and yet so dangerous. Somehow she
managed to slip through all his barriers.

As he watched her back he realized something else. He
might think she was dangerous, but now there was someone
else far more likely to betray him. Himself.

It was the longest day he'd ever spent in his life. Neither of
them could go out. From time to time as the day wore on
they heard loudhailers and the roar of trucks down on the
beach. The dog, puzzled that no one would accompany him,
circled the hut, occasionally poking his lean grey nose
through the crack in the door.

Without the fire it was cold, even in the cramped confines
of the tiny room. Rose busied herself with the provisions.
She never spoke a word, respecting his silence, but every one
of his senses was alive to her every movement. She plucked
the rooster, her cheeks flushed with the effort. The old dog
snapped at the falling feathers, sneezed as they tickled his
nose, but neither of them laughed at his antics.

With a sense of surprise, as the day wore on, he realized
that he'd never spent so long at any one time alone with his
thoughts. He was used to a crammed, active schedule. Even
his quiet moments were spent in some pursuit or other,
fishing in a mountain stream, hunting on the moor. Unable
to go out, unable even to move much without getting in
Rose's way, the silence of the hill all round him, he began to

feel disorientated, as if the outside world didn't exist. The rustle of water in the burn, the perpetual sigh of wind in the door, became almost hypnotic. Time stretched interminably in front of him.

And still darkness refused to come. He found himself longing for it. Then at least he would be able to sleep and the time would pass more quickly. Then he wouldn't be haunted by the awareness of the swish of her soft woollen skirt as she moved about the hut, the faint fragrance – rain, sea air, mountain flowers – that accompanied her every movement.

Late in the afternoon they ate, a cold, silent, unappetizing meal of oatmeal biscuits and salty cheese. He could hardly eat, the dry crumbs stuck in his throat, the silence oppressed him. It was full of so many things that couldn't be said, must not be said. He found himself longing to know the right time, his own watch had stopped. She cleared away the battered tin plates. He found himself watching her again. She never looked up. It was just as she'd said, she almost wasn't there. Quiet, discreet, unobtrusive.

'Can I ask you something?'

The silence was shattered into a million pieces.

'Of course.' His own voice almost deafened him. In the pause that followed she still didn't turn and look at him. He felt his heart racing, dreading her answer. There were so many questions she could put to him which he would find impossible to answer. Simple questions. Where is my locket? Why didn't you tell me who you were? Why did you leave me? Why did you never come back?

'What should I call you?' Oh God. Shame and relief and something else ... could it be a strange sort of disappointment? ... almost took his breath away. Suddenly he felt an insane desire to laugh. With an effort he kept his voice light.

'Well, you have a choice. Your Royal Highness, if you want to be formal. Most people just call me Sir.' He paused, irresolute. He wanted to hear her call him Charles, as she had before, but he had no right to ask.

'Sir ...' She nodded, just once, then stood up briskly and

230

dusted off her skirt. 'Yes, Sir.' She still wouldn't meet his eyes. Perfectly proper behaviour, but it was beginning to irritate him.

Silence again. Quietly she went to the pallet she'd prepared in the corner and lay down, pulling the blanket over her.

'Is it all right if I fall asleep, Sir?'

'Of course. You don't need my permission.'

'Oh. Thank you, Sir.' Her voice was small, drowsy, muffled against the blanket. Belatedly he realized how tired she'd seemed. No wonder, getting up at dawn after the long night. Sleep was the best thing for her. He only wished he could do the same.

'Wait.' What could he have been thinking of? Quickly he reached behind him, took the pile of blankets off the bed. She'd be cold with only one. 'Take these.'

She had her eyes closed, she was obviously half asleep already, but she shook her head. 'No. You're ill. You need them.'

He stood with the blankets in his arms, exasperated.

'Don't be ridiculous.'

'It's no good.' Her jaw set mutinously. 'I won't take them, Sir.' Again he felt that wild desire to laugh, or cry, or both.

'Here.' He spoke quietly, reasonably. 'Here's what I'll do. I'll split them with you.' A pause, while she digested this proposal, then a small sigh of acquiescence.

Scrupulously he divided the blankets into two piles.

'There. How's that.' One sleepy eye opened, appraised the two piles.

'That's OK.'

Hiding a smile, he spread the blankets one by one over her. Sure she was asleep, he added an extra one from his pile. But he was wrong.

'Don't cheat, Sir.' Her voice, though drowsy, was scandalized.

Shaking his head at her obstinacy, he removed the offending blanket and replaced it with the others on his bed. Still smiling, he stretched out on top of the covers, eyes fixed on the square edge of light round the ill-fitting door. Comforted by the thought that it would soon be dark, soon the day would be over, he let his aching body relax. The small sounds she made while she was asleep were somehow reassuring. Freed from the pressure of trying not to meet her eyes his mind could drift away, range free, even dream a little ...

He must have fallen asleep, because when he next opened his eyes the edge of light round the door had disappeared. He looked over towards her makeshift bed but it was empty. An irrational surge of panic filled him.

'Rose?'

Silence. The room was empty. He sat up, noticed that his share of blankets had been spread over him carefully while he slept and that a lighted candle on a tin plate was set beside the bed. His panic eased a little. He'd been foolish. It was dark now, safe for her at least to go out. He got up, stretched, refreshed after his sleep, looked round the room. It was beginning to seem familiar to him, reassuring. Left alone, he began to see for the first time the practicality of it. Solid stone walls, thick enough to keep out a gale or a regiment of troops. No more furniture than strictly necessary. No frills – just the answer to all the basic human needs. Shelter. Privacy. Warmth.

He glanced at the hearth. She'd been busy. The old ashes had been swept away. Above the hearth, wedged into a crevice in the stone, was an enamel mug full of small bright yellow flowers, candle-bright. And he could have sworn that the floor had been newly sanded and swept. The morning seemed a hundred years ago. Remembering his jaundiced impressions he felt faintly ashamed. Now he could see that even though the stone hut was simply, even crudely furnished, it was as much of a home as anywhere he'd ever been. Flowers. Kitchen tools neatly stacked in the wooden crate, each in its proper place. The kettle shining above the earth. Nothing magical about it, just ...

The door swung open behind him. Rory rushed in, frisked

around his ankles. Surprised, he almost lost his grip on the
tin plate, and a dollop of hot candle wax hit the dog square
on the nose. He yelped in astonishment, pawed at himself,
then trotted to his corner, shaking his head in disbelief.

A peal of laughter from the doorway. She was there. Her
arms full of peat squares, her eyes spilling over with gaiety.
He lifted the candle. Hastily she tried to smother her
laughter. He was glad she didn't quite succeed.

'Welcome home.' Her eyes widened for an instant, then
she ducked her head and hurried past him.

'Thank you, Sir.' He closed the door behind her and
latched it. Somehow the simple gesture gave him enormous
satisfaction.

She busied herself at the hearth, stacking the peats. Her
fingers moved swiftly and surely as she built the fire. He
watched her in fascination. He'd never seen a peat fire laid.
There was clearly quite a science to it. With a brisk,
housewifely air she dusted off her hands and leaned back.
They both admired the construction silently for a minute.

He felt almost dizzy with relief at seeing her again.
Refreshed by sleep, his mind was beginning to pound with
questions. There was so much he wanted to ask her and yet
here they were, forced to behave like strangers. I looked for
you, he wanted to say. Why did you leave, why didn't you
wait for me? But he had no right ...

Still, there was one thing he had to know.

'Rose?' She looked up questioningly. 'Your mother ... did
you find her?' Perhaps that was the reason for the change in
her, the new confidence in her bearing.

'No, Sir.' She saw the expression on his face. 'But it
doesn't matter ... not so much as it used to.' She looked
thoughtfully down at the unlit fire. 'I looked for her. That's
what brought me here. But I didn't find her. I think ...
maybe ... she didn't want to be found.' Her direct gaze met
his. 'That's possible, isn't it?'

He nodded. It was what he'd thought all along, and hadn't
dared tell her.

'It's funny, though.' Her eyes were faraway. 'I used to think that if I didn't find her I would die.' She looked up at him shyly. 'Do you remember?'

'Yes, I remember.' I remember everything you've ever said to me, he thought silently.

'But now I know better.' A shadow flitted across her face and was gone. 'Things change, people change. You just have to get used to it.'

The words sent a pang through him. She looked so quaintly philosophical, sitting there by the hearth. Like a little old lady with all her life behind her. He wanted to sweep her up in his arms, prove to her that life could be a carnival ... He restrained himself with an effort. She'd reached some kind of peace inside herself, he mustn't destroy it.

She reached out and picked up the matches. Without meaning to, he took a step closer. Such a simple, old-fashioned thing, lighting a fire, but somehow, with the cold and dark outside, it became more than just a chore, almost a ceremony. As he watched her strike the match and touch it to the peats he realized that, half unconsciously, he'd been waiting for this moment all day. Silently they watched the charcoal brown peat catch light. A plume of scented white smoke spiralled upward. The small flame crackled, rustled, grew magically before their eyes. The first faint waves of heat reached out to them from the hearth. He knelt down beside her, mesmerized by the flames. He looked at her, their eyes met. One side of her face was edged in gold by the light of the fire. More firelight was dancing in her eyes.

A small core of warmth began to grow deep inside his body. Both their hands reached out tentatively towards the flames. The warmth grew, enfolded them both. For a second they looked in each other's eyes and saw they were the same. Two human animals comforted by the warmth of the fire .. warm blood, warm skin, warm lips, nothing separating them but air ...

Then, hurriedly, she rose to her feet. He blinked. It was as if a cold wind had suddenly blown through the room. The moment was broken. He shivered, stretched his hands out again to the fire. The light glinted off the gold signet ring on his little finger. Still dazzled by the fire, he stared at it, his mind refusing to work. The ring. The ring she'd sent back to him, the ring that proved she hadn't lied. He'd forgotten all about it. But she'd seen it. And now she must think . . .

He should never have let her see it. How could she understand? How could he explain? If only he'd noticed it earlier, realized how it must look. He stared at it. By the light of the fire, so much warmer and brighter, the gold metal seemed unreal, trumpery. With a muffled oath he tugged it off and thrust it into the zipper pocket of his jacket. It was too late, the damage had been done, but he couldn't bear to be reminded of it. Bitterly he watched her bent head as she busied herself over the plucked bird. She was the real thing, the light of the fire. It was a pity it had taken him so long to tell false metal from true.

Rose blinked fiercely as she struggled with the cold, damp flesh of the rooster. Her vision was blurred, she could hardly see what she was doing. She told herself that it was the smoke from the newly-lit fire making her eyes water. Her face felt flushed. Behind her, she was aware that he'd got up and was striding impatiently round the room.

She risked a quick glance over her shoulder. His face was set and frowning. The dark stubble on his chin made him look a bit like a pirate, but there the resemblance ended. Even angry and ill-at-ease, he looked what he was. Imprisoned but somehow unreachable, like a caged lion. Pacing to and fro, alert for the first chance to escape.

Her eyes burned as she reached for the big cast-iron pot and filled it with water. He couldn't wait to get away. She didn't blame him. This wasn't what he was used to. She stared sadly down into the pot where the pale chicken joints floated. He'd be used to French cooking, sauces and spices and elaborate desserts. Iain Dhu's stringy old rooster couldn't compete. Blotting her eyes surreptitiously she hung the big pot above the fire with a dash of salt and wedged four scrubbed potatoes into the peat embers. Deep inside she knew it wasn't the cooking that was upsetting her. She bit her lip fiercely. How many times did she have to be told? Even Iain Dhu had tried to explain it to her, but she still couldn't get it into her head. It took the sight of the ring to drive it home to her for the last time.

She meant nothing to him, nothing at all.

Her hands shook as she stoked up the flames. Even now, knowing that he'd forgotten all about her as soon as the ring was safely back on his finger, she couldn't seem to break the link. Even now that she knew who he was, knew how impossible it had all been. She shuddered inside. He must have found it very amusing, her not knowing who he was. The things she'd told him, things she'd never told anyone else. And he'd listened so patiently. It must have been easy for him, he knew he'd never see her again. He'd go back to his own expensive world and forget all about her. And now he couldn't wait to get away again.

'The sign ... was it there when you went down to the burn?'

He'd stopped pacing for a few seconds, his face was drawn and impatient. She shook her head, not trusting herself to speak. His words proved it. He couldn't wait to leave.

'I can't stay here much longer. It's impossible.' The anger was back in his face now.

'Tomorrow ... perhaps tomorrow, Sir.' She managed to get the words past the lump in her throat. He rounded on her.

'Don't call me that!' She stared back at him, hot tears rising. He shot a quick look at her face. His mouth twisted, he turned away, flung himself on the bed. 'I'm sorry, I shouldn't have said that.' His voice was muffled. 'Call me ... call me anything you like.' He was staring savagely up at the rafters.

Confused, she knelt back and waited for him to explain. The silence stretched between them tautly, broken only by the rustle and hiss of the fire.

'Is ... is your shoulder hurting you, Sir?'

He turned towards her, his face unreadable. He gave a short, bitter laugh.

'Yes. That's it.'

'I could make you something to ease the pain, Sir.' She gestured at the row of herbs hanging above the hearth.

'No.' His voice was clipped and harsh. 'There's no need. There's nothing you can do.'

The silence stretched between them again. He lay motionless on the bed, she stirred the pot over the fire and turned the potatoes in the ashes. Dimly she wondered how much of this she could take before her heart broke clean in two. Deep inside she knew the answer. Her heart belonged to him. It was his to break whenever he liked.

'Follow your heart ...' That's what Catriona had said. 'Promise me you'll follow your heart.' She'd promised. But she hadn't realized just how painful it could be.

She served the meal in silence. The chicken stew was hot and delicately flavoured, the potatoes melting inside their crisp roasted skins. When they'd finished he sat back. The pain must still be bad, his face still had that drawn expression.

'Tell me more about Iain Dhu.' His voice was abrupt. Startled, she felt her face get hot. He saw her surprise, looked down and toyed with one of the chicken bones on his plate. He gave a small ironic smile.

'I've eaten his rooster. I'd like to know more about him.'

'Well ...' she didn't known how to begin. 'There's not much to tell, Sir. He lives four miles away. He has his own croft. Twenty-five black-faced sheep and a ram of his own.' Without meaning to she mimicked the gentle note of pride Iain Dhu's voice had had in it when he told her.

'I see.' He looked down again. She couldn't see his face. 'That wasn't quite what I meant. Tell me ... about the man himself.'

'Oh.' The conversation was beginning to make her feel uncomfortable, she didn't know why. Perhaps he was still worried that Iain Dhu couldn't be trusted. 'He's very loyal, Sir.' She tried to reassure him. 'And strong too. I've seen him with a full-grown sheep under each arm.'

A wry smile flitted over his face. He touched his shoulder lightly.

'I know.' His smile faded. 'So he's a good friend to have. Strong and loyal.' That odd note was in his voice again.

'Yes, Sir.'

'The sort of man who'd never let you down.'

'No, Sir.'

'I see.'

No, she wanted to say to him, no, you don't see at all. But loyalty to Iain Dhu kept her silent.

Another pause. This time his face was distant, he looked as if he was somewhere else. It seemed as if that was the end of his interest in Iain Dhu. She relaxed a bit, trying to hold on to the memory of them sitting like this with the firelight playing over them. The last time ...

'What was that name he called you?' The question was so sudden and unexpected that she jumped.

'Floraidh.' She stumbled a little over the Gaelic pronunciation.

'Floraidh ...' He said it musingly, softly. It made her heart miss a beat. 'But that wasn't all.'

She felt herself blushing again.

'No. There's another bit, but it's just, well, sort of a nickname. Only Iain Dhu uses it. It doesn't mean anything.' She spoke too hurriedly. He looked at her without speaking.

'I see.' His mouth twisted again. His face hurt her, she didn't know why. Hurriedly she got up and began to clear away the dishes.

'It's late.' His voice was flat, all the life seemed to have gone out of it.

'Yes, Sir.'

He must be tired, that was it. Quickly she stacked away the dishes, gave Rory his scraps, banked up the fire, so that it would burn all night. When she next looked he was lying on top of his bed, his eyes closed, apparently asleep. As quietly as she could she doused the candles, settled Rory in his corner and then went to her own. She burrowed under the covers and pulled the blankets over her head. That way he wouldn't hear her when she cried.

Through his closed eyes he was achingly conscious of the firelit room and everything it contained. He could see it in his mind's eye, every small, endearing detail. So familiar now, but never to belong to him. He had no right to any of it. He was heir to a kingdom, but couldn't lay claim to what he most wanted.

He opened his eyes, stared unseeingly up at the shadowed rafters. Another man would lie here, king of this tiny principality. A draughty hut. An old dog. A girl with rain in her eyes. Burning awareness of his unforgivable behaviour flooded through him. He'd been rude, churlish, the perfect boor, pursuing his interrogation to the bitter end. Well, now he knew, and the bitterness of that knowledge was no more than he deserved. Her hesitancy, her blushes, they'd told the whole story. Strong, loyal Iain Dhu. With his twenty-five black-faced sheep. The simple words burnt into his brain. Strong. Loyal. Lucky . . .

He listened for a noise from her bed. Nothing. He almost called out her name, fought back the impulse with a physical effort. It was no use. She felt nothing for him now, how could she? She had her home, her Iain Dhu. His throat aching, he lay rigid on the rough blankets. The fire burned on, smouldering under its banked ash. He couldn't sleep. The hut, her sleeping form in the corner, kept tantalising him with its promises of what might have been. If he'd been someone else, if she'd been someone else. In the glowing half dark he felt himself drifting away from his moorings, losing track of himself. Her soft breathing filled his mind with the illusion that outside there was nothing . . . all the life and warmth in the world was concentrated in this one room.

Moving in a dream, he bent down and picked up the unlit

candle from his bedside. His bare feet made no noise as he padded across the sand and lit it at the fire. Still in a dream, he crossed to her bed and looked down. I must see her face, he thought. I still haven't seen her face properly . . . only in the half-dark, only by candlelight. No one could grudge me that. Just once. So I can remember. For auld lang syne. He raised the candle, looked down.

She was lying on her side, just her nose showing above the blanket edge, one hand curled under her cheek like a baby's. He lifted the candle higher, reached out a hand to uncover her face. Rory shifted in his nest beside the fire and looked up at him with bright eyes. I won't hurt her, he promised him silently. Just one more look. The blanket fell back. Her cheeks were flushed, her eyelashes soft, her lips slightly parted. She looked warm and defenceless and very young. Against his will he reached out a hand to touch her cheek. Then he noticed something that made him draw his hand back. Tearstains down the soft skin; in the corner of her eye, catching the light from the candle, one tear that hadn't fallen.

Suddenly cold, he turned away. What could he have been thinking of? He'd been in a dream. He drew a shaking hand down his face. He'd brought her enough pain already. Let her sleep, and forget he'd made her cry.

He looked round the hut in sudden desperation. He couldn't stay with her now, here, in the same room. It was too much to ask. Just the sight of her made him forget everything . . . he was only human after all. Quickly he tugged the blankets off his bed and threw one round his shoulders. Cursing to himself, he plunged outside into the cold and darkness. He couldn't trust himself alone in this room with her. He'd spend the night in the open, even if he died of pneumonia in the process. The way he felt now, he didn't really care.

She was dreaming. The old lament she'd sung at Catriona's ceilidh echoed in her mind.

'S mise tha fo mhingean,
Mu'n ghille dhonn ...
Oh but my heart cries for my dark-haired lad,
he smiled at me so fine,
For he lies cold in his bed,
and I in mine ...

No! She wrenched herself away from sleep, her heart racing. The old woman was trying to tell her something through the song. The words echoed in her mind ... she hadn't understood them before. He lies cold in his bed and I in mine ... she's thought it was just another sad song about separated lovers. But now she knew it said more than that. It said that if one died, the other did too. When you lost your love you lost yourself as well.

She sat up, strained her eyes into the darkness. The fire had almost gone out, hours must have gone by, but it wasn't yet dawn. It was the worst time of the night, when it felt as if the sun would never come up again. When water kelpies rose dripping out of the ocean to carry you away while you were asleep ...

'Are you awake, Sir?'

No reply. Nothing but the beating of her heart. Suddenly anxious she slipped out from under the covers. He in his cold bed and I in mine ... She shivered as her bare feet touched the ground.

'Sir?' Her voice echoed in the emptiness. Rory stirred in his corner, whimpered. Gone, gone ... Suddenly afraid, she crossed to his bed, half knowing what she would see. The bed was stripped bare, empty.

Gone. She pressed her hands to her mouth. Rory watched her anxiously from the corner.

'What shall I do?' She stared wide-eyed into the darkness. In his weakened state he wouldn't be able to go far. And it was no night to be out on the hill alone. Rory whined, heaved himself out of his nest and came across to her, pressing his head against her knee.

241

'What shall I do?' She looked down at his wise grey face. The wind rattled the door, cold air nipped her bare ankles. Catriona's face came back to her. Behind it, so faint she could hardly see it, was the face of the young girl she'd been, before the light had gone out of her eyes. 'Follow your heart . . .'

The wind rattled the door again. Quickly she reached down by the bed and pulled on her shoes. There wasn't a moment to lose.

CHAPTER SIXTEEN

All around him the night was full of noises. The rustle of the wind in the grass, the distant sound of the sea on the coastline below. The wind was cold, but he didn't feel it. Above him the round, hostile face of the full moon stared down, its flat light illuminating the whole mountainside with a strange ghostly glow.

He was cold, but he wasn't unhappy. Out here, disorientated by the moonlight, by the wind, constantly changing direction, by the small, unidentifiable noises, he felt strangely at peace. The impersonal blank face of the moon made a mockery of his petty confusions. The moon didn't know who he was, wasn't remotely interested. Neither were the crickets. The mountainside was solid underneath him.

He closed his eyes. Nothing stopped. The busy secret life of the mountainside went on regardless, the moon went on shining. Out here he was nothing and nobody. No house, no servants, no protocol to follow, no appointments to keep.

He let his mind drift. If only, if only ... if only he could stay here forever. But he'd have to leave, there was no choice. The ship was calling for him at dawn. Half-asleep, he frowned in confusion. The ship ... what ship? What was he thinking of? There was no ship. The image faded, but something else took its place. The strange feeling that he'd been here before, out in the open under the full moon, a plaid round his shoulders, homeless, penniless, hunted. But, feeling none of those things. Feeling instead richer, safer than he'd ever been. Rich because though the land might never be his, the hearts of its people were.

How could he feel cold or lonely when he was surrounded by so much love and loyalty?

Deep in sleep he felt the cold recede, felt warmth surround him on all sides. As if the mountain itself had opened its arms to him. So much love ... and all it asked for in return was not to be forgotten. He stirred in his sleep, the warmth radiating right through to his bones. How could he have forgotten? His word was his bond. But the mountain hadn't forgotten. The past melted away as if it had never been. He smiled, reaching out in his sleep to his sleeping people. 'Look. I have kept the old promise. I have come back.'

When he woke he was still warm. Two solid bands of warmth down either side, more warmth pressing golden against his closed eyelids. Slowly, luxuriously, he stretched, breathed in deeply, sweet cold air lightly scented with salt. He savoured it, keeping his eyes closed. He didn't want to wake up and break the spell. It seemed familiar somehow. Salt air. A heather bed. Coming home ...

'I keep my health better in these wild mountains than I used to do in the Campagnie Felice, and sleep sounder lying on the ground than I used to do in the palaces at Rome ...' He frowned. The words seemed to come out of nowhere, spoken straight into his mind. They seemed familiar too, perhaps he'd read them somewhere. He stretched again. They were certainly very apposite. He hadn't slept so warmly and deeply in years.

Then he heard it again, the sound that had woken him. Bells, church bells, pealing unmistakably through the clear air. Puzzled, he opened his eyes. Above him the sky was almost light, it must be nearly dawn. The first few rays of the rising sun were warm on his face. To the east, above the sea, the sky glowed gold. Around him everything seemed to be waiting breathlessly for the sunrise. No birds, nothing stirring, not even a breath of wind.

Slowly, inexorably, the sun edged above the sea, opening up a dazzling fiery path across the water. The new day. Again he had that strange feeling that he'd been here before, waiting for the dawn on this very mountainside, wishing the moment would last forever ... The light was too bright. It

244

dazzled him, brought a lump into his throat. He closed his eyes, as if that would help him freeze the moment in his memory. But of course it wouldn't. Nothing would. Despite himself, he sighed.

Another, answering sigh came from his right. Startled, he shifted round in his blanket cocoon. Only inches away another face, black and white with bright brown eyes, reared up and confronted him.

'Rory!'

The dog nudged him, swept a cursory tongue across his face, then scrambled to his feet. A cold blast of air filled the warm space where he'd lain. Head down, he trotted off down the hill.

Astonished, he watched him go. How long had the dog been there? No wonder he'd felt so warm all night. But that wasn't all. There was another source of warmth all down his left side. Half knowing what he would see he turned his head carefully to the left. Another mound of blanket, tightly rolled. Sticking out at the bottom of the roll, a pair of small bare feet. He turned further, half sat up. His heart seemed to have stopped beating. The warm bundle stirred, whimpered softly, sighed. Very gently he tweaked back the fold of blanket at the top of the cocoon. More blanket. It was like unwrapping an Easter egg. Chocolate before breakfast. A miracle, breaking all the rules. He could feel his heart melting inside. The light was growing all around him. He could feel the warmth of her body through the coverings.

He reached for the last bit of blanket hiding her face. She still didn't wake. Holding his breath, he eased it back, knowing he was on the brink of some enormous discovery. Once he saw her face he'd know, one way or the other. For better or worse. For richer or poorer ...

For the first few seconds he couldn't look. The dawn light was cruel. In the dimness of the shieling he'd found her beautiful, but maybe once he saw her clearly it would be the end. He didn't know what would be worse, if it was the end or the beginning. Maybe, in the clear light of day,

)
that haunting, aching sense of recognition would be gone.
Maybe ...

He looked down. Her eyes were closed, her breath just
fluttering a wisp of hair by her cheek. Time stood still. Gently
he moved the wisp aside. The light showed up every tiny
freckle on her skin. The rest of her face was tanned golden,
flushed with pink like a wild bird's egg. She looked as if she'd
break if he touched her. He felt like a nest-robber, but he
couldn't look away. He found himself counting her eyelashes. They were soft and brown and very straight. He felt a
ridiculous desire to brush them with his finger. She was so
close ... her mouth was only inches from his, he could feel
her breath on his cheek. There was no one watching. Just the
two of them, alone on the cool flower-scented mountainside,
church bells echoing in the stillness.

Very gently, taking care not to scratch her with his
stubble, he kissed her on her warm, parted lips.

Slowly her eyes opened. He leaned back. It was like
watching a flower opening. At first her eyes were blurred and
unfocused. She blinked, then she saw him. He smiled. She
smiled. He saw the colour of her eyes, the colour he'd tried to
forget. Green and brown and gold. Like mountain water
running over speckled pebbles. The dawn light was in them,
she was lit up inside. His Easter morning girl.

The brightness took her breath away, for a moment she
didn't know where she was. Then she felt the hard earth
under her and remembered. Against the dazzling sky she saw
the shape of his dark head, his sun-tanned neck, his blue-
shadowed chin. His eyes were looking straight into hers.

She felt the shock run through her body. His face looked
different. Something had happened to him. He looked,
somehow, as if he belonged, here in the open. The blue of his
eyes was dazzling. There were bits of grass in his tousled hair.

'What is it?' He looked as if he'd discovered some kind of
secret. Suddenly she realized what had happened to his face.
The armour had fallen off it. She blinked. It was almost too

246

much. He was there, all of him, laughing in his eyes.

'The dawn.' His voice had changed too. He looked suddenly young, free, reckless. Like a knight going on a crusade. Instinctively she looked towards the east. There was no mistaking that brightness over the water. It was dawn. The Sabbath bells were tolling. Soon there'd be a trickle of people across the machair on their way to early service ...

'Oh no!'

Icy realization rushed in on her, clearing the last drowsiness from her mind. Hurriedly she struggled to her feet. She'd meant to stay on guard but she'd fallen asleep. And now it was nearly light. At any moment they could be spotted.

She shot a quick glance towards the small grey shape of the shieling, just visible in the distance. Suddenly it looked very far away. Here on the braeside they'd be clearly visible, and there was nowhere to hide. Not even a tree or a clump of boulders. Just bare grassy slopes, windswept and exposed, rolling down to the sea below.

But there might still be enough time, if they followed the quickest way down, the narrow track beside the burn that the sheep always used. She strained her eyes into the distance, trying to pick out the irregular rocky banks. It took her longer than she expected. She felt strangely disorientated, still dazed with sleep, half-dazzled by the light. She picked it up at last further up the mountain and traced it quickly down. There wasn't any time to lose, no room for any mistakes.

Then she saw it. A small, workmanlike, unmistakable shape, outlined in light. Neatly placed just where Iain Dhu had said it would be. Someone who wasn't looking for it would never even notice it, but to her it seemed to be etched into her brain. The cairn. The sign. Suddenly cold she pulled the blanket closer round her shoulders. All the warmth seemed to have gone out of the sun.

'What is it?' His voice was soft, with a note in it she'd never heard before. It made her feel soft inside, when she'd meant to be strong and determined. She didn't dare look at him, she didn't know what might happen to her if she did.

'It's the sign, Sir.' She tried to keep her voice level, pretend it didn't matter. She tried not to think what it meant.

'The sign?' He sounded puzzled. Maybe he'd forgotten. She waited, fixed her eyes on a bit of rock mossed over with tiny flowers, and hoped he'd remember. She didn't think she'd have the strength to explain.

'You mean ... it's all clear? They've gone?'

She nodded, hardly trusting herself to speak. He sounded so relieved. It was obvious that he couldn't wait to get away. She bit her lip. This was the moment she'd feared and dreaded, pretended to herself would never happen. But she'd have to face up to it now. Well, she'd managed to last this far, maybe she could go on a bit longer. Catriona did.

She turned round, forcing herself to keep steady. It would be all right, she could be brave, as long as she didn't meet his eyes. He was on his feet now, the plaid thrown carelessly over his shoulder. His blue-black hair was ruffled by the wind, his head flung back. His skin was tan against the crumpled white of his shirt, his eyes bluer than anything she'd ever seen. She felt her heart flutter inside her chest. For a moment her vision blurred, the distant bells came through a dream-like haze. The dawn light and the mountainside were the same, but she was someone else. Today he might be lost to her, but she had his promise. He would come back. She trusted him. He was her King. Tousled, unshaven, but unmistakable. Her King.

Love and loss welled up inside her, threatening to spill over. In a dream she felt herself sink down till the hem of her skirt brushed the wiry mountain grass, heard her own voice – or was it a voice on the wind – say,

'I am your servant always, Sire.'

Slowly her eyes lifted, met his. Through the blur of tears his face looked strangely different. And yet every line was familiar to her. And his eyes, his eyes were the same always, nothing could change them, not time or death or loss of all their hopes ...

248

'No.' He reached out his arm, she felt the warm steady pressure of his hand under her elbow. 'We have shared so much together. You must never kneel to me.'

His voice was low, but there was something in it that took her breath away. It took her a moment to realize what it was, and when she did the realization convinced her she must be dreaming after all. He'd spoken in Gaelic.

What is happening to me? His mind whirling, he drew his palm across his unshaven chin. He felt as if he was losing control, forgetting everything. Or was it remembering? He frowned. The dawn light was dazzling, it must be playing tricks with his eyesight, turning everything upside down. Nothing had changed, and yet everything had changed. He was himself, marooned here in the wrong place with the wrong girl, and yet deep inside everything seemed familiar and right. Something he'd promised himself long ago ... the sense of recognition, warm and bone-deep, was everywhere.

Another chance ... he felt the warmth inside him grow, begin to flood his body. A chance to make good the old bitterness, salve the old wounds. The loneliness, the disappointment, the gnawing canker of regret ... Broken promises, lost causes, the sea running red with tears and blood. Loss and grief. A ship in the bay. Safety without honour. The choice was his. And time was running out.

In a dream he felt himself turn and plunge down the mountainside. His feet seemed to know the way, treading unerringly over the uneven surface. He didn't even look down. His eyes were fixed on the eastern horizon and the path of fire across the water. She followed, as he knew she would. Somewhere, somehow, they'd done this before. The same sense of poignant urgency was in the air, the same goodbye feeling. Only this time ... this time he knew where he was going, even if he didn't know why. There was something he had to do.

The wind lifted his hair, he felt a wild surge of exhilaration. The standing stone was still there. Tall and proud and indomitable, rising out of the bare scree like the spirit of the land itself. Deep down he'd hoped and prayed it would be there. Against all the odds, battered by the wind and spray, it had survived. It remembered. He rested his hand on the rough stone surface. It was taller than he was, taller than any mere man. Already the surface was warm from the sun.

Without looking round he felt her take up her position beside him. Down by the sea here the sun looked close enough to touch. If they took one step forward they'd leave the land behind, step right on to the fiery path across the water. He had to suppress a crazy impulse to do just that. The light drew his eyes, he couldn't look away.

He narrowed his eyes, blinked, then looked again. Something was happening. The sun's outlines were rippling through the golden haze above the water, vibrating with energy. It looked as if it would leave its moorings at any minute and escape to freedom, break the chains that held it fixed and soar away. If that happened, anything would be possible. All the old rules would be swept away. All past losses and gains would be cancelled out, meaningless. Time as they knew it would come to an end . . . there would be just this moment, the two of them side by side by the standing stone, for eternity.

'What is happening?' His voice sounded strange in his own ears, hoarse, disbelieving. He felt the world dissolving round him, all the outlines melting and running into one. Inside him too something was dissolving and reforming, his old self melting away.

'It's just like she said . . . only I didn't know it could be so beautiful.' Her voice was awed, almost a whisper. So she saw it too. He was glad, for a moment he'd felt he was losing his sanity.

'What is it?'

'It's the sun dance.' Her voice slowed, took on a singsong quality as if she was reciting. 'Since the beginning of time it's only been seen half a dozen times, and no one who sees it can

250

find words to say what it is they've seen. You can only see it once in your life, and then only if you are fearless and take what comes. There was an old man at Stulaval who stayed out on the mountain on Easter Eve looking for a lost ewe and in the morning he saw the sun dance for joy in honour of the reborn King. And they say it will happen again when the island King returns to his faithful people. But you can only ever see it once.'

Breathlessly they watched, trying to hold on to the image. He willed himself to remember it. How could something so beautiful ever be forgotten? It seemed impossible, but fairy gold slipped through the fingers in the light of day . . . If only he could remember. The huge bright disc pulsed and flowed, struggled to free itself from the water, struggled to be born. Its lower edge was almost free now. He felt its energy coursing through his body, reaching into all the dark crannies and crevices, stirring him to life. Now . . . now he knew what he had to do. To bring the wheel full circle one last time, to free himself and her.

The realization burst inside him with a blaze of light. The talisman. How could he have forgotten. The one bright spot in two centuries of dark, lonely years. The one link that time could not destroy. He must give it to her, now, quickly, while they were still both outside time. So that she would know that he'd kept his promise, that he'd come back. Just as he'd given it to her then, all those bitter years go, he must give it to her again. The circle must be completed, before they were both thrown off the wheel once more.

There wasn't much time left, the sun was almost up. Quickly he fumbled through his pockets. The locket had to be there, it was hers, he would never have given it to anyone else. But he couldn't find it. His pockets were empty, apart from the gold signet ring. A small cold chill went over him, a memory stirred. But that was from another life, it had nothing to do with him. His sense of urgency deepened. Time was slipping away, it was almost too late. But the locket was lost. His pockets were empty. And without the locket, the link – his only chance to mend the broken past, to keep his promise – was gone.

Anguished, he turned towards her. Already his awareness of her seemed to be blurring, he was losing the sharp edge of it, she was fading away before his eyes. He couldn't hold her now, he'd betrayed her trust in him. The talisman was gone. He had failed to keep the tryst, laid down all those years ago. He had failed to keep faith with himself and her, and now she was lost to him forever ...

Already his inner strength was fading. Once the sun was high the last fragile links would be destroyed. Then, he knew, he would forget everything. The ultimate betrayal.

He mustn't let that happen. With the last remnants of his strength he willed himself to hold on. There must be some way, something he could do. He couldn't lose her again, not when she was so near. But despite his effort he felt himself slipping. The outside world was filtering in, extraneous noises and images edging into his consciousness. The buzz of an outboard motor in the bay. A dog barking. The past was fading, fading ... He pressed his hand harder onto the stone, it was the only thing that kept the past alive. It had seen and survived it all. Nothing, not the baking sun or the bitter wind or the salt spray had worn it away. It had kept the faith. He pressed harder. From deep inside the stone he drew some kind of strength, right from the earth's core.

With a last desperate effort, using that strength, he reached out his hand through the worn grey hollow in the stone. As he did it he had a sudden image of hundreds, thousands of hands reaching out to each other just like his over the years, in fear and longing and blind hope. His other hand clenched tight on the gold ring. It was all he had, he hoped it would be enough. Her small pale face turned towards him, he saw the doubt and fear mirrored in her eyes as she saw his outstretched hand. Please trust me, he said silently in his mind, please trust me this one last time. Before it's too late.

Slowly, hesitantly, her hand reached out towards him,

clasped his through the hollowed out stone, fingers laced round fingers, palm to palm. In the same instant the sun quivered one last time and freed itself from the water's edge. They stared at each other over their clasped hands. Now the sun was still, the dance was over. Any minute now he'd begin to forget. But there was one more thing he could do. The locket was lost, he couldn't give her that, but ...

He opened his right hand. The ring rolled on his palm, caught the light. Gently he unlaced her fingers, held them in his own. The warmth of her hand was real, it gave him strength. Hurriedly, almost clumsily, he slipped the heavy gold seal on to the middle finger of her left hand. It hung loose, far too big for her, but it would have to do. He doubled her hand over it to keep it safe. His heart was hammering so hard he could hardly breathe. A wave of doubt and guilt and fear rose up inside him but he fought it back. What have I done? he thought. And the answer came back, what I had to do. Or die inside.

He tried to blank out the enormity of what he'd just done by looking at her face. Her eyes were huge, her lips parted. Again he had that feeling she was part of him, right inside his body. Gently she drew back her hand, touched the ring, looked up at him. He felt she was looking right into his soul.

'Why?' There was a catch in her voice.

He wanted so much to tell her, but he couldn't. A lifetime's discretion wasn't so easily brushed away. The reasons why ... they were so many and so foolish. Because I was dazzled by the sun. Because I had to. Because I want to make up to you for everything that's happened in the past. Because I don't trust myself. Because I want to keep you close to my heart. Because I need you with me to face whatever comes. Because I want to take care of you. Because I want to give you my name ... Because I love you.

She was waiting for her answer. He smiled shakily.

'Why? Because. Just because.'

She was silent. The beginnings of the little smile he loved

253

so much curved her mouth. She understood. She'd seen the sun dance too. He took back her hand.

'Here.' He turned the seal to the light, just as he'd done once before so it showed up the intricate intaglio engraving. 'See those three plumes encircled by a coronet?' She nodded. 'Yes, Sir.' Her eyes were fixed on his face, eager to learn. 'What does it mean?'

Her voice was soft, close to his ear. It means everything, he wanted to say to her. It means generation after generation of royal descent, centuries of power and privilege, grace and favour. It means the divine right of kings, an ancient tradition going back to the Black Prince. It means history books gilded with royal dynasties – Tudor, Plantagenet, Stuart. It means the power and pressure of the Crown itself – all resting lightly on the slender finger of a girl with no name.

'It's the crest of the Prince of Wales.' And there's more, more that you can't see. The three lions of England, the lion rampant of Scotland, the golden harp of Ireland, the red dragon of Wales. The blue buckled garter of the Most Noble Order, the Royal Helm overflowing with gold and ermine, the lion and unicorn, differenced, the shield of arms of the Duchy of Cornwall ... There was so much she didn't, couldn't know. Another wave of doubt, stronger now, surged over him. The outside world, with its castes and precedents and formalities, couldn't be kept out forever ...

'What does this say?'

A shadow went over his face. She was pointing at the two words engraved at the base of the crest.

'That's the motto of the Prince of Wales. Ich Dien.'

'What does it mean, Ich Dien?'

Against his will he felt the vision slipping away from him, the outside world crowding in.

'It means, I Serve.'

Her face was puzzled.

'Serve? You? I don't understand.'

He allowed himself a bitter smile. It would take a thousand years to explain the subtle distinctions of the English social system.

'I suppose ... in my own way ... I am a servant. To my people.'

But that's an ideal, he thought. In reality there's a world of difference between upstairs and belowstairs. Not even the King of England can spirit that difference away.

She'd sensed his withdrawal now, there was no hiding it. But he hadn't realized how much it hurt him to draw back. He felt as if he was being split in two. There had to be a way, there had to be something he could do. If only he could think.

'Are you tired? Does your shoulder hurt?' Her face was anxious. With an effort he shook his head.

'Go back to the shieling. Leave me here. There's something I've got to work out. I need time to think.' His voice was rougher than he intended, he felt her flinch at her dismissal.

'Yes, Sir.' She whistled once and Rory came flying down the hillside, his tail fluttering like a banner.

'Stay, Rory.' She looked up at him as she patted the dog. 'You'll be all right with him, Sir. He'll take care of you. He knows the way back.'

I wish I did, he thought. She was so gentle with the dog. The wind whipped a lock of golden brown hair into her face, he felt an absurd desire to brush it away. She rose to leave.

'Wait!' There was something he had to ask her, something that lingered at the back of his mind. 'What was that you said ... about the sun dance ... about taking what comes? What is it, some kind of penalty?'

She hesitated.

'It's only an old story, Sir. Maybe it's not true, no one knows for sure.'

He sensed her reluctance but pressed on. He had to know.

'You must have some idea. What happened to the old man, for instance, the one who saw it at Easter?'

He waited tensely for her answer. It was a long time coming.

'He never saw the sun rise again.'

'What? You mean he died?'

'No, not exactly.' She shook her head sadly. 'When he came down from the mountain he was blind.'

So that was it. He watched her begin the long climb back up the hillside towards the shieling. Blind. A supremely fitting penalty. A lifetime's payment for just one moment out of time. And maybe, just maybe, the old man had thought it was worth it.

His mind racing, he turned round and stared blindly out past the standing stone to the steadily climbing sun. The path of fire across the water had disappeared . . . but maybe there was still a way.

CHAPTER SEVENTEEN

By the time she reached the burn she was tired and out of breath. Her feet seemed to get heavier with every step she took. She looked back over her shoulder, just once. He was standing very still by the stone. He looked as if he belonged there somehow.

She paused to catch her breath and pick up the day's provisions. Only three eggs this time, in a brown clay bowl. And wedged underneath, one of Iain Dhu's cutthroat razors. He couldn't have made it clearer. It was time for her guest to leave. For everything to go back to normal. Only things would never be the same ...

She bit her lip and picked up the milk pail, tucking the eggs under her arm. Nothing would be the same without him. But she'd always known he'd have to go in the end. It had just come sooner than she'd expected. The idea of Sunday on the island must have been too much for all those journalists and newsmen. Everything closed down on a Sunday, even the hotel in Lochmaddy. Not a drop of whisky or petrol to be had on the whole island. The islanders wouldn't even fetch peat or find a lost lamb on the Sabbath; all that had to wait. Some wouldn't even cook hot food.

She looked down at the eggs. Just this once, she didn't think they'd mind, even the strictest of them, if she boiled up the kettle to cook his breakfast. It was the last thing she'd be able to do for him. Even on a Sunday the islanders would never send a guest away hungry.

She tucked the razor in its worn leather holder into the waistband of her skirt and set off up the last bit of slope towards the shieling. The sun was high in the sky now, it was going to be a fine day. With a faint sense of surprise she saw that the shieling door was open, half ajar. She must have left it like that in her hurry last night. But it didn't matter. Whether the door was open or shut, none of the islanders would go in without permission.

The last few steps of the climb left her giddy. The night on the hillside had taken more out of her than she thought. Exhausted, she leaned against the door jamb for a second and put down the pail. The gold ring slid forward on her finger, threatened to fall off. She rescued it in time and hugged it to her chest.

At last she allowed herself to think back to that moment on the hillside when he'd held her hand in his through the stone. She'd never forget it. For the first time she'd felt they really belonged together, that there was a future for them somewhere. She'd had the strange idea that if only they could remember something, very important, neither tide nor time could ever part them again ...

She touched the ring gently. Something of that other-worldly feeling had stayed with her. The gold still seemed to glow with the warmth and certainty of that one moment stolen out of time. It made her remember the dawn light reflected in his eyes. There had neen just the two of them in the whole world ...

But she couldn't let herself go on dreaming. Of course he hadn't known about the old lovers' custom, the handfasting. How could he have known? But all the same it meant more to her than he'd ever realize. Even when she was a very old woman it would shine as clear and bright in her memory as the ring now did on her finger.

With a sigh she picked up the pail again and pushed the door wide. The shieling smelled strange, stale and musty after the fresh pure air outside. With a chill she wondered how it must have looked to him. Poky, shabby, dirty even – she hadn't had a chance to fetch up new sand for the floor. But before he came back she'd have all that straightened out. No matter how tired she felt. 'Well, well, this is an un-expected pleasure.'

Her heart in her mouth she spun round. The bowl slipped out of her grasp and fell. One by one she heard the eggs strike the floor and break. Surely she recognized that voice, that subtle, possessive blend of curiosity and caution that sent cold shivers all over her body. She looked frantically round, caught a pale blur of movement.

'You haven't forgotten me, I hope. Earnshaw, Richard Earnshaw.' A figure moved forward out of the shadows. A lean, eager face above a shabby beige waterproof.

'You.' She recognized him instantly.

'Dear me, I seem to have startled you. I do apologize.' He looked down at the broken eggs. Quickly she bent and retrieved one yolk, still swimming intact in its half shell. Conscious of his curious eyes on her she propped it up on the table, then turned casually towards the door.

'I must go now.' She kept her voice level with an effort. There was only a few feet between her and the door and safety.

'Wait a minute!' Suddenly his arm was across the door, swinging it shut. 'I want to talk to you. It won't take a moment.'

He smiled, his eyes flicking round the room. In one glance he took in the wild flowers in their can of water, the two rumpled beds, the unwashed dishes stacked by the fire. She had the strange feeling he was putting a price on everything. 'It's not for sale,' she wanted to say.

'Been here long?' She shook her head, she couldn't speak. He gave her a knowing look, his gaze lingered on the two mugs side by side. 'Must be lonely, all by yourself.' She shook her head again. He watched her brightly, like a greedy bird. He looked down at the bed, then back at her. Slowly he ran his eyes over her, making her suddenly conscious of her rumpled skirt and tangled hair. But she refused to drop her own gaze and look away. She had to outface him. At all costs she mustn't let him suspect the truth. Let him jump to conclusions, anything, so long as he didn't guess the truth.

'But that's neither here nor there .. ' With one last

fastidious glance at the rumpled sheets he sat down and propped his legs casually on the makeshift table. He looked completely relaxed. Only his eyes, alert, restless, constantly assessing her, betrayed him.

'Well now Rose ... may I call you Rose? ...' He didn't wait for an answer. 'What an elusive young lady you are.' He looked at her consideringly. 'You know, I hardly recognized you. You've changed. It must be the sea air.'

'Why have you come here?' She tried to mimic his self control but it didn't work. Instinctively she knew that this man never went anywhere without a purpose, without something to gain. And that whenever he stood to gain something, someone else stood to lose it ...

'To find you of course.' He neamed widely. 'I'd given up hope. But when they mentioned at the Post Office a girl with a scar, living up here on the mountain, I had to check it out. I've always been lucky.' He rubbed his hands together briskly. 'Now, we must turn over a new leaf. There's a whole different angle to cover.'

He glanced at her. A shadow of irritation crossed his face. 'I'm not trying to corrupt you, for heaven's sake. After all, your objections are no longer valid, how could they be?' He turned a spent match over in his fingers, flicked it expertly away. 'I'll be frank. Now that he's dead, the price has gone up. The public will soon get tired of headlines with black borders, they'll be ready for a little touch of pink. So anything you can tell me about your ... er ... brief relationship with him will be worth its weight in gold.' She flinched, tucked her hand with the ring behind her back. He watched her curiously.

'After all, it can't matter now, surely – either to you or to him, poor fellow. It's an advantage really – there'll be no routine denials from the Palace.' He paused. When he spoke again his tone was softer, almost sympathetic. 'If you'd rather, we can dress it all up a bit. Make it a great romance. Tristan and Isolde. The prince and the beggarmaid. No one will be any the wiser.' He smiled encouragingly.

260

She shrank back into the shadows. His smile began to fray.

'Unless you prefer living in total squalor?' He regained control of himself with an effort. With exaggerated casualness he leaned back and half-closed his eyes. 'Perhaps I'd better wait till the boy-friend comes back. Perhaps he can change your mind.'

'No.' She darted a quick look towards the door. At all costs she had to get rid of him before then. 'No, I'll tell you.' Something, anything. 'What do you want to know?'

'Well . . .' A small light of triumph flared in his eyes then was gone. He took out his notebook. 'Let's start with something fairly easy. Just some background detail about yourself, where you come from, your family, that sort of thing.' He paused expectantly. She stared back at him, her mind racing, her throat locked tight.

'Well, come on then. It can't be that difficult. You must know who you are, everyone knows that.' His eyes narrowed. 'But that's not it, is it? There's something else ... You're hiding something.' His gaze fell on her left hand, hidden behind her back. In one quick stride he crossed the room. With a swift movement he wrenched her hand up to the light. She just had time to clench her fist over the betraying signet ring so only the gold band showed.

'I see . . .' His grip tightened. 'Well, that does make things a little difficult. My word, you are a quick worker. Gold too.' She clenched her fist tighter. His eyes were burning into her face, he was so close she would smell last night's whisky on his breath. His grip tightened again, her hand was slowly going numb. 'There's something in this I don't quite understand . . .' His voice was quiet, almost thoughtful. Somehow that made his iron grip more terrifying.

He turned her fist palm upwards. 'What are you afraid of? What are you afraid I'll find out?' He tried to loosen her fingers, she tried to tug her hand away. He kept his grip. 'Come on, Rose. There's no crime in wearing a ring ... even if you're not married. You can tell me. I'm not one of the locals. Lots of people do it.' His voice was persuasive, reasonable. So were his fingers – only they were harder, they dug viciously into her palm.

'You're going to have to show me sooner or later.' He was using all his strength now, she could see from his eyes that he was really angry. She began to struggle in earnest. He was strong, he was used to getting his own way no matter what he had to do. She'd sensed that dangerous aura round him from the first time she'd seen him, and now the disguise was off. He was breathing hard, she could feel her fingers bending, beginning to open.

'No!' She kicked wildly at his shins, but he held her away from him, laughing out of the side of his mouth. He seemed to be enjoying himself, he knew he would win, he was just holding off till the right moment. And there was no one she could call on for help, unless ...

'Rory, Rory!' She shouted with a last desperate effort, but deep down she knew that he wouldn't hear. He'd been told to stand guard and he wouldn't leave his post for anything. The waterproof man seemed to know it too.

'It's no use, you know. No one can hear you.' One strong, sinewy hand forced her wrist against the table, the other prised excruciatingly at her fingers, bending them back. The pain made her gasp. His voice, alight with triumph, was loud in her ear. 'Make all the noise you want. There's no one to hear us. We're all alone.'

'Not entirely.'

A shaft of light knifed through the room, dazzling them both. They froze. The grip on Rose's wrist slackened, with a sickening plunge of relief and dread she heard Rory's whine.

'And who are you, may I ask?' The waterproof man squinted against the light. The door swung open fully. All he could see was a tall silhouette, alarmingly large and somehow wild-looking. Barefoot, wind-blown, a blanket thrown carelessly round the shoulders – the image of a wild Highlander, stepped straight across the centuries ... lawless, pagan, dangerous. He regained his aplomb with a struggle.

'The boy-friend, I presume.' He turned to the girl and made no attempt to keep the jibing tone out of his voice. He was off balance, but he still had the upper hand. The light fell full on her face. There was something in the way she was looking at the figure in the doorway that sent a thrill of doubt down his spine. There was something here that he didn't understand. He tightened his grip on her wrist again.

The figure took a step into the room. Against his will Earnshaw felt himself flinch. He was used to summing up people in an instant, his livelihood depended on it. But this man had something he'd come across only rarely – a sort of natural authority, a presence that had nothing to do with physical strength.

'Rose. Has he hurt you?'

The girl shook her head. The man touched her once, lightly but somehow possessively, on the arm. Earnshaw's mind began to reel. The voice ... it wasn't what he'd expected. No rough Highland brogue there.

'Kindly release her.' This was addressed to him. His hand on the girl's wrist seemed to go nerveless all of a sudden. The voice was low, quiet and controlled, but underneath there was a vibrant undercurrent of pure command.

'Thank you so much.' The irony burned, the blue eyes seared into his. 'Mr Earnshaw, isn't it?' He nodded dumbly. The blue eyes watched him coldly. In their depths was a hot spark. For once, looking into those eyes in the split second before they turned away, he had nothing to say. Then he cleared his throat, and wiped the sweaty palms of his hands on the side of his trousers. He was always one to take a gamble, and life had handed him a real turn-up for the books this time. There was only one thing for it.

He drew a deep breath and turned to face the music. Automatically he noted that her head barely reached his shoulder, that they didn't touch each other but seemed somehow invisibly welded together. And their eyes – even though hers were brown and his were blue they were somehow alike. As if they'd seen something other people

263

hadn't seen. But there was no time to work out what.

He bowed stiffly from the waist. To the tall, tanned figure with the tousled black hair and deep blue eyes he said, 'Your Royal Highness.' To himself he said, Earnshaw, if you live in the dirt sooner or later you're going to have to eat it. That time has come. So eat.

They both froze as they listened to the sound of footsteps going down the hillside. She could feel his hand trembling on her shoulder, feel her own body shaking with relief. She hardly dared look at his face. She'd never seen him so angry.

'Are you all right?'

She nodded wordlessly. There was a new note in his voice, raw and uncontrolled. She rubbed her bruised wrist, but that wasn't what hurt most. She looked round the shieling, seeing it with Earnshaw's scornful eyes. He'd violated her home, it would never be the same. He'd broken into her dream.

She swallowed hard. Charles' eyes probed into hers.

'Are you sure you're all right?'

She looked up into his face. Just seeing the concern in his eyes made her feel better somehow. The tension began to leave her body. He smiled back at her.

'In that case . . .' He released her, glanced at his watch. His face changed, suddenly he was business-like and matter-of-fact. 'We haven't got much time. By the time Mr Earnshaw picks up the nearest telephone I'd better be out of here. The further the better.'

Her heart sank. This was it. To hide her dismay she bent down and began to clear up the broken eggs, putting them in Rory's bowl. He loved raw eggs. But it was no use pretending to herself that everything would go on as usual. They weren't even going to have a last meal together, like she'd imagined. The peace and serenity of the morning had vanished. There was no going back, not since Earnshaw.

'It's my fault. I'm sorry, Sir.'

He shot her a preoccupied glance.

'No. Someone was bound to find out sooner or later. It

just happened to be sooner.' He paused. 'In a way, I'm glad it's happened.'

She looked down, concentrated on the last fragments of broken eggshell. Of course he was glad. He was longing to get away.

'What about the ferry?'

Treacherous hope flared for a moment inside her.

'There are no sailings on a Sunday.'

He frowned.

'There's one early on Monday morning, Sir.'

His frown deepened. 'No, that's too late.' He turned on his heel, began to stride up and down in the confined space. Rory watched him expectantly from the hearth. 'It must be today, it's the only chance.'

He was determined to leave. There was no getting away from it. She bit her lip and tried to help.

'Wouldn't they . . . couldn't they send someone to pick you up?'

He looked at her. His expression was difficult to read.

'Yes, they could.' He paused. 'But I don't want that. Only as a last resort.' He hesitated again. 'I don't want to involve the islanders any more than I can help it.'

She flushed. She'd almost forgotten, but he hadn't. Even in this emergency he found time to remember his obligation to Iain Dhu. She bowed her head.

'Thank you, Sir.'

His face softened.

'It's your island, Rose. I want it to stay that way.'

But it won't be the same without you, she thought confusedly. Nothing will.

He turned away again, pacing restlessly.

'There must be another way, there has to be.'

Slowly the glimmerings of an idea came to her. It would be risky, but . . .

'I think there may be a way.'

He looked at her in surprise.

'How?'

265

'The same way you came, Sir.'

He looked puzzled.

'By navy helicopter? But I told you, that's just what I want to avoid ...'

She shook her head.

'No. There's a better way.'

'What is it?'

She took a deep breath.

'My boat, Sir. *Love and Honour*. It's small, but –'

He stared at her incredulously.

'You mean cross the Minch in an open boat?'

'Yes. It's been done before.'

He began to smile then, his blue eyes lighting up.

'All right Rose. Lead the way. *Love and Honour* it shall be.' His face was reckless now, bright with exhilaration. He shot a swift glance round the shieling.

'Look, you'd better pack what you need. Not too much, we'll be travelling light.'

She stared at him in disbelief.

'Me, Sir?'

He gave a brief, dazzling smile.

'Of course. You're coming with me. You can't stay here now. They'll be back, in force next time. And next time I might not be here to rescue you.'

He was right. If she stayed here, she'd go on being a danger to him.

'You'd better hurry. There isn't a moment to lose. I'll wait for you outside.'

Torn, she looked round the little shieling. Earnshaw had spoilt it, but it was still all she had. It was her home. She heard the door swing to as Charles went out and drew a deep breath. How could she decide what to take, what to leave behind? What the shieling had meant to her couldn't just be packed into a suitcase and taken away.

But there was no time to lose.

Hurriedly she slipped out of the clothes Catriona had given her and changed back into her blue print dress.

266

Travelling light ... somehow it seemed fitting that she was going to leave the island with nothing more than she had when she arrived. She stuffed the rest of her few possessions into the cardboard case, then straightened the bed and tidied the hearth. At least if someone came up the brae needing shelter they'd find things neat and welcoming. Peats in the creel, the kettle on its hook, two mugs upended in the wooden crate ... On a last impulse she picked up the enamel mug Catriona had given her, with its faded inscription. 'My heart is fix't, I cannot range, I love my choice too well to change.' She knew what that meant now. Quickly she slipped it into the case along with three bunches of dried herbs.

She snapped the case shut and looked round one last time. Already the shieling looked different, it seemed to know she wasn't coming back. There'd be no one to take care of it, to put flowers above the hearth and sprinkle the floor with new sand, let the sunshine in to scour out the stale air. Soon it would begin to smell damp and musty. In the end no one would know she'd even lived there.

Quickly she turned away to the door. It was no use looking back, that was one thing she should know by now. She'd never really had the right to stay there in the first place. She'd never really belonged.

Her eyes blurred, she almost bumped into him as she closed the door behind her. He was doing something to the crooked block of sea-whitened wood above the low doorway. His face was serious and intent. He had a rough stone in his hand and with its point he'd gouged out a sort of pattern in the old wood. She stared at it. It was rough, difficult to make out, but somehow familiar. She stared at it. The pattern blurred and shimmered in front of her eyes. Two initials woven together, just under the eaves, above the threshold. Where had she seen that pattern before? A long time ago ... so much had happened since then ... She looked up at him, confused. The wide broad curve of the capital C sheltering the small letter F ...

267

'Isn't it dangerous, Sir? Supposing someone sees?' Her voice had shrunk to a whisper, almost as if there were enemies all around them.

He looked down at her. A strange, rueful little smile touched his lips.

'Very probably.' His voice was gentle, his eyes had a faraway look in them as he brushed away a few splinters. 'But I'll let you into a secret, Rose. At this moment, I really couldn't care.'

Their eyes met, entwined. For a moment she felt as if it wasn't just their initials tangled together there above the threshold for everyone to see, but something deeper, that couldn't be pulled apart. Memories, betrayals, ancient loyalties ... woven together forever.

'We must go.' She looked up at him.

'Yes, Sir.' She hoped he wouldn't mind what she was going to do next, but she couldn't let him stop her. 'Only ... there's something I've got to do first.'

CHAPTER EIGHTEEN

The door was open. Rory, with the ease of long familiarity, nosed through and disappeared inside. Her heart in her mouth, Rose followed him, remembering just in time to warn Charles to duck under the lintel. He followed her silently.

There was a rustle of movement from the back room, a surprised voice as Rory made himself known. Taking a deep breath, Rose pushed open the door. Iain Dhu was standing by the table. It was laid with just one plate, a pile of oatcakes and a knob of cheese. Carefully laid out square beside the plate was a red polished apple and a foil-wrapped chocolate biscuit, the kind he liked so much. A lump came into Rose's throat as she remembered their picnic in the ruined cottage. It had all seemed to simple then.

Iain Dhu's eyes went from one to the other. A slow flush rose up in his face but he didn't speak. The three of them seemed frozen into immobility. In the aching silence she had time to see that he was wearing his Sunday clothes. He must have just come back from church. His hair was brushed hard back and wetted to keep it down, his face was scrubbed and shaven so close it looked painful. He looked stiff and uncomfortable in the close-fitting suit and hard collar, he hated wearing it, she knew, but Sunday was Sunday. Best clothes and cold food, no matter the weather. His voice came back to her, stating the facts simply and calmly. That was the way things were here. Safe and orderly and reassuring. And she could have had a part of that, if only things had been different ...

Rory was eyeing the knob of cheese greedily. Her voice shaky, she called him to her. It broke the tension, but still no one spoke. Desperately she tried to put into words what she'd come to say, but it was too difficult. She wanted to make everything right again between herself and Iain Dhu, but that was impossible. Then Charles laid a hand on her shoulder and gently moved her aside. He stepped forward into the small room and held out his hand.

'I want to thank you for all you've done for us in the last few days. I know how diffucult it must have been.'

Iain Dhu looked at the extended hand, hesitated, then took it. The two men met each other's eyes and the tension in the room slackened a bit.

'It was nothing.' Iain Dhu's voice was gruff, but his face relaxed for a moment. He glanced at Charles' shoulder, with the same appraising look Rose had seen him give an ailing ewe. Charles caught his meaning and flexed the damaged joint.

'A little stiff still, but otherwise as good as new. I have you to thank for that too.' Iain Dhu looked down and flushed a dull brick-red. Charles saw his embarrassment and went on smoothly.

'There's one more favour I'd like to ask you, if I may.' Quickly he explained the plan for leaving the island. Iain Dhu listened, his face serious. When Charles had finished he paused for a long moment, then nodded his head.

'Will it work?'

Iain Dhu nodded again.

'It'll be a long haul, mind, six or seven hours.' He glanced towards the small window. 'But you have the day for it.' He turned back to Rose. 'You'll need a sheltered spot to land. Once you reach Trotternish you'd best follow the coast due South till you meet Loch Snizort Beag. It's quiet there.'

'I see.' Charles hesitated for a second. 'There's one more thing.' He took a slip of paper out of his pocket and handed it to Iain Dhu. 'Six or ... seven hours, you think?' Iain Dhu nodded. Charles glanced at his watch. 'In that case ... yes.' He paused, then made up his mind. 'Give us five hours. Then

270

ring the number on that piece of paper and tell them what I've told you. They'll send someone to meet us.'

'But how will they know I'm telling the truth?' Iain Dhu's voice was doubtful. The glimmer of a smile crossed Charles' face. 'They won't need to know. They'll send someone anyway.' He paused, then added gently. 'There's no need to give your name.'

Iain Dhu nodded once more, biting his lip. Carefully he folded the piece of paper in half and stowed it away in the top pocket of his jacket.

'You'd trust me with this?' His voice was harsh and abrupt.

'Of course.'

There was a long pause. Iain Dhu drummed awkwardly with his fingers on the deal table, then suddenly seemed to make up his mind. He swung round and delved into the back of a shelf. With a determined thud he set down a dusty bottle and two large glasses. Deftly he uncapped the bottle and wiped one of the glasses with a clean cloth. Then, very slowly and steadily, he poured the glowing amber liquid, two large measures, right to the top of the glasses. He handed the wiped one to Charles and took a deep breath.

'Slainthe mhor.'

'Your health.'

The two glasses met, the two men looked at each other steadily. Then Iain Dhu spoke. The sonorous Gaelic syllables rang out in the small room. Charles smiled, puzzled, looked questioningly at Rose. She smiled back, caught Iain Dhu's eye, saw the mischief mixed in with the sadness in it, and began to laugh. After all, it was very apt.

'What is it, Rose?'

'It's the old toast. To the king over the water, Sir.'

'Of course.' Comprehension spread over Charles' face. With a steady hand he lifted his glass and drank deeply. Iain Dhu drained his glass in one; Charles matched him valiantly. Both set their glasses down on the table with a ring.

Wordlessly they shook hands, this time as equals. Charles smiled.

'Thank you, Iain Dhu. For everything.' His smile faded. He looked round the room, at the sunlight streaming in through the window, the simple meal set out on the table. 'You know ... I envy you your island, Iain Dhu.' The other man's eyes widened in surprise. 'Air like wine, and whisky fit for a king.' Their eyes met again. 'I am honoured to have been your guest.' He turned to Rose, Looked slowly from her to Iain Dhu and back again.

'I'll wait for you outside, Rose.'

Quietly he turned away and left the room without a backward glance. She looked after him. There'd been something in his eyes, as if he understood about her and Iain Dhu, as if he too sensed the sadness and wished he could help. But there was nothing he could do. Except leave them together, this last time.

They heard the door click to behind him. The room seemed very quiet and small with just the two of them in it. It was almost like old times.

'Well, Floraidh Donn ...' His use of the old name made tears come to her eyes. But there was nothing she could say. The silence stretched between them. Iain Dhu sighed and gave a nod of his head towards the door.

'He's no such a bad laddie after all.' He tapped his pockets awkwardly, pretending to look for his pipe. She nodded. From Iain Dhu that was high praise. 'He has a way with him. He may be a Sassenach, but he's not completely without understanding.' He gave up looking for his pipe and picked up the two glasses from the table. He turned to the cracked china sink that served as his scullery, rinsed them both out slowly and carefully. 'He knows a good dram when he sees one.' He set the glasses to drain, turned back. 'And a good lass.'

She felt herself blush. He shot her a glance, then looked away. He leant against the table, suddenly he looked tired.

'It was always the way. I think I knew ... always ... that

272

you'd not be staying here with me. I felt it, that you'd have to go. It was like Catriona said, you were too good for me.' His shoulders slumped.

'No, no, Iain Dhu, that's not true.' She couldn't bear to see him like that. 'I'm not too good for you, how could I be? I'm nothing, I'm nobody.' She hesitated. 'You'll soon find someone much better than me.' She touched her scarred cheek. 'Prettier too.'

He stared at her for a long moment.

'No, Floraidh Donn. 'Tis yourself I wanted.'

A lump came into her throat. The expression in his eyes was like Rory after the new cheese. It would have been so easy to make him happy. She couldn't look at his face any more. Instead she lifted up the case and opened it out. Carefully she lifted out the three bunches of dried herbs and held them out to him.

'These are for you.' Her voice shook a bit. He looked puzzled for a moment. 'For your whisky heads.' Gently she laid them on the table. 'All you have to remember is to take one handful of each of these two, and just a pinch of this prickly one. And not to boil it too long.' He was staring at her strangely. She stumbled on, trying to make him smile. 'It doesn't taste too good, but it'll clear your head on Sunday morning. I don't want you to miss early service just because I'm not here to brew up your cure.'

He looked down, his mouth twisted. A pang of anxiety seized her. This was worse than she'd thought. What she was saying seemed to be making him feel worse instead of better.

'Please, Iain Dhu ... you'll use them, won't you? Promise me?'

He shook his head violently.

'No. I canna promise anything. I'm no good at keeping promises.' Something had happened to his face. Suddenly, bewildering her, he turned away. Without a word he went into the back bedroom. She heard a cupboard door open, the rustle of paper, and then he was back with something in his hands. He set it on the table

273

'Here.' His voice was almost inaudible. 'I should have given it to you before. But I thought . . . I thought as long as I had it you'd come back.' He took a step back from the table as if it might explode. His face was scarlet.

'What is it?' She stared at it. It looked like the keg of salt he'd brought up with him yesterday, for the sheep.

'Take it. It belongs to you.' His voice was rough, he looked almost guilty. Wonderingly she picked it up, saw the envelope loosely taped onto the brass studded lid. Her heart missed a beat as she recognized the faint, spidery writing. Faint but fierce. Catriona.

Her heart missed a beat. She held the casket tight against her body, as if somehow that could make the old woman come alive again.

'Are ye no going to open it?' There was a pleading, left-out look in Iain Dhu's eyes. He must be longing to find out what was inside the mysterious box. She smiled at him and nodded. After all, he'd shared everything he'd had with her, she wanted to share this with him.

Ceremonially she put the box on the kitchen table and drew back a chair. In the slanting light from the small window she could see that it must be very old. The wood was dark and stained and coarse-grained, the brass hinges and corner mountings worn thin. It didn't weigh much but it wasn't empty, she could hear something rattle inside.

For some reason her heart began to beat faster. It was only a box but there was something special about it, something special about the three of them being gathered together in the small room. Catriona's three friends. Rory with his nose pressed against her leg, Iain Dhu with his eyes fixed on the casket. For a moment it seemed as if Catriona herself was in the room.

With clumsy fingers she lifted away the envelope on top. She couldn't help smiling as she noticed it was a used one. Thrifty as ever, Catriona had steamed off the stamp and saved it for a rainy day. There was no message inside, no

274

explanation, just a worn brass key. That was like Catriona too, mysterious to the end.

The key was loose in the lock but it turned easily. The lid swung back. The inside was lined with faded rose-pink velvet. There was a faint scent of old wood, cloves, dried flowers.

She put her hand inside, touched something smooth and cold. It was a photograph, carefully framed and mounted but faded like the velvet, mottled with moisture behind the glass. She rubbed at it gently, looked closer. It was a young girl's portrait, a small smiling face under a crop of dark curly hair, arranged for the photograph in stiff formal waves, slender neck and shoulders rising out of a low-necked, narrow-strapped frothy dress that flared out into fullness at the waist, making her look like a little doll.

She stared at the bright-eyed face, childlike under the formal hairstyle and frock. The girl couldn't be more than fifteen or sixteen. She'd never seen her before, and yet ... there was something familiar about her. Something in the eyes ...

'Who is it?'

Iain Dhu looked down at the girl's face and shook his head blankly. Then he turned the portrait over and stared at something on the back. A shadow crossed his face.

'Do you recognize her?'

He gave her a long slow look. Then he set the portrait down carefully on the table. He shook his head again, looked up, then made up his mind.

'Aye, well ... I suppose it canna matter now.' His face was sad. 'The auld woman must have wanted you to know after all.'

A thrill of fear went through her. The way he'd looked at the girl ... the way he'd put the portrait down ... carefully, with an odd sense of finality. Suddenly she knew what it meant.

'She's dead, isn't she.'

275

She looked down at the smiling face, so young and sure behind the smudged glass. He nodded.

'Aye. A long time ago. Nearly twenty years. I was only a bairn, but I remember the talk.'

Twenty years ... before she was born, almost. And yet the girl's face smiled as if it was only yesterday.

'What happened?'

'She was coming home. A train through the mountains. It was winter, there was snow on the high ground. There was an accident, a derailment. They never found the driver. She was killed.'

'But why ... what is her portrait doing inside Catriona's box? Who is she?' Without a word Iain Dhu turned the portrait over and pointed to a line of scratchy writing on the back, above the name of a studio in Fort William. Just one word and a date. Floraidh. July, 1956.

'But ...' She stared at the name in confusion. It was Catriona's writing all right. But it didn't make sense. Why had she given her this other girl's name?

'I don't understand ...'

He paused. When he spoke his voice was gruff and matter-of-fact.

'How could you. She was Catriona's daughter.'

The room reeled. She found herself clutching the casket with both hands, only the touch of the old wood told her she wasn't dreaming. Iain Dhu spoke again.

'Maybe I shouldna' ha' told you. But she must have wanted you to know.'

She heard his voice from a long way away. Dazed, she stared at the portrait. Of course, how could she have missed it? Now she knew, the resemblance was unmistakable. The tilt of the chin, the defiant line of the mouth, they were Catriona to the life.

Iain Dhu sighed.

'It was a terrible scandal at the time ... you know what people are. And Catriona made it worse, she wouldn't stand for pity. My mother told me how it was when the child was born. With her being so proud and all, and the last of a long

276

line. The talk was terrible.' He shook his head. 'She never told who the father was, but of course everyone knew. There was only one man it could be.'

'Callum.' Of course. Now it was all beginning to make sense. The old woman's conviction that one day he would come back ... her crotchety independent ways.

'Aye. A quiet man by all accounts. Everyone was surprised. Just before the war it was. The worst time for the island. There was no work for the young men, nothing at all. So they went away across the sea, one by one. Canada, America, Australia. From what I heard Callum was one of the last to go, because he wanted Catriona to come with him. But she was too proud to go. "When you're a rich man you can come back and claim me," she said to him.' He shook his head again. 'Vain auld woman. She never thought he'd go. But in the end he did.'

'Poor Callum.'

He glanced up in surprise.

'Why ... I never thought of it quite like that. It was poor Catriona everyone was thinking ... until she put a stop to it.'

'Yes ... but he never knew. About his daughter.'

He shrugged.

'You knew the auld woman as well as I did. I doubt she'd have told him. Not till he came back to claim her, with gold spilling out of his pockets ... And he never did. Not that I blame him.'

A sudden surge of sympathy for Callum welled up in her.

'If he'd known ... he'd have come back, I know he would.' He loved her, she wanted to say, but it sounded foolish.

'Aye, maybe.' He tapped the portrait. 'She'd maybe have lived if he had.'

'Oh no ...' Her heart began to ache thinking of it. 'Why? What happened?'

'Well ... she grew up, as young girls do – fanciful. And nothing would do but she must go and find her father. That was the way of it. Stubborn as her mother she was.' He gave a wry half-smile.

'I'd have done the same!'

He looked at her appraisingly, then nodded.

'Yes, I think you would.'

'Did she find him?'

'No, I don't think so. But no one knows exactly what happened. There was no word, you see. She wouldn't admit she couldn't find him. And then, three years later came word that she was dead. But if she'd never left home she'd be alive today. Catriona never spoke of her again.'

Rose shook her head sadly. Now it wasn't the young Floraidh she felt sorry for, or even Callum. They'd done what they had to do. But it was Catriona who'd been left behind. Waiting, with only her pride to keep her warm. Blaming herself, but pretending not to care. Left alone in the end. Fifty years of waiting . . . and nothing to show for it but a faded photograph.

Iain Dhu had the portrait in his hands again, he was looking at it in a puzzled sort of way.

'There's something else . . .' His voice trailed away, then strengthened. 'Yes, I'm sure of it.' He held out the photograph. 'Look at her closely now. Forget about the dress and the hair.'

Still dazed, she took it, looked again into the direct dark eyes.

'There . . . who does she remind you of?'

'I don't know.'

He shook his head impatiently.

'. . . Look again.' His big hand blocked out half the portrait, framing the face. 'I didn't see it at first, but she looks like you. She could be your twin sister.'

The image swam in front of her eyes. For a moment it was as if she was really looking into a mirror. The girl's colouring was like hers, so was the shape of her face.

Then she saw something else. Round the girl's neck, half hidden in the filmy folds of her neckline. A silver locket.

She gripped the portrait frame so hard she thought it would break apart in her hands. The room went black. She looked into the dark eyes. They were familiar now.

'No ... she's not my twin sister.' Her voice was a whisper. 'Look. The locket. It used to be mine.'

Iain Dhu reached forward and took the portrait from her.

'Well, well ... so that's the famous locket. Catriona was always boasting about it, saying it had been in her family for six generations. Handed down by each mother to her eldest daughter when she was of an age to be married. Many a time I asked to see it. "Are you not yet of an age to be married then?" I used to ask her. Now I wish I had held my tongue. No wonder she never showed it to me.' He frowned. 'But how did you come by it?'

She took a deep breath. 'My mother left it with me when I was only a baby. Don't you see?' She took back the portrait, stared down at that wide-eyed face.

'Catriona's daughter ... she was my mother.'

There. It was said. The unbelievable, impossible truth. She'd found her at last. Stunned, she tried to absorb the knowledge. Her mother hadn't abandoned her after all. She'd been telling the truth. She'd been going home, braving the long dangerous journey, to prepare the way. And then she'd have come back just as she promised.

Joy flooded through her, followed almost immediately by a surge of pain. She'd found her only to lose her yet again. She was dead. And Catriona ... The pain intensified ... Catriona was her grandmother. If only she'd known in time, if only she'd trusted that strange link between them, the way they understood each other without speaking. If only ... but it was too late.

She looked up, met Iain Dhu's eyes. His face was ablaze with triumph. Suddenly he reached across the table and clasped both her hands in his.

'Don't be so sad, Floraidh Donn ... don't you see what this means? It means you are one of us, one of the clan.' Words came tumbling out of him in his excitement. 'Catriona's cottage, her bit of land, it belongs to you by right.' Again she was aware of the depth of feeling behind his quiet exterior. 'I won't let you go. You belong here. With me.'

His hands were very warm. A flush of warmth spread up from them through her body, touching her frozen heart. What he said was true. A tempting vision opened up in front of her. Perhaps it was right after all, to stay here and be happy. There might be people who remembered, who could tell her more about her mother, about who she was. Perhaps she'd even find out something about her father. Little by little she'd build up a picture of her family. She'd be somebody. She'd belong. She'd live in Catriona's cottage, in the house her mother had grown up in, with Rory and a bit of land to work and Iain Dhu just a few miles down the machair. One day they'd marry, and the two ajoining crofts could be worked as one. She wouldn't come empty-handed to the marriage after all – Catriona's land would be her dowry. It would be like all her dreams come true.

Then, as suddenly as it had come, the warmth faded. Very gently she withdrew her hands and rested them on the casket. The old wood was hard and rough under her fingers. And inside was the past, with all its sadness and lost hopes. She drew a deep breath. Now she knew why Catriona had given it to her. The old woman's voice rang in her ears. 'Follow your heart, Floraidh. Or it will shrivel up inside. Like mine.' If only she knew for certain where her heart lay ...

Quickly, before she lost her courage, she slipped the portrait back inside the casket. She was her mother's daughter after all. Ready to gamble everything, throw away certain happiness and safety ... for what? A man with blue eyes, an unknown country, danger ... She shivered, but it was too late. Her choice was made. It had been made all those years ago, it was in her blood. For better or worse, she had to follow this road to the end.

Iain Dhu must have read her face. All the light and warmth went out of his eyes, but he didn't flinch. Slowly, silently, he rose to his feet and held out his hand.

'Goodbye Miss Floraidh.'

A cold chill went over her. It was the first time he'd ever called her that. The formality put distance between them already. There'd be no more picnics in the dunes, no more of the old stories, no more Floraidh Donn. Only memories, dreams of how things might have been.

Heavy-hearted, she picked up the casket and went towards the door. Maybe she'd never have the chance to be so happy again. Soon the cold grey water of the Minch would come between her and happiness, that sort of happiness, forever. And there was no way of knowing what be waiting for her on the other side ...

CHAPTER NINETEEN

To the West the sun was dipping slowly down. The vast shining expanse of the Minch was almost empty. Nothing moved on the calm water except a small open boat, forcing resolutely on with an escort of gulls wheeling lazily overhead. Not a breath of air stirred. The gulls looked down curiously at the man and the girl in the boat. They were huddled together like castaways, hardly moving. But they were singing.

'Speed, bonny boat, like a bird on the wing,
Over the sea to Skye,
Carry the lad that was born to be King,
Over the sea to Skye ...'

Charles' hand tightened on the tiller. He was cold, but the familiar haunting words of the old ballad lifted his spirits, gave him an odd sense of exhilaration. They were so apposite, after all. Two hundred years ago another hunted prince and the Highland girl who saved his life must have taken this self-same route, throwing their lives in the balance to be free.

'Baffled our foes stand by the shore, follow they will not dare ...' His arm curled closer round the girl. She must be exhausted after the long cold hours at sea, but her voice rang out strongly in counterpoint to his own.

He glanced ahead, and the song died on his lips. The grey craggy mass of the Cuillins, gaunt and somehow formidable, loomed on the horizon. They'd be in Skye within the hour.

'We're nearly there.' Their eyes met, then suddenly she looked away.

'I'd better take the tiller then, Sir.'

Silently they changed places. Charles took up a seat by the

283

oars in the bows. For the first time the cold sank into his bones. He looked over the way they'd come. There was no trace of the island now, they'd left it far behind them. The journey was almost over.

Reluctantly he forced himself to think of what lay ahead. Iain Dhu's call would have gone through by now. At first they might think it was some sort of hoax. But they would send someone to meet him all the same. No matter how slight the chance, how unreliable the source of information, someone would be sent.

And then ... He gave an unconscious shiver. He was above all relieved that his family's ordeal was nearly over, but mixed with his relief was a sort of dread. The day of reckoning was coming closer. When he'd have to account for these two stolen days of freedom. Not only to the world but to himself.

His eyes went back to the girl with the dog at her feet. She'd been reluctant to let him take over the tiller. That had made him smile, thinking of his years of Navy training. But now she was sitting quietly, her face intent and serious, her small feet braced against the side, the wind whipping the golden-brown hair into a cloud round her head. All her energies were concentrated on getting him safely home. Her eyes were narrowed against the light, one hand steadied the tiller. The battered little case was stowed away under the bench, but the casket she'd had with her ever since they'd left Iain Dhu was carefully tucked into her lap. What was in it he didn't know and had no right to ask. Some last goodbye gift from the crofter probably. He winced as he remembered the look in the man's eyes. He'd destroyed something there unwittingly but nonetheless thoroughly. If only he could make it up to her ...

His eyes went back to the sea. Silence, emptiness, peace. If only it could stay that way forever, with them both sailing on together, never reaching land. But journey's end was coming closer by the minute.

'Baffled our foes stand by the shore, follow they will no

dare . . .' If only that could be true for him too. But unlike the young Stuart prince he was sailing right into the enemy's hands. And he knew what would be waiting for him . . . explanations, press conferences, an endless round of procedures and formalities. He could cope . . . but could she?

A wave of anxiety went through him. What had he done? He'd thought only of himself, his need to keep her with him. But perhaps like a fragile mountain flower she couldn't be transplanted. Ripped up by the roots, she'd fade and die in his clumsy hands. If only he could protect her somehow, teach her in the few minutes left to them a lifetime's quota of reticence, evasion, double-think . . .

He looked at her again. And changed his mind. No matter what happened, he wanted her to stay herself. Clear and transparent as mountain water running over stones. Maybe he was dazzled by hours on the open water, maybe he was still dazed from his concussion, but to him she was beautiful. Golden and perfect as a small wild berry.

He gritted his teeth. If only other people could see her as he did, there was a chance. If only they could forget about names and position and status for long enough to see her as she really was.

Dimly, at the back of his mind, he knew he was asking too much. Even the prince couldn't make a princess out of beggarmaid. In fairytales, yes, but in real life? Not any more. But he thrust the knowledge away and clung grimly to the mad, wild, foolish hope that just once the fairytale would come true.

She cut the engine. Automatically he picked up the oars. To the North over his shoulder he could just see the tiny white-painted houses above the bay at Uig, where the ferry steamers docked during the week. Just as they were when e'd flown over them two days ago. It felt more like two undred years.

Journey's end. With a sudden flash of insight he thought ack to the Bonnie Prince, growing old and fat and embittered in lonely exile, outliving his legend along with his

hopes, far from the land and the people he loved. Perhaps he
too, looked back to his fugitive highland days and wished
he'd never reached journey's end ...

Slowly, inexorably, they edged South, following the rocky
coastline towards the inlet Iain Dhu had described, Loch
Snizort Beg. Silence was all around them, broken only by the
plash of the oars. He pulled hard, welcoming the pain in his
stiff shoulder. It took his mind off the knowledge that his
time alone with her was running out.

'We're here, Sir.' Her voice was a whisper. He rested the
oars, turned round, looked up in amazement. It wasn't what
he'd expected at all. The coastline rose briefly above them
but that wasn't the surprising thing. The bare grey rocks
were topped by a tumbledown wall, above which the tops of
trees danced in the evening light.

'Are you sure this is the right place?'

'Yes, it must be.' She turned towards him, her eyes
luminous, full of green lights from the overhanging leaves.
The wild beauty of the place, so incongruous and sudden on
the bleak coastline, was affecting him oddly. He had a
strange feeling of recognition, almost familiarity. A flicker of
memory came back to him, something he'd read. A walled
garden just like this one ... Dr Johnson and his faithful
Boswell sitting there, deep in conversation with the great
Flora herself, reliving the old days ... The learned doctor as
proud as a small boy to sleep in the very four-poster that had
sheltered the Bonnie Prince after the Forty-Five ... Was this
could it be the same place, the same garden, after two
hundred years? Surely there couldn't be two walled gardens
carved out of the stone on the island? He gazed upward in
awe. History was alive in this place ... The trees waved
enigmatically above the sheltering wall. Only the rustle of
their leaves and the lap of water against the sides of the boat
answered him.

A last ray of sunlight dappled them with green and gold
through the leaves. There was an aura of peace and welcome
about the place, safe harbour after storm. For a moment he

had the illusion that if only they could disappear under the overhanging branches the trees would keep them safe forever.

'Is there a way up through the trees?'

She nodded. His heart tugged inside him as he watched her make the boat carefully fast. Who would be coming back for it, after all? Probably it would just rot away, hidden in the rocks.

'Lead the way.'

The dog at her heels, she began to make her way up the rocky incline. She was right, there was a path, though it was so well hidden among the rocks that he would never have suspected it. It brought them right under the shadow of the cliff, where there was a small opening in the wall. She hesitated there until he caught up with her. When he reached her side she saw why. Ahead there was nothing but green gloom; near to, the trees seemed infinitely taller, a forest one could get lost in. And the silence . . . even the noise of the sea behind them was muffled, absorbed in the dry, dusty, stillness.

Without thinking, he took her hand. It was small and cold in his; he felt the dog press against his leg on the other side. Close together, their feet noisless in the thick carpet of leaf mould on the forest floor, they went forward. Slowly his eyes grew accustomed to the gloom; he saw with a pang that many of the trees, though tall, were obviously neglected and uncared-for, dead and dying branches hanging awkwardly like broken limbs, others fallen and rotting away to dust. Someone had broken a promise to this garden; even though the trees still lived, their hope was gone. Decay was everywhere. Decay, dust and silence. It seemed impossible that so much beauty should be allowed to die.

Far away, in the topmost branches of the trees, he could hear the wind from the sea, so distant it was just a whisper. It seemed like the saddest sound he'd ever heard. Soon, he thought, this will all be gone. And no-one will even know what was once here. One by one the trees will fall, choked by their own dust, like that huge oak over there. And there's nothing anyone can do now to save them.

Obeying an impulse he didn't understand, he paused by the fallen oak. He shook his head in amazement. It was a vain hope surely to expect an English oak, better suited to the sheltered green pastures of Somerset, to take root and flourish in these bitterly exposed surroundings. But it had grown and survived all the same against all the odds. From the look of the wood it had stood till only recently. With a sudden surge of pain he wished he could have seen it standing. It must have been the largest tree in the garden, the King. And now ... he edged closer. Strange, the trunk had been marked in some way, perhaps to indicate that it was the first tree planted all those years ago. He frowned, trying to make sense of the markings.

As he traced the letters he felt the girl at his side stiffen with tension. They were hardly there at all, mossed over and eroded in the crumbling bark; even as he traced them fragments of wood puffed into dust under his hand. But all the same the entwined initials were unmistakable. The large C sheltering the smaller F, exactly like the ones he'd carved that morning in the wind-whitened lintel above the shieling door.

For a long, aching moment they stared at each other. What could it mean?

Then, abruptly, with a violence that wrenched them painfully into the present, the calm was shattered. Above them, from beyond the trees, came the slam of a car door, the sound of urgent voices, the scrape of footsteps on stone. Irrational panic surged inside him. For a moment he felt hunted, betrayed. He had a wild impulse to flee, race back to the boat, grab up the oars and escape like a common fugitive. Her face, pale and wide-eyed, mirrored his.

With an effort he fought to stay calm. This was nothing more or less than he'd arranged, after all. The moment of reckoning. But he hadn't reckoned on how it would make him feel. Like a man going to his execution.

It was the sight of her white, shocked face that saved him.
At all costs he must protect her. This moment must be far
worse for her than it was for him. So much depended on
exactly who or what was waiting for them up there. And
there was no time to lose.

His heart racing, he took her hand and plunged up the
incline, leaving the fallen oak behind. He could almost feel
the huge prostrate shape reproaching him, as if he was
leaving a wounded friend behind on the battlefield, but he
pressed on regardless. There was no time ...

The light as they emerged was dazzling. He blinked, trying
to scan the sunlit expanse of scrubby grass that stretched
ahead of them. With one hand he signed to Rose to keep out
of sight.

When he saw what kind of reception committee was
waiting for him he was glad he'd taken that simple pre-
cautionary measure. His heart sinking, he realized the worst.
The official car he'd hoped for was there. But so too, looking
oddly incongruous in their city clothes, were the gentlemen
of the press – the last men in the world he wanted to see at
this moment. Earnshaw, solid professional that he was, had
betrayed them. Once the news that he was alive was out, it
must have been all too easy for them to wait for an envoy
from Balmoral and then follow.

He turned back, the blood thundering in his veins.

'They're there, aren't they, Sir.'

Her voice was small but firm, the quiver in it hardly
noticeable.

He took a deep breath.

'I'm afraid so, Rose.'

She bit her lip.

'You'd better leave me here, Sir. It's the best way. Don't
worry, I'll be all right. I've got Rory.'

She lifted her chin in that defiant way he'd come to
recognize. For a moment he was tempted. If he left her here
he could send someone later, it would be the best, the most
discreet thing to do. But in the same instant he realized he

couldn't do it. If he let her go now he felt sure he'd never see her again. If he abandoned her once more she'd disappear into the midsummer twilight like a sea maiden and he'd have lost her forever. He couldn't take that risk.

Desperately he scanned the assembled cars. There had to be a way out. Then it came to him. Dangerous, very dangerous, but it was the only alternative. And if he timed it right ...

Quickly he explained to the girl. When he'd finished he watched her face anxiously. There was no reason why she should trust him one more time, but she had to. Her eyes dropped, her lips quivered.

'I'd rather go with you, Sir.'

A lump rose in his throat. How could he explain? What he was thinking of was such a wild gamble, he didn't dare to raise her hopes.

'I know.' He gripped her by both arms, she felt small and light, as if she'd blow away. 'But this is the only way.'

Her eyes looked up at him, trying so hard to believe that he felt his own eyes burning.

'Is this goodbye, then?' Please, tell me the truth, her eyes said. A snatch of the old ballad the Highlanders used to sing for their absent King drifted unbidden into his head. 'Will ye no' come back again ...' He felt he understood it for the first time. The longing, the hoping against hope ...

Her head lifted, ready to face the worst. She had more courage than he did.

'No.' How could this be goodbye, after all that had happened? If only his courage held out ... He faced her squarely, taking in her small pale face, the smudge of dirt on one cheek, the mop of sea-tangled hair, the way she stood there braced, her head high, like a little queen.

Suddenly, obeying an impulse that seemed to come from somewhere outside himself – from the ancient walled wood perhaps – he took her hand and lifted it to his lips. Her eyes widened, her small roughened fingers trembled in his. If only he could find the words.

290

'Yes, it's goodbye. But only for a little while. I can't explain, but it has to be like this. Please believe me.'

Doubt still flickered in her eyes. Desperately he searched for something that would convince her. Make her believe that this time, this time he would keep his word. He gripped the small hand tighter, their eyes met. Remember, please remember, what's between us can't be forgotten. He willed her silently to remember. The night on the brae, the sun dancing ... and before that, their last goodbye, in the rainy scented darkness of the park, with the gas lamps glowing pale just before the dawn, all around them the sleeping mass of London but only the two of them in the whole world. He hadn't believed then, he'd thought it could only be a dream, but now he knew ... Somehow, deep in himself, he knew he'd been given one last chance, to redeem all the broken promises. To go walking in the rain once more.

'Please. Trust me.'

Silence quivered between them, broken only by the murmur of voices beyond the wood. Then her lips trembled, parted, finally broke into a smile. With a shudder of relief he released her hand. She believed him. She understood.

Without a backward glance he turned away and walked steadily up the slope towards the waiting cars.

She watched him go until her vision blurred. Then, obediently, she retreated back against the gate, under the protective shadow of the trees. Rory, shivering, pressed against her legs. The warmth comforted her a bit. She felt strange, cold inside, as if the sun had gone down already. There were so many things she hadn't said to him, things he'd wanted to say. And now he was gone. Desolation gripped her. Soon he'd be back among his friends, where he belonged.

For a moment she was wildly tempted to creep back into the wood. If she hid there no one would ever find her. After a while, when it got dark, they'd give up looking, and then she could make her way back to *Love and Honour*, and maybe, tonight or early tomorrow, sail her back to the island. The shieling would be waiting for her, the door open ... and above the door, waiting to remind her, the initials he'd carved. Just like the ones carved into the rotten bark of the fallen oak. Only those must have been carved hundred of years ago.

She shivered. What could it mean? Whoever had carved those initials all that time ago must have wanted desperately to be remembered ... but who, and why? And why on just one tree, the oldest, and so far up, almost hidden, where no one would have seen it before the oak fell?

The dog at her feet growled deep in his throat as a subdued roar of voices went up from beyond the trees. She shivered again. There was something animal-like about that roar, something hungry. She closed her eyes. The roar seemed to go on forever. Then, quite suddenly, it was cut off. There was a short silence, then a frantic slamming of car doors. Engines revved violently, someone shouted. She opened her eyes. It was almost dark; along the narrow track in the distance she saw a crazy procession, cars jolting and bumping along, headlights blazing, horns going, almost nose to tail in their eagnerness. One by one they jolted away and disappeared into the twilight.

In the silence they left behind them she heard her heart hammering. The seconds lengthened into minutes. She didn't dare peer out from the cover of the trees in case someone saw her. Crazy thoughts chased through her mind – perhaps he hadn't been able to make the arrangements he'd told her about, perhaps she'd been forgotten already. Suddenly, as the warmth began to leave the air, the idea of sailing back alone across the Minch began to seem less attractive. She was so tired and cold and hungry ...

Rory growled again, this time rising to his feet, hackles quivering. She stiffened, listened. Then she heard it. Soft but determined footfalls, coming nearer. She could hear the swish of grass, the creak of leather. Stiffly she got to her feet.

292

tried to straighten her hair with her hands. Her heart was pounding.

'Miss?' She strained her eyes into the twilight, made out a uniformed man standing at a respectful distance beyond the gate. She took a step forward, hushed the dog. Now she could make out his face, clean-shaven, the brim of his peaked cap hiding his eyes.

'Yes?'

He glanced at her once, then looked away immediately, his face expressionless.

'If you'd be so good as to follow me, Miss.'

Trust me, he'd said. There was no going back now. Helplessly, she followed.

CHAPTER TWENTY

By the time he reached Ballochbuie forest it was well into the night. The car headlights reflected off the startled eyes of deer, glowing like fireflies in the darkness. But at last the long journey eastwards to Balmoral was over.

As the car swept up the familiar gravelled drive between the low hedges that framed the lion-headed fountain he looked out of the side window and was almost dazzled. The whole castle was a blaze of light from top to bottom. None of the curtains had been drawn and light streamed out of every tall mullioned window, making the gravelled forecourt as bright as day. He blinked, a lump rising in his throat. He was expected. They were waiting for him. He was home.

As he clambered stiffly out of the car he noticed the expression on the chauffeur's face. Excitement and relief were blended with something else, a sort of stunned disbelief. What it must have been like, what it must be like now for those he'd left behind. They'd thought he was dead, how could they have thought otherwise? And now . . . here he was returned from the grave. No wonder every light was blazing.

'Thank you, Matthews.' The man was rooted to the spot, his eyes fixed on his passenger's face as the light from the castle fell full on it. With a sudden shock Charles realized that until this moment Matthews himself, who'd known him since he was a boy, hadn't been able to believe the evidence of his own eyes.

'Very glad to see you back, Sir.' Matthews' voice was a croak. He was so overcome that he'd forgotten to close the car door. Charles smiled.

'Thank you. It's good to be back.' He turned and looked up at the tower, with its gold-faced clocks and bartizan turrets. Lit up like this, the delicate stone battlements and corbels glowing pearly white, the castle looked more than ever like a fairytale palace. For a moment an extraordinary sense of unreality came over him. Was he, after all, the Prince of Wales, or someone else, a changeling prince, his soul stolen forever by the sea? He swayed slightly on his feet with exhaustion. He could almost hear the swell of the sea in his blood, beating in his ears. With an effort he came back to himself. He was on solid ground now. He was home.

He willed himself to move towards the light. Doors opened in front of him by magic, he heard the murmur of voices, the sudden stunned silence as he passed under the arched porchway and entered the hall. For the first time in his life he was acutely aware of the footmen lined by the door, each pale face bearing the shock of recognition. He was right. Even up to the last minute, they hadn't been sure.

The senior footman took a step forward. He too seemed to be having trouble with his voice, it came out almost a whisper.

'Her Majesty is in the library, Sir.'

Charles nodded. The sense of unreality was back. Maybe it was the dazzling lights of the chandeliers, pooling on the highly polished parquet ... he'd grown used to the dim glow of tallow candles, a sand-strewn floor ... He straightened his shoulders and followed the two footmen towards the tall mahogany double doors. In the deafening silence the click as the doors swung back sounded like the crack of doom. He stepped inside.

In here there was more silence, broken only by the crackle of the logs in the fireplace. For a long, electric moment the only thing that moved was the firelight, flickering off the tall book-lined walls. The room was empty except for one solitary figure, small and straight-backed in the deep brocade-covered armchair in front of the fire. For a whole minute her head didn't turn, her eyes apparently fixed on the flames. Then, with what seemed like an enormous effort of will, she looked up. Charles took another step into the room. The silence deepened. In the firelight the Queen's face looked drawn and grey. Her eyes searched, probed. One hand gripped the arm of her chair, but her face didn't change.

A log spat, sending up a jet of flame, then toppled with a crash into the fender. The spell was broken. Suddenly the Queen's composure crumbled. Just as suddenly they were in each others' arms, hardly knowing which of them needed the more support. They embraced silently. At last they drew apart. He looked down into her face. She looked worn and pale, but the blue of her eyes was indomitable.

'It is you . . . I was so afraid . . .' She held him tightly by the arms. 'Welcome Charles. Welcome home.'

As if it was a signal, suddenly the room was full of people. They were all here, all his family, despite the lateness of the hour. Suddenly the air was full of voices, laughter, questions. First Philip, his bronzed face alight with irony: wordlessly he clasped his hand.

'It seems that a quick dip in the Minch is as good as a rest cure. You look very fit!' Philip shook him almost fiercely by the shoulder, then turned away, trying to regain his composure. Now it was Andrew's turn to shake his hand. His eyes were brimming with mischief as usual.

'You've no idea how glad I am to see you, old man,' he choked. 'Being next in line was giving me nightmares!'

Charles shook his head in sympathy.

'Playing havoc with your social life. I know.' Andrew's handclasp was warm and hard. Edward was next. His face was wreathed in smiles. There'd always been a special relationship between the eldest and youngest brothers. He cocked his head on one side, put his hands on his hips and beamed round at the assembled family.

'Well, was I right or was I right?'

There was general laughter as the tension began to dissolve. The Queen shook her head in mock disapproval. Her face was beginning to come alive again now and some of the old strength was back in her voice.

'You see, Charles, he was the only one who never once believed you were dead.'

Edward nodded vigorously.

'You couldn't have been dead. I told them, but they didn't believe me. But I was right, wasn't I?'

Charles grinned.

'You were indeed. But how did you know?'

'Oh, that was easy. You couldn't have been dead because it wouldn't have been ...' he searched for a word and found one which he pronounced with an important flourish, 'it wouldn't have been historical!'

The family, drunk with relief, erupted in laughter. Charles laughed with them, but there was a dark shade to his amusement. Edward had put his finger on it all right. Historical. That was the one thing the heir to the throne must always be. History, tradition, it had to be stronger than a mere prince's wishes. The survival of the monarchy depended on it.

'You must be tired.' The Queen laid her hand on his arm. She must have read his face.

'No, Ma'am.' He was tired, dizzy with exhaustion, but that must wait. He put his hand over hers, looked round the assembled faces. All of them, young and old, blazing with warmth, interest, relief and – yes – love. Telling him he mattered, he belonged. Not just because he was the Prince of Wales and the heir to the throne, but because he was one of the family, one of their own. Here he was, warm. secure, surrounded by his family, while somewhere in the castle, smuggled in through a back door, cold, tired and possibly afraid, with only strangers to welcome her, was Rose.

He turned to the Queen, speaking to her only. She was the Head of State as well as his mother; he was well enough aware of the dual burden of their positions to know that she must be the first to be consulted.

'There's something very important I have to talk to you about.' She looked up at him.

'But surely it can wait till tomorrow? You look so tired . .

surely nothing can be that important.' She squeezed his arm. 'You're alive, you're back, and that's all that matters.'

'No. Not to me.' He smiled down at her, but his eyes were serious. 'There's nothing I'd like better than to fall asleep for the next fortnight, but there's something I must tell you first.' His eyes softened. 'That is, unless you're too tired.'

The Queen looked up at him unsmiling, noting the determination in his face. 'If it's that important, then of course it must be dealt with at once.'

They exchanged a rueful glance of complete understanding. Affairs of state, as they both well knew, must come first, no matter how emotional the occasion.

Tactfully the rest of the family said their goodnights and left the library. Charles heard the excited buzz and murmur of their voices as they made their way upstairs, and he was left alone with the Queen. She motioned him to sit down, but he shook his head. He was so tired that he felt he'd fall asleep as soon as he relaxed. He crossed to the terrace window overlooking the garden, trying to gather his thoughts and find the right words. There was a moon, outlining the garden with silver, so bright he could almost imagine he could see the mountains beyond.

'You've changed, Charles.' The Queen's voice was soft, tentative, almost like a young girl's. How quick she was. It was impossible to hide anything from her.

He turned back from the window.

'I know. That's what I wanted to tell you about. Why I've changed.'

The Queen searched his face. His dark head was outlined against the rose garden beyond. White rose of Lancaster, red rose of York ... all the battles and plots that had gone into the making of the monarchy ... and now it rested in his hands. Her first-born son.

With a sudden flash of foresight she realized what a King he would make. The perfect prince, the parfit gentil knight had somehow, mysteriously, come into his own. What could have happened in a mere two days to change him so? The brush with death, perhaps. Whatever it was, something had signed him, marked him out.

Quietly, Charles began to speak. He told her first about the little stone cabin on the hill, the icy water in the burn, the sound of the curlew and the wheatear and the faraway gulls. The velvet green rim of the machair, the tiny lochans that reflected the sky, the silver line of the Atlantic beyond the sheer white sand. The air that in the day was soft as spring water and at night so clear you could count the stars. He told her about the sunlight making jewels out of plain grey stone. Knowing her countrywoman's interest he told her about the small black island cattle, so dark they turned silver in the sunlight. He told her about the dog Rory, who knew more about sheep than a sheep itself. Finally, his voice just a murmur in the dimly-lit library, he told her about Rose.

When he'd finished, there was silence. The Queen drew in her breath. Her mind was in tumult. Her whole nature rebelled at the thought of this girl, sprung from nowhere to capture her son's heart. What was there solid and real about a relationship formed in haste and continued when Charles was in his most vulnerable state? It just wasn't fair, either to her son or to the monarchy. And the girl herself . . . a nobody, an orphan even – it was impossible.

And yet . . . deeper down, in the carefully hidden part of her soul that she could call her own, something responded to the note in Charles' voice when he said the girl's name. That small, deeply-hidden part of herself couldn't help remembering her own first glimpse of a tanned, bright-eyed naval rating, over thirty years ago, that had made up her heart forever.

Quickly she banished that rebellious memory. After all, she was being hasty, jumping to conclusions. There was still time; in the cold light of day, away from the island and the spell of castaway solitude, this girl would appear very differently to him, she was sure. Above all, she must tread very carefully. It was in her power to forbid, but that power must be used only as a last resort.

'Well, what do you want me to do?'

He turned towards her eagerly, his eyes shining with relief.

'I'd like you to meet her, get to know her for yourself.'

She took a quick breath. He was so urgent . . . but he was right. She must meet the girl. There was no sense in avoiding the issue, it must be faced. Forewarned would be forearmed . . . and once she knew the worst something could be done about it.

'Of course.' She pressed her hands together to stop their trembling. 'A meeting must be arranged. You have my permission.'

Without a word he strode to the bell-pull on the wall and tugged it. She watched him, astonished. Then he came to her side and took both her hands in his.

'She's here now.'

'Here?' Shock and apprehension began to race through her veins. 'In the castle?'

'Yes.' She tried to withdraw her hands, but he wouldn't let her.

'Oh Charles . . . I can't, not now.'

'Please.' His voice was compelling, the eyes in his tired face brilliant with energy. Suddenly the fatigue, the alternating hope and despair of the last two days, overwhelmed her. Tears came into her eyes. Helplessly, she returned the pressure of his hands.

'You'll see her?'

She nodded, halfway between tears and laughter.

'How can I refuse, when my eldest son has been given back to me?'

He released her. Triumph and gratitude shone in his eyes.

'I knew you would. You have to. You see, I want to marry her.'

CHAPTER TWENTY-ONE

The bell peal jangled through the castle. In the vast empty kitchen belowstairs it shrilled so loud it was almost deafening. Rose, seated at the long scrubbed table, half rose to her feet and Rory growled.

She met the eyes of the stout middle-aged woman standing, arms folded, by the range. The woman shook her head She was wearing a thick woollen robe hastily thrown over a long nightgown and had obviously been dragged from bed and wasn't best pleased about it. Her plump pink-cheeked face wore a look of long-suffering disapproval.

Rose subsided back into her seat. The man who'd brought her through the back entrance had disappeared. She'd had barely a glimpse of the place she was in before she was hurried out of sight. But what she'd seen had been enough . . . Her few tentative questions had been met with tart answers.

'It's big, isn't it?'

'Aye. Sleeps one hundred and thirty people.'

Concious of the woman's disapproving gaze on her crumpled dress and tangled hair, she hadn't dared ask more. The kitchen was cold, and she wished her coat and case hadn't been whisked away by an impassive footman. But she still had the casket. She held it close to her. One hundred and thirty people . . . She'd never find him again in a place this big. She fought down a rising tide of despair.

A young footman appeared in the doorway. He was hardly older than she was, but his expression was forbidding.

'Miss? The Queen will see you now.'

Her heart leapt into her mouth and choked her. She rose, brushed down her skirt. The woman and the man exchanged a speaking look. Rory pressed close against her legs.

'Best leave the dog here.'

She looked from one to the other, and her courage almost failed her. Then she braced herself.

'I'm sorry, I can't do that.'

The footman's jaw dropped. For a moment he looked his age, then a reluctant gleam of admiration crept into his eyes. He exchanged another expressive glance with the woman and shrugged.

'Please follow me.'

Her heart pounding, she followed him through what seemed like a maze of dimly-lit passages and corridors. As the servant's quarters were left behind she began to notice the opulence of her surroundings. Rich carpets were soft under her feet, the light picked out the gleam of polished parquet, elaborate brocade hangings, ornate woodcarvings . . . and everywhere the glowing jewel colours of tartan, the vibrant green and red of Royal Stewart.

As they passed room after high-ceilinged room her heart sank lower and lower. She began to feel shabby and small; she longed for Charles' hand in hers. But all she had was the stern erect back of the footman ahead of her, looking neither to left or right. You don't belong here, it said, as clearly as words.

They emerged into a vast parquet-floored hall. On either side of tall mahogany doors were stationed two more footmen. She'd thought the one leading her was forbidding enough, but these were elderly men, who managed to convey exactly what they thought of her appearance without moving a single muscle.

A pang of pure terror seized her. She couldn't do it, she couldn't go in. She knew they would understand, be pleased even, if she turned tail and fled.

The young footman disappeared without a backward glance. She was left alone in the great hall. The two remaining footmen waited impassively for her to step towards the doors. She looked desperately round her for something, anything to tell her this wasn't some kind of nightmare.

Then she saw something that made her smile. On either side of the great doors were two candelabra mounted on the wall. They were supported by the marble figures of Highland chieftains, thrusting proudly out with the lights above like torchbearers. Suddenly she was reminded of what Iain Dhu had said, that day in the ruined cottage, about the clan chief's men. 'Where, with all your silver and gold, will you find finer candle bearers than these ...'

She straightened her shoulders. The same Highland blood ran in her veins and she wouldn't disgrace it now. Rory at her side, she advanced towards the door.

'As soon as you meet her you'll understand.'

The Queen turned away from the eagerness in her son's voice. Marriage ... had it gone so far? Her heart was racing with alarm. Never, she longed to say, but caution prevented her. It was too soon for a direct confrontation on such a delicate subject. Besides, Charles was tired, overwrought, disorientated. Sooner or later, he would see reason.

But the expression on his face ... Heavy with misgiving, she crossed to the mantelpiece and held out her hands to the blaze. Despite the warmth she felt cold inside. But she must speak, say something, anything to break the silence.

Her eyes fell on a small wax-sealed package propped up against the mirror. It had arrived for him two days ago, and in the commotion after his disappearance it had given her an odd sort of comfort to have it by her. With an inward sigh of relief she picked it up. The distraction was just what they both needed.

'I almost forgot. This came for you, I believe it's urgent.'

For a moment the Prince looked puzzled, then his face cleared. With eager fingers he tore the wrappings. Something silver spilled out into his hand. He looked down at it and smiled. Then he unfolded the letter that accompanied it and began to read.

The Queen watched his bent head and gave way for the first time to her anxiety. Every nerve in her being dreaded the approaching encounter. What would the girl be like? Glamorous, of course. That was something that all her son's girlfriends, whether blonde or dark, frivolous or intellectual, had in common. But this one must have some added ingredient to slip past his defences so cleverly . . .

Suddenly Charles lifted his head from the letter. The expression on his face was indescribable. Joy, hope, disbelief, all mingled.

'What is it? Good news, I hope?'

He stared down at the letter, his eyes faraway.

'Good news . . . yes. Better than any I could have expected. Better than I deserve.

Silently he handed her the paper.

A premonition went through her. Matters seemed to be moving inexorably out of her control. The print blurred for a second before her eyes. She reached for her reading glasses, keeping her hand steady with an enormous effort of will. As she read she felt the room – the night outside the drawn curtains, the crackle of logs in the fire, her son's eager face – recede to a great distance away.

When she'd finished she handed the letter back to him.

'If this is true . . . if it can be proved . . .' She was unable to complete the sentence, but he did it for her.

'Then it changes everything.' His voice was gentle but it throbbed with conviction.

She bowed her head in acknowledgement. 'Yes. Of course.'

He took a deep breath. 'But please . . . don't let it affect your decision. I want you to see Rose for yourself. Talk to her.' He hesitated. She could see how much the words were costing him. 'I won't interfere . . . I won't try to influence you in any way. I trust your judgement.'

She didn't know what to reply. How could he suspect tha

she'd already judged this unknown girl, already made her decision, not as a Queen, but as a mother?

A sudden commotion outside the library door saved her. Startled, they both swung round. There seemed to be some sort of altercation going on in the great hall. Two voices were concerned, one the smooth tones of Morris the head footman, still calm and urbane even at this late hour, the other so low that she could hardly make out what it was saying. The two of them froze, helpless to intervene, as Morris' tone grew shriller. Now they could catch some of the words. 'Below stairs . . . inadvisable . . . the custom of the house . . .' Then his voice tailed away. There was a short, electric silence. The altercation seemed to have reached an impasse. Then a small voice with a tremble of pure indignation in it said clearly.

'You wouldn't like it if you were a dog.'

Against her will the Queen's mouth twitched. Any girl who could defy Morris must have the build or at least the presence of an all-in wrestler . . . But before she could collect her thoughts further there was the patter of a dog's claws on the parquet outside and the doors swung wide.

The Queen's eyes widened in surprise. The figure that stood in the doorway had nothing to do with any of her preconceptions. For a start she was small and slight, hardly taller than a child. In her old-fashioned blue and white print dress with its white collar and cuffs she looked as if she'd stepped straight out of a Victorian lithograph. A mass of golden-brown sun-streaked hair tumbled down her back. Above the white collar her face was flushed with embarrassment and determination, the small chin held defiantly high, the dark eyes under their level brows almost fierce. Tucked under her arm was a small wooden casket; by her side, silent as a shadow, was an old black dog.

For the first time since girlhood the Queen was at a loss for words. She saw the girl's eyes go straight to Charles like a homing pigeon. He took an instinctive step towards her, then halted, keeping his promise not to interfere. But his face . . . it was lit up from inside. And the answering light in the girl's eyes transformed her. With a pang the Queen realized she'd forgotten how much could be said without words.

But words were necessary now.

'Come to the fire, my dear. You must be cold after your long journey.'

The girl wrenched her eyes away from Charles, blushed, and advanced into the room. The dog followed her. There was something wild and yet oddly dignified about them both. Shyly she held out her hand.

'How do you do, Ma'am. I'm very pleased to meet you.' Her voice was soft, with an accent that reminded the Queen of her country childhood. Bobo Macdonald, her beloved Scots governess, had spoken with that same lilt. The girl's hand was surprisingly warm and firm. Instinctively, from a lifetime's experience of judging character by the sound of a voice and the clasp of a hand, the Queen knew that she was to be trusted.

'You must be Rose.' She patted the brocade sofa beside her. 'Sit down, my dear. Charles has told me so much about you.'

Now, in the light from the fire, she could see what Charles hadn't told her. Across one cheek stretched the fine line of a scar. For a moment her heart went out to the girl in unwilling sympathy. To be marked out like that, for life ... But somehow it didn't detract from the wide golden-brown eyes.

The girl sat down gingerly, the dog curled at her feet.

'I hope you don't mind Rory, Ma'am. I couldn't leave him behind, he would have fretted.'

'I know. I have dogs myself.' Automatically the Queen bent to caress the dog's rough head. In the same moment she realized that she was coming dangerously close to liking this girl. 'Has he been fed?'

The girl's face lightened. 'Yes, thank you Ma'am.' Some of the tension seemed to leave her body, though she still sat very erect and straight-backed in the soft chair, refusing to give way to her obvious fatigue. There was something gallant in that ... it reminded the Queen of her own small, indomitabl

308

mother. The first commoner to marry a King's son for two hundred years . . . And there was something very touching in the way the girl refused to look to Charles for help, as if she sensed that this was a test he wanted her to pass on her own.

'What a beautiful casket. It must be very old.'

'Yes Ma'am.' She noticed how gently the girl's small hands touched the battered wood. 'I believe it is. It belonged to my grandmother.'

'Your grandmother?' The Queen heard Charles' sharp intake of breath, saw his shoulders stiffen.

'Yes, Ma'am.' The girl hesitated, sensing the tension in the room. 'Would you like to see inside?' She drew a key from the pocket of her dress and inserted it in the lock. The lid swung open. Very gently she drew out something and held it for a second in her hands. Then she handed it to the Queen.

'That is my mother.' The Queen was touched by the unconscious pride in her voice. 'When she was my age. I never knew her. But she looks nice, doesn't she?'

The Queen nodded.

'And the locket she's wearing . . .' the note of pride in the girl's voice grew stronger, '. . . it's been in my family for six generations.'

Six generations. The Queen was aware of Charles at her side, leaning over her shoulder, looking down at the faded portrait. Wordlessly their eyes met. Her it was, the proof he'd needed. The glowing certainty in his eyes made her feel suddenly very old.

The girl's puzzled face roused her from her reverie. Slowly she rose to her feet. The girl followed suit, her eyes alarmed.

'I think Charles has something to show you, my dear.'

Charles held out his hand. The silver locket gleamed there, catching the light of the fire.

'Come here Rose.' Charles voice was low, almost instinct. The girl obeyed, her eyes never leaving his. Gently he lifted the hair from her neck and clasped the locket round. Her hand went to it instinctively.

309

'You've mended the chain, Sir. Thank you.' He shook his head.

'But that's not all.' He took her hand. With a pang the Queen saw that the girl wore his signet ring on the third finger of her left hand. 'Do you know who you are?'

Her head lifted proudly. 'Yes, Sir. I'm Catriona Ruadh's granddaughter. I only wish ... I only wish you could have met her. You would have liked her.'

He smiled. 'I know But there's something else.' He reached forward, lifted the locket where it hung over her heart. It fell open like the wings of a butterfly under his hands.

She watched him, puzzled.

'There's nothing inside, Sir. I've looked.'

'Wait.' His long fingers moved over the interior, testing, probing. There was a tiny almost inaudible click. 'Now look.' Their two heads bent together, almost touching. The Queen felt her eyes mist. It was a supremely private moment.

'There ... what do you see?'

The girl caught her breath in astonishment. The Queen knew what she was seeing. The laughing, mocking face of a young man, golden hair falling over his lace collar, over his shoulder a tartan plaid. Unmistakable ... a secret portrait as fresh and vibrant as the day it was first painted, every tiny brushstroke full of love and loyalty.

The girl laughed, a sudden joyous sound.

'To think I've been carrying him round my neck all my life and I never knew. But who is he?'

Charles laughed with her. 'That's not difficult. He's signed his name for you, here on the other side. It looks rough – think it's been done with a point of a dirk – but it's clear enough.'

Slowly she traced the two initials, the entwined C and F. Her face went suddenly pale. 'I don't understand.'

'Yes you do.' He gripped her by the shoulders. 'Remember the walled garden? I should have known then. The initials on the tree, the C and the F together ... And now the locket proves it.' He took a deep breath. 'There's only one Charles it could be. The Bonnie Prince. And that garden ... it belonged to Flora Macdonald, the girl who saved his life. She must have carved the initials there all those years ago, where no one would see them ... to remember him by. And the locket. It's been passed down from mother to daughter for two hundred years.'

She frowned. 'But that means ...'

'Yes.' He couldn't keep the exhilaration out of his voice. It means that you're not just Catriona's granddaughter. You're a member of one of the great Scottish clans. And more than that. You're the last direct descendant of Flora Macdonald herself. Your line goes back as far as mine, further probably. To clan chiefs and great landowners. All of two hundred years and more.'

He took in her anxious face with one glance.

'Oh Rose, don't you understand? It changes everything.' He whirled on his heel, met the Queen's eyes. The challenge in his was unmistakable. For a moment she trembled on the brink of denying him. Then she remembered, not only her own youth, but the tragedy of the abdication, her sister's broken romance with Townsend, and knew she couldn't do it. Too much had already been sacrificed for duty. She would not stand in his way.

'You have my approval, Charles.'

He turned to the girl. Suddenly the warm, brightly-lit library seemed stuffy and alien to him. He had to get out, into the open. He'd never find the right words here for what he had to ask her.

He strode to the terrace doors and threw them wide. Cool night air drifted in, bearing with it the scent of dew and flowers and the sound of water splashing in the fountain.

'With your permission, Ma'am?' His face was stern. The Queen nodded.

'Rose?' He looked towards the girl. Obediently she went to his side. The Queen, adrift on her own memories, watched

311

him usher her onto the terrace. Then, quietly, she closed the door behind them and turned back to the fire.

Outside, Charles proffered his arm. She took it. He breathed in deeply. The scented darkness brought back images that had been stifled inside ... Another terrace, deep in the heart of London, where he and the girl beside him had plunged into the darkness like a pair of fugitives. He'd hardly known her then. But now she was as much a part of him as his heart. And the roses were pouring out their fragrance for them again, just as they'd done in St James' Park. With a flash of memory he recalled Bonnie Prince Charlie's last words to Flora Macdonald. 'We shall meet again, at St James's.' He shivered. What strange forces had brought them together he didn't know and he didn't care. She was beside him at last, and the roses were in bloom, just as they would have been for any pair of lovers, safe and anonymous in the night ...

He led her to the wrought-iron bench that overlooked the rose garden. The air was cold, but he could feel the heat from her presence beside him consuming him.

'Rose.' She looked up at him questioningly. One half of her face was in shadow, but he didn't care. He knew every line of her face, it was written on his heart.

'Rose ...' His voice strengthened. 'No, not Rose. Floraidh Macdonald ... Will you do me the honour of becoming my wife?'

He felt rather than heard her sharp intake of breath. A minute stretched into a century. Then, in a voice so small it was hardly audible, he heard her reply.

'No, Sir.'

A chill of disbelief ran through his body. The feeling between them was so strong ... surely he couldn't have been mistaken. He felt as if the ground had suddenly been cut away from under his feet. He stared at her bent head.

'Here.' She slipped off the ring. His heart twisted in his chest as he saw how easily it came off her finger. She held out to him. The gold looked pale and insubstantial in the moonlight.

'I'm sorry, so sorry. But I can't marry you.'

Numbly he took the ring.

'Rose . . .' He didn't know what else to say. He felt as if half of himself had been torn away. He ached to put his arms round those small shoulders, now drooping with fatigue. But she was out of reach, withdrawn into herself.

'Rose . . .' This time she quivered at the sound of her name. Hope stirred in him. How could he lose her now? Her head was still down, her lips set, but there was a tear trembling on the end of her eyelashes. Those ridiculously straight eyelashes . . . Like an owl's.

'What's the matter?'

'Nothing.' She shook her head. The tear trembled but didn't fall.

'You're crying.' Suddenly there was no one but her in the whole world.

'No I'm not. I'm just tired.' She looked up at him imploringly. A wave of tenderness went through him. He'd been too hasty. He must tread carefully, so carefully . . . Gently he touched her hand.

'I suppose we should start again, really.' A quiver of surprise went through her. 'After all, you're a new person now. We should introduce ourselves.'

She looked down at her lap.

'No I'm not. I'm just me.' The desolation in her voice cut him to the bone.

'But I thought that was what you always wanted. To be somebody. Have a family of your own. Somewhere to belong.'

'So did I.' A small sob escaped her. 'But that doesn't matter now.'

A moth blundered into one of the late blooms ahead of them, dislodging a shower of snowy petals. In his own way he felt just as lost, just as clumsy.

313

'Please don't cry. I never meant to make you cry. I'm sorry I asked you to marry me. I thought ... I thought perhaps you might like to.'

She fought back her tears. She couldn't afford to cry, not now. Somehow she had to make him see.

'You don't understand, Sir. It's not that, it's something else. You belong here, I don't. You're used to it, you probably don't even notice it any more. It's your world, your life. But it isn't mine, it could never be mine.' She paused, thinking back to what she'd seen of the castle. The jewel colours of tartan, the glow of gilding everywhere, the long carpeted corridor leading to the imposing book-lined room with its profusion of satin and brocade. And then her final meeting with the poised, perfectly dressed woman who wore her royalty so easily. She'd known then. She could never live in that world. But how could she explain? She lifted a hand to take in the moonlit garden and the gleaming silver bulk of the castle behind them. 'You see ... you have all this. You don't need me.'

'Oh Rose ... it's just because of all this that I do need you.' He paused, at a loss for words. How could he explain to her that she belonged here, that only she could bring the fairytale palace to life for him? Victoria's 'dear Paradise', built for lovers ... it would be a mockery without her. Desperately he looked round him for inspiration.

Something, ruffled by the night breeze, touched his shoulder. It was one of the climbing roses trained against the trellis behind them. Acting on impulse he reached out and gently detached one heavy bloom from its stem.

'Here. This is for you.' He handed it to her. In the darkness the bloom was so deep a red it was almost black. The moth, attracted by the scent of bruised petals, flitted forward to reconnoitre.

Her eyes dropped, one finger touched the dewy petals.

'What kind of rose is this?' Her voice was a whisper. 'Does it have a name?'

He fixed his eyes on her bent head and prayed for the right

words. 'Yes ...' He gestured towards the garden. 'All the roses have names, even the hedgerow ones. That one over there, the pale pink one, is Queen Elizabeth.'

'And this one?'

'That one ... don't laugh ... it's called after me. Prince Charles. It's a Bourbon rose.' With a pang he remembered its catalogue description. 'Expanded form, muddled centre.' How often he'd felt like that, now most of all.

'Prince Charles ...' Again she touched it, almost tenderly.

'Yes.' If only words would come. 'It takes years, decades even, to breed one rose like that. The nurserymen raise hundreds, thousands of seedlings, but only one at most will be worth keeping and giving a name.'

'I see.' Her voice was sad, a little shiver ran through her. 'What happens to the others?'

'I'm not sure ... I suppose they get thrown away.'

'Yes, of course.' The unconscious desolation in her voice was more than he could bear. 'That's not what I wanted to say.' She tried to draw her hand away, but he held firm.

'That rose ... cuttings from the mother plant go out all over the world ... it goes down in the nurserymen's catalogues ... it becomes famous. But do you think it cares where it grows or what its name is? All it needs is sunlight and air and rain. Without them it would die.'

He forced her to face him. The words were coming easier now.

'Don't you see, that's what would happen to me if you left me. You're my sunlight and air and rain. I can't live without you.' Holding tight to her hands, he willed her to meet his eyes. It was now or never.

'So you see, Rose, you're holding my life in your hands.' His voice strengthened. Words he'd never said to anyone before, words that he thought he'd never say, flooded into his mind.

'You see, I've never felt like this before. You belong with me ... you're like part of myself. Without you I'd be only half alive. Because I've been waiting for you all my life, only I

315

didn't know it. Because I can breathe when I'm with you. Because you're real. Because you're you.' He felt himself begin to tremble, felt her response. 'Because it will take me the rest of my life to tell you how beautiful you are. Because I love you.' He took a deep breath. 'And that's why I have to ask you again. As yourself this time. Just Rose, will you marry me?'

She raised her head. Echoing silence stretched between them. He heard the sound of his own blood beat in his ears. Her upturned face seemed to reflect all the moonlight in the world.

'No, Sir.' It was almost a whisper. She looked down at the lovely rose in her hand. When she spoke her voice seemed to him to come from a thousand miles away. As if she'd already said goodbye ...

'Do you remember, Sir, on the island ... You asked me what my name meant. Floraidh Donn. I didn't tell you then, but now I will.' She lifted the rose and very gently inserted it in the collar of her dress. It showed dark, blood-red against the pale fabric. 'It is the name of a flower, a mountain flower that only grows on the island. It's not very big, in fact you'd hardly notice it. Its colour is difficult to describe ... it changes with the light ... sometimes grey, sometimes cream, sometimes no colour at all.' Iain Dhu's words came back to her, with the sound of the sea as their background. 'The colour of a bird on the wing.'

She looked up. 'That's the kind of person I am, Sir. If I was here, after a while, I'd begin to fade. Like one of those wild flowers you sometimes find pressed in an old book. I'd forget who I was and where I came from. And then ...' Her voice faltered momentarily. 'And then ... you wouldn't love me any more.'

'That's not true, Rose.' With a pang he noticed that she'd pricked herself on the rose thorns. Blood was welling out of her finger. Silently he dug out his handkerchief and wrapped it round the wound. Her hand still in his, she met his eyes.

'Yes it is, Sir.' Her voice was soft, but it held an age-old certainty. 'You see . . .' she looked out sadly over the moonlit garden once more. 'You see . . . you have so many roses.'

He bent his head. Suddenly he realized how tired he was. And something else, too. She was right. But if only she knew . . . all the roses in all the gardens of the world couldn't make up for the one he was losing now.

And he was going to lose her, he could feel it. Against his will he remembered his own doubts and fears on the journey back from the island. Now he knew what journey's end had brought him. It was as he'd feared. His mountain flower couldn't be transplanted after all. And he loved her too well to try to change her mind.

'So this is goodbye.' She nodded. Another sob, valiantly swallowed.

'Its for the best, Sir.' She smiled at him, but it was a sad shadow of a smile.

'Yes.' With an effort he found an answering smile. 'But you know, Rose . . .' he searched her face, willing himself to fix it in his memory. 'I think I preferred it when you were a nobody.'

'Don't, Sir.' Her eyes were full of tears. If only, they said. If only we could go back. But it's too late. Perhaps it was always too late for us.

'What will you do now?' He knew what she would answer before she spoke.

'I shall go back to the island. It's where I belong.' She touched the locket round her neck. 'Now more than ever.' She hesitated. 'And you, Sir?' Her voice was tentative. 'What will you do?'

'I don't know.' The concern on her small face touched him almost more than he could bear. 'One day . . . maybe . . . a long time from now, I'll fall in love again.'

'With a girl like me?' She looked up at him anxiously.

'Perhaps. If I can find one.'

'And you'll live happily ever after?'

Against his will, he smiled. 'Like the Prince in the fairytales?' His face grew serious again. 'I don't know. I'll do

my best.' If I can find the right girl, he thought. Another girl
with the dawn in her eyes. Perhaps it's too much to hope, but
now I know what I'm looking for.

'And then you'll forget me.' He heard the unconcscious
note of desolation in her voice and all his love for her welled
up in a tide. He took her by the shoulders, almost shaking her
in the intensity of his feeling.

'Rose – please – you must never think that. Even though
we may never see each other again, I shall never forget one
minute of the time I've spent with you. And ...' he took a
deep breath – 'Even though it has to end like this, I'm glad ...
yes, glad that I could help you find your freedom. Because it
means you'll be taking a little piece of me with you back to
the island. Wherever I am, whoever I'm with, I'll be able to
remember that.'

'Oh Sir.' She began to cry, silent tears coursing down her
face. 'How can you say that? You've given me so much ... I
haven't given you anything.' He took her hands in his. His
face was intent. He had to make her understand.

'That's not true. You've given me something I'll never
forget as long as I live. The courage always to follow my
heart.'

She looked up at him, reaching out to him with her eyes,
just as she had that night in St James's Park. Without a word
he took her into his arms. Her lips were warm and trembled
under his. For a dizzying, spinning moment he forgot
everything – the cold night air, the future ahead, even his
own name. All that was real was the girl in his arms.

Then it was over. She drew away. In the breathless silence
they stared at each other.

Suddenly she reached round her neck and unclasped the
locket.

'I want you to have this.' She thrust it clumsily into his
hand.

'Rose ... I can't take this.'

'Please, you must. I want you to keep it.' Her voice
trembled, just once.

Wordlessly he let the locket fall open in his hands, slipped the catch that opened the secret compartment. The laughing eyes of the long-dead prince met his. What must he have felt, two centuries ago, dying in exile from everything he loved? Surely nothing worse than this.

'Will you keep it?' Her voice was anxious.

He nodded. For a moment he couldn't speak. But there was something he had to know. 'Why, Rose? The locket . . . it meant so much to you once. And now you're giving it away. Why?'

For a moment her resolve wavered. Because I love you, she longed to say. Because, when I'm far away, I want you to have something that once belonged to me. For auld lang syne.

But she caught herself in time. He must never know how much she loved him. That way it would be easier for them both.

His eyes met hers. She saw mirrored in them her own sadness for all the might-have-beens. In any other world they could have shared a lifetime. But this world, these last few minutes, were all they had.

It was almost more than she could bear. She had to answer.

'Why, Sir?' She tried to smile 'Close your eyes and I'll tell you.'

It was the faintest whisper. He closed his eyes, making himself blind for her, like the old man she'd once told him about. He was aware of the cold light of dawn against his closed eyelids. Low to the East the pale disc of the sun would be rising over the hills. Where had all the time gone? The wheel had come full circle . . . the nights would pass, dawn would follow dawn, but the sun would never dance for them again.

Then, even fainter than before, came her answer.

'Because, Sir. Just because.'

His own words. One more echo in a wilderness of echoes . . .

Then, suddenly, he understood. This was no ordinary gift

that she was giving him. He closed his hand around the locket. It was a gift beyond price. She loved him. And even though they would never meet again, the memory of that love would be warm against his heart for all the days to come.

He felt her lips brush lightly across his, sensed again the faint perfume he'd never been able to define. Rain, flowers, tears ...

A fallen petal touched his hand.

When he opened his eyes, she was gone.

EPILOGUE

A small figure flies across the sand, a black and white dog at her heels. Ahead of her, roofless and windowless, is the ruined cottage which Flora Macdonald left one stormy midsummer night, never to return. There is a man standing there, his back to her, facing the sea.

He turns. His face is drawn with tiredness. The girl and the dog career to a stop. The man and the girl look at each other. They do not touch.

'It's me, Iain Dhu.'

'I know it is, Floraidh Donn.' His face is grave. 'I was waiting for you.' She looks up at him.

'How did you know I was coming back?'

'I did not know ... But I waited all the same.'

She smiles. After a long moment he returns her smile. Slowly, hand in hand, they walk away across the sand.